THE PUCKING WRONG DATE

THE PUCKING WRONG BOOK #3

DALLAS KNIGHTS

USA TODAY & AMAZON BESTSELLING AUTHOR

C.R. JANE

The Pucking Wrong Date by C. R. Jane

Copyright © 2024 by C. R. Jane

All rights reserved.

For permissions contact:

crjaneauthor@gmail.com

This book is a work of fiction. Names, characters, businesses, places, events, locales, and incidents are either the products of the author's imagination or used in a fictitious manner. Any resemblance to actual persons, living or dead, or actual events is purely coincidental.

Cover Design: Cassie Chapman/Opulent Designs

Photographer: Cadwallader Photography

Editing: Jasmine J.

JOIN C.R. JANE'S READERS' GROUP

Stay up to date with C.R. Jane by joining her Facebook readers' group, C.R.'s Fated Realm. Ask questions, get first looks at new books/series, and have fun with other book lovers!

Join C.R.'s Fated Realm

To my red flag readers who see handcuffs as a plus...

PLEASE READ...

Dear readers, please be aware that this is a dark romance and as such can and will contain possible triggering content. Elements of this story are purely fantasy, and should not be taken as acceptable behavior in real life. Our love interest is possessive, obsessive, and the perfect shade of red for all you red flags renegades out there. There is absolutely no shade of pink involved when it comes to what Walker Davis will do to get his girl.

Themes include ice hockey, stalking, manipulation, dark obsessive themes, birth control tampering, sexual scenes, prescription drug addiction, physical abuse-NOT FROM THE LOVE INTEREST, and references to previous sexual assault references-NOT INVOLVING THE LOVE INTEREST. There are no harems, cheating, or sharing involved. Walker Davis only has eyes for her.

Prepare to enter the world of the Dallas Knights...you've been warned.

THE PUCKING WRONG DATE

Walker Davis is going to ruin me...but for once, it might be worth it.

I'm a pariah, an outcast, and my life is not my own.

I went to that hockey game hoping for an escape and found one in *him*.

They call Walker Davis "Disney" for a reason, because the superstar goalie is the "Prince Charming" of every girl's dreams.

He told me he understood I just wanted one perfect night...

But now he's everywhere I go.

He seems to know everything about me.

He keeps saying I'm the one.

And he's trying to change my last name.

He's crazy...

A **wrong date** can never be a happily ever after though...right?

DALLAS
KNIGHTS

TEAM ROSTER

LINCOLN DANIELS, CAPTAIN,	#13, CENTER
ARI LANCASTER, CAPTAIN,	#24, DEFENSEMAN
WALKER DAVIS, CAPTAIN	#1, GOALIE
CAS PETERS,	#42, DEFENSEMAN
KY JONES,	#18, LEFT WING
ED FREDERICKS,	#22, DEFENSEMAN
CAMDEN JAMES,	#63, DEFENSEMAN
SAM HARKNESS,	#2, GOALIE
NICK ANGELO,	#12, DEFENSEMAN
ALEXEI IVANOV,	#10, CENTER
MATTY CLIFTON,	#5, DEFENSEMAN
CAM LARSSON,	#25, LEFT WING
KEL MARSTEN,	#26, DEFENSEMAN
DEX MARSDEN,	#8, CENTER
ALEXANDER PORTIERE,	#11, RIGHT WING
LOGAN YORK,	#42, GOALIE
COLT JOHNS,	#30, WING
DANIEL STUBBS,	#60, WING
ALEX TURNER,	#53, CENTER
PORTERS MAST,	#6, DEFENSEMAN
LOGAN EDWARDS,	#9, DEFENSEMAN
CLARK DOBBINS,	#16, WING
KYLE NETHERLAND,	#20, DEFENSEMAN

COACHES

TIM PORTER, HEAD COACH
COLLIER WATTS, ASSISTANT COACH
VANCE CONNOLLY, ASSISTANT COACH
CHARLEY HAMMOND, ASSISTANT COACH

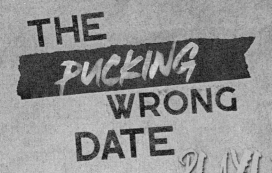

THE PUCKING WRONG DATE PLAYLIST

"SLUT!" (TAYLOR'S VERSION)
Taylor Swift

SKIN AND BONES
David Kushner

BEAUTIFUL THINGS
Benson Boone

FALLING APART
Michael Schulte

SELFISH
Justin Timberlake

HEARTBROKEN (FEAT. JESSIE MURPH)
Diplo, Jessie Murph, Polo G

I'M YOURS SPED UP
Isabel LaRosa

STICK SEASON
Noah Kahan

WHAT WAS I MADE FOR?
Billie Eilish

DEEPER WELL
Kacey Musgraves

MAKE YOU MINE
Madison Beer

DEVIL DOESN'T BARGAIN
Alec Benjamin

SHAMELESS
Camila Cabello

CAN I BE HIM
James Arthur

LOVE SONG
Lana Del Rey

THE LONELY
Christina Perri

BAD REPUTATION
Shawn Mendes

NOT AFRAID ANYMORE
Halsey

MASTERMIND
Taylor Swift

LISTEN TO THE FULL PLAYLIST HERE:
HTTPS://OPEN.SPOTIFY.COM/PLAYLIST/20PFVLAK53FJXP9HO6HOAK?SI=7F7B936B10EC4FB7

"I guarantee we'll win tonight."

—Mark Messier before Game 6 of the 1994 Eastern Conference Finals.

Hockey Boyfriends Anonymous ✓
@hockeyboyfriends_anonymous

Bunnies, hold onto your hat tricks, because we have news for you! The Knights yummy new star goalie @walker_davis1 may be a taken man.#IWantDisneyBabies 📖🔍 Sources say Davis might be sniping hearts off the ice with Olivia Darling-- yeah, the Olivia Darling--the songbird who supposedly went crazy two years ago... #adarlingscandal Can't confirm if he's blocking pucks or blocking hearts. But evidently they're being seen all around Dallas #LoveOnIce 🏒 I'll be over here crying. #truelovehurts #iwantdisney

12:00 PM · Jun 1, 2021

24K Retweets   **247K** Likes

PROLOGUE
OLIVIA

9 YEARS OLD

I stood there, my heart pounding like a drum, my small hands trembling at my sides.

The waiting room felt frigid, the harsh overhead lights casting a stark glare on the blank beige walls.

Mama had curled my hair that morning. She'd used a lot of hairspray, and the tight curls tugged at my scalp, making me wish I could scratch my head. She'd also spent the little money we had on a pretty, frilly dress that looked like it belonged to a princess. But it itched, and I was scared.

I didn't want to be here.

I'd only ever sung at church and at home. I didn't like this.

Mama and I stood there in uneasy silence, waiting for our turn. The tension in the room was so thick that it was suffocating. She finally turned her attention to my face, her gaze boring into me, her brown eyes filled with a cold determination that made me really nervous. She grabbed my shoulders firmly, her grip almost painful. "Olivia," she began, her voice low and sharp, "I need you to grasp just how vital this audition is. Our entire future hinges on this. You *cannot* make any mistakes."

I nodded hesitantly, trying to hide the fear that was bubbling up inside me. I didn't even know what she meant. Did she mean I had to get all the words right? I could do that.

At least I thought I could.

"I understand, Mama," I whispered, hating how her lips curled up in disgust at the sound of the nervousness in my voice.

She was pretty, like a movie star, with her hair all done up and her best dress on. Her eyes were always angry though, and her mouth was in a tight line, like she was trying to hold back. I wished she ever smiled at me. Her fingers dug into my arms, and she leaned in closer, her voice turning even colder. "You have a talent, Olivia, and I've spent everything to get you here. If you mess this up, if you embarrass us in front of those people in there, you'll ruin everything I've worked for. Can your little brain understand that?"

Tears welled up in my eyes as her words washed over me. If there was one thing that I hated doing, it was disappointing her. And it seemed like I was always doing that. "I'll do my best. I promise."

She didn't smile or show any sign of warmth. Instead, she released her grip on me and said, "You'd better. Because if you don't, if you waste this opportunity, I won't forgive you, Olivia. I won't forget it."

With that chilling warning, she straightened up.

Her cold words were still lingering in the air when there was a knock on the door. A second later it opened, revealing a young woman with short, dark hair and a serious demeanor, like this place never let her have any fun.

"My name's Kylie. If you would follow me, please," she said as she turned and started down the hallway, not bothering to look back and see if we were still behind her.

Mama pushed me forward and I followed Kylie down a dimly lit hallway adorned with framed pictures of famous musicians who had once graced the same record label. Their faces stared down at us, and my nerves crept up my skin even more.

My fingers smoothed the frills of my itchy dress anxiously as we continued down the hallway. I could feel Mama's tension radiating from her, and it made the silence between us feel even heavier.

We finally stopped in front of a metal door, and the assistant turned to me with a faint, sympathetic smile. She leaned in closer, her voice hushed, and whispered, "Good luck."

A second later, I was being pushed through a door, Mama close behind me. The huge room had walls that stretched up so high they seemed to touch the sky. There were big windows that let in the sunlight, making everything seem brighter. But even with all that light, the room felt dark and scary. There were men in suits sitting around a long table, their faces serious and their voices low. They looked important, like they could make things happen with just a word. I felt small and out of place standing in front of them. As the door closed, Mama's words were still echoing around in my head, and knowing this was so important was making me even more nervous.

"Go on, Olivia," she whispered frantically, her voice strained and desperate. She stood behind me, her hands on my shoulders, but they felt heavy, like they were pushing me forward. "Sing."

As I looked at the men in their fancy suits and stern faces, I couldn't help but feel like a little mouse caught in a room full of hungry cats.

The way that they were staring at me...their eyes sharp, like they were trying to see inside my soul. Mama had told me they were important people from a record label. Was this how all rich people were? Intimidating? They were way more scary than the principal at my school, Mr. Henry.

I took a deep breath, trying to find the courage to start. The room was so quiet that I could hear the hum of the fluorescent lights above us. I squeezed my eyes shut and began to sing, my voice trembling like a leaf in the wind.

But something was wrong. The words caught in my throat, and my voice cracked. I couldn't breathe, and I felt like I was choking. My heart raced, and I opened my eyes to see the men still watching me, their faces unreadable.

Tears were welling in my eyes, and I wanted to run out of the room and hide. But I couldn't. Mama had said this was our chance, and I couldn't let her down. Not like I always did.

I tried to sing again, but all that came out was a soft, shaky whisper.

The men exchanged glances, and a few of them shook their heads. Another cleared his throat, and they all stood up.

"I think we've seen all we need to. She's a cute kid," one of the men offered as he walked out of the room. He was the only one who said anything.

Mama's fingers dug into my shoulders, the harsh bite of her nails pricking me with pain. Her anger was a tangible thing, and I was terrified of what was going to happen once we left here today.

"She's just nervous!" she practically shouted at the suited men as they filed out one by one. "She can sing, I promise."

But the men just kept walking, their expensive shoes clicking on the tile floor. Mama let go of my shoulders and took a few steps after them, her voice pleading and desperate. I stood there, feeling small and insignificant, like a bug that had been squashed.

The door slammed shut behind them all.

And then there was only silence.

Dark, terrible silence. That felt like the end.

Mama was still, her lips pressed into a thin line, and her face was flushed red. Her whole body was trembling, and her eyes were wet with tears.

She didn't look at me. But maybe that was worse.

I was the worst daughter in the world.

She didn't speak for a few long, torturous minutes.

"You ruined everything, you stupid little bitch," she finally whispered, her voice shaking with the fury she was trying to contain. I held in the sob throbbing in my chest—she *hated* when I cried.

This was a moment where she would have normally been screaming at me. But of course she couldn't do that here. "Our whole future was in that moment, and you couldn't even sing a simple, stupid song."

She squeezed the bridge of her nose and stared off at the wall, lost in thought. Taking a deep breath, she patted down her still perfect hair.

And then she glanced down at me, like I was a worm, writhing there under the ground beneath her. "I will fix this. And if you disappoint me again...if you fuck it up...I am done with you."

I shuddered under her gaze, the hate in it soaking into my skin and making my tummy hurt even more than it already was.

She said things like that to me all the time. But right now...it felt like she really meant it.

Mama walked me down the hall, past the harried looking employees whose frantic movements reminded me of bees swarming around a hive like they used to do at grandpa's old farm when I was really little.

She didn't speak to me, not while she was frog marching me to the car, not when she threw the door open, not when she tossed me inside like a pile of luggage.

And not when she slammed the door closed, clicking the lock behind her as she stalked off in her high heels.

———

I sat alone in the car, the cold seeping into my bones as the minutes turned into hours. My breath formed frosty clouds in the frigid air, and I wrapped my arms around myself, shivering uncontrollably. The car was freezing, and it felt like I was never going to be warm again. I didn't dare move though, didn't dare even consider leaving the car. Her anger was already scary and unpredictable...I couldn't afford to do anything else.

The darkness outside deepened as night fell, and the street-lights cast long, eerie shadows that danced across the windows. I'd always been scared of the dark. Every person that passed the car was a potential murderer or monster. I slapped a hand over my mouth to hold in my whimpers...even though no one was in the car to hear them.

I had no idea how much time passed. I only knew that I had to pee...really really badly. My hands felt numb, and my teeth chattered as I huddled in the backseat.

Finally, when it seemed like an eternity had passed, the car door opened. I looked up, startled, and there she was—dressed in a tight black dress, her lips painted a mean looking red color. Her expression was unreadable, and I couldn't help but feel a pang of fear deep in my chest as she stared down at me.

"Get out," she hissed, and I stiffly slid out of the car into the even colder night.

I didn't bother asking where we were going. I'd learned long ago she didn't like that sort of thing...where it seemed like I was questioning her.

Mama led me down a dimly lit street, and I shivered, still feeling cold all the way into my bones. After a couple of minutes of walking, we arrived at a fancy-looking restaurant, with a sign done in pretty cursive letters. She ushered me inside, the heavy door closing behind us with a soft thud.

Once in the building, she let me go to the bathroom, and then had me sit on a plush leather bench near the entrance before disappearing again, with a stern look thrown over her shoulder that warned me I shouldn't move. People passing by gave me side glances, and I squirmed uncomfortably on the bench.

I hated people looking at me.

As I stared around, I realized that I was the only child in the place. The lighting was dim, casting long shadows that danced across the walls, and weird, unfamiliar music played softly in the background. All the adults were dressed in fancy clothes, holding drinks in their hands, and talking in hushed conversations.

I stared at my scuffed shoes. Mama had tried to make them look better with some permanent marker, but there was only so much you could do.

A flash of blonde, and I saw her—Mama—laughing and smiling at a man I could have sworn was at the meeting this morning. What was she doing?

I'd never seen her like that...so happy. She was never like that around me.

Minutes turned into what felt like hours, and I watched as my mother eventually took the man's hand, leading him away from the bar and deeper into the dimly lit restaurant. My stomach was growling–I was so hungry, and I wanted to leave... something about this place made me feel nervous.

I continued to wait in the dimly lit corner, feeling like a forgotten piece of furniture as I sat there. The low, unfamiliar music played on, and I glanced around uneasily, wishing that she would return soon.

Finally, after what felt like an eternity, they came out from wherever they had disappeared to. Mama's hair was messy, and her lipstick was smeared, the edges of the red visible on her perfectly powdered skin.

But it was the smile on her face that scared me. There was something unsettling about it, something that made me fidgety. Although I didn't quite know why.

The man leaned in to kiss her, grabbing her butt as he did so, and my belly churned as I watched in confusion. After a minute, she slowly pulled away and winked at him before striding towards where I was sitting.

Her smile was gone once she got to me. She grabbed my arm, her grip strong and painful like it had been all day, and she dragged me out of the restaurant and back to the car.

We started to drive, and then finally Mama turned to me, her voice low and menacing. "You're getting another chance tomorrow," she said, her words cutting through the air like a razor.

I nodded, unsure of what to say. How had she gotten me another chance? I couldn't ask though, she'd just get mad at that.

"Look at me," she growled, and then, without warning, she backhanded me across the face. It was a sharp, stinging pain that brought tears to my eyes. She'd screamed at me before obviously, dug her nails into my skin, shook me to get a point across…but she'd never hit me.

The shock of it twisted something inside me, leaving a strange, tingly feeling that spread throughout my chest.

Mama's eyes bored into mine, and her voice was cold and threatening when she spoke again. "This is just the beginning, Olivia. If you mess up again, it won't be just a slap. You hear me? I'll make you wish you were dead."

I nodded, the tears I'd been doing my best to hold in all day now streaming down my cheeks.

She scoffed at the sight of my pain, and the rest of the drive was done in silence.

─────

The next morning found us back at the same place, and I couldn't shake the numbness that had settled over me since she'd slapped me. But maybe that was better than the scary feeling I'd felt yesterday.

Maybe.

Just like before, there was another knock on the door and the same assistant was there, her eyes widening when she saw us. "I've never seen someone get a second chance," she commented as she gestured us out into the hallway, clearly trying to get answers from my mother. "Lucky girl."

Mama simply hummed, a slight smirk on her lips as we walked.

We were led into the same room where I had failed so badly

the previous day, but this time…something had changed within me. The nerves that had bothered me were gone, replaced by that odd sense of detachment, like I wasn't really standing there, and they weren't really watching me. The men in suits stared at me with blank faces, the expectation from yesterday completely gone, like they were ready for me to fail again. The man from last night was seated on the right, and I saw him shoot my mother a wink.

I studied it all for a long moment, until my mother shifted, panic starting to creep into her features.

And then I opened my mouth…and I sang.

The notes flowed effortlessly from my lips, filling the room. I could do this. As Mama always told me, I wasn't smart, and I wasn't good for much else.

But I could sing.

I closed my eyes as the song flowed out, allowing the music to carry me away. I was singing "I Dreamed a Dream." It had been Grandma's favorite song, and she'd taught it to me when we would sing together at her house. She cried every time I sang it.

When I finally opened my eyes, I saw a glimmer of approval in the faces of the men who had watched me so closely. The man from last night nodded at Mama, and her whole body seemed to slump in relief.

Did that mean I'd done good…that she wasn't going to be mad at me anymore?

The rest of the room got up, and just like yesterday, they started to leave.

The man from last night stopped in front of us, though. He was really handsome, with nice combed black hair and a suit that was sharp and crisp, like the fancy ones you saw on people in the movies.

But there was something about him that made my skin feel like bugs were crawling all over it.

Everything about him seemed too polished, too perfect, and

his dark brown eyes...they were the worst part. They were cold like Mama's, and I hated how they seemed to measure and judge everything about me.

With a faint smile that didn't quite reach his eyes, he leaned down, "You're going to be a big star, sweetheart." His words were silky and smooth, and oily feeling. I didn't like the way they slid across my skin. I especially didn't like the way he was staring at me. I shivered and Mama's nails dug into my shoulder, silently telling me that wasn't allowed.

The man held out his hand. "I'm Marco. And you and I... we're going to be best friends."

I shook his hand, not sure what I was supposed to say. "I'm Olivia," I finally said...dumbly. Because surely everyone had known who I was before I sang...right?

He chuckled, but there wasn't any happiness in the sound. It felt like he was laughing *at* me.

I hated when grownups did that.

After he let go of my hand, he patted my head. His touch was too firm, too possessive, and I shifted uncomfortably under his grip.

Mama, as usual, didn't catch on to my uncomfortableness.

Or maybe it was that she just didn't care.

That was probably it.

"So what's next?" she purred, clasping her hands under her chin and beaming at Marco like he was the most wonderful person she'd ever met.

Marco started to captivate her with a bunch of stuff I didn't fully understand—recording a Christmas album, TV show auditions, photo shoots, and more. When he mentioned something about a tour, I blinked a couple of times. Because I couldn't do that. I had school and my friends, and I had my choir concert coming up in the spring.

"What about school?" I stuttered when they mentioned a bunch of cities. Besides this trip, I'd never been outside the county line. The cities he was mentioning were all over the country.

Marco stared down at me, his expression blank. Mama's face was a mixture of rage and annoyance, neither of which were good for me.

His grip in my hair tightened for a moment, and then he patted my head in a condescending way. "None of that matters now, Olivia," he said dismissively, his voice dripping with superiority. "We've got much more fun things on the horizon than a little bit of formal education." He chuckled again, that wrong feeling slicing down my back. "And besides...aren't your classmates going to be so jealous when you're a big star?"

My eyes widened. I didn't care about any of that. Lottie and Megan didn't care about that. I wasn't going to see my best friends anymore?

They continued to talk about plans, and with their words, the numbness I'd been feeling was sliding into panic.

What was happening?

When was my mother going to explain to me what was going on? Leading up to yesterday, Mama had been nothing but vague, talking about this "life changing moment" without telling me what was so life changing about it.

"We'll need to give her some highlights, and a much better haircut," Marco drawled, directing my attention from my nerves, to the fact that he was staring at me again. "And those clothes..." his voice trailed off, but that mocking tone was there, fixed in every word he spoke.

I glanced down at my dress, wondering what was wrong with it. I glanced at Mama and saw her cheeks were flushed, like she was embarrassed.

"And she'll need to gain a few pounds," Marco continued. "We can't have her looking like a street urchin."

I smoothed down my dress as they continued to talk about all the things they wanted to change about me, like I wasn't even there.

Marco's gaze was still focused on me, his eyes *still* cold, like there wasn't anything inside him. Grandpa used to tell me you could tell a lot about a person from their eyes.

I hadn't understood that until today.

Finally, Marco seemed to be done, glancing down at his watch and swearing when he saw what time it was. "I've got to run to a meeting. Marsha will send all the paperwork," he tossed at us, already striding towards the door.

"Sounds good," Mama called after him, still speaking in that weird, overly excited voice—one I'd never heard from her before.

Marco paused in the doorway, staring back at me. "Olivia, *princess*, we're going to make you a star. You'll have everything you've ever dreamed of," he told me with a smug looking smile before he disappeared from the room.

"And you *are* going to become a star, little girl," Mama said through gritted teeth, no sign of the friendliness and happiness she'd possessed just a second ago.

"You have no choice."

CHAPTER 1

OLIVIA

19 YEARS OLD

I stared at the picture on the dressing room table, a snapshot from the day I'd signed my first contract.

From the day I'd signed my life away.

Or should I say the day *Mama* had signed my life away. Because at nine years old I hadn't been old enough to do that for myself.

In the picture, my mother–Jolette as she liked me to call her now–and I were both wearing twin smiles, a pen in her hand. Her smile was because she was about to make millions off me. My smile…was because she seemed happy with me for once in my life.

I would have given anything to go back in time, to right before that contract was signed. I would have torn it up, and run from the room. I would have disappeared.

I wouldn't have even cared if I'd died.

Because it would have meant…I was free.

I flung the picture down in disgust, enjoying the sound of glass breaking. Not that it would matter.

Somewhere, there was a dressing room rider, that I'd never

seen, that made it so this stupid fucking picture was waiting for me at every venue.

I rubbed at my chest. At nineteen you weren't supposed to have chest pain, but here we were.

We were in New York tonight, and I was about to play for a packed house at Madison Square Garden.

But if this chest pain kept up, I wasn't going to be playing anywhere.

I sank down on the padded bench, exhaustion seeping through my bones. I'd been on tour for…how long?

It felt like forever. It felt like I was a rat on one of those wheels, destined to collapse because I couldn't stop running myself to death.

I rubbed my hands along my legs, struggling to find my composure. I could hear the faint sound of the roaring crowd, and I was already dreading the blinding lights.

This was a small venue compared to where they normally had me play, but there were still twenty thousand people out there.

Jolette and Marco were furious about the size.

When was the last time I'd eaten? When was the last time I'd done anything remotely in the realm of taking care of myself?

I was so fucking tired.

The door to the dressing room swung open, and my mother entered. She was dressed in her usual outfit of the most expensive designer clothes money could buy, her demeanor as cold and demanding as ever.

"Get up. You're on in five," she hissed, staring down at me with her nose wrinkled up, like I was a splash of mud that had gotten on her pristine white Chanel coat.

"And while you're getting ready, think about this shitshow." She threw down her phone where there was an article displayed from some news site, speculating I'd been high at a recent show.

They weren't wrong.

"If you have to be a weak little brat…" she said snidely,

tossing me the bottle of pills she'd forced down my throat for years. I took them willingly now before shows and appearances; I couldn't get through a show without them. "Then you need to control yourself better. That's all you need is more bad fucking publicity."

A wave of shame sliced through my skin, like it always did when she pointed out all my deficiencies. No matter what I did…I was a disappointment.

There was a knock on the door and Marco opened it without waiting for anyone to tell him to come in. I stiffened at his appearance. He wasn't supposed to be at this show tonight. I wasn't supposed to have to deal with him too. A bead of sweat dripped down my spine and my hands began to tremble.

Marco's gaze darted to the bottle in my hand and his smarmy grin widened. "Getting ready for the show, princess?"

The word "princess" made me want to vomit. It's what he whispered to me when he…a sob built up in my chest and the edges of my vision darkened.

Stop it, I told myself fiercely. I couldn't think about *that* right now. I had to go out on stage.

I unscrewed the cap and swallowed a few of the pills, hoping it would bring the calm I so desperately needed.

The problem was that it was starting to take more and more of the pills to give me the numbness I craved.

My mother watched me, a small, smug smile on her face that made me want to scream, destroy the room…destroy myself.

Even more than I already was.

"A shot or two will finish the job," Marco said casually as he walked over and grabbed a bottle of vodka and poured it into a shot glass. He meant that it would kick in with the pills and get me to the numbness I required for the show…but it fit right in with my current thought process. Finish the job…

He handed the shot glass to me, making sure his fingers slid against mine when he did it, and I tried to hold in the revulsion and fear his touch gave me.

I threw the vodka back, not even noticing the burn. Or maybe it wasn't that I didn't notice it. Maybe it was that I liked the hurt.

There it was.

I could feel the numbness sliding through me, erasing all the nerves, and the nausea, and the pain.

My high always started with a subtle warmth spreading through my body, like a comforting embrace that chased away the cold that had gripped me just moments before. The trembling in my hands subsided, and a sense of calm settled in.

But it didn't stop there. The calm deepened into a soothing euphoria, like a gentle wave washing over me. My senses seemed to sharpen, and the world around me became more vibrant, as if I were seeing it through a new lens. The colors in the dressing room seemed to pop, and the soft hum of the fluorescent lights became a melodic symphony.

My heart rate steadied, and the knot of tension in my stomach loosened. It was as though a weight had been lifted from my shoulders, and I felt lighter, freer. The anxiety that had plagued me was like a distant memory, replaced by a sense of invincibility, like I was flying high above myself. All my problems were drowned out by the euphoria slicing across my skin.

"That's it, princess," Marco purred as my mother adjusted my outfit.

I stared at myself in the mirror, admiring the way the liquid silver of my form-fitting, sleeveless gown shimmered under the dressing room's lights. My chest had intricate beadwork that caught the light, creating a dazzling effect that seemed to rival the stars themselves.

Or maybe that was just my high talking.

After she was satisfied with how I looked, they led me out of the dressing room. We got into a golf cart, and then I was driven to where I'd enter the arena.

"Try not to embarrass me," Jolette snarked as I got out of the cart.

I normally would flinch at her words. But right then, there

was nothing that could touch me, nothing that could make me feel anything but *this*.

I grinned at her and she scoffed. "Did we give her too much?" she muttered to Marco as he stared at me with greedy, glimmering eyes.

"She's fine," he answered, handing me my guitar. I hummed under my breath as my fingers brushed the strings.

It was time.

I walked down the tunnel and emerged into the brightly lit arena, and a deafening roar erupted from the crowd. The screams and applause battered against me as I moved, but my high acted as a barrier, protecting me from the anxiety that it would have given me otherwise.

I stepped onto the stage, the spotlight capturing me in its brilliant glow, and I leaned towards the microphone with a confident smile that had come from doing this what seemed like a million times over the years. "My name is Olivia," I announced, my voice carrying over the enthusiastic cheers of the audience. "And welcome to my show."

With that introduction, I launched into my first song. The lyrics flowed effortlessly from my lips, and my voice soared through the arena, filling every corner. The crowd, caught in the magic of the moment, sang along, their voices blending with mine in a soundtrack that I both adored and hated at the same time.

Minutes stretched into hours, and I sang to them. And they sang to me.

And for a little while, I felt happy.

——————

After the show, I walked back into the dressing room, and I stared at myself, not recognizing the girl glaring back at me.

My once dark auburn hair had been bleached to a harsh, unnatural shade of blonde, its tips brittle and fried from constant styling and coloring. It was a far cry from the healthy, vibrant locks that I'd had as a little girl. My eyes, normally a shade of hazel with gold rims…just like my grandmother's, were blown out and ringed with kohl, their intensity dulled by layers of makeup. My cheeks, once filled with youthful vitality, now appeared gaunt and hollow. Like a skeleton.

My face was caked with layers of foundation, concealer, and powder, a mask that concealed every imperfection and blemish.

I looked sick.

No wonder the gossip rags were always talking about me.

I *was* sick.

I pulled on one of my curls, staring at the stranger in the mirror.

My high was almost gone, and with its demise, a creeping sense of unease was settling in. The rush of euphoria and confidence was giving way to an unsettling emptiness, a void that seemed to grow with each passing moment. The world around me had lost its luster, and all that was left was the stark reality of my existence.

A subtle restlessness gnawed at the edges of my consciousness, making it difficult to find comfort in my own skin. My limbs felt heavy and sluggish, a stark contrast to the heightened energy and alertness I'd had just hours before.

I needed to go home.

Marco and my mother were long gone. They'd probably only stayed to make sure I made it out to the stage. Laura, one of my hired handlers, was waiting outside the dressing room to escort me to my ride. One of my houses was nearby, and for the first time in a long time, I didn't have to sleep in a hotel, or on a bus.

If only the house felt more like a home.

Laura didn't say a word to me during the forty-five minute ride to the outskirts of the city. But I was used to that.

I never would have thought you could be lonely while constantly surrounded by people.

But my life was testament to that.

I shifted in my seat as the mansion came into view. It seemed to loom before me, its opulent facade illuminated by a cascade of vibrant lights. It was ridiculous looking, too big, too flashy..too excessive. My mother had forced me to buy it for us a few years ago, saying that I needed it to reflect my fame.

Really, though, it was an extravagant testament to her insatiable hunger for status and prestige. Everything about it was hers, from the ostentatious decorations, to the servile staff that catered to her every whim. Even the food in the kitchen was carefully selected and monitored by her.

I'd always felt like a stranger every minute that I spent between its walls.

I stepped through the imposing double doors, rubbing at my pounding head.

All I wanted to do was climb into bed after performing for hours. But of course that wasn't possible.

Jolette had guests over. A mansion full of them.

All of them a carefully curated collection of individuals who had one thing in common: they had used me as a stepping stone to further their own ambitions. They were the hangers-on, the sycophants who clung to my mother as a means to climb the social ladder, and they had little interest in me beyond the status boost my name provided.

They moved through the opulent rooms with an air of entitlement, their designer outfits and expensive accessories on full display. They laughed too loudly, their voices filled with false enthusiasm, as if they were all trying to outdo each other in their quest to get noticed.

They were opportunists, all of them. All they cared about was getting the chance to say they were at a party at my mansion, because it would make them seem more important than they actually were.

Someone's phone camera flashed as I walked through the room, and I grimaced as they took a picture of me. I'd changed into a pair of comfy sweats after the show, since my dress had been drenched in sweat.

They smiled at me and waved, all of them wanting my attention. They were vipers wearing suits of skin, and I hated them all.

Fuck. My head was throbbing.

I turned a corner...and there was Marco, leaned over a wannabe C list actress that had been trying to get his attention for weeks. I only knew that because she'd been my assistant at one time. Before she'd sold a lying sack of crap sob story about what a horrible brat I was to the media and got a spot on a soap opera because of it.

Of course she'd be allowed in my home.

Her dress was pulled down and his hand was squeezing her enormous fake boob. I grimaced and he saw me, immediately straightening up and shooing her away. She shot me a phony smile and waved like we were the best of friends before she trounced out of the room. Because why wouldn't she?

"There you are, princess. I've been looking all over for you. I have some contracts for you to sign."

"We need to wait until morning. I've got a headache," I croaked, my head pounding and my eyes feeling like they were going to melt out of my head.

He took my arm and began to lead me down a hallway that led to the office he used in the mansion. "We need to go over them now. Especially with the recent headlines about you, we need to lock these agreements in place before the companies decide to revoke them based on bad publicity."

I pulled on my arm, but he was holding it in a firm grip. It at least got him to slow down. "I don't think I'm going to be signing up for the next tour. I need a break. I'm exhausted. And if I do play, I want it to be at smaller venues, like at music clubs or something. Places that feel more intimate."

His face curled up in disgust. "Why the fuck would you want something like that? You're at the top of your game. You need to keep pushing. They won't always want you, so you have to take advantage while they do."

That was a threat he and my mother always had. Everything was about the next big thing in music. It was *me* right now, but in a moment's notice…it could be someone else. So I had to push, push, push until that other person came along.

My headache pulsed and a wave of nausea built up in my throat. When was the last time I'd eaten? Were pills and alcohol really all I'd had today?

I yanked on my arm this time, forcing him to let me go. "I'm not signing up for the tour. I'm tired. I—" my voice hitched. "I can't continue like this."

There was no sign of understanding in his gaze, no sign that he empathized…or that he cared. Instead his gaze grew hard and flinty, filling me with a sense of unease.

"Marco?" my mother said, coming around the corner and making the situation even worse. "What's the problem with the brat now?"

"*Princess* here is saying she needs a break. She's refusing to head out on the next tour..despite all the time that's already been put into planning it. Despite all the people that are counting on it to put food on the table for their families."

That was also something they used quite often, the threat of all the jobs that would be lost if "Olivia Darling" was no longer in business.

Except I was so tired at the moment, so out of sorts, so done…I couldn't find it in myself to really care.

"They'll understand that I'm human, and sometimes, I need a break."

My mother's red polished fingernails dug into my skin. "Spoken like a girl who doesn't understand how lucky she is," she spat.

Vomit filled my mouth, and I choked it back. I pulled my arm from her grasp and started to back away from the two snarling assholes in front of me.

"What's wrong, princess, need another hit?" Marco asked cajolingly, holding up the pills that he and my mother kept control over so they were my only access point.

Believe me, I'd tried to get ahold of some of those myself, and somehow they blocked me successfully at every attempt.

"I'm going to bed. And you can tell everyone, AS MY AGENT, that I'm taking a break. I'm not deciding on tours, or music...or my next record deal until I'm ready."

My heart was fluttering like mad around me, sweat beading on my forehead with the effort to stand up to them like this.

But I couldn't do it anymore. Something had to change.

Marco patted my mother's back, and his face gentled. "You know, you're completely right. You have been working hard... you need a break. You *deserve* a break."

I wrinkled my nose in confusion at his about face, waiting for him to add one of those all important "buts" to his sentence.

"We shouldn't be talking about what's next. We should be celebrating what you've just accomplished! A sold out tour, including ten football stadiums...you've truly catapulted to new heights."

My mother side-eyed him and then shrugged. "It's true, Olivia. We owe you an apology. You have been working so hard."

Had aliens invaded their bodies? Why was my mother's tone so nice? I eyed them suspiciously.

"Thank you for understanding," I said slowly, not trusting a word coming out of their mouths. "I'm just going to head to bed now."

"Nonsense," Marco said, beckoning me to his office. "We need to have a celebration drink, just a nightcap to celebrate a job well done."

No way was I taking alcohol from him. He'd probably spike my drink. But the way they were so intently watching me...I would just go in and sit with them for five minutes. Then I would excuse myself. I'd stood up to them, I'd actually done it. I could do this.

Marco gestured to his office and I followed him into the room that he'd had completely redone to suit his taste—despite the fact that this wasn't his house...and I wasn't his only client. It wasn't normal that he was here like this. But he and Jolette had insisted on it..so it had been done.

The room was out of place in the rest of the mansion, which was the epitome of traditional. His office had been done with clean lines and a monochromatic color scheme that screamed "modern." The walls were covered with abstract artwork, their bold strokes and vibrant colors providing a striking contrast to the otherwise muted palette of the room. His desk was a polished slab of dark wood, adorned only with a few essential items—a sleek computer, a designer lamp, and a stack of contracts and scripts. Shelves lined one wall of the office, displaying an array of awards and accolades...all thanks to my work. Golden statuettes, glistening trophies, and framed certificates sparkled in the ambient light.

The fact that they were in here, and not in my room, told a clear picture of who he attributed my success to—himself.

"Brandy?" he asked, holding up a decanter from his bar cart on the far wall. My hands were trembling, and my mouth was watering...but I couldn't be a fool.

Ignorance was only acceptable for so long.

"Just one of those water bottles," I murmured, watching his eyes flash down to my shaking hands in my lap.

"Suit yourself. It's not very celebratory," my mother said, pouring herself some of the brandy with a smirk, like she was mocking my paranoia about the drink.

Marco handed me a sealed water bottle out of his mini fridge, and I opened the lid and gulped down the cool liquid. My throat was raw from singing for hours.

"To you, princess," Marco hummed, lifting up his glass of brandy. I smiled weakly, trying to convince myself to stay in the room for one more minute. They were taking this a lot better than I thought they would. Maybe they finally understood how close to the edge I was.

Probably not. But…maybe.

"So tell me, Olivia. What are you going to do on your little… break?" my mother asked. Her voice was still mocking, but without the usual rancor she had when she spoke to me.

"Rest," I croaked, my headache getting worse.

"How wonderful," she giggled. Giggled. She usually saved that for people she was trying to impress.

Wait…what was happening to her?

I blinked and leaned forward, trying to focus on her head because…something was wrong with it. Her eyes were sliding down her face. "What's—" I whispered, rubbing at my eyes. The room was blurring and warping. The artwork on the walls was melting and shifting in a nightmarish display. Panic clawed at my throat and I lurched out of my seat, pulling on my sweatshirt as I struggled to stand.

"What's happening to me?" I stammered, my voice coming out garbled and distorted. My body felt heavy and uncooperative, like my limbs didn't actually belong to me.

Laughter surrounded me, but it was demonic laughter, and it seemed to be coming from everywhere, like the room had suddenly filled with people while I'd been sitting in my chair.

"Help me," I rasped, but I couldn't make out faces anymore, everything seemed to be melting like hot wax, puddling onto the floor around me.

And still that laughter continued.

I needed to get out of here…call for help. I lurched towards what vaguely looked like an opening in the room, my movements clumsy and unsteady.

In the hallway, I clung to the cold, unforgiving walls for support, my breath coming in ragged gasps. My steps were faltering, and it felt like my legs were encased in concrete.

I tried to scream, but it was trapped inside me.

Step after step, I forced my way forward.

So many distorted faces. All wearing eerie masks of laughter. There were flashes of light, erratic and blinding...everywhere.

———

Beep. Beep. Beep.

I slid into consciousness, trying to open my eyes. But it was as if they'd been superglued shut. It took what felt like forever to finally open them, and then even longer until the room came into focus.

White. It was on every surface. White walls and a white ceiling. White tiles on the floor.

White sheets.

Sheets? I stared at them, trying to figure out where I was. A hotel?

Some kind of weird, monochromatic one?

I tried to move my arm and something chafed my skin.

There was a scratchy band around my wrist.

It took me a second to realize that it was holding me to the bed.

Panicked, I pulled on my arm, trying to dislodge it. A moment later I realized that my ankles were also bound.

As I continued to struggle, a nurse entered the room, of course wearing a meticulous white uniform.

I'd obviously realized by now that something bad had happened. And the pitying way she was staring at me wasn't making me feel any better.

"Can you please undo these?" I asked desperately, even though I had a feeling I knew what the answer was going to be.

"Don't you worry, darlin," she cooed. "We're going to get you the help you need. That's a promise. Your family is working very hard."

My family?

"What...?" I whispered in confusion. The door to the room swung open and my mother and Marco rushed into the room.

"Oh you're awake. Thank God!" my mother said, almost hysterically, as she squeezed Marco's arm like she'd fall over without his support.

"We're going to help you," said Marco gravely.

I blinked up at them owlishly, trying to understand what they were saying. It felt like I was the punchline of some kind of joke...and I didn't get it.

I bit down on my lip, trying to think of how I'd gotten here. I'd been performing right? And then I'd gone home. We'd been celebrating the last show and...

"You drugged me!" I screeched, pulling at the bindings desperately and thrashing around. I had to get out of here. I had to tell someone.

"Is this from the drugs?" my mother cried pathetically at the nurse, one hand still clutching Marco.

The woman nodded her head. "Coming down from that amount of ketamine can cause delusions. And combined with the other drugs she had in her system...she's so lucky you were able to get her here in time."

Ketamine?! "I've never taken ketamine in my life," I snapped, hating how the nurse kept looking at me.

"Can we have a minute?" sniffed my mother.

The nurse hesitated and then nodded. "I'll be back in a few minutes to check some more vitals."

Marco and my mother waited until the nurse had closed the door behind her before their masks slipped. Gone was the concern, and in its place...pure evil.

"Did you really think we were going to let you destroy all of our hard work with one of your tantrums?"

"What have you done?" I whispered, desperately yanking again at the bindings. What was this fabric? It wouldn't even budge.

"Well, we started with a 5150 psych hold," Marco offered

with a grin. "And tomorrow we'll be appearing in front of a judge to start the conservatorship process."

"I won't let you get away with this," I said…as fiercely as I could manage in a hospital gown, tied to a bed with all my basic rights stripped away.

"*Okay*," my mother snickered sarcastically.

Marco opened up the briefcase he had with him and began to throw newspapers and magazines on the bed. All of them covered in pictures…of me.

From that night.

I was in my sweats, with a bottle in my hand, vomit stains on the front of my top. In one of the pictures my sleeve was rolled up and there was a needle in my hand that I was pressing into my arm. In another of the pictures, I was on my knees in front of some guy…On and on they went. Like I'd had a personal photographer witness to my downfall.

The headlines were just as bad.

"Pop Princess Olivia's Shocking Downfall: A Tragic Tale of Drug Scandal and Despair!"

"Olivia's Dark Descent: From Chart-Topping Sensation to the Depths of Addiction."

"The Rise and Fall of America's Darling: Inside Her Drug-Fueled Spiral."

"Olivia's Drowning in Fame: The Scandal That Rocked the Music World!"

"From Sweet Melodies to Bitter Pills: Olivia's Troubling Journey."

"Behind the Curtains: Olivia's Hidden Battle with Addiction."

"The Tragic Ballad of Olivia Darling: How Fame Led to Her Downfall."

"From Pop Stardom to Rock Bottom: The Shocking Truth About Olivia Darling's Struggle."

"Olivia's Last Note: The Pop Princess's Drug Scandal That Shook Hollywood!"

I stared at them all, a strange numbness sliding through me, greasy and thick.

"This isn't true," I whimpered. "Why would you do this?"

"We'll have all the control. We'll have all the money. You won't be able to do anything without our permission." My mother's voice was so gleeful, it was like a cartoon villain.

And as I sat there staring at them…all I could think was…

My life was over.

CHAPTER 2

WALKER

"Hello Disney," my brother's voice crowed at me mockingly through the speaker.

Fucking asshole.

"Should I be more specific than calling you 'Disney?' Like is this a situation where I need to ask you to let down your hair so I can come upstairs, like what's that chick's name?" continued Cole.

Rapunzel. "That chick" was Rapunzel. *Obviously.*

"I have no idea," I drawled, deciding that Ari fucking Lancaster needed a puck to the dick now that the nickname "Disney" was spreading across the news. "But if you want me to let you up, 'Walker' better be the only thing you're calling me."

"Come on, little brother. Let me in," he singsonged. I sighed and then pressed the button that allowed him through.

A few minutes later the elevator dinged, and Cole emerged, that effortless coolness surrounding him that had become his trademark. His longish, sun-kissed blonde hair fell to his shoulders, held back from his face with a dark blue bandana. His shirt was unbuttoned halfway down his chest and he was wearing some long necklace with a blue stone that matched his bandana. And the cowboy hat he was carrying…

Completely ridiculous.

"You look like a fucking hippie," I commented, and he snorted, removing his sunglasses and revealing the dark brown eyes that reminded me of Mom in a way that made my heart ache. He strode toward me, a carefree smile curved on his lips.

"Love you too, Walkie Poo," he cooed as he threw an arm around my neck and squeezed me into a hug.

He'd been on tour for the last six months with the Sounds of Us and our visits had been few and far between.

He was annoying. But it was good to see him.

Cole let me go and headed in the direction of my kitchen like he owned the place. "So ya ready for the big game tonight?" he asked as he opened my pantry and surveyed the contents.

"Make yourself at home," I said sarcastically.

He grinned. "I'm a growing boy, Disney. I need nutritional substance after weeks of living off whiskey."

I threw my keys at him, and he chuckled as he ducked just in time to avoid being hit.

I picked up my phone and shot off a text.

> Me: YOU'VE RUINED MY LIFE.

Ari answered immediately like he'd been waiting with bated breath since Sports Illustrated had released this morning.

> Ari: Excellent. We're doing this. I love a good drama scene.

> King Linc: What's the problem?

I grinned like I always did when Lincoln answered one of my texts. Because Lincoln Daniels was a god.

"Why do you have Lincoln in there as King Linc?" Cole asked over my shoulder. I jumped at the sound of his voice and hid my phone. My brother was like a cat.

"Don't you have a pantry to raid?" I snarled.

"Well, I couldn't help but notice that your rock god of a

brother isn't holding your attention at the moment," Cole grinned, folding his arms in front of him.

I scoffed. "Did you just call yourself a 'rock god'?"

"It's confidence. Not cockiness, little brother."

"Did you also rip your sleeves on purpose to make your arms look bigger?"

My phone buzzed, but there was a blush on my brother's cheeks so I ignored it for the moment.

This was too good.

"If you got it, flaunt it, Walkie," he finally said with a sniff, burying himself in the pantry again.

> Me: From hereforth "Disney" is not allowed in your vocabulary.

> Ari: I think the word you're looking for is 'henceforth,' Disney.

> King Linc: It's definitely henceforth.

"I agree. Definitely 'henceforth'," Cole said as he bit into an apple with a crunch.

"Fuck!" I cried, jumping again at the fact he'd managed to sneak up on me once more. "I hate you all," I growled.

Cole continued to eat his apple, completely unaffected by my ribbing.

My phone alarm went off and nerves spiked in my chest.

"Game time?" Cole asked and I nodded, rubbing my hand down my face.

Tonight was a big game. One of the biggest of my career. We were playing to get into the playoffs. But more importantly...I was playing to have a chance at a contract with Dallas for next year. Ari was leaving after this season, he'd been very clear about that.

I may have sounded like a pussy...but the chance to play with Ari and Lincoln...it was career goals for me.

L.A. had been good to me. But I was ready for change. And

I'd always felt like a fish out of water here. For a Tennessee boy, L.A. was an alien world.

I smirked as Cole fiddled with some kind of falcon feather in his pretentious cowboy hat that was more rockstar than ranch. Maybe *one* of the Davis brothers felt at home in L.A.

But it wasn't me.

"Parker's being a jealous prick that I'm going to the game and he's not," Cole smirked, looking decidedly delighted about that.

Our little brother had spring practice starting this week, and although it was a complete waste of time, Parker had the NFL draft in his sights and he was trying to do everything right to prepare for it.

"Interesting place for lingerie, Walkie," Cole commented, bending over and using a beef jerky stick to pick up a pair of black lacy panties. I blinked at them.

"I mean I knew you were a freak in the sheets, the nice ones always are, but the pantry? What would Mom say?" he drawled.

I scoffed, my cheeks burning, even though I knew his tour bus probably had to be scrubbed of DNA at the end of the tour because of all the tail he got after shows.

"Who was the lucky girl?" he asked, swinging the panties around on the tip of the beef jerky.

"Give me those." I grabbed them and stuffed them in the trash.

"I'm going to get ready," I called to him as I strode towards my room. "Please don't eat that jerky."

"I want names."

I threw a middle finger over my shoulder and hid in my room.

I actually had no idea whose underwear those were. I'd been on a bit of a dry streak as of late. Watching your best friends with their soulmates would do that to you.

One night stands or trying with puck bunnies who were with

me for all the wrong reasons wasn't having quite the same effect as it used to.

And there was the whole Davis family curse thing. Parker and Cole swore it wasn't true. But you couldn't help but think about it when every male relative that you'd ever heard of had experienced it. That moment when they locked eyes with a special woman and they were instantly in love.

My phone buzzed, saving me from my fucking pathetic thoughts.

> Ari: Blake just told me my dick looks bigger than normal. So we're definitely going to win tonight.

> Me: I didn't want to hear that.

> King Linc: What happened to not nutting before a big game?

> Ari: Like you haven't.

> King Linc: ...

> Ari:...

> Me: Again. I'm still here.

I snorted and went to take my pre-game shower where I decidedly was not going to nut.

Because it was a big game.

———

I was so glad that Cole couldn't see me right now. I was a terrible dancer, first of all, and he'd be offended that I was dancing to Taylor Swift instead of one of his songs.

But he just didn't have that infectious beat.

Ari's dance ritual got the team out of the funk they'd been in for the past hour and with one last "Cobras!", it was game time.

Ari slapped me on the ass as we waited in the tunnel, preparing to skate out.

I winked at him. "I thought you said no ass tap tonight?" I snorted.

Ari rolled his eyes, pushing his dark hair out of his face and slamming on his helmet. "Tonight's game is bigger than that, Disney," he retorted, getting his game face on.

I nodded and got my head in the game.

We skated out for warm-ups and I took my customary loop around the ice, counting to sixty-five as I did so. It was a weird ritual I did every game, and everyone knew not to talk to me until I made it back to the goal. Then they just had to wait a few more minutes so I could do twenty up downs. And then I was ready.

Hey...it was only weird if it didn't work. And it did work... like 75% of the time...at least this season.

"Have I ever told you you're kind of odd for a Disney prince," Ari commented as he skated by.

"I'm flipping you off right now," I yelled after him, even though that was impossible with my gloves on.

Across the way, Seattle's goalie was stretching and I glared, envisioning a million goals going past him, because if you didn't think it, you couldn't manifest it.

Hmmm. Maybe I was a little weird.

I was also...the fucking best, I told myself as warm-ups continued.

Because again, positive thinking was key.

"You're a wall, Disney. A fucking brick wall," Ari told me as he skated by, obviously getting it.

I nodded, keeping my focus on Coach Markov, who, armed with a bucket of pucks, was testing my reflexes from every angle.

Warmups ended and I skated over to the bench to grab a water bottle, lifting up my helmet to spray it on my face.

"Let's go, Disney," Cole yelled from nearby. I groaned and

put my best snarly face on as I glared at him through the glass. I had seats for the game that I'd given him, and he'd somehow filled three of the extra ones with *chicks*. They were hanging on him like he was a god. I groaned and he grinned and winked, the smug fuck.

Ari skated up beside me and grabbed some water. "This is going to be a good fucking time," he yelled at the team and all of them lifted a glove and roared with him.

And then it was time.

The puck dropped, and the first period was underway. Seattle was known for their aggressive offense, and I braced myself for an onslaught of shots. The rink echoed with the sounds of skates cutting the ice and sticks clashing. Within the first minute, Seattle's star forward burst through our defense, attempting a breakaway. I tracked his every move, staying square to the shooter. He released a quick wrist shot, but I snapped my glove hand out, snagging the puck mid-air. The crowd roared their approval.

Ari gave me a fist pump and I nodded at him, adrenaline spiking through my veins.

Moments later, a scramble in front of our net resulted in a point-blank shot. I dropped into the butterfly position, covering the lower portion of the net. Ryan Taylors, one of Seattle's forwards, fired a low shot, aiming for the five-hole, but I sealed the gap with my pads, denying him any daylight. The rebound was quickly cleared by Ari.

As the period progressed, Seattle gained momentum, creating a flurry of chances. A wicked slap shot from the blue line rocketed toward the top corner of the net. I read the play, tracking the puck's trajectory. With a desperate leap, I reached out and snagged it with my glove, robbing the shooter of a goal.

Fucking hell. How many saves was that already?

"That's my goalie," Ari called, right before he stole the puck from Taylors.

With less than five minutes left in the first period, Seattle executed a swift breakaway. Their forward skated in alone, and I could feel the collective tension in the arena mounting. As he unleashed a shot, I reacted instinctively, positioning myself to make the save.

The puck struck me squarely in the chest, and I quickly smothered it, anticipating a whistle from the ref. But it fucking never came. Play continued, and Seattle regained possession.

"Hey stripes, the whistle ain't a dick, you can blow it," Ari snarled as he knocked a player into the boards, struggling for the puck.

I snorted and shook my head.

But it was true. What the fuck.

The game continued, and with two minutes left, Sullivan made a sharp move towards Seattle's net, attempting to cut through their defense. One of Seattle's defensemen attempted to intercept the play but instead slammed Sullivan's facemask with the blade of his stick.

The resounding crack of the impact echoed through the arena and refs were blowing their whistles immediately, signaling a penalty. The crowd roared, screaming "Shame," over and over as the player skated to the penalty box.

Fucking loved when they did that.

It also meant it was powerplay time and I watched as Tommy skated towards the net, weaving in and out deftly despite his injured leg. He shot and...

Fuck yes. 1-0.

I stood at the net, getting ready for the second period, stretching my back and getting a drink of water. I was feeling antsy from all the adrenaline spiking through me.

I lived for this game.

I'd stopped every puck that came my way so far, and the anticipation was building as we inched closer to securing our playoff spot.

Hopefully Lincoln was coming through for us.

Not that I doubted him for a second.

That man was a god after all.

Ari shot me a thumbs up as he skated by and I readied myself for the next period to begin. "Good fucking job, Disney. Circle of trust behavior for sure."

I rolled my eyes, but I was feeling pretty proud of myself. I was a shoo-in for the Circle of Trust.

If it was actually a thing.

Hadn't quite figured that out yet.

I took in the crowd for a minute, listening to the cheers and the trash talk. My mom was big about taking in the moment. She always said that she wished she had taken in more of the small moments with Dad.

Fucking hell, why am I thinking about that?

I turned my focus back to the crowd and there was a distinct, piercing voice that cut through the noise. "You fucking suck, Davis!"

I mean, I'd heard that a million times. Fans trash talked me all the fucking time obviously…but something had me turning my head.

And there she was, standing on the other side of the glass.

Our eyes locked.

Mine.

I felt lightheaded as I stared at her, the world rearranging around me until all I could see…all I could feel…was her. I had no idea who she was. But for a heartbeat, I forgot about the game, the score…the pressure. I was entranced. Nothing else mattered.

I stared at her angelic face in blind amazement until I lost my mind and I blew her a kiss, watching in awe as her gorgeous face screwed up in disgust, gold flecked eyes unaware that she'd just changed my fucking world.

The buzzer sounded and I reluctantly dragged my gaze away from hers and towards the action happening on the other side of the ice, feeling like I was going to choke with all the nervous energy I was experiencing.

What if she left? What if I never knew who she was?

Fucking hell.

It felt like I would die if that happened. And yes, I was well aware I was being crazy.

"All good, Walk?" Ari called as he slid by.

I nodded, words escaping me at the moment.

"Hey Davis, anyone ever tell you you're just like a tampon? Only good for one period," Taylors called as he skated by.

"Heard you were the worst player on your last team too, asswipe," Ari said to Taylors through gritted teeth, knocking him in the boards before he stole the puck from him.

I loved that guy.

When the puck was safely on the other side, I dared to glance behind me to the beautiful girl who'd just rewritten my fucking stars. She wasn't paying any attention to me. Her focus was on what was happening on the other side of the ice.

She had no idea what she'd just done.

But she would.

"Walker!" someone choked out, and I pulled my attention back to the game.

Fuck.

A Seattle player was on a breakaway.

As he closed in, I did my best to cut down his angles. He tried to slip the puck through my legs, but I dropped into the butterfly, trapping the puck under my pads. Our fans erupted with applause.

"A little close there, Dis," Ari commented as he moved past me.

"Now I'm getting nicknames of my fucking nickname?" I called out as I tossed the puck to the ref.

"It's all about how I feel in the moment," he shot back as he lined up near Tommy who was getting ready for a face-off.

Another glance back at the girl. She was up on her feet, arms crossed in front of a rack that not even her loose Seattle jersey could hide.

Fuck. I was not about to get a woody in the middle of this fucking game.

Ari would never let me live that down.

I also was not going to rip off that Seattle jersey in the middle of the game.

Because I was a fucking gentleman.

At that moment Soto, our so-called enforcer, decided it was a good idea to throw his gloves off and throw some punches. I couldn't help but roll my eyes watching him go at it with the grace of an elephant. Predictably, he was banished to the penalty box, which meant our team was effectively down a player.

Seattle's power play unit moved the puck with precision, weaving a web of passes right through our defense. I braced myself for the shot.

But it happened. A swift pass, perfectly timed, and the puck whizzed past me, finding the back of the net. Seattle's fans erupted as the red light behind me illuminated.

Fuck. Fuck. Fuck.

"Hey tender, your legs are so wide open you make your mama look like a saint," Taylors called as he shot me a smug grin.

"Taylors', your mama's so nasty, they used to call them "jumpolines" 'til she bounced on one," Tommy called back as he skated by with a nod.

Ari snorted. "Tommy, I didn't know you were funny." He patted me on the helmet. "Not another shot, *Walker Disney Davis*. You're a fucking wall."

I nodded, feeling like the girl's eyes were staring into the back of my helmet. She was going to think I sucked.

I'm a fucking wall. I'm a fucking wall, I chanted to myself, determined *not* to suck anymore.

The next play Seattle executed a perfectly timed cross-ice pass, setting up a one-timer from the faceoff circle. I kicked out my left leg in a sweeping motion, deflecting the puck away from the net.

"Very nice, Disney," Ari screamed. "Good fucking boy."

Praise kink unlocked. I'd have to examine that later.

Second period ended without another score, and I skated desperately off the ice as soon as the buzzer sounded. My teammates were trying to talk to me, but I was a man on a mission.

"Hey, Fargo," I called out to one of the security guards by the box. He frowned and looked at me. "There's a girl over there," I told him, gesturing to the blonde. "Second row, towards the middle." He squinted and then finally nodded.

"Davis—in the locker room," Coach Gretz yelled as he walked by. I waved at him, unable to go in for the break until I knew she couldn't get away.

"Fargo, for the love of all that is holy. Find a way to keep that girl here after the game. I don't care what it takes."

He stared at me like I'd lost my mind. And I was pretty sure if he was thinking that...he'd be right.

"Kid, what do you want me to do, kidnap her?" he asked, confused. "And what are you doing thinking about pussy in the middle of a game? Don't you get fucking laid enough?"

For a second I was tempted to rip his vocal chords out for calling my girl "pussy," but I held myself back. That wouldn't get me what I wanted.

"Fargo. Figure it out. $1000 for you if you do it."

His eyes widened. "Are you shitting me?"

"No. I'm not shitting you," I snapped, riding the edge of desperation.

"Davis—what the fuck is going on?" Coach Gretz yelled again, popping his head back in from the tunnel.

"Fargo," I pleaded with the old man, feeling like my life fucking hung in the balance. If he didn't say yes, I didn't know what I was going to do. Quit the game? Fake an injury?

Fuck, I couldn't let Ari and the others down like that.

But this moment felt like I was holding fate in my hands.

"Fine, kid. I'll figure something out. But you're going to owe me a thousand fucking dollars."

I nodded, only feeling slightly better as I stomped my way into the locker room where I was most definitely going to get reamed by Gretz for taking so long.

————

Three minutes left in the third period and we were ahead by one, I'd kept sneaking glances at her when I could, but I hadn't let another goal pass.

Was she impressed?

I'd lifted my mask up multiple times, trying to see if I could attract her attention. But nothing. It was like I didn't exist outside of that one moment where she'd told me I'd fucking sucked.

Cole had noticed me looking at her and was now waggling his eyebrows every time I glanced over.

Fucking prick.

Desperation hung thick in the air as Seattle continued their offensive onslaught. They were like a wounded animal backed into a corner, and Ari and I were having to play fucking lights out to stop them.

Taylors unleashed a blistering slapshot, and I reacted instinctively. My glove shot up, snatching the puck.

Fuck. That was close.

"What a fucking king," Ari shouted, doing a little dance on the ice. I saluted him and pretended I needed a drink...for the five hundredth time...so I could make sure she was still there.

She was fucking staring at me. She raised both hands slowly and flipped me off and I almost passed out on the ice, just from having her attention.

Because evidently I had forgotten how to interact with someone of the opposite sex, I once again blew her a fucking kiss.

Thank fuck Linc wasn't here, and Ari wasn't paying attention.

They would be so ashamed of my current game.

But then she blushed and averted her eyes.

And fuck...was I swooning?

The seconds ticked down and then Seattle was pulling their goalie. Ari knocked the puck loose from Taylors and sent it to Tommy.

Goal!!!!!

I shook my fist and screamed as the buzzer sounded, signaling the end of the game and a fucking victory.

A victory that would mean nothing if Dallas didn't win.

I hesitated, feeling fucking frozen in the net as my whole team skated towards the bench to watch the rest of the Dallas game. She was standing up, she was getting ready to go...and then Fargo was there, stopping her from leaving.

Thank fuck.

Praying that a thousand dollars was a good enough incentive for him to keep her there, I skated towards the bench. Cole was up on his feet, screaming as I skated by. "One to one," he mouthed and I nodded, feeling sick to my stomach. Dallas and Detroit were tied.

The fans were already celebrating as our whole team watched the game on someone's iPhone.

Lincoln was a god. He could fucking do it.

And then he did do it. Breaking away, he slipped a shot right in between the Detroit tender's legs.

Fuckkk.

Like I hadn't worshiped him enough before.

Linc skated up to a camera and blew it a kiss. And Ari snatched it up like it belonged to him.

I scooped it up behind him, pretending it was for me.

Because it could have been. Or at least I could dream.

Security was letting fans onto the ice to celebrate like we'd just won the Stanley Cup, and I searched desperately to see where the girl was.

Fargo was leading her onto the ice!

Nervous butterflies about knocked me over.

"Disney, you fucking rocked," Cole shouted as he scrambled onto the ice with everyone else. "Let's get druunk!" He slung an arm around my neck, not minding at all that I was a sweaty mess and possibly smelled like balls.

Fuck. If I went over to her smelling like this...she was probably going to run away.

Cole kept raving about the game, holding up his phone where he had Parker on Facetime.

Any other day before today, this would have been my dream. Celebrating with my brothers and Ari.

But today...today I was desperate to get to her.

My girl.

Mine.

CHAPTER 3
OLIVIA

"It's a big game, Liv…and you always have excuses. Just come tonight, pleaseeeee," Harley wheedled.

Harley was the only family member I could stand, and even rarer, one of the only people that I trusted in the world. "You can wear one of your disguises and sit next to Maddie, no one will ever suspect that the great Olivia Darling is at a hockey game. Especially since you've been a ghost for the last two years."

I didn't know how long it would take for the world to forget what had happened…but maybe.

"It's a big fucking deal, Liv. I wouldn't ask you if it wasn't."

I winced. More from what he wasn't saying than what he was. Harley and his girlfriend had basically been my only support since I'd woken up in that hospital. They were the only ones to believe me when I said I'd been drugged…the only ones not to make me feel like I was crazy.

Public events were *definitely* not my thing anymore, but he was right…with a little disguise, who would know?

I grabbed a wig and a Seattle jersey he'd sent me, making sure to hide every lock of my dark auburn hair. Frowning, I stared in the mirror. I couldn't wear sunglasses, that would be a surefire way to get noticed at an L.A. event. It was basically the

M.O. of all the celebrities after all. And I hadn't replenished my stock of colored contacts. I slipped on a baseball cap, hoping that would help hide me more. Between that and the fact that my face was bare of the heavy makeup I used to wear every day... would that be enough?

Staring at myself, I couldn't help but start to think about all the things that could go wrong. My heart thundered against my ribcage. My trembling hands tried to adjust the baseball cap, but there was no hiding my face.

My chest tightened, each breath becoming shallower, more erratic, as anxiety wrapped around me like a tightening vice. The room felt smaller, like it was closing in on me. Flashing lights filled my vision and then the questions began...all of the questions.

The moment the heavy courthouse doors swung open, a barrage of piercing flashes assaulted me. Blinding and relentless, they broke through the carefully constructed façade I had worn for the courtroom.

The air was filled with the deafening roar of paparazzi voices. They swarmed like vultures, eager to catch any hint of weakness or vulnerability.

"What did you take this morning, Olivia?" one of them had shouted, a twisted grin on his face as he elbowed past my bodyguard. "Why are you lying?"

"Stop," I screamed at my reflection, feeling in that moment that maybe I was actually as crazy as everyone thought I was.

I turned away from the mirror in disgust and strode towards the door before I could have second thoughts.

Fuck this. I was going to the game. I was a "has been". A nobody. With nothing.

One night out wasn't going to change that.

I didn't call for my driver. He would tell Jolette and Marco I'd left and then there would be questions.

I walked a few blocks down from my place and waited for Maddie to swing by to pick me up in her Uber.

Maddie's enthusiasm was infectious as she hopped out of the

car, her blue eyes sparkling with excitement. Her short blonde bob framed her face perfectly, and she was also wearing Harley's jersey.

"Liv!" Maddie all but screeched, throwing her arms around me. "You ready for the game? Your cousin's a nervous wreck!"

I glanced anxiously down the sidewalk, like any minute now someone would pop out and come at me.

But of course, no one was paying attention.

Relaxing slightly, I nodded at Maddie and climbed into the car with her as she immediately chatted away on all the latest WAG gossip.

As we drove through the city, I held onto the seat like the nervous wreck I was, glancing at the Uber driver every couple of seconds, sure that he would recognize me.

But he didn't even spare me a second glance…

My nerves only increased as we pulled into the arena's parking lot and I saw the swarms of people everywhere.

"Hey," Maddie whispered, putting a hand on top of my shaking one. Her eyes were filled with concern…and pity.

That was what I hated most of all. The fact that the whole world pitied me now.

"We don't have to do this. Harley will survive. He'll pout and complain because he's a big baby, but he loves you. He'll understand."

I shook my head. "No. I'm fine. I just…don't get out much," I whispered back lamely, sneaking another glance at the driver who still seemed to not be paying attention to me.

For some reason, the offer to leave was enough to settle me so that I could get out of the car and walk with her into the arena.

As we walked, my confidence slowly increased.

I was just one of the masses. No one was giving me a second look. And if they were giving me a second look, it wasn't one filled with recognition.

Which meant…I could just live. In the moment. Like everyone else.

A grin touched my lips. Because wow…

After grabbing some popcorn, we made our way to our third-row seats, right behind the L.A. Cobras' goalie.

I took it all in.

The electrifying atmosphere. The crowd's excitement. The cheers and roars echoing through the arena. The way the ice glistened under the bright lights. The players doing drills as they warmed up.

And through it all, there was no one screaming my name, no one in my face. I was just one of the crowd.

It was heaven.

Harley skated by with a confident grin on his face. I waved at him, and he shot us a thumbs-up before focusing back on the game. Maddie squealed and tucked her arm in mine, her legs bouncing in anticipation.

The game began, the competition on the ice was insane. I'd been to Harley's games in college, but they'd been nothing like this. He'd been in the league for two years now, which happened to coincide with me hiding for the most part, so this was the first professional game I'd actually been to. Watching him on TV definitely didn't give the same vibes and excitement as actually being at the arena.

"Is every NHL game like this?" I whisper-yelled as Harley was slammed into the boards by an L.A. player.

"Mmmh. I think everyone's playing harder because of the playoff implications. They both have to have a win tonight to even have a chance," she explained, shrieking in my ear when Harley made a shot and it was saved by the L.A. goalie.

"Fuck, Walker Davis is good," she growled as we watched him make another save after that.

I rubbed at my ear, wondering if I'd ever regain the hearing I'd just lost with her screeching. "He does seem pretty good," I murmured, watching him move.

"Don't ever tell Harley I said this, but it's pretty freaking cool that we're getting to watch Ari Lancaster and Walker Davis play.

I mean, they're basically the best in their positions…and they're eye candy in the yummiest possible way."

She shot me a side glance.

"Like I said…don't ever tell Harley I said that."

I snorted and shook my head, staring at the two players in question.

It was hard to tell with their helmets on.

"Lancaster is new to L.A. this year. He used to play for Dallas and then after they won the Cup last year, he abruptly asked to be traded here."

I frowned. "How come?"

She giggled and pretended to swoon. Pointing over towards the L.A. bench, my eyes caught on a sign being held up behind a beautiful girl.

"Mrs. Lancaster is my baby angel face. Do Not Touch," I read out loud, snorting and then staring at Maddie with wide eyes. "What the heck?"

"I know. It's the cutest. That's the girl he requested the trade for. And now they're married." She squirmed in her seat. "It's a love story right out of a book or something."

"Mmmh," I responded, wondering what it would feel like to be loved like that. It was certainly something I'd never experience.

I couldn't get anyone to love me.

With each cheer and roar of the crowd, I was getting more into the game, the excitement feeding my own. Maddie screamed and yelled at every play, and her energy was contagious. I settled into my seat and found myself relaxing, the tension and worries I'd been feeling melting away.

Harley got slammed into the boards again, this time by Lancaster, and we both winced. Maddie leaped to her feet, "Fucking asshole!" she screamed at the L.A. player.

I snorted. This was actually pretty fun.

To rub more salt in the wound, the goalie blocked another

shot, right as the buzzer sounded, signaling the end of the period.

As if possessed by the spirit of a die-hard fan, I shot up from my seat and screamed at the L.A. goalie, "You fucking suck, Davis!" The words slipped out of my mouth before I even realized what I was doing, and once I did, I was dying. What the fuck was I doing? People were going to look at me.

But it was the person I didn't expect that actually did...

The goalie turned and stared at me, our eyes locking in a silent exchange that sent a shiver down my spine.

Wow.

He was pretty.

The kind of pretty that made you dizzy, and slightly obsessed. And wondering what having that for yourself would even be like.

I didn't know that people existed like that in real life.

And I'd been surrounded by pretty people for years.

But not like that.

How had I not heard about this guy before? His name should have been all over L.A.?

He had lifted his helmet, revealing a mess of brown hair, tousled in a way that looked more like he'd just rolled around in bed after a hot night of sex rather than played a period of a hockey game with a helmet on. He had a sharp jawline and intense blue eyes that seemed to pierce right through me.

But it was more than his looks that was getting me. He also had some kind of undeniable magnetism, an allure that was holding me captive.

I couldn't help but stare, enchanted by his beauty, as if he were a work of art on display for my eyes only.

And then...he blew me a kiss.

A fucking kiss. One that had fans squealing all around me.

I was immediately jealous of them seeing it. An insane part of me wanted to snatch it out of the air so that no one else could claim it for themselves.

I wanted to keep it for myself, like a dragon hoarding its jewels.

For the second time today, I wondered if I had actually gone crazy.

I glared at him for drawing attention to me...even though it was my own fault...and then I yanked my gaze away, pretending to stare disinterestedly at the banners hanging in the rafters of the arena.

"Wow," Maddie whispered, elbowing me in the gut.

I grunted and shot her a look.

"I feel like I need a smoke after watching that interaction," she commented with a smug grin, her eyebrows rising and falling lecherously.

"He was just egging me on," I told her, but it felt like I could still feel his gaze. Like he was tracing the lines of my body, doing something to me that I wasn't going to come back from.

It was official. I'd been without human companionship really for so long, that I was creating something that couldn't possibly exist.

That was all it was.

Out of the corner of my eye, I watched the goalie skate towards his bench. He stopped to talk to someone in a Cobras polo for a minute and then he disappeared from sight for the period break.

Had they been looking over here?

Surely not.

What if he was trying to get me removed from the game for yelling at him?

No...I wasn't yelling anything that anyone else wasn't.

I was pretty sure that was how sports events went.

"Too bad he's going to be on the other side for the next period," Maddie commented, still watching me closely like she could see the crazy thoughts in my head.

"Mmmh," I muttered non-committedly.

Her answering grin was honestly a little feral.

I ignored her and happily glanced around the arena. I hadn't had fun like this in...forever. The thrill of being out in the open, surrounded by the anonymity of the crowd...it was like a breath of fresh air. For once, I was simply blending in. I loved it.

The game proceeded on and as the clock wound down, I was feeling pretty bad for Harley. He'd played a great game, but L.A. was just better.

I was also feeling a strange sense of sadness about leaving.

Which I was not about to admit may have had something to do with having to leave Walker Davis's presence.

I'd found myself tracking his every move...for the entire game.

I had the strangest urge to curse him out again, just to see if he'd blow me another kiss.

Which was crazy. I was an under-the-radar kind of girl now. Something in this stadium had definitely gotten to me.

It had almost seemed like he'd glanced at me several times during the game. But that had probably been wishful thinking.

Not that I wanted anyone to pay attention to me.

It was a weird thing that for the first time in years, I was rethinking that.

The buzzer sounded and Harley and the rest of Seattle skated off the ice dejectedly as the L.A players moved towards their bench like their asses were on fire.

"What are they doing?" I asked Maddie as we stood up and prepared to leave—or I prepared to leave. Maddie was going to go meet up with Harley before they both flew home.

"I bet they're watching the Dallas game," she answered, pulling up the score between Dallas and Detroit on her phone. "L.A. had to beat Seattle to have a chance at all, but then Dallas had to win too." She huffed. "All Seattle had to do was win to get to the playoffs. I can't believe they blew it."

We watched as Dallas's #13 did some kind of crazy puck handling and scored a goal for the win. The fans around us had already been going crazy, but now the players were too.

Maddie stood up. "Let's get out of here. I hate watching other teams celebrate." I stood up to follow her and all of a sudden a grizzled old security guard was standing at our row.

Maddie and I stared at him, unsure.

"Please exit through the ice, ladies," he said in a no-nonsense voice, gesturing to where fans were pouring onto the ice in celebration.

Maddie pointed to the people who were also filing up the stairs…the normal way. "We can just go up that way. It's not a big deal."

"We're asking everyone in the first five rows to exit through there. For safety concerns," he added…almost as an afterthought.

"You want us to exit on the ice?" I asked, confused. Maddie's forehead was also scrunched up. Evidently this was a new one for her as well.

"Okayyyy," Maddie murmured, grabbing my head and leading me down a few steps and around, to where people were flooding the ice.

"This doesn't feel like a safety precaution," I called to her as I narrowly missed getting my nose bashed in by an eager fan holding a giant "I Love You, Lancaster" sign, my feet slipping as I tried to walk on the slippery surface. I'd never been particularly coordinated.

"It's fun to be out on the ice. Fuck…there's Ari Lancaster," she whispered, coming to a sudden stop and grabbing onto my arm like she needed it to keep her from jumping at him.

"You're hopelessly in love with Harley and Ari's married!" I reminded her, feeling my own kind of shaky in the face at how good looking Ari was.

But he wasn't as good looking as that goalie.

Walker. That's what she said his name was.

"I know I love Harley. I'm just having a fangirl moment," Maddie retorted.

"Can you fangirl after we get off the ice? It's getting full." My gaze watched everyone nervously.

"Give me one more moment," she hissed, and I said a silent prayer.

I'd gotten comfortable during the game, but being on the ice with everyone walking around and yelling, nearly bowling into us...it was making me nervous again. It just took one person recognizing me to set everyone off.

And I wanted to keep this night for myself. I didn't want to have to explain it to Jolette and have her ruin it...just because she could tell it brought me joy.

Suddenly an arm swung around my waist and carried me forward.

"Eeeek!" I shrieked, only to be set down a little bit away. "What the hell?" I snarled, prepared to have a hissy fit on whoever had dared to grab me like that.

But when I swung around, all the anger immediately fled my body. Replaced by white hot...lust.

It was him.

The L.A. Goalie.

Walker Davis.

He was staring at me, an amused smirk on his full, perfect lips.

I felt dizzy. Confused. Caught...

A weird feeling, but there was something almost predatory about him. Not in a gross way. But in a way that told me this was the way man had meant to be created. Like all the DNA in the world had come together in its most perfect form...and come up with him.

I'd thought his eyes were just blue, but this close to him, I could see a kaleidoscope of colors. The blue was interwoven with subtle hints of emerald green and flecks of steel gray, and I was beginning to think that magical powers were real because he seemed to have ensnared me with his gaze.

His brown waves actually had sun-kissed highlights adding

depth to the strands. Even in the harsh lighting of the arena, his locks seemed to shimmer. Like he was some kind of mystical god or something.

"Wow," he murmured, and I ached, because maybe a part of me had just fallen in love with the sound of his voice.

It was like honey, warm and smooth as it slid across my skin. Wow indeed.

I'd never written a song about a real man. But Walker Davis may have changed my mind.

"Ahem," Maddie inserted, clearing her throat in an over the top way and bringing me crashing back to reality.

A reality where I was standing way too close to this stranger. And the reality that his arms were still around me.

I shivered, but not from the cold of the ice. I shivered from the need pulsing through my body. Need I hadn't experienced since…

The old memory creeped in and like a bucket of ice water, everything was gone. And I was the numb void I'd been for years once again.

"Excuse me," I murmured, attempting to extricate myself from his embrace. Even though a part of me wanted to snuggle into him.

"Sorry, you were—ah—about to be knocked over, and I guess I got a little carried away trying to save you," he said with a grin. His voice was a low, husky rumble, like his words were just for me. Like this was an intimate moment he was trying to make our own.

I'd always had a wild imagination. It's what had made me so good at writing songs. But the scenarios my brain was coming up with at the moment were on a whole other level.

"I'll see you later," Maddie mouthed just beyond him, pointing to the exit. "You stay here with the hottie."

Or at least I think that's what she'd just said.

The crowd was starting to dissipate…at least a little. And glancing around, the ratio of players to fans was improving. But a lot of the ones left were yelling Walker's name...asking for autographs. I didn't want them to notice me.

Which meant I needed to leave.

Besides large crowds...and small crowds...I also didn't do celebrities.

And staring at Walker Davis's beautiful face, the face that hadn't strayed from mine since the moment I'd turned around... I was definitely looking at a celebrity.

"I'm Walker," he offered, his voice low and still way too sexy...

I opened my mouth automatically, a part of me prepared to give this stranger whatever he wanted...his voice and face and everything way too convincing...

And then I slammed it shut. An idea forming...

This god of a man was clearly attracted to me.

The way he was leaning towards me...how he couldn't tear his gaze from my face...the way he was biting down on that bottom lip...

He at least wanted a minute of my time...and maybe I could give him a little bit of that. If given the chance—what woman on this planet wouldn't?

But not as myself.

He was too beautiful for my brokenness.

"Violet," I finally murmured. His eyes flashed in response to my name, but he didn't challenge it.

"Walkie," a deep voice called out, and then an arm was slung around Walker's neck, a tattooed arm...that led to another gorgeous face...with very similar features.

A familiar face.

Cole Davis. Frontman for Anarchy...an up and coming band I'd been obsessed with over the past year. Their show with the Sounds of Us was the only show I'd been tempted to sneak out for last year.

What was my life right now?

There was something almost disappointing about the way his

eyes slid over me, no recognition that I'd once been his peer.

That I'd once been bigger than him.

"You did so fucking good, bro. You were a killa," he drawled in a light southern accent that matched his brother's. A second later his gaze met mine. "Well helloooo," Cole crooned with the signature charm that he was known for.

My eyes couldn't stay focused on him for more than a few seconds though. His brother's face was like a tractor beam, pulling me in. Still giving me that light, overwhelming, woozy, delirious feeling.

Beguiled curiosity. That was how I would describe the way Walker was staring at me. Like I was a puzzle he had to figure out.

I'm not going to tell him that there's nothing to see. That I'm an empty husk that's been sucked dry of anything redeeming or worthy.

Tonight, I'm going to be Violet, free of my past...free to have fun.

In a couple of hours I can go back to misery.

"I need to get laid," Cole complained, dragging my attention back to him. "If it was possible, I'd be pregnant right now from the way you two are looking at each other."

Walker's eyes gleamed and he seemed to preen. Like that was the biggest compliment his brother could have given him.

My whole body flushed in embarrassment, because Cole was right...I was definitely eye fucking his brother.

"I'll just leave you two to...celebrate," Cole murmured, whispering something in Walker's ear before he ambled away, immediately surrounded by three beautiful girls.

"Disney," a sexy voice called, and then the guy that Maddie had been dying over skated next to us. The beautiful blonde she'd said was his wife was wrapped tight in his arms. I cocked my head, confused at the nickname.

"I've got Linc on the phoneeee," Ari Lancaster sang.

Walker immediately paled and all the smooth confidence

disappeared. In its place was a stuttering, nervous, *adorable* mess. "He's on the phone? Did you tell him he was amazing? I—"

"Good job to you too, Walk," a deep voice drawled. Ari turned the phone and there was a majorly gorgeous blonde guy on the screen. Golden. Not blonde. That was a better word to describe his hair...and his face. Wait...it was the #13 that Maddie had pulled up on her phone. The one that scored that crazy amazing goal.

Seriously, how had I been missing out on the fact that hockey players were this gorgeous? Forget actors and models...this was where it was at. My gaze flickered over to an L.A. player nearby who seemed to be glaring at the back of Ari's head. Ok, maybe *some* hockey players were this gorgeous. That guy definitely wasn't.

"Golden Boy," Ari said suddenly, like he could read my mind. "I think you broke Disney. He's got this crazy look in his eyes."

Ari turned and winked at me, like I was in on the joke, and then his gaze dropped back to his wife, a besotted, slightly insane look on his handsome face as he stared down at her.

"We're going to get drunk," Ari commented to the guy on his phone. He held it up in front of Walker. "Say goodbye, Linc."

"Bye Lincoln," Walker stammered. And I finally got it. Walker totally had a guy crush on this dude. I cocked my head. At least I thought it was *just* a guy crush...

They left, but Walker's attention went back to me. Was this where he told he had to go? That he needed to celebrate with his team? I wanted him to stay...just a little bit longer.

"So what happens next?" I asked tentatively.

Walker

I marry you.

That was the first thing that popped into my fucking mind

when she'd asked that.

Which meant that I'd officially lost it.

But I couldn't imagine the man who could look at her and not crave her. Need her. Be desperate to own her all to himself.

I'd only gotten high once. Cole had gotten ahold of some verrry potent weed when we were teenagers. And the three of us, Parker, Cole, and I...we'd gotten so stoned we couldn't move. I'd never done it again. I'd hated losing control, being unable to restrain myself.

But I was feeling that way again. Like maybe I wasn't calling the shots over my body anymore. Like maybe some other part of me had taken over.

She was like a petite fairy princess, like something out of a movie—and yes I was aware how that matched my new nick-name. Fucking perfectly.

Or an angel...yeah, that was a good description for her.

She was tiny, with a delicate look about her, like a precious porcelain doll. And those eyes. They were this crazy shade of... gold and green with a stunning golden ring around the irises that I'd never seen before.

She had full lips that were made for my cock and—alright... that took a turn.

Or maybe it hadn't taken a turn. I'd been fucking dying for her since the moment I'd seen her. And now up close...

Well, let's just say if I didn't get inside her tonight, I would in fact cease to exist.

"We should get drunk," she said suddenly, almost desper-ately, actually, as she looked around.

I kind of didn't want to get drunk. I just wanted to go home and touch her and fuck her and keep her...

Okay, down boy.

But if she really wanted to...I think maybe I'd give her what-ever she wanted from me.

"Walker," a voice called out. I sighed, wishing everyone but Violet would disappear. And then I forced myself to glance over at Sam Williamson, one of our rookies, who was running out on the ice shirtless with a bottle of Jack. "I scored a fucking goalllll!" he slurred, somehow already drunk.

I glanced around, realizing that the stands and the ice had almost cleared. Hmm. I guess time goes fast when you meet your new reason for existing.

"Fuck yes, you did," I told him, mustering some enthusiasm as I reached out and pulled Violet into me when his gaze happened to fall on her.

"It's time to *collect*, Davis," he said seriously, offering me the bottle.

Collect?

Oh fuck.

Why did I let Ari *fucking* Lancaster get me in these situations?

"Maybe we can do this after practice or something..." I suggested, an edge of panic creeping in.

I glanced around desperately. Where even was Ari? Getting drunk I could understand. But this was his fucking fault.

"A deal's a deal, Walker," Sam said. Some more of my teammates started to file out onto the ice, catcalling and all well on their way to getting wasted.

I glanced down at Violet. "I'm really sorry in advance about this," I muttered, thinking she was adorable when she was confused.

I picked her up, and she squeaked. As I skated her a few feet away, a safe distance from my rowdy teammates...I was thinking it was a dangerous thing. Touching her.

It was the kind of thing you could get addicted to.

She stared up at me with a bemused little grin, like she wasn't sure how she'd gotten herself in this situation, and I was confident she had flight risk all over her.

"Please don't leave. And please remember that it's not usually like this," I begged, wishing there was some sort of, I don't know, handcuff, around...? So I could prevent her from leaving.

That was a weird thought.

She was still staring at me, confused, biting down on that full bottom lip of hers and making me feel slightly feral.

I dragged myself back over to Sam, shooting looks at her every few feet to make sure she was still there. Yanking the Jack Daniels out of Sam's hands, I started gulping it down for some liquid courage.

Not that I particularly cared about streaking. Other men seeing your balls was basically part of the athlete life.

But I did care what *she* thought about the whole thing.

Somehow, a few months ago, Sam had gotten drunk and started practically bawling about not getting a goal. He'd been on the team for a month, just brought up from the AHL, and he was convinced that he was going to get kicked off if he didn't make it happen.

Ari had decided that Sam needed some encouragement in the form of us streaking or...I actually wasn't sure what the motivating factor was.

But the point was, that *I* was the only one on the ice, about to freeze my balls off in front of the prettiest girl I'd ever seen.

And Ari fucking Lancaster was nowhere to be seen.

So okay...maybe Ari and I had also both been really, really drunk when this bet had taken place.

But still...

Sam handed me a large sock with a chin nod, like he was doing me a huge favor by helping me avoid a dicksickle.

Okay, fuck, maybe he was.

"Take it off," Tommy called, waving a shirt above his head and chugging a beer.

I flipped him off.

Glancing back at Violet, she was still there...and she was still eyeing me, a confused...and hungry gleam in her gaze.

The hunger I could work with.

And for her patience...I should at least give her a show.

I peeled off my jersey, revealing the chiseled contours of my chest…keeping my eyes on her the entire time. Normally I'd be cold, and my nipples could cut a dick being shirtless out on the ice. But I was feeling rather toasty at the moment.

Her eyes were glazed and she looked a bit shaky as she stared at me, like I was actually the eighth wonder of the world.

It was probably how I'd been looking at her too, though.

And fuck, I was getting hard. She couldn't look at me like that. Popping a boner in front of my teammates was not my idea of a good time.

Sauerkraut, bunnies, crushed turtle shells, green peas…

I went through my usual list of things that were sure fire ways to get rid of a hard on.

But they weren't fucking working.

Lincoln Daniels telling me I have a small dick!!!!

Phew, that thought was actually terrifying. My dick went down…at least a little bit.

"Stunna," another of my teammates called out, but I couldn't give them my attention even if I tried.

Look, the amount of times I'd gone streaking in my life was not something I was proud of or would ever admit. Guys are idiots, and streaking came with the idiot territory.

But this was actually torture. I'd already taken off my pads while we'd been watching the Dallas game, but it was still a process to get the rest of my fucking clothes off.

I turned away from everyone and undid my pants, pulling off my jock strap and cup and sliding the yellow and purple sock on my cock, because that obviously had to be done first. Thank fuck it was a proper size.

Hercules had to be taken care of.

The pants came all the way off and there I was, standing in my skates with nothing but a striped sock on.

I turned around and her eyes widened, a rosy glow hitting her cheeks. Her gaze was focused on my socked cock, and her mouth dropped open.

That was a good sign.

THE PUCKING WRONG DATE 63

Well, I thought it was. Or she could just be embarrassed for me. I tried not to think about that.

Also...I was pretty sure there was nothing to be embarrassed about.

Violet made a choking sound and she swayed in place.

Fuck, no. Maybe she was thinking I was hideous? I mean, I'd never had confidence issues before. But I was experiencing them now.

I swung by Sam and grabbed the bottle of Jack out of his hand while I made my loop around the ice, my teammates cheering and yelling ridiculous things as I skated.

Was this real life right now?

Also, if anyone was recording this, I was going to break my stick over their head.

Except Violet. She could record it for her spank bank if she wanted.

Streaking around the ice, butt-naked, with a bottle of Jack in hand? It had to be the most ridiculous bet I'd ever agreed to.

I really hoped that fucking Coach didn't come out and see this.

The cold air hit my skin as I skated, and I shook my head as my idiotic teammates howled with laughter and threw their jerseys onto the ice as if it were some kind of bizarre approval ceremony.

"No shrinkage!" one of them yelled, and I rolled my eyes as I glided past.

I mean, even if I did have shrinkage...I'd still be bigger than all of *them*.

I took a long swig to drown the growing embarrassment. The fiery burn in my throat seemed to offset the chill, or maybe that was just the alcohol messing with my senses.

Violet had her hands in front of her mouth, and her body was shaking as she laughed at me.

"Having fun?" I called out to her, trying to sound casual despite the fact that I was skating around in my birthday suit.

She nodded, bending over as her laughter increased. "This is really weird," she finally giggled.

I stuck my tongue out at her as I passed, shaking my ass a bit for good measure. But that made my dick swing, which made the situation even more embarrassing.

One more lap and I called it. Honestly, I couldn't even remember all the terms of the bet, but I was done.

If they wanted more, they could go get Ari.

The guys hooted and hollered for a bit longer before someone yelled something about shots and they filed off the ice.

And then...it was just Violet and I.

She was standing where I'd set her down, her arms wrapped around her body...shivering.

"Fuck, sweetheart," I murmured, rushing over...only to remember that I was just wearing a cock sock when her eyes widened.

"Right...give me one second and then we can get off the ice and get warm," I told her hurriedly, grabbing my stuff and almost falling over as I tried to put on clothes.

In my hurry to try and put pants on...my sock got pulled off.

"Holy dick," she breathed as my dick popped into view and, to my horror, I got an erection.

"Fuck. I'm sorry!" I screeched.

She squeaked and covered her eyes as I scrambled to put something over my dick.

But then I did fucking slip, my skates going over my head as I fell to the ice, my dick flopping around at half mast for her to see.

"I'm sorry!" I screamed, a note of hysteria in my voice.

"I mean, congratulations," she sputtered, waving the hand around that wasn't covering her eyes. "That's, really, big. It's a big...deal...fuck." Her words gave out in an embarrassed whisper.

Look, I wasn't exactly Mr. Cool twenty four seven.

But I had never, *never* in my life done anything as remotely awkward and humiliating as what was happening right now.

And in front of the girl I was desperately trying to impress… and keep.

Violet still had her hands in front of her eyes as I struggled to my feet and spun around so my dick was out of sight. A minute later I'd managed to get my pants, and my shirt on.

"Is it safe?" she called out, and I snorted. I could just see it now in the headlines…"Marked safe from Walker Davis's freakishly huge dick."

"I'm dressed," I answered instead. Because she wasn't safe from my dick.

Not by a long shot.

She slowly lowered her hands like she was expecting me to have lied and still be prancing around with my dick out.

"I can't say, in my wildest dreams…did I imagine tonight going like this," she mused.

I laughed, pushing my hair out of my face. "I would agree with you on that—your first time seeing my cock should have been a much less shameful experience."

She flushed and I examined her for a moment, noting the perfect pinkness of her lips, trying to ignore the lust licking at my veins. Her gaze flicked down to my…pants…like she was afraid *Hercules* was going to make an appearance again.

Fortunately, he was locked up tight.

Violet's cheeks were still rosy and embarrassed…almost like she hadn't seen very many dicks in her life.

I studied her closer, unable to stop myself. Her face was bare of the heavy makeup most girls I knew wore. And she looked young.

Fuck.

Really young…

I bit my lip, a roar of satisfaction in my gut at the way she tracked the movement.

"You're legal…right?" I finally blurted out, not sure for the first time in my life if I really cared. We could move to North Carolina.

Violet snorted. "Yes," she said, like the question was funny. But she didn't tell me how old she was.

The sound of laughter reverberated from the tunnel just then, and a flash of what looked awfully like terror streaked across her perfect features.

I finally skated closer to her, unable to keep myself away.

She was staring at me warily now, like the sound of other people had broken a spell.

"Hey Walk, there's a huge party upstairs, you coming?" Tommy called, his arm around a puck bunny that stalked the team relentlessly.

"In a minute," I said back, raising my eyebrows in what I hoped was the sign for...*you should put three condoms on if you touch that girl's pussy.*

He just smirked and disappeared out of sight.

"I should probably head home," she murmured, a note of dejection in her pretty voice.

A knot formed in the pit of my stomach at her words, and panic surged through me, like an electric shock—the trifecta complete when a cold sweat broke out on my forehead.

"No—I mean...why?" I finally managed to choke out.

"So you can go celebrate?" she said slowly, like she didn't know why she was leaving either.

"I think you should celebrate with me."

Again that fear, that I desperately wanted to understand, spilled across her features.

"You've seen most of us at our worst already," I cajoled. "Everyone will get much dumber and much drunker, but that's about it."

I grabbed her hand, trying to keep the awe off my face at how fucking soft her skin was.

She didn't need to know that I would be the only hand she'd be holding for the rest of her life.

CHAPTER 4
WALKER

"Just for a minute, maybe," she murmured, her gaze dancing around the arena like she was looking for someone. Everyone not allowed to stay would be out of the building by now. Was she looking for a guy she'd come with?

I gritted my teeth, jealousy splitting through me at the thought.

Okay…that was weird.

I was not the jealous type.

Never had been.

But right now I was dying at the thought there could be someone else.

It didn't matter if there was someone else. I would fix that.

Okay crazy…

"We could go somewhere quieter if you didn't want to go to the party," I said hesitantly.

Her beautiful eyes flashed with interest. "What did you have in mind?"

Back to my place was honestly all I had. I wasn't exactly one of those cool people that knew all the quiet, sexy places in town where no one bothered you.

Taco trucks were more my jam if I was going to go out.

I lifted my hands in the universal "don't freak out" motion, which probably only made everyone freak out more.

"We could go to my place."

Her first instinct was to scoff, which was only a little bit offensive. So far my actions had screamed unhinged wackadoodle. With a big dick thrown in.

Scoffing was probably a correct way to respond.

She stared at me for a long moment, and it kind of felt like she was holding my destiny in her hands. A scary thing to think for sure.

"Okay, let's do it," she finally said, everything about her posture and her voice completely unsure and...scared.

"Let me just get out of my skates and change real quick," I told her, grabbing her hand and leading her toward the locker rooms. All of my movements were slow, designed not to scare her off.

But what would I do if she did get jumpy...I couldn't exactly grab her and never let go. I took a deep breath, telling myself to get my shit together.

Definitely not circle of trust behavior right now.

She seemed not to notice that I was freaking the fuck out though. Her gaze was curious as I led her down the tunnel and into the locker room. Thank fuck there wasn't anyone in here. I don't think I could take it if she saw any other dicks.

I needed to think ahead in the future. Probably wouldn't do well to maim and torture my teammates because she got an eyeful of something I didn't want her to.

"Okay, I'll be right back," I murmured, before my gaze fell on her Seattle jersey again.

Fuck. I wasn't going to be able to handle that.

"What? Why are you staring at me like that?" she asked, smoothing her hair down self consciously.

"Okay, well, it's not a big deal...actually, wait...sorry. It is a big fucking deal. Can you please put on my jersey? I can't—I can't deal with what you've got on."

I want to kick myself for how that came out, but it's honestly the nicest way I could say it. If she didn't take that off...I wasn't sure what I'd do.

I'm pretty sure she would go running for the hills if I tear it off with my teeth like I really want to.

"You realize we just met," she answered with a slight, teasing smile that made my head spin.

"What can I say...I make friends fast."

"Are you always so bossy with your *friends*?" Her tongue peeked out to lick at her lip and I wondered how such a simple movement could literally threaten to drive me insane.

"Mmh, that's more of Linc's thing, I guess. But he must have inspired me." She huffed and crinkled her nose adorably, like she didn't understand a thing I was saying.

I honestly didn't understand a thing about myself at the moment either.

She gestured around the locker room. "Okay, *friend*...where's the jersey I'm supposed to wear?"

I grinned at her and made a big show of taking off my jersey like I was going to make her wear mine.

She held up her hands. "Look, my cousin plays for Seattle. I absolutely know how stinky you guys are after games. There is no way that I'm putting that on."

My smile only widened. "I dare you to smell it."

"What are we...twelve? I am not smelling that."

"Have you smelled me yet?"

"I mean—" Her mouth opened and closed.

I tossed the jersey at her, confident in myself since I'd done a smell check while getting redressed out on the ice. Then I headed for the showers for what was going to be the quickest shower of my life, all while convincing myself I didn't need to drag her in with me so I could make sure she didn't run.

The water pelted my skin, the coldest setting I could get, and I was still hard just knowing she was on the other side of the wall. Who knew that frozen balls could still make an erection?

Not me.

What the fuck was it going to be like once I was actually inside of her?

Ten seconds.

If I was lucky.

Lincoln and Ari would somehow find out. I'd never live it down.

Violet would never want anything to do with me.

The only answer was a little hand session. In the freezing cold water. While she was a few feet away.

Fuck, this felt pathetic.

But necessary.

Gripping my dick tightly, I slowly worked my hand up and down, hissing out my breath as the cold water hit my skin.

This was a handjob that would go down in infamy for me.

A moment I could pinpoint as the exact second I'd lost my mind.

But it was so easy to think of her...in my jersey, on her knees. Soaking wet as she stared up at me with those crazy, beautiful eyes...those pink, pouty lips.

Her tongue slipped out, the tip of it touching my dick...

"How the fuck does your jersey not smell?" Her voice cut through my daydream. And I was coming...unable to stop myself as ropes of cum hit the tiled wall in front of me.

"Holy fuck," I whispered as I literally trembled from the force of my orgasm...and the freezing cold.

Ten seconds.

That's how long it had taken.

Fucking embarrassing.

Maybe I could hope for *twenty* seconds for the real thing.

I turned off the water, grabbing a towel and wrapping it around my waist. I knew I'd just heard her voice, but I needed to see for myself she was there.

A few steps out and there she was...in my fucking jersey. It drowned her and she fidgeted with it self consciously as her golden gaze fucking devoured me.

"Umm...I'm wearing it," she stammered, her gaze trapped on my chest. A bead of water slid down my skin and she tracked it all..the way...down.

"Wow," she murmured.

"What was that?" I asked teasingly. "Did you just say 'wow'?"

She stuck her tongue out at me, waving her hands around frantically. "I mean, it's really not fair, that you get all of that..." she gestured to my face, "and all of that...." pointing to my chest, "and, all of freaking that!" Her gaze was definitely on my dick again.

"Don't stare at my dick," I yelped, putting my hands in front of it, because fuck...the towel was rising. What was this girl doing to me?

"Get dressed," she groaned. "I'm dying."

I pushed some of my wet hair out of my face, still covering my dick area with my other hand because Hercules was as OBSESSED with her as the rest of me was.

"Two minutes, don't move," I told her, striding to the other side where my locker and a clean pair of sweats were.

"There you go again...being bossy."

"Only for you," I muttered.

I may have been a captain on the team, and a goalie...but "bossy" had never been a character trait I'd been accused of prior to meeting her.

After I pulled on my sweats, I took her hand, wondering how it could feel so right.

She stared down at our clasped hands for a beat, before finally glancing up at me...an awestruck vulnerability in her starry depths.

Say it. Tell me you feel it too.

But she didn't.

I led her down the hallway and out the back doors to the

team parking lot. We could hear shouting and celebrating from nearby, but we didn't see anyone. Which I liked. I didn't want to share her. I wanted her to myself. I wanted to bask in the light she was giving off. Take all that gorgeous perfection for myself.

Fucking hell. I was acting like Lincoln.

That thought kept me occupied all the way to the truck.

"I would say you're overcompensating, but I know you're not," she suddenly said, bringing my attention away from my crazy...and back to her perfect face.

"Huh?"

"Your truck. It's got a lot of Big Dick Energy," she mused as I helped her into the cab.

I groaned and adjusted myself. "Don't say 'dick' please," I begged.

She just giggled, and I wanted to capture the sound. Play it back over and over again.

Violet's face shuttered at the sound though, a blank mask taking over her smile. Like the sound of her laugh had offended her.

This girl was a mystery, a labyrinthine maze of secrets and hidden passages, with each layer waiting to be unraveled like the pages of a long-forgotten manuscript.

And I couldn't wait to discover all of it.

I smiled gently at her and closed the door, taking my time walking around the front of the truck so she could have a second to collect herself.

If she was feeling even a little bit like I was, like she'd been flayed open and her insides were being overhauled with every second that passed...then she needed a minute. I didn't expect her to embrace the insanity instantly like I was.

I'd help her get there.

Stepping up into the cab, my head started spinning as I caught her scent. In such close quarters, it was overwhelming. She smelled like wildflowers and summer rain...like Tennessee after a thunderstorm.

I stared at her for a second and she blushed, lifting an eyebrow in a "what are you staring at, weirdo" kind of way.

Start the truck, Walk. Start the fucking truck.

I dragged my gaze away and turned the key, the rumble of the exhaust surrounding us as we started towards my place. I couldn't help but sneak glances at her every few seconds.

She didn't seem to have the same problem as me though, her gaze was firmly out the window.

"So…" I said lamely. "It's kind of dumb to ask you to tell me all about yourself…so let's play a game."

"A game," she repeated slowly, finally giving me the attention I wanted.

I came up to a red light, and turned towards her. "Games are kind of my thing if you hadn't realized."

Her eyes flashed with amusement and I gave myself a mental high five.

Because I believed in rewarding myself for success.

And getting this girl to smile was the definition of success.

"Okay, what are the rules?" she asked.

Hoooonnnnk!

I cursed and waved sheepishly at the car behind us, even though L.A. drivers could care less about that kind of thing. Who knows how long the light had been green for.

"You have to tell me five truths about you. And one lie…"

"And then we guess?" she drawled.

I acted shocked. "No. We keep that lie to ourselves forever and ever."

She giggled again…and once again touched her lips, like she couldn't believe she'd allowed such a sound to escape.

"Okay, I'm in."

"That's my girl." Her face flushed and she fidgeted in her seat.

"What's making you blush?" I questioned, wanting to hear her say she'd liked being called "my girl." I put my arm over her seat and dragged my fingers over her skin.

She shivered and shot me a look. "Is that one of my six things?"

My attention snagged on how fucking perfect her skin felt against my fingers and it took me a second to respond.

"No. I'll get it out of you later," I said, reluctantly staring back at the road. Death by car crash wasn't going to do it for me. Death by pussy was the only way I wanted to go.

"Alright, do your six things."

She scoffed. "This was your idea. I'm not going first."

"Fiiiine," I drawled as I made a left hand turn.

"I'm Tennessee born and bred, and I miss it every day. I'm hoping that I get signed by Dallas next year. I'm better at baseball than I am at hockey, but I love hockey more, so here I am. I hate scary movies and literally shriek whenever I'm forced to watch one. Diet Dr. Pepper is one of my main food groups... and...I don't believe in love at first sight." I gave her a challenging grin when I finished and she flushed again.

"You want to get signed with Dallas?" she said softly. "I'm actually a Texas girl. I'd love to go back."

"Could have been a lie, angel face," I told her with a wink and she smiled.

I hoped she could see through me. See everything I was trying to tell her.

"Alright, your turn," I said. "And you'd better hurry because we're almost to my place."

"Are we not allowed to talk when we get there?"

I smirked as we pulled up to the underground garage of my complex and waited for it to open. "I personally don't plan to do very much talking."

She gaped at me and I gently tapped her chin to close her mouth. "You'll need to be a little wider than that, sweetheart."

Holy fuck, what was I saying right now? Abort. Abort. Keep your fucking mouth closed.

"Alrighttt," she finally said in a deliciously breathy voice, obviously deciding to ignore my loss of all societal niceties. "I—

I'm a huge Cowboys fan. I also consider Diet Dr. Pepper to be an essential food group. I've been to every major arena in the country. My favorite color is pink. I have nothing to offer anyone. And I don't believe in happily ever afters," her voice trailed off in a whisper at that last line, and I was stuck, soaking in the snippets she'd given me. Especially those last two...which one was the lie? Had to be the "nothing to offer", right...hopefully. Because she had plenty to offer me. And I could change her mind about happily ever afters. It would become my mission in fact. Firmly above my previous number one goal of winning a Stanley Cup.

What a fucking night.

I pulled the truck into my spot and we sat there for a beat in silence.

The moment felt heavy, like we both knew we were on the precipice of something big, standing on the edge and waiting to dive off into the unknown.

I hopped out of the truck and raced around, like my life depended on her not opening the door for herself.

Fuck, I really was a fucking simp.

I caught the door just as she tried to open it, and then I helped her out of the vehicle.

The same silence followed us into the elevator, and up as the floors beeped by. I tapped my foot nervously. Had I cleaned up my clothes? Put my dishes in the sink? Had Cole done anything stupid while I was getting ready?

He was known for that.

I opened my mouth to warn her, but decided that would just be worse.

The doors slid open, revealing the giant living room that looked out onto the L.A. skyline.

"Wow, that's quite a view," she whispered, her gaze intent on the skyline showing from the floor to ceiling windows—the whole reason I rented this fucking place.

"I hate feeling caged in. I grew up on a farm with nothing but rolling hills for miles. This was the best I could do while staying close to the arena," I explained as I watched her look out with an almost...devastated look on her face.

"Please stop. I—I don't need to know any of those things about you. Whatever this is. It's just for tonight," she finally snapped in a hard voice far different than how she'd been sounding. Violet wouldn't look at me, her gaze was glued ahead of her. "You don't need to know me. I don't need to know you. I —my life is complicated. I just want...tonight."

My chest tightened as Violet's words sank in.

Just one night?

It was as if the ground had been ripped out from beneath my feet, leaving me stumbling.

I'd never been more sure of anything in my life than I was in our connection.

How could she give up on us so easily, before we'd even had a chance to truly begin? Didn't she feel this—this thing between us?

It was a once in a lifetime kind of feeling...anyone would realize that.

I took a deep breath, fighting against the surge of frustration in my gut. Why was she making this seem like nothing?

This was real, raw, and unyielding, a force of nature that defied logic and reason.

This was *everything*.

What usually would be a hockey dick's favorite thing to hear was actually the second most fucking awful thing I'd ever heard in my life.

I didn't think about what was number one on that list. Because unlike what she'd just said, there was nothing I could do to change that.

I gently turned her chin so she had no choice but to look at me.

"If tonight's all I get, then I'd better make it good," I whispered, memorizing the way she nuzzled into my hand like she couldn't help herself. She could say whatever she wanted, but she was affected by me. Her body was telling me what her heart didn't want to.

Grabbing her hand, I led her to my bedroom. I had planned for champagne or wine...maybe some pre sex snacks because I always performed best when I wasn't starving.

But that didn't fit the vibe she was giving me.

So straight to sex it was.

Hercules, don't fail me now.

"Condom," she murmured, glancing around my bedroom once I'd led her inside. She was pulling on the jersey, obviously uncomfortable, everything about her saying that she could choose to bolt any minute.

"They're in the bathroom...I'll be right back," I told her, leaving out the "please don't leave," I wanted to throw in there.

I all but ran into the bathroom, glancing back over my shoulder to make sure she hadn't made a mad dash for the exit.

Sliding open the drawer where I kept them, I grabbed a condom package.

And then I stared at it.

There was a strange ringing in my ears all of a sudden...and my heart was pounding in my chest. The bathroom's light seemed to intensify whatever...insanity I was feeling.

What if...

Something took hold of me, the addiction that had been building inside me all night, unfurled, stretching its wings and transforming into...desperation.

Uncontrollable desperation.

She wanted to pretend this was a one night thing, but I knew better. And I knew she knew it on some instinctual level too. She wanted to run, because she was scared.

I couldn't let her run.

So this uncontrollable desperation inside me...turned into something else.

There was one way I could keep her.

Trap her so to speak...

I was having an out of body experience.

That was the only way to describe what was happening as I reached back into the drawer, and pulled out the sewing kit I kept in there. I pulled out one of the needles, watching as it glinted ominously under the unforgiving light.

No turning back now.

Carefully, almost mechanically, I began to puncture the condom package with the needle. One hole, then two, and soon a pattern of tiny punctures formed.

The voice of reason in my head screamed at me to stop, but the obsession, the overwhelming need to possess her, drowned out those voices.

I continued to poke holes, my heart pounding louder in my chest. Each puncture felt like a step further down a path I'd never envisioned...one I was never going to come back from.

Finally, I was done.

The condom package was riddled with holes that she wouldn't notice, and I felt a strange mixture of triumph and guilt. My fingers trembled as I closed the sewing kit and tucked it back in the drawer.

Obviously it was still a million in one chance she'd get pregnant.

But if we were meant to be, which I knew we were... wouldn't it be my lucky day.

With every step back to the bedroom, I felt more sure, like I was shedding the weight of trying to be the good guy all the time.

I'd be that good guy eventually. I'd make all her dreams—whatever they were—come true.

But in order to have the chance to be the good guy...I was going to have to be the villain first.

CHAPTER 5

OLIVIA

There was something different about him when he stepped out of the bathroom, something more intense...darker.

And the damaged parts of me made me even more interested in this new side of him.

Just for tonight. That's what I'd said. But as I stared at his perfection, I was wishing it was possible to have more.

When I'd left the house this afternoon, there was no part of me that would have ever fathomed I'd end up here. But somewhere along the way, as the night had progressed, something inside me, the part I kept locked away out of necessity...it had wanted to be free.

I wanted to choose that out of control lust, where all you wanted was *that* moment, where all you wanted was *that* guy.

Just for tonight.

"I've never—I've never done this before," I told him, pulling on the jersey and patting my wig to make sure it was still in place.

He hadn't recognized me yet, but if he did...it would ruin *everything*.

"You're a—" his eyes were wide, a crazy gleam in them.

"Oh! No. I mean—I just mean that I've never done a one

night stand before," I blurted out. "I mean, I've never just gone home with a guy."

The word vomit coming out of my mouth was a thing to behold. For someone who had made millions with my ability to write and sing flowery, perfect words...I'd evidently lost that skill.

What I didn't say, was that I didn't know how to explain my sexual status. I couldn't exactly tell him what Marco had done to me growing up, or the fact that some of the pictures taken the night I'd lost everything had been of me in a bed with some druggie...completely naked.

They'd given me a morning after pill, just in case, but they hadn't checked. I guess it was just assumed by what the media said about me that I must be some slutty singer, spreading my legs for everyone...and honestly...I guess the stupid part of me hadn't wanted to know. Like maybe if I didn't know, then that night hadn't actually—

"Hey, I lost you," Walker murmured, tipping up my chin so I had to look at him. He seemed to like doing that, having my attention on him.

But staring at him was a dangerous thing. Up close like this, it was like I was staring into the sun, destined to burn.

His gaze was laser focused on me, like out of everything in the world, I was the only thing that mattered.

The feeling was heady, panty-melting. Like the feverish lust I could see in his blue depths was contagious.

"Touch me," I finally whispered, wanting to break whatever spell he was weaving on me.

Apparently that was the only invitation he needed.

Walker's firm grip encircled the nape of my neck, he squeezed gently, just enough for me to feel grounded.

Like I could trust him to lead the way for us. Like I didn't have to worry...just for tonight.

He leaned closer and I had to remember to breathe.

I'd been kissed before.

But I was very sure that any kiss I'd ever had wasn't going to come close with what I was about to experience.

Walker Davis was going to ruin me.

And maybe it was going to be worth it for once.

The first brush of his lips against mine felt like a fever dream. His lips moved gently, his tongue pushing in, electricity shocking my senses as it slid against mine.

Magic.

That's what this kiss was.

Like whiskey and moonlight, and hot summer nights. Like strawberry wine and wildest dreams.

His kiss felt like a tattoo, branding me in a way I'd never come back from.

I moaned and he caught the sound, breathing it in as he expertly worked my mouth.

"My sweet girl," he murmured in between kisses. "My gorgeous, perfect girl."

I was drunk on him. Addicted. Desperate in fact.

His grip on my neck tightened, a dark dominant possessiveness seeping into his kiss. I could feel my core softening, my panties growing damp with desire.

Walker feasted on me like I was his favorite thing, his hot tongue licking into me like he couldn't get enough. I sucked on his tongue and he groaned, like it was the best thing he'd ever experienced.

I was light-headed, destroyed…over just a kiss.

What was going to happen when he actually got inside me?

Walker lifted me into his arms, and I wrapped my arms and legs around him as we continued to kiss, each step towards his bed rubbing his huge, hard length on that perfect spot between my legs.

"I'm not going to be good at this," I told him, an edge of panic slipping through the lust because everything he was doing was so perfect.

The opposite of everything about me.

He laid me on the bed, and I immediately missed his warmth.

I'd always thought I'd hate a lover who was dominant. I'd imagined myself marrying some paper pusher, who said yes to me on everything and let me make all the decisions.

After years of not making any decisions, that seemed like the only thing I could stand.

But as he handled me like I was his own personal doll, like he owned me…

I wasn't sure I could ever go back.

Just more confirmation there was something broken inside me.

He sat me down on the bed and stared at my face with glittering, gleaming, lust-fueled eyes.

"Take the jersey off," he murmured in a thick, rough voice. A voice like that, you couldn't help but do what he wanted.

With shaky hands I peeled the jersey up over my head, trying to look sexy while I did it—but failing miserably.

I was wearing a thin black tank top underneath the jersey… and my nipples pebbled under his watching, wanting gaze.

"You're an angel," he whispered, awe all over his face. It made me want to cry, which would be completely embarrassing. But no one in my life had ever looked at me like that.

I wish I could keep you. The words repeated themselves over and over and over again.

I wish you could keep *me.*

"I don't know if I can be gentle, baby. I want you too much," he growled, the words seeming to touch every part of me.

"Bring it on, Disney," I teased, remembering the nickname I'd heard a few times tonight.

Evidently his nickname unlocked something inside of him because one minute he was staring at me, and the next he…pounced.

"Mine," he whispered gruffly.

Oh fuck.

Something about just *imagining* myself belonging to him was an aphrodisiac in its most potent form.

He pushed me down on the bed, one hand roughly moving down my chest, in between my breasts.

"All fucking mine."

Abruptly, my tanktop was ripped, my bra snapping off like it was made of nothing.

My core gushed and he grinned smugly, like he knew exactly what he'd just done to me.

"Fuck," he murmured then, his grin fading as his eyes latched onto my chest.

He stared as if my boobs were the most fascinating thing he'd ever seen. Which couldn't be the case. There was no way this man hadn't seen a million breasts, way more perfect than mine.

The thought made me sick.

His hand slowly covered my breast, gently kneading it. Leaning down, he bit softly at one of my tips before his mouth returned to mine, capturing my answering moan like he wanted every part of me. He licked and sucked at my lips as his fingers expertly mimicked the movements on my breasts. Walker's hot tongue slid down my throat, sucking at my pulse point as I gasped for breath.

My body had always betrayed me in the past. This was the first time it felt like it was doing what it was supposed to. Like this god was made to bring me pleasure, and it was my purpose to enjoy it.

He gently suckled my nipple into his mouth, creating magic as pleasure built deep inside me.

The rough pads of his fingers glided down my skin. My breath came out in gasps as he again bit down on the top of my breast this time…like he was trying to mark me. He soothed away the pain with his tongue, a puzzled frown on his face as I glanced down at him, as if he hadn't expected to do that either.

His hand reached the band of my leggings and he tugged

them down, yanking and pulling until he'd gotten them down under my ass.

"If you don't want me to tear them, angel, you might want to help me get these off," he said silkily as his mouth and other hand continued to torture my breasts with pleasure.

I would need them when I ran away.

That was the thought in my head as I feverishly pulled my pants the rest of the way off, taking a second to realize that I was now completely bare underneath him, and he was still fully dressed.

As soon as I was done, my fingers tangled in his hair, needing something to hold onto as his hips rolled against my core. He was hard and huge against me. My mouth was literally watering just thinking of that giant, perfect dick I'd glimpsed earlier being anywhere near me.

A hand slid to my sex, Walker's fingers rubbing through my *dripping* folds.

His other hand was still tugging and pinching at my nipple and a small orgasm rolled through my insides, completely shocking me.

"Did you just cum?" he asked, a hint of wonder in his voice.

I flushed, feeling it all across my chest, pinpricks of pleasure all over.

Pleasure was something I never got, not since I'd stopped those pills. But this was ten times better than the high they'd given me. An orgasm from Walker was a buzz I'd never stop craving.

"Fuck, you're sexy," he muttered as his talented fingers pressed and rubbed at my clit like he was actually some kind of sex god magician instead of a hockey player. "I'm going to ruin you…"

I was only faintly aware of what he'd just said, and I certainly didn't understand it. I arched against him, grabbing desperately at his shirt as my insides coiled tight.

"Ahh," I screamed as a much stronger orgasm hit me, the edges of my vision going white as euphoria splashed over me.

"You're really good for my ego, baby. I think that was twice in twenty seconds."

I blinked at him, slowly coming back to earth.

He lifted off his shirt, revealing inch by inch of the most glorious body I'd ever seen. Up close I could take in the tattoos that I hadn't gotten a look at while we'd been on the ice. Like the replica of a human heart etched over the skin where his actual one was beating. The heart itself appeared as though it had been plucked from a living, beating chest, with every vein and artery meticulously etched into existence.

I hungrily traced the rest of his inked artistry. Watercolor-inspired designs splashed across his strong, broad right shoulder. The soft lines of the artwork at odds with the macabre images; hauntingly beautiful skulls with hollow eyes that seemed to stare out at me.

His tattoos didn't seem to match what I'd seen of him so far, and I was even more...interested.

Just for tonight, I told myself fiercely, trying to memorize the cut of his abs and how protected I felt underneath him like this.

"You're unreal," I murmured, kind of wondering if I was actually dreaming. Men like him didn't exist.

His abs were a masterpiece, each muscle sharply delineated, creating a mesmerizing pattern of ridges and valleys. They rippled as he pushed off his sweatpants, and I couldn't help but reach out and run my fingers along his skin.

He shivered as if my hands were cold, but when I tried to move away, he grabbed my wrist, holding it against him.

"Please touch me," he begged in a pained voice that made me feel...powerful.

This beautiful god was desperate for me.

Me.

Olivia Jones. The fuck-up. The pariah.

That someone like him could want me...at least for a night... it was almost unbelievable.

Not that he knew any of that about me. I frowned at that reminder.

My gaze got caught on his arms though as he moved, all that delicious corded muscle.

I wanted to lick his forearms. Was that weird?

Ooop. And there it was. Peeking out from the top of his sweatpants like there was no way to contain it.

Holy dick had been the right reaction.

Look, I'd seen dicks before. Kind of came with the performing thing. People just changed right in front of you. Or the parties at the mansion that got out of control where guys would whip them out. Or...*don't think about that.*

Most of the time it had been a very unfortunate sighting.

But Walker's dick...my pussy was aching just thinking of putting that beast inside me.

Ridged veins along its thick, silky looking length. It was a dusky color, the smooth, rounded head, broad and angry-looking. It was leaking copiously, a glistening, milky fluid I was suddenly starving for.

I hated giving head. Loathed it in fact.

But I was suddenly very interested in having *him* in my mouth.

"Now where was I?" Walker murmured roughly, not seeming to notice how entranced I was by his cock. He moved down my body until he was practically eye level with my slit, tracing my folds with just the tip of his finger. I gushed all over his hand, just from the slight touch, and he grinned at me wickedly.

"Please," I called out, and now I was the one who was begging, desperate to have some part of him inside me. Finger, tongue, cock...just fucking give it to me. He watched me avidly as his thumb skated over my clit, another finger *finally* slipping inside. I squirmed against the bed, my hips desperate for more friction because he was going so achingly slow.

Fast enough to torture me. But too slow to push me over the edge.

I'd already had two orgasms, but I'd decided that on my one night of freedom...I deserved to be a greedy girl.

"Please what, *angel?* Tell me what you want, and I'll give it to you," he teased with a low laugh.

Words were failing me at the moment though.

My eyes rolled to the back of my head as he pushed another finger in...and then another. A tear slid down my cheek at the feeling of fullness. Evidently, goalies had big hands because I was filled to the brim.

That gigantic cock of his was *definitely* not going to fit.

"Mmh, I guess we'll see about that," he growled as he suddenly withdrew his fingers. Guess I'd said that part out loud...whoops.

I was about to start crying over the extreme edging I was enduring until he slid his fingers into his mouth, the ones covered in my gleaming arousal. He watched me, the electric blue of his eyes holding me hostage as he sucked, licking his fingers like he had to make sure and get every...last...drop.

"I have one more thing to add to my list," he mused as gave his finger one last lick.

"Huh?" I murmured, my brain not functioning on all cylinders because of how freaking turned on I was.

"My favorite flavor, I didn't give you that before."

This was a weird time to talk about flavors of ice cream, but I guess he couldn't be perfect.

"Your cunt is without a doubt, the most delicious thing I've ever tasted, baby," he growled. "And since I was such a good boy at my game, and we won, I think I need more of it."

Before I could say anything in response, he pushed my thighs wide, his hands bracing them apart so that I couldn't move. His eyes darkened as he stared for a long minute, long enough that you start to think about things like...what if one of my vagina lips is longer than the other and looks funny? Or what if...

"Ahh," I yelped as he suddenly gave me a long, slow lick, definitely tasting every inch of me. His tongue was everywhere, dirty and messy as he dragged it through my folds, spearing it inside me as his fingers plucked and pulled at my clit like I actually had some kind of freaking pleasure button that only he knew how to operate.

The stubble of his scruff scraped against the skin of my thighs and I dragged my fingers through his hair, my hips moving desperately against his face as my whimpers filled the air.

His tongue was relentless, like his only goal tonight was tasting every inch of me.

I was possibly fine with that.

Okay, scratch that…I was *definitely* fine with that.

"That's it, baby. Ride my face, give me all that sweetness. I want to die in this pussy."

His dirty mouth sent me over the edge, pleasure surging down my spine as he lapped at my clit while his fingers pushed into me. I quivered and writhed against his mouth, my cries filling my ears as bliss bloomed inside my core.

I came so hard I almost passed out.

And we hadn't even had sex yet.

He kept on licking my clit, like he couldn't drag himself away, until I desperately pulled on his hair.

Walker grinned, the whole lower half of his face glistening with…me.

What a sight.

"Walker, please," I murmured, pulling on his hair because I needed him. Enough was enough. "Come here."

"But I'm living my best fucking life right now, sweetheart," he purred as he made his way up my stomach, kissing and licking his way across my skin until finally he was staring down at me.

"You should have a taste," he whispered right before giving me a dirty, wet kiss…his tongue dragging my essence across my tastebuds.

Another rush of heat hit my insides. I could only imagine how wet the bed was underneath me, but fuck, he was hot.

While he kissed me, he grabbed his dick and rubbed it through my folds, bumping into my clit with the head on every pass. I moaned into his mouth and he chuckled…like the best part of this whole thing was how he was destroying me with his sexual prowess.

I bit down on his lip…hard…and that got his attention. He growled, his gaze glittering with just a hint of madness.

He started to push in and I froze—"Condom," I blurted out, even though his dick was well on its way to making my dreams come true.

Walker pulled out without complaint, grabbing the condom he'd tossed on the nightstand when he'd come back in from the bathroom. He angled his body, turning slightly away from me as he put it on…which only led to me ogling what must be the most biteable ass I'd ever seen. Hockey players were stacked from all that leg work…but he was on another level.

I would say it was a goalie thing, but something told me Walker Davis was over here playing with a much fuller deck of cards than the average guy. He was a god. Even among professional athletes.

He turned back around, eyebrows wagging when he saw the way I was obviously lusting after him, his cock encased in what must have been an XL condom—it wasn't fitting otherwise.

"Ready for me, angel?" he murmured as he prowled towards me. My heart rate picked up, it suddenly felt like I was being hunted, and for once I was the prey that *wanted* to be caught.

"Not sure you should call me that with what's about to go down."

He snorted at my comment, a lock of his mussed up hair falling in his face like he was some sort of fucking model.

No one should have talent and looks like that. It wasn't fair to the rest of us.

Walker crawled over me, pushing my legs open like he'd done before, only this time it was to line up his cock.

Grand finale, Olivia. Don't fuck it up now.

He pushed inside and I'd really begun to believe that I could handle it. I mean, I had handled three fingers like a champ...but just his tip was inside me and I was decidedly no longer sure.

"That's it, sweetheart," he murmured, "look at you...taking my big dick so fucking good. Your sweet cunt was made for me. I'm positive about that."

He pushed further in as I grabbed onto the sheets, squeezing my eyes closed and trying not to be *too* obvious that I might rip in half after he pushed that monster into me. The dirty talk was helping though.

It was keeping me dripping wet. Even with the condom, I was going to soak him.

A whimper spilled out of me as he carefully continued to push. Was his dick a mile long? Every inch felt like a *journey*.

"You're doing so well, angel. My perfect fucking girl," he praised as he reached between us and caressed my clit, the instant ecstasy relaxing me enough that he could finally push all the way in...

"Holy dick. I can't breathe. You broke me," I gasped, my head thrashing from the fact that a nine or ten inch pole had just been stuffed inside me.

He laughed, the sound transforming into a groan as he slowly pulled out...and then slammed back in.

His mouth descended on mine, his tongue sliding inside in an almost lazy way, at odds with how his hips were now pistoning in and out of me.

"You're stunning. Too beautiful to be real," he murmured as he held my gaze.

I closed my eyes and turned my head, unable to deal with how he was looking at me. Nothing like how you were supposed to look at a one night stand, or at least not the way I imagined you were supposed to.

He wasn't supposed to look at me like the sun set and rose because of me, that I was the best thing that had ever happened to him.

He wasn't supposed to look at me like he was in love...

A hand came up and caressed my pulse, like he was memorizing the pattern of my heartbeat.

And then his hold tightened.

"You're going to look at me while I fuck that perfect pussy. I need to make sure you know exactly who's inside you," he growled. I had no choice but to stare up at him, take in every greedy, savage sound as it left his chest. I had no choice but to watch him, watch me.

His cock hammered into me, over and over again, hitting a sensitive spot inside me that I'd thought was just a myth.

Walker's hand was still wrapped around my throat, like he was afraid if he moved it, I'd disappear.

"Your pretty pussy is choking my big dick. Your cunt is so fucking tight."

Once again words were failing me. All I could do was hang on for the ride, and what a ride it was.

I convulsed around his cock, my insides squeezing as I came, gushing all over him, just like I was worried I would.

"Fuck, that's hot," he grunted, thrusting in and out of me, his pace never faltering. "And I'm so fucking close." His hand went to my clit once again. "But I want to come with your pussy milking my dick. So I need one more."

"I can't," I moaned in a strained, tired voice. How many times had I come by now? I'd lost count. I was a rag doll at this point, the pleasure in my core never actually leaving because my nerves were so sensitive.

"Just one more, baby. I need it. I need you to cum with me," he said desperately, playing my clit while he talked.

He leaned down and sucked on my breasts, his teeth gently grazing my nipple.

My pussy clenched again and he pressed his forehead to

mine. "Good girl," he whispered roughly as his movements became erratic and his cock twitched inside me.

He stayed nose to nose with me as his hips slowed. "Wow," he huffed, before he did some kind of superhero roll thing that ended up with me laying on his chest and him beneath me, his dick still buried inside me.

"I don't think I can move. You're going to have to wait to kick me out," I joked as I slumped against his chest, listening to his heart beat under me.

He stiffened for a second at my words, taking a moment to resume tracing patterns on my back.

"I would never kick you out," he finally murmured, and my eyes widened as I stared at the wall next to us.

I didn't say anything in return.

And he didn't try and ask me anything else.

Not when he pulled out slowly and walked to the bathroom. Or when he came back with a warm cloth that he used to clean up my arousal that had dripped down my thighs.

And not when he pulled me into his arms, fussing with me until he had me exactly where he wanted.

It wasn't until I was fading into sleep that I thought I heard him ask something.

But by then I was too far into unconsciousness to hear what it was.

Walker

I watched her sleep, my heart in my throat, a mix of awe and fear churning inside me after the best fucking sex I'd ever had in my life.

Violet lay there, peaceful and vulnerable, her chest rising and falling slowly. She looked ethereal, like she couldn't possibly be real, like she was too beautiful to belong to this world.

As my gaze lingered on her, I noticed something out of place

—was that a glint of red? Leaning forward, my fingers lightly brushed her hair as I tried to figure out what I was seeing.

My jaw dropped when I realized she was wearing a wig.

A blonde fucking wig.

That was a plot twist I hadn't seen coming.

Underneath the blonde was a rich and vibrant auburn. Absolutely fucking stunning. I was suddenly desperate to see those golden eyes of hers with that color hair. I'd thought she was gorgeous before, but this was on a whole other level.

My breath caught in my throat as I watched her, my dick hardening again as I took in her perfect face.

Would she care if I just slipped inside her again while she was sleeping? Fuck. That would probably be weird for a stranger to do.

I'd do that eventually. When she was mine.

My gaze drifted to her flat stomach. There'd been quite a bit of cum leaking out of the condom I'd fucked up. She hadn't seemed to notice since she'd been fucking soaked with her own arousal.

I winced, adjusting myself, because just thinking of it made me want to die a little bit.

So fucking hot.

I had a million questions for my golden-gazed girl, but I didn't wake her up. She'd probably run away the second I did.

Her clutch caught my attention, sitting innocently on the nightstand, next to the bed.

Maybe just a peek…

Taking one more glance at Violet to make sure she was still sleeping deeply, I slipped off the bed and grabbed the small bag. I didn't make a habit of going through my date's purses, but the situation called for it.

Besides, I wasn't going through just my "date's" purse, I was going through my future *wife's*.

I'd heard that sharing was caring when it came to successful marriages. We were just starting that early on in the process.

There wasn't anything inside that revealed any secrets to the universe—a lip gloss, a few crumpled ten-dollar bills, and a credit card that read "Lucky Pic, LLC." Intriguing, but hardly enough to uncover the enigma of my angel girl.

I set the purse back where I'd gotten it and then pulled out my phone, carefully taking a picture of her perfect face, okay...a few pictures.

I didn't think it was possible to forget what she looked like, but the picture could help me if she really did wake up and decide one night was all she wanted.

And I had to go hunting for her.

Crawling back in bed, I laid on my pillow and watched her sleep. Would it be weird if I cuddled her? I could just pretend it had happened while we were sleeping. That shit happened all the time in rom-coms.

I decided to risk it. She'd let me hold her right after we'd had sex. It was probably okay now. Pulling her into my arms, I buried my nose into her neck, wishing I was burying my dick inside her instead. My lips tracked her pulse for a long minute, some weird part of me obsessed with the feel of it. I reluctantly stopped when she stirred in my arms.

Waking her up was the last thing I wanted to do. If she did wake up, then she could decide we were done, and she could leave.

I blinked my eyes wearily, trying to stay awake. I'd been riding a high since the moment I'd seen her tonight, adrenaline from the game and everything else keeping me wired.

But...that was a whole fucking lot for one night and...my eyelids grew heavy. I'd just close them for a second. I couldn't go to sleep...not until I convinced her she was meant to stay instead of to leave.

CHAPTER 6

OLIVIA

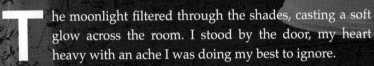

The moonlight filtered through the shades, casting a soft glow across the room. I stood by the door, my heart heavy with an ache I was doing my best to ignore.

Walker lay in bed, his features etched with a frown, his hand clutching the sheets as if searching for something that had slipped away.

Everything inside me was screaming at me to stay, to crawl back into bed with him, to drown in the intensity of whatever this was.

But that wasn't an option. Because good things never were for me.

I didn't know almost anything about him, but the little I did know made it clear he was too good for my shit. He deserved so much more than the chaos that clung to me.

Tears welled in my eyes as I stared at him one last time, committing his image to memory. His disheveled hair, the way his lips curled in his sleep. I wanted to keep it with me, help me get past what waited for me after I left here.

With a heavy heart, I turned away, my footsteps silent as I slipped out of the penthouse and into the elevator. As I pressed the button for the lobby, I whispered a silent goodbye.

It was better this way, I murmured for the millionth time.

The city outside was already waking up, cars honking and racing by, a stark contrast to the stillness I had left behind. Each step I took away from him felt like pain.

The ache in my chest wasn't real, I told myself.

But it tasted like a lie.

———

I slipped out of the Uber, the ever present hole inside of me feeling even wider for some reason, the emptiness clawing at my insides and making it hard to breathe.

I stood on the sidewalk, taking a few deep breaths. Trying to get ahold of myself, rebuild my armor before I returned back to my real life. Where I couldn't feel, couldn't smile, couldn't be anything but what they wanted.

I could feel him inside me, and on my skin, like somehow he'd managed to coat every part of me with...him. The ache between my legs, I didn't want it to fade.

Like maybe if I carried part of last night with me, it could help me...

Survive.

I sighed, because I knew better than to have anything that resembled...hope. Hope was for fools.

And after that one night, the one where I had dared to hope, my whole life had been ruined.

I'd never be foolish enough to hope again.

I pulled off my wig as the elevators opened and I stepped inside my apartment, somehow not surprised at all to see Jolette and Marco sitting in the living room, lounging on my furniture like they lived here.

Resigned.

That was the only thing I could feel with what I knew was coming.

Jolette was checking her fingernails as I slowly trudged in, not bothering to give me attention. The anticipation of her disapproval was what she liked the most. It was an art form for her. Dragging out the dread.

Marco typed on his phone, controlling his empire even at five fucking thirty a.m.

"Olivia," Jolette finally said, her voice oozing disdain. "So nice of you to join us."

"It is *my* apartment," I said lightly.

Her eyes finally snapped to mine at my tone, her red lips pursing in displeasure. Disrespect may have been the only way to immediately get her attention.

Marco slipped his phone in his pocket, his tone dripping with condescension. "You know better than to leave without notifying us. It's all about security, princess."

I held in the shiver his pet name gave me, trying to think instead of what it had felt like for Walker to whisper "angel," as he thrust inside me, his soft expression as he stared.

"Are you listening?" Jolette snarled.

I clenched my teeth, trying to hold myself back, because this was a situation I couldn't win. I didn't need to make it even worse—like her putting a guard at the door. I'd just gotten rid of that six months ago.

"I went out, alright? I needed some air," I snapped back, my defiance cutting through the tension.

Jolette's icy blue eyes bore into me, her perfectly styled hair framing her face like a judgmental halo. "And where exactly did you go for *air*?"

"Harley's hockey game. It was a big game," I finally whispered, hating the way her eyes flashed with disdain. Harley was her nephew through my father—and since she loathed that man almost as much as she hated me, Harley wasn't her favorite person either.

I didn't give her any other details. I wouldn't... Everything she touched turned to ashes, all the good about anything burned away.

Jolette's laugh was a mockery. "Did the hockey game last all night, Olivia?" She held up her phone and the 5:30am that was blaring from the homescreen.

I blinked at her slowly, my hands fisted at my side.

"Like I said...I needed some air," I said through clenched teeth.

I was embarrassed standing there. Pretending to be someone else for a night...it was dangerous. It had made me forget for a second how life really was. It had given me a taste of...freedom.

And that was as dangerous as having...hope.

There was a beat of silence, like both of them were waiting for me to break and spill my secrets.

But I stayed quiet.

"Being stubborn this morning, are you? I guess we're being too lenient, Marco. She's getting a wild hare again."

Dread filled my gut at the reminder of what happened the last time they'd thought I was trying to break away.

Marco was still staring at me, tracing his bottom lip idly like he was deep in thought.

"Let's remember to give someone a head's up next time you leave, princess," he finally said dismissively, shocking me with how he seemed to be simply letting it go. But his next words were like ice water in my veins. "Jolette, why don't you go home and get some sleep. Olivia and I have some things to discuss."

Jolette's gaze hardened. "You're too lenient on her," she snapped, like I was an unruly child instead of a fucking adult.

Shame turned my insides like spoiled milk.

Shame and rage.

There'd never been anyone to help me. My mother and Marco had manipulated everything around them to keep me under their thumb.

No one would listen to me.

What little freedom I had came from giving up *everything* I'd worked so hard to get.

Those feelings slipped into fear as she left the room without a look back.

And then, it was just me and *him*.

Marco was back to looking at his phone, letting the anticipation peak—he and Jolette had that skillset in common.

Finally he slipped his phone into his pocket...and that's when my hands began to shake.

"Tell me what you were really up to last night, princess," he ordered silkily.

I gulped, trying to keep my face blank. "I already told you," I whispered. "And there may have also been a late night taco truck run in there as well," I said the words lightly, like maybe they'd tamp down the madness seeping out of him.

He prowled towards me in long, slow steps...until he was standing just a breath away. It was all I could do not to back up.

But he'd like that too much.

Seeing my fear.

"You smell like sex," he whispered, leaning forward, his lips brushing against my ear and making me want to vomit. "You must have lost your mind if you think you could give that pussy to someone else and expect there wouldn't be consequences."

I should have been prepared, but the blow from his fist still took me off guard. I staggered back, the searing pain in my face radiating through me. The metallic tang of blood flooded my mouth. My vision swam as I struggled to stay on my feet, my legs wobbling beneath me.

My lips were trembling as I held in my tears. It was the only thing I had—not giving him the reaction that he wanted.

My defiance only made him more furious.

He loomed over me, his face twisted with anger and frustration, his chest heaving with each ragged breath.

"Who does that pussy belong to?" he growled, the words hanging in the air like a heavy shroud of doom. A hand darted between my legs, digging into my core painfully. "Who?" he shouted.

Without waiting for an answer, his fist hit me again in the stomach. Each blow was like a sledgehammer, raining down on me in sickening punches that echoed around the room. Each impact sent shockwaves of pain coursing through my body, and like every time…

All I could do was survive it.

I collapsed to the floor, my consciousness slipping away, my vision narrowing to a pinprick of light. My body was nothing but a battered and broken vessel, aching with every heartbeat. The room seemed to spin around me, the world fading into a nightmarish blur.

I clung to the last vestiges of my consciousness. What he'd do if I passed out wasn't something I could survive.

I could survive a fist. But I couldn't survive *that*.

Not after last night.

Finally, he stopped. Marco stood over me, his breathing heavy, his fists clenched at his sides like he was having to hold himself back from more.

I laid on the carpeted floor, now sullied with my blood, gasping for air, my body trembling with pain.

Without a word, he walked away, leaving me there in a pool of misery and relief…because at least he wasn't going to rape me. The room was silent, save for my labored breaths and the distant sounds of the world outside.

When the door finally slammed, and I let myself slip into unconsciousness, all I could think was.

Last night had been worth it.

CHAPTER 7
WALKER

Ari: Disney, there were rumors a cock sock was involved in last night's festivities.

King Linc: It's too fucking early for this.

Ari: Blake and I haven't gone to sleep yet, so maybe it's actually too fucking late.

Ari: Walker. Please tell me the cock sock was at least big enough. The anaconda you're packing needs some breathing room.

King Linc: I definitely know it's too early to talk about Walker's cock size.

Ari: Don't worry, Golden Boy. You've got the whole dick tattoo thing happening. You've definitely got Monroe dickmatized. You can do one of those Facebook things for her. "Marked safe from Walker Davis's dick."

King Linc: Do not ever mention Monroe's name and another man's dick again.

Ari: You're a little scary, Linc.

King Linc:...

scrolled through the texts, not able to even grin because I was so devastated that she was gone.

Whoever *she* even fucking was. She was wearing a wig. She didn't have an I.D. I was pretty sure "Violet" hadn't even been her name.

> **Me:** Either of you know how to find missing people?

> **Ari:** That was a weird segue. Did you make someone disappear with your dick? OMG. Has your dick disappeared?

> **King Linc:** STOP TALKING ABOUT DICKS.

> **Ari:** Oooh, he pulled out the shouty caps, Disney. I'm a little nervous.

> **Me:** FOCUS. I need to find…someone.

> **King Linc:** Does this…someone…have something to do with the cock sock?

> **Ari:** I thought we weren't allowed to talk about cocks anymore.

I threw my phone on the bed, huffing as I flopped down in the sheets, trying to soak myself in the scent she'd left all over.

A second later, my phone buzzed. Glancing over dejectedly, I sat straight up…because Lincoln Fucking Daniels was calling. Me!!!!

I cleared my throat as I fumbled for the phone. *Act cool, Walker. Act cool.*

"Hey," I said, wanting to throw myself off a cliff at the way my voice had just squeaked.

Fucking *squeaked.*

"Tell me about this girl," he demanded.

"There's nothing to tell," I said. "I just wondered if you guys knew someone who could find people."

"If you don't give me details, I can't help," he said in a silky, smooth voice. Holy fuck. I could not imagine people said no to him very often.

"This girl left without giving me her last name. And I'm not sure she gave me her real first name either."

"Okay, well, my last P.I. was a piece of shit. But this new one has been doing a good job."

"Ummm...I mean, I'll take the info...but....what are you using a P.I. for?"

"Oh Disney...." he purred.

He *fucking* purred.

Click. The bastard hung up on me.

The brilliant, perfect, god-like bastard.

And now...I was even more intrigued.

A second later, a text came through with the contact information for some guy named Jeff.

What kind of P.I.'s name was Jeff?

––––––

The wait took forever. Apparently when you only had a first name and where someone had been sitting at a hockey game...it was difficult to find a person. I hadn't given him the picture I'd taken of her sleeping...even in my desperation. I couldn't share that moment with someone else.

It was mine.

We lost the first round of the playoffs. I searched the stands for her each home game, trying to see if she would make an appearance.

But she never did.

The loss was even worse than usual because now I didn't have the season to distract me. Not from the silence from Dallas, not from L.A. pushing me to re-sign...not from the lack of...her.

I clicked through the channels on the tv, scoffing when I saw NHL Network was playing a replay of our game against Seattle.

Because of course they were. The universe just loved fucking with me.

Wait…Seattle. She'd said something about them.

She'd said she'd been at the game because she knew someone from Seattle! Her cousin!

How the fuck had I forgotten that?

Probably because I was trying to block out the fact that she was wearing another man's jersey.

I'd only just allowed my sheets and the jersey she'd worn to be washed last week…and only because the smell of her had finally faded.

Fucking hell.

I dialed Jeff, who was probably going to ban me as a client soon with how many times I called him on a daily basis.

"Her cousin's on the team," I blurted out the moment he picked up.

"Relax, kid, I finally figured that out last night," he muttered grumpily. "No thanks to you. I could have gotten you something fucking sooner if you'd remembered that important little tidbit." He huffed dramatically like he wasn't fucking charging me a gazillion dollars for every hour that he worked. "Check your texts."

Was it okay for my heart to be beating this fast? Because it was. It was beating out of my fucking ribcage as I pulled up the text he'd just sent.

The fucking *video* actually.

There she was in a vid that must have been from a security camera in the arena, sitting next to the girl I vaguely remembered from that night. Looking fucking adorable. And perfect.

And mine.

"What's her last name?" I said in a weird sounding voice.

"She's *Harley Jacobs'* cousin," he explained, not answering my question. "Or at least I assume you've been looking for the one on the left, and you're not boning Jacobs' girlfriend. The girlfriend's the chick to the right of her."

"Nope, not that one," I muttered, feeling dazed as I continued to stare at her, replaying the fucking clip over and over again like a lovesick crazy person.

"The tickets were in his name obviously, so I had to do a deep dive into his family history. You're lucky she wasn't just a friend. I'd never have been able to find that shit."

"Who is she?" I growled. If he were in the room, I would have had my hands wrapped around his fucking throat, trying to shake the information out of him since he was obviously enjoying keeping me hanging.

"You're going to want to sit down for this."

"Fucking hell, JUST TELL ME."

"That girl. She ain't no Violet. Her name is Olivia Jones…also known as…" He took a deep inhale and paused…because this guy must thrive on fucking with me.

"Olivia Darling."

"Olivia," I said the name out loud, thinking how good it tasted on my lips.

That fit her way better than "Violet".

Wait a second…Olivia Darling. Where did I know that name from?

"Why aren't you freaking out more about this? You fuck crazy superstars on a regular basis, kid?"

"Watch your fucking mouth," I growled, as the story came to me. No one was allowed to talk about her like that.

Olivia Darling. Now I knew why that name sounded so familiar.

She was a singer. She'd supposedly been addicted to tons of shit and lost her mind. Something about a conservatorship.

"I might have found her address…" he said slyly, and I realized I hadn't said anything for a long time.

"Send it over."

"That's going to be worth double…I had to use my contacts at the court because her case is sealed."

"Fine. Just give it to me."

A second later there was an address in my texts.

Gotcha.

"The stuff that's out there about her is *bad*. You sure you want to go there?" he asked.

"Just find out more," I snapped. He decidedly was *not* in the circle of trust. Which meant he was definitely *not* getting that answer.

"Alright. Alright, you can thank me later," he grumbled as I hung up.

A quick Google search of the address and I was out the door, driving like a mad man to find her. To do what...I wasn't sure. But I at least needed to be near her.

———

Three days. That's how long I'd spent in my fucking truck, parked near her high rise, my eyes fixed on her building like a fucking crazy person.

I couldn't exactly just waltz up to her front door and say hi... remember me...I mean, at least I *knew that now,* after the doorman had laughed in my face and threatened to call the police on me if I didn't "leave the premises immediately."

Asshole.

Hence why I was now living in my truck. Waiting to get a glimpse of her.

The P.I.'s file was my bible during the long hours. I pored over every article, every scrap of information about her. Googling whatever questions I had.

It was an obsession, one that I accepted more and more every day.

I'd also become obsessed with her music.

I was a country boy, a lifelong listener to country music...and Taylor Swift. But Olivia's music had become like a lifeline to me, the soundtrack to my days and the lullaby to my restless nights. I'd memorized every song in her catalog, listening to each one on repeat, each note wrapping around my soul like a lover's caress. They were raw, honest, and hauntingly beautiful, just like her. Each lyric felt like a glimpse into her soul, a part of her that she'd shared with the world.

Olivia Darling was my addiction and I didn't want anything to make me better.

My phone buzzed.

> Ari: Disney aka Dis aka Not Walker Texas Ranger…where the fuck are you? I have news.

I'd been ignoring my phone. Not bothering with anything unless it was Jeff sending me information. But the idea of *news* was intriguing…

> Me: What's up?

> Ari: What's up? That's what I get? No, "I love you the mostest." Or "thanks for finding this out."

> King Linc: Just tell him the news, Lancaster.

> Ari: Ooh…pulling out the big guns. A little last name action.

> Me: Thanks for finding this out. Now what am I finding out?

I sat up straight when the door to her complex opened and… a seventy year old woman stepped out.

Buzzz.

Slumping back in my seat, I glanced at my phone.

> Ari: Dallas called your agent.

I tensed, staring at the text.

> **Me:** You better not be joking with me, Lancaster.

> **Ari:** Hah. Nice try. But that doesn't do it for me like it does when golden boy says it. There's simply not enough simping coming from you at the moment over the fact that I just told you DALLAS CALLED YOUR AGENT.

My phone buzzed, this time with an incoming call. Fuck. It was my agent.

Was it hot in here? Did I have a fever? Was my truck leaking gas and I was going crazy from the fumes?

Actually something to consider. I kicked at a chip bag that had fallen to the cab floor.

"Hello," I said, trying to keep my voice steady despite the fact that I might have been about to spontaneously combust.

My agent's voice crackled through the line. "Walker, Dallas reached out."

"Fuck. Tell me they want me," I begged...sounding a little hysterical.

The door opened again and honestly, thank fuck it was another gray haired, hundred year old looking granny, because I may have died from excitement between seeing Olivia and this phone call.

"They sent over an offer."

I was dying, about to melt into my seat.

My phone buzzed as texts came in.

> **Ari:** WALKER PUCKING DISNEY DAVIS, WHY AREN'T YOU RESPONDING?

> **King Linc:** Maybe he's not interested in Dallas.

I pretended like he'd said that in a very sullen, distraught, devastated voice.

Ari: Psshh. Disney would never.

"Six years. Sixty million," Tucker said, obviously done with the blank silence I was giving him.

"Fuck," I whispered, and the fucker laughed at me.

The door to Olivia's building opened again and I glanced up, watching it almost absentmindedly, expecting it to be another old lady...since Olivia apparently lived in some kind of retirement home judging by the ages of the other residents in the building.

But it was her.

My angel.

It was like I could breathe again. Like I'd been jolted back to life. Like the blood had returned to my veins.

And to my dick.

I stared at her like a lovesick puppy, memorizing every detail about her, from her long, wavy dark auburn hair which I was actually obsessed with...to the L.A. Cobras hat she was wearing.

That hat had to be a sign. She was thinking of me. She was missing me too.

Or at least that's what I was telling myself.

My agent was giving me what were probably *very* important details about the deal, but I was catching maybe every tenth word as I studied my girl.

A second later, a man in a three piece suit emerged from the building. Olivia had stopped just outside the entrance, and I watched with sick dread as the slick haired, slimy looking DEAD man grabbed her arm, leading her to a car waiting at the curb.

I could hear my heartbeat in my ears as I watched them. Who the fuck was that? And why was he handling her like he *owned* her?

He slid into the car after her and it pulled away.

And I followed it.

"Walker! Are you listening?" Tucker snapped, exasperation clear in his tone.

"Yeah, just get the deal done, Tuck. I'm good with it."

"I just told you L.A. beat Dallas's offer."

"They beat sixty million?"

I stared at the phone, wondering how this was real life. And why this was all happening at the same fucking time.

Keeping one eye on the road and the car I was tailing like I was some kind of James Bond character, I flipped through a couple of pictures in the file Jeff had sent me, trying to see if the guy was in there.

"Gotcha!" I snarled. Marco Davine. Olivia's agent and one of her conservators, along with her mother. From what I'd read, it had been shocking when the judge had appointed him as co-conservator. A lot of financial ethical issues with that one.

"Gotcha what? Do I need to call you fucking back? It's not like I'm over here trying to get your *dream* deal on your *dream* team, Walker."

The sass on this one.

"Sorry," I muttered unrepentantly as I turned left after the car.

I was terrible at this. Fuck.

For the first time...I wondered if Dallas was the right move. Because I couldn't leave her here.

No. I would just have to figure that out. She would come with me. Somehow.

"So what's the plan, Tuck? I want Dallas," I finally got out as Olivia's car pulled into the parking lot for Ray Therapy Center.

"I already countered, asshole. I should have a response by tomorrow."

I grinned as I parked on the other side of the street. "That's why you're my guy."

"Yeah, yeah," he barked, trying to sound grumpy. I could hear the smug smile in his voice though. Tucker knew he was the best. The rest of his clientele agreed.

But my smile faded as Olivia got out of the car, everything about her body language defeated as she trudged into the clinic.

"I'll talk to you later," I said, my voice trailing off before I hung up.

I sat there in tense silence, ignoring my phone, and watching the doors. An hour later, she came out, her head turned down, her arms wrapped around herself.

I picked up the docs again, looking at the terms of the conservatorship that Jeff had gotten from the court file.

Davine and Olivia's bitch looking mother basically had complete control over her.

What the fuck?

Nothing about that woman had seemed like she needed to be watched over. She'd been sad, flighty, twitchy…yes. But nothing that even hinted at the claims the two fuckers had presented to the court.

Drug addict.

Mentally incompetent.

A danger to herself and others.

I trailed the car back to her apartment, dying inside as I watched her walk into the building…at least without Marco.

I stayed there, waiting for any sign of her.

Minutes turned into hours, and still, she didn't reappear. Eventually, I went home.

I tossed and turned that night for hours, one of her songs playing on repeat, the soundtrack to my agony…and what must have been hers.

I'm trapped in a cage of my own design,
Lost in a world where the sun won't shine.
My heart cries out, but my voice is stilled,
In this prison of sorrow, my dreams are killed.
Every day, I paint on a smile,
Hiding the tears that I've cried for a while.
I'm a bird with clipped wings, unable to soar,
In this cage of regrets, forevermore.

CHAPTER 8
OLIVIA

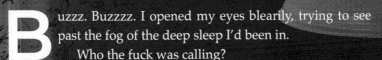

B uzzz. Buzzzz. I opened my eyes blearily, trying to see past the fog of the deep sleep I'd been in.

Who the fuck was calling?

No one ever called me.

No one I really ever *wanted* to call me at least.

I squinted at my phone, finally coherent enough to press accept when I saw that it was Harley calling.

The screen lit up, Maddie and Harley's smiling faces filling the phone as soon as I accepted the video call.

Maddie held up her hand, an enormous sparkling rock on her finger. She was like an excited puppy as she danced on the couch next to Harley.

"We're getting married!" she squealed, her voice echoing through the connection. Harley's grin was equally as wide as he slung an arm around her shoulders and pulled her into his chest, pressing a soft kiss on her hair.

I forgot all about being tired, my jaw dropping...even as a pang hit my chest as I watched how in love they were.

The way he'd held me that night, the feel of his lips...the way he'd looked at me like he could love me to my soul...

"Harley. You're finally making an honest woman out of her.

I'm so proud of you," I cooed, trying to push away all my other thoughts.

"Hey! I've been trying to get her to marry me for the last year, Jones. You should be proud."

I snorted, my eyes widening. I hadn't known that little tidbit.

"I'm really happy for you both," I said in a softer voice, feeling oddly like I was going to cry.

There was a pause on the other end, and Maddie shot a glance at Harley before looking at me again.

"What? You're making me nervous!"

"Olivia," Maddie began tentatively, "I—I want you to be one of my bridesmaids."

I blinked in surprise, my heart fluttering. The offer was unexpected, and I was more touched than I would have...thought.

Until I remembered what the realities of my life were and why they'd been so hesitant to even ask.

I stared at the happy couple, two of the only people in the world that had been on my side throughout all the shit.

I wanted to go to their wedding.

Desperately actually, which was a weird thing to think. I stared at them, probably resembling a crazy person. How had they managed that, even after everything—getting under my skin?

It sucked because now I was going to have to do whatever it took to make it happen.

Even if I had to beg.

"Maddie. I would be absolutely honored," I finally replied.

Maddie didn't seem to mind my long pause, she just let out another delighted squeal that had Harley wrinkling his nose because he was probably deaf now.

"Yes, yes, yes. I'm so happy right now. Liv, it's going to be the best!"

"Okay, so when's the big day?"

Maddie and Harley exchanged another one of those glances,

where they were communicating silently. They didn't have to say the words out loud, because they knew each other so well.

The ache inside me grew. I could only dream about having that kind of relationship with someone.

"So...it's in two months...in Dallas. We wanted to do it before the start of the season. And since most of Harley's and my family are there...it just makes sense." She bit down on her lip. "But we're doing the shower, the bachelorette/bachelor parties, and everything else over that three day weekend so that no one has to travel twice," she added, like she was making a sales pitch.

Maddie was still beaming, but her smile had dimmed some, like she was waiting for the inevitable pushback or for me to say I couldn't do it.

"Okay then...in two months I will see you in Dallas," I said, forcing a brightness to my tone even though I was dreading the conversations that were going to have to take place to get me there.

When I'd refused to perform as a pushback against the conservatorship, it had also meant the end of my freedom. Besides trips around town, I hadn't gone anywhere. Not vacations, not day trips. Nothing.

So this would be a big jump.

But as they signed off and I promised to keep them updated on my travel plans, I decided it would be worth it.

That seemed to be happening a lot these days.

———

The click of the lock signaled Jolette was here.

Two freaking days after I'd told her I needed to discuss something with her.

The sudden intrusion into what was supposed to be my private sanctuary grated on my nerves like it always did, like the screechy sound when nails met a chalkboard. I couldn't remember her ever knocking before coming in, and the fact that she and Marco both had a key and could come and go as they pleased—under the guise of safety concerns, of course—had always made sure this place never felt like home.

It was just another way they constantly rubbed in my face how little control I had over my own life.

As she let herself in without a second thought, I fought the urge to lash out, knowing anything I did would be futile.

"Well, I'm here. Taking time from my busy schedule to deal with you. Once again," she snapped.

Right...her busy schedule of spa treatments and private planes to the vineyard to get drunk with her vapid friends—all using my money.

Such a busy schedule.

I stared at her as she finished whatever she was doing on her phone.

Her long, perfectly coiffed hair cascaded down her back in a glossy, blonde waterfall. Her skin was flawless, but it had that telltale plastic sheen that came from too many cosmetic procedures. Her designer clothing clung to her figure, emphasizing her slender physique, carved by Dr. Rothingham on 5th Avenue himself. Diamonds flashed at me from her ears down to her hands.

A beautiful plastic exterior housing the poisonous snake inside.

"Harley's getting married," I said, cutting straight to the chase.

"And," she drawled...still not looking at me.

"Maddie has asked me to be a bridesmaid for their wedding in two months...in Dallas."

"Who's Maddie?"

"His fiancée," I said slowly, since that should be obvious.

"No," she said simply, spinning around and heading back to the door, the click of her heels reverberating through the room.

"Wait...what do you mean no?" I called after her, jumping up from the couch where I'd sat to try and pretend nonchalance.

Obviously that plan was out the window.

"You've shown time and time again, Olivia, that you can't be trusted around Harley. Wasn't he the little reason for your temper tantrum the other morning?" she said with an unyielding tone, *finally* glancing at me with a perfectly shaped eyebrow raised.

My hands were shaking, and I swallowed, trying to get control of my voice. "I've given you and Marco *everything*. What more do you want from me? What can I do to get this madness to stop? You can't just keep me a prisoner until I die!"

It was more than I wanted to reveal, this desperation sitting in my chest. It was the weakness I had tried my best never to show her, and now here it was, splayed open for her to use.

And Jolette knew it too.

"I think you know what would help your 'little situation'," she purred, her eyes gleaming as she went in for the kill. "Your refusal to cooperate with our terms has been sooo...*disappointing*."

I closed my eyes, trying to hold in the scream burning in my chest.

Oh, I knew exactly what she was talking about. The only thing they couldn't get a court to force me to do.

Sing.

"I'll perform in Dallas the day after the wedding," I finally offered softly, feeling like I was losing something important even as I said it.

I'd vowed that I would never give them what they wanted like this—access to my voice.

I guess they'd finally, truly broken me.

Jolette's smile was victorious and cold, and I could practically see the dollar signs stacking up in that psychotic brain of hers. "Marco will set it up," she said dismissively, like she hadn't just won the war we'd been waging for the last two years.

She turned on her heel to leave.

"Wait, so that means I'm going to the wedding, right? Because that's the only way I'll perform," I called after her.

Jolette gave me a sickening grin over her shoulder. "Yes, you can go to that little wedding of yours. But if you try anything, if you don't do that show..." Her grin widened and cold sweat slicked across my forehead at the warning.

She left the apartment after that happy little thought, leaving me alone with my dread and my demons. I felt sick, the walls of my world closing in on me. I wanted to call her back, tell her the deal was off.

But I needed that one weekend of freedom. I needed it like I needed water...to survive.

I would just perform one show. And then I could say no again. I already knew that was one thing I had in my power.

This was Walker's fault.

If I hadn't had that night with him, if I hadn't tasted that one night of liberation, I could have kept going as I had been. I could have accepted my fate.

I wouldn't have given in.

My eyes landed on the bathroom door, and unlike every other day over the last two years...I didn't resist.

With shaky hands, I retrieved the pill bottle I had tried so hard to stay away from. Jolette and Marco had started to keep the bottles in the apartment over the last year, to tempt me so to speak.

But I'd already given in on so much today—what was one more thing?

The tiny white tablets offered a cruel sense of comfort, and I sighed at the bitter taste they left on my tongue as I put them in my mouth.

The bitter taste was a perfect reflection for the *bitter* life I experienced each day.

The high slid through my senses much faster than it had a few years ago, when I'd depended on it multiple times a day.

I laid on my bed, feeling pathetic, feeling *so* out of control of my life, until finally, the numbness swooped in and took it away...and I could breathe again.

"**D**isney's in the house," Ari whooped as I strolled into the Dallas bar. I'd just signed a record breaking contract as a goalie with Dallas, and tonight...we were celebrating. I was also breaking some very important news to the "circle of trust." And in my humble opinion, one of them was much more exciting than the other.

Although I was really fucking excited about *finally* being a Dallas Knight.

Ari held up a glass, a sheen to his gaze that told me he and Linc had already thrown a few back. He'd signed with Dallas a week before, also a very nice contract, and I could practically taste the beer I was going to drink from the Stanley Cup when we won it this year.

They had their phones out, and as I passed behind them to head to the empty seat at the table, I saw they were both watching video footage of Blake and Monroe hanging out in Lincoln's living room.

"Are you guys stalking your wives right now?" I drawled, nodding at the waitress who'd popped up by the table like she'd been waiting with bated breath to get me whatever I needed.

Judging by the way she was looking at me, that was probably the offer on the table.

"Is that a real question, Disney?" Ari answered, a small smile on his face from whatever he was seeing.

"Whatever they're having," I told the waitress dismissively, wishing I had my own camera on Olivia.

I'd been following her every day, living for the small glimpses I got when she went to therapy...basically the only place she ever went. Unless she was going out at night—which I didn't think she was—since I'd also spent two nights outside her place...to make sure.

The waitress came back with my beer and some chips, queso, and wings.

I fucking loved Texas. And since Olivia had said she was originally from here, I was positive I could get her to love it too.

"Blake's sitting too close to Monroe," Lincoln grumbled suddenly, his gaze still locked on his screen. It was the closest thing to whining that I'd ever heard out of the glorious god.

"They're watching a movie," snorted Ari, giving him a dramatic eye roll. "They're just keeping warm."

"That's where *we* watch movies. I don't like it."

"Golden Boy, are you jealous of my wife right now? Because I promise, she's all about the dick. Correction—she's all about *my* dick."

Linc rolled his eyes. "I'm just saying."

My phone buzzed and I glanced down to see that my group chat with my brothers was picking up steam.

> Cole: Hell yeah my baby brother just signed a contract for seventy million fucking dollars!

> Parker: Show us your ways, Disney.

I rolled my eyes.

> Me: I hate you.

> Cole: Why aren't you drunk yet, Walkie-poo? This kind of news deserves alcohol.

Correction, I hated both of them.

Me: I'm working on it.

Parker: Good boy.

"I have some big news," I told Ari and Linc, leaning over to grab a few wings.

"Give it to us, Disney," Ari said in a muffled voice as he stuffed some chips and queso in his mouth.

Lincoln went for a chip and Ari stabbed him with a fork. "I ordered all of this for myself. I've got months to make up for."

"Why didn't you tell me that?" he snarled, going to dip his chip again.

"I will stab you again. And then you won't be able to hold your stick. Of any kind."

"Monroe will hold my stick," Lincoln said cockily, and Ari mimed throwing up.

"I'm going to be a daddy," I announced, taking the chance to get my own queso covered chip as they both stared at me with slow blinks and gaping mouths that reminded me of a frog's.

Ari made a choking sound, coughing dramatically like he was fucking dying. "Sorry. What was that? Are we talking about sex kinks right now? Because I need to prepare myself before I think about some puck bunny calling you "daddy." Or are you and golden boy doing some reverse role play...because I was sure you'd be the one calling *him* 'Daddy.'"

Lincoln also took advantage of Ari's hysterics to dip his chip in the queso.

"No, I mean a real dad," I grinned, thinking of Olivia.

"Okay...Walker. And are you adopting? Because I haven't seen any ladies around, and I know you were taught better than to not double wrap when it comes to those stage five clingers," Ari said, continuing to sound very concerned about this news.

"It's a new thing. But you'll meet her soon," I said, munching on another chip.

Lincoln winked at me and dipped again, Ari seeming to have completely forgotten about his queso obsession in the face of my news.

"So you got a one night stand pregnant?" he asked slowly, still very confused.

"Naw. She's the love of my life." It was the very first time that I was saying it out loud. And I fucking loved it. It felt right.

Even if she had forgotten that I existed.

Lincoln and Ari side-eyed each other, grins sneaking on their faces.

"What's her name? Is she excited about the baby?" Lincoln asked as he went in for more queso. Ari had woken up from his temporary daze though, and he smacked his hand right before he got in there with his chip.

I thought about his question. Excited was probably not the right word for what Olivia was feeling at the moment.

But I was hoping I could change her mind.

Yes, I'd poked the condom a million times to make sure my swimmers got in there, but the idea had really taken root when I saw an interview she'd done with Diane Klossrud, a fucking genius at getting things out of even the most difficult subjects.

The interview would have taken place about a year before the conservatorship had kicked in, when she was still performing. Diane had asked Olivia what she wanted for the future, I'm sure expecting something like "winning a million Grammy's, or touring every country," or something else like that. Instead, Olivia had said, "I want to have a family someday."

Believe me, the statement had surprised me as much as it had surprised Diane.

"She *will* be excited," I finally announced to Lincoln and Ari as I snagged some more queso and started snacking on it.

They stared at me like I'd said something crazy, so I decided to just give it all to them..."When she finds out..."

We were drunk.

More than drunk. We were wasted.

"If you love this girl, you have to pwooove it," Lincoln was explaining, waving his hands around in the air.

I studied his hand movements, wondering if there was like a secret message in them or something.

"How do I do that?" I slurred, blinking a few times so I could stop seeing double of him. I could barely speak right in front of *one* of him, I couldn't handle two of Lincoln Daniels.

"Disney, you little simp," Ari said loudly, throwing a shot back. I frowned, because that was my shot.

"Oh fuck," I whispered as the room spun.

"Walker," Ari whisper-yelled. "They've just started playing our song!"

"What song?" Lincoln asked, throwing back the shot that the waitress had just given him.

"It's Tay-Tay!" Ari announced, jumping from his stool and doing some kind of weird hip thrust thing.

"You look ridiculous," slurred Lincoln.

"I call this the Blake WallBanger." Ari almost fell over as he started laughing like he'd said something *hilarious*.

I realized finally what he'd just said. "It is Tay-Tay!" I said, my voice coming out really high-pitched. "I'm going to do it. I'm going to dance on the fucking table. She deserves it," I told them, and they both nodded seriously, like I'd had the best idea of all time.

I kneed up on my chair and then crawled onto the table, my unsteady legs carrying me like they were guided by some unseen force.

Players gonna play, play, play, I hummed as I struggled to my feet.

"Shit, that's good," said Ari, and I glanced over to see him doing this weird spin move that made me dizzy. Lincoln was bobbing his head, unable to withstand the force of the infectious beat as I finally got to my feet, the table swaying underneath me.

The chorus was about to hit, fuck yes.

I threw my hands in the air, swaying my hips as plates and glasses clanged together on the table as I moved.

"Disney! Disney! Disney!" Ari chanted, pointing at Lincoln as he sang along.

"Sir. Sir!" the waitress called. "Sir, can you come down, please?"

"I love Olivia," I told her. "This dick is hers."

"Uhhh," she said, her gaze dipping to my dick. I made a slicing motion in front of it.

"That's not yours."

She got all red for some reason. "Sir, can you please come down."

Whoops, I thought as the table started to tip and I fell forward onto…

Lincoln Fucking Daniels.

"My hero," I wheezed as I started to laugh hysterically about the fact that I'd fallen into Lincoln's lap.

He was even more golden up close.

"That's it. I'm a motherfucking genius. Without the mother part though," Ari added seriously, leaning between us like it wasn't odd at all that I was sitting in Lincoln's lap.

Lincoln pushed me off and I fell to the floor with a plop. I collapsed backwards in hysterical sounding laughter.

"Listen, Linda," Ari said, leaning over me, and not looking confused at all why he was talking to me on the floor of a bar.

"Who's Linda?"

"It's a YouTube thing," Lincoln called, frowning as he started typing on his phone.

A second later he held up a video of this cute little kid talking to his mom. I moved my hand and felt something sticky.

Oh, I was still on the floor.

Ari heaved me up and I staggered, thinking maybe I should get some water or something.

"He has to prove that he loves her," Ari said, his hand

cupping the front of his jeans for some reason. "And there's only one way to do that."

Lincoln nodded seriously, and I perked up because if Lincoln said it was the only way, I had to do it.

"What's the way?"

"Let's go," Ari slurred, pulling on my arm and starting to heave me towards the door. "It's the only way."

I threw my arms up in the air as we burst through the door into the humid night air. "Where are we going?"

Lincoln slung an arm around my shoulder and I froze while Ari fiddled with the Uber app. "The only way to prove it," he said, his voice pitched low, "is through...your dick."

I stared at him, completely confused as the Uber pulled up. "I can't really do that right now," I tried to explain as I got into the car. "My dick tried to prove it, and she still left."

The driver gave me a weird look. "It's a dick thing," Ari told him. "You understand."

"Stupid fools," the driver muttered under his breath as we pulled away from the bar. "Inked on Main Street. Let me guess, you guys decided to get matching tattoos."

I gave Lincoln the side-eye. "Why are we going to a tattoo parlor?"

Ari patted my shoulder. "Don't worry about it. It's what must be done, young padawan."

Lincoln snorted. "I thought it was young grasshopper."

"Stars Wars seemed more Disney-ish."

"True," Lincoln replied, pulling up a video of Monroe on his phone. She was passed out on the couch and Blake was stretched out on another couch, the TV still playing a movie.

The car stopped in front of a place called Inked, which was clearly a tattoo parlor, even if the name didn't give it away.

"Does this mean I'm in the 'Circle of Trust'?" I asked hopefully as I hopped out of the car. "Because matching tattoos seems like a 'Circle of Trust' kind of thing for sure."

I started to fall over as I stood on the sidewalk because the neon lights were making me all sorts of dizzy. That last shot was definitely not a good idea.

"Just trust us. It will only hurt for a few weeks. A month max," said Lincoln as he opened the door to the shop.

"A month max?" I asked, horrified. "What kind of tattoo are we getting?"

"I actually think it will be a few months, but it should be healed by the start of the season."

"What the fuck," I muttered as I followed Ari and Lincoln to the front desk, the bright lights spinning and swirling as I dazedly stared at them.

"Yes, we're here for a dick tattoo," said Lincoln to the goth looking girl with tattoos swirling up her cheeks and huge gauges in her ears big enough to fit a ping pong ball through.

Wait a second. I stared at him incredulously. Had he just said a "dick tattoo?"

"Or a dick piercing," added Ari, doing a weird little dance shuffle to whatever techno song was blaring.

"A dick piercing," I murmured, staring at the two of them and wondering if I was having a drunk dream right now.

Because everyone knew drunk dreams were ten times more intense than regular dreams.

That's what was definitely happening.

I told myself that as we were led to a back room.

I told myself that as I sat in the padded chair.

And I told myself that as Lincoln and Ari discussed options with the tattoo artist, who was nodding seriously like everything they were saying made perfect sense.

"Disney, just take deep breaths. We'll be sitting over there," Ari said happily, patting my shoulder as he pointed to some chairs facing the opposite direction.

"Can you pull down your pants and I'll sanitize the area," the guy said.

And that's when I started to stare at him in horror.

Because I was pretty sure this wasn't a dream.

THE PUCKING WRONG DATE

"Don't worry. I did Lincoln's. It's going to be perfect." He waggled his eyebrows. "And rumor is his wife lovvvvves it."

"Don't talk about my wife, Dave," Lincoln called, giving him the side eye while I tried to wrap my drunk as fuck brain about what was happening.

"Walker, just do as he says," Ari told me, popping some M&Ms in his mouth he'd gotten from who knows where.

I could use some M&Ms at the moment.

Dave laughed at me, like he thought I was joking. "Don't worry. I use lots of numbing cream," he told me. "It won't hurt until tomorrow."

"I don't want to be in the 'Circle of Trust,'" I called out as I somehow found myself unzipping my jeans.

"Holy hell, that's a big guy," Dave said with wide-eyes.

"Stop looking at it!" I hissed.

"It's a dick tattoo. He kind of has to look at it," drawled Lincoln, sipping from the beer he'd somehow gotten hold of.

"I object!" I screeched, but they all laughed at me, like I'd said something funny.

"Here, dude, have a hit. You need to calm the fuck down," Dave muttered, offering me a bong he'd pulled from who the fuck knows where. I inhaled and then inhaled again–forgetting why I didn't like being high.

I clearly needed it for this.

"She's going to love it!" called out Ari.

"True love hurts, Walk," added Lincoln as he watched the weather report on the tv on the wall like it was the most fascinating thing he'd ever seen.

That may have been the truest thing I'd ever heard.

The buzz of the tattoo gun filled the air...and that's about when I blacked out.

CHAPTER 10
WALKER

Fuck, my dick hurt.

And so did my back.

Why exactly had they decided I should get a butterfly tattoo too?

Wasn't the piercing enough?

My phone buzzed and I winced, adjusting the ice on my cock as I answered the phone. Three days later and my dick *still* felt like it might fall off.

"She's going to a wedding in Dallas," Jeff said without preamble as soon as I'd picked up. He sounded very proud of himself.

"What?" I asked, completely shocked by the news. I was beginning to think I was going to have to pose as a therapist to ever be able to see her again since she never left her apartment.

"Yep. Her cousin Harley's wedding. The cousin from Seattle."

Like I had forgotten that.

"She's in the wedding. It's completely top secret that she's going to be there."

"How did you find out?" I asked, thinking it was creepy—and useful—how these P.I.s could get access to this kind of information.

"This one kind of fell in my lap. Her mom and that agent of hers were discussing it at The Ivy last night. I just happened to be in the booth behind them."

"Just happened to be?"

"You're going to get a huge bill," he said, and I could hear the smile in his voice. "But before you go into sticker shock...check the links I just sent you."

The links were internet articles and I immediately clicked the first one.

Olivia Darling's Return?

The headline blared at me as I scanned the article speculating that Olivia would be performing for the first time in years in Dallas.

"In a surprising turn of events, it seems that the elusive Olivia Darling is set to grace her hometown of Dallas with a secret performance. An insider from Olivia's camp has confirmed that the highly anticipated show is indeed in the works. While details remain top secret, fans are buzzing with excitement, eager to catch a glimpse of the missing in action singer-songwriter. Stay tuned for further updates on this intriguing development that promises to be a musical event like no other. One can't help but wonder though, with Darling's past...is this the return of a superstar...or the beginning of another disaster?"

I ground my teeth at the article's mocking tone about my girl, but went on to the next one.

Harley Jacobs Engaged!

"For some off-ice development, Seattle's hockey sensation, Harley Jacobs, is taking a break from his on-ice battles to score a victory of a different kind—tying the knot with his longtime sweetheart, Maddie Cascio. The Seattle star forward is set to trade in his jersey for a dapper tuxedo in his hometown of Dallas."

"You wouldn't happen to know when these things are taking

place...would you?" I asked, my heart beating faster as a batshit crazy plan formed in my mind.

"August 16th it looks like."

"Two weeks," I whispered to myself.

"Find out where Harley Jacobs is right now," I ordered, trying to keep the desperation...and crazy out of my voice. You never wanted someone like *Jeff* knowing how much you needed something.

I heard some papers ruffling. "I actually know that one already. He and his girl are in Dallas until the wedding, getting everything prepared," Jeff said after a minute.

"Perfect."

"Whatcha going to do?" he asked, intrigued.

"Thanks," I said in response, hanging up as I texted my assistant to book me a flight and start getting my place packed up to start the move to Dallas.

Texas was calling my name.

———

I navigated the rental truck through the winding streets of the upscale Dallas suburb, tall oak trees lining the roads and casting dappled shadows. Turning left, I glanced at my GPS as it guided me to the house that Harley Jacobs called home during the offseason.

"Buh-buh-buh-buh-buh-buh-buh-buh, buh-buh, buh-buh, buh-buh, buh-buh-buh-buh-buh-buh-buh." The "Mission Impossible" Theme song blared out of Ari's phone and I glanced at him with my best "what the fuck" expression.

He smirked at me. "Just setting the mood for our secret special spy mission."

I snorted.

"Stop calling it a 'secret special spy mission,'" drawled Lincoln from the phone. Ari had insisted that Linc participate in…whatever we were calling this…while he stalked Monroe on campus.

I was only fifty percent sure he had been kidding when he'd said that's what he was doing today.

Stalking seemed to be *approved* behavior in the "circle of trust."

"So what's the plan, Dis?" Ari said as he bopped along to the rest of the song.

"You going to use that info I told you about?" asked Lincoln.

"If that's what it takes."

"What do you mean 'if that's what it takes?'" snorted Ari. "I highly doubt he's going to give you a spot in his wedding without some…persuasiveness."

"This information does feel very persuasive," I noted.

"Park here!" Ari said frantically. "You can't just park in front of the person you're trying to blackmail's house. Everyone knows that!"

"Everyone does know that," agreed Lincoln.

I pulled the truck over and stared at Ari. "Why do you guys sound like you've done these things before?"

Ari smirked at me, and if a smirk could be heard, I was pretty sure Lincoln had the same look on his face…wherever he was.

"There comes a point when you have to decide what your line is, Walk. This is the point."

Actually, I think the needle I'd used to poke holes in the condom for a girl that was just looking for a one night stand was the point…

But semantics.

"Alright. I've got this."

"Can I hang up now?" asked Lincoln. "I'm a little…busy."

Ari frowned at the phone even though Lincoln couldn't see him. "We have to do our cheer first."

"What do you mean we have to do a cheer? I'm not doing a cheer." Lincoln sounded very insistent on that…

"I'm not doing a cheer either," I said quickly, and Ari smirked at me—because yeah...I would totally do a cheer.

"Simp," he mouthed at me.

I flipped him off.

We froze when Harley's fiancée walked out the front door, giving Harley a kiss before she strode toward the car parked at the end of the drive.

"Well, that was convenient," Ari muttered.

"What—what's convenient?" Lincoln pressed.

"Wouldn't you like to know. You should have been here. For our super secret spy mission," Ari taunted.

"Okay...I'm going in," I said, feeling slightly queasy at what I was about to do.

"Wait, you need a pump up speech," Ari said, throwing a flask at me. "Drink some of that first."

I nodded. That was probably a good idea. I took a deep draw from the flask, wincing at the burn.

"What is this?" I gasped, feeling like my esophagus had caught on fire.

"Moonshine. A batch that Bill put together."

"Monroe's homeless friend?" I screeched.

"Shhh. It's perfectly fine. Keep drinking, I'm going over my speech," Ari urged.

I kept drinking...until I was feeling much better about everything.

"Alright. Here it goes..." Ari said, shaking a fist in the air. "Perhaps it's fate that today is the 4th of July, and you will once again be fighting for our freedom, not from tyranny, oppression, or persecution -- but from annihilation. We're fighting for our right to live, to exist—"

"Why the fuck are you quoting 'Independence Day' right now?" asked Lincoln, sounding horrified.

Ah, I knew it sounded familiar.

"Because that's the most inspirational speech in cinematic

history," Ari said indignantly, forcing me to knock back another drink.

"Oooh I have a good one," I said, sitting up straighter in my seat. "In Greek mythology, the Titans were greater even than the gods. They ruled their universe with absolute power. Well that football field out there, that's our universe. Let's rule it like titans."

Ari grinned. "Remember the Titans." Oh...that's a good one too."

Lincoln sighed...heavily.

"Disney, just get it fucking done," he growled.

Best pump up speech ever.

I took a deep breath and opened the door. After weeks of being unable to do anything about this little obsession of mine... it was nice to finally be taking a step.

Even if it was a crazy step.

I walked up the sidewalk towards Harley's red brick mansion, the streetlights casting shadows across the lawn that made what I was doing feel a little spooky. Good thing this alcohol floating through my veins was making me feel free and easy.

Taking a breath, I rang the doorbell, aiming for casual as I heard the lock disengage.

Harley swung open the door, his face registering shock when he saw me standing there. "Um...what the hell are you doing at my house, Davis?" he asked, his voice laced with confusion.

"I was just in the neighborhood and thought I would stop by," I told him, pushing past him into the house.

It was a nice place. Very homey feeling—

"What the fuck?" Harley hissed. I turned, frowning when I saw that he was still standing by the door, gaping at me. He was dressed in workout clothes and I grimaced at the Seattle shirt he was wearing—it reminded me of the fact that Olivia had been wearing *his* jersey that night.

The thought made me feel a bit twitchy inside.

"Have any beer?" I asked, making myself comfortable on the couch. TV was a little small, but I guess the house couldn't be perfect.

Harley blinked at me and I was afraid that I'd broken him.

"Sit the fuck down," I murmured, since he obviously wasn't going to just be cool about this.

A very rational response to a random person he barely knew showing up to his house late at night.

"I feel like I should call the police...should I call the police?" Harley asked haltingly, finally walking into the living room... moving as slowly as he was talking.

I couldn't believe this guy was Olivia's cousin.

"First of all, congrats on the wedding, dude. That's awesome. I hope to be married soon, too."

Ari had told me to go in all charming like...but it didn't seem to be working. Harley was staring at me and it was honestly a little bit unsettling, because he wasn't blinking that much.

"Um...thanks?" he finally said.

I nodded. Alright, that was a good sign.

"Are you sure you don't have any beer?" I asked, because this was really awkward. "Maybe some whiskey or something..."

Hmm...maybe I should have brought in Ari's flask. Harley here could have used some moonshine...obviously.

"Weed, maybe? It came in clutch when I had my dick done. You should try it. Not the dick obviously...the weed."

Harley's eyes bugged out like I'd said something weird.

I licked my lip, catching some of the moonshine's aftertaste... it actually wasn't that bad.

"I'm still waiting for the punchline, Davis. My fiancée is going to be back in twenty minutes...and I really don't want you still here because you're creeping me out."

I scoffed. He was the one staring at me without blinking. Who was he calling creepy?

Focus, Walker. Focus, I told myself.

Fuck, my dick hurt. I really wanted to adjust it...but I obviously couldn't do that with him watching me like that.

"Okay...I'll just cut to the chase then. I need you to make me a groomsman in your wedding." I sat up straight, glad to have just gotten it out.

He gaped at me.

"Man, you gotta blink. You're scaring me. Your eyeballs are going to fall out or something," I told him, very serious about it.

"Did you just ask me to make you a groomsman in my wedding?" he spat, completely ignoring my helpful words of advice.

Rude.

"Well...there's actually a little more to it than that," I told him, trying to get comfortable because the couch wasn't nearly comfy enough for my tortured dick. "I need you to match me up with your cousin. I assume you're doing it the traditional way where people are paired up in the wedding—"

Harley sat on the couch and leaned forward, pulling out his phone. "Walker, dude. Who can I call? Are you okay? Have you hit your head recently? Because there's no fucking way that I'm having you as a groomsman in my wedding. And it's even a bigger no fucking way that you're going to have anything to do with my cousin."

I sighed, because honestly, I really hadn't wanted to do this the hard way. Just based on the fact that Olivia never left her place, the fact that she'd gone to Harley's game meant that she liked her cousin. A lot. This was going to be a temporary setback to me forming a friendship with Harley for Olivia, but I was sure we would eventually recover.

Possibly we would recover.

It honestly could go either way.

"Look Harley, this is an easy peasy thing. I have the best intentions when it comes to Olivia. We've already met. This is a good thing."

"That's it. I'm calling the police," he snarled, beginning to type in the dreaded 9-1-1.

I leapt up and snagged the phone out of his hand, quickly holding up my phone where I'd started a video.

A distraction was definitely needed at the moment. I was a little bit bigger than him, and obviously much more of a badass. But I really didn't want any visible bruising on either of us before the big weekend, and I really didn't want to have to beat the shit out of Olivia's favorite cousin.

I watched as the color drained out of his face as he watched himself makeout with Maddie's best friend in a dark corner of a club.

"This was about a year ago, right? At the NHL All Star game?" I remarked casually, not feeling remotely guilty.

All was fair in love and war after all. And this was definitely for love.

"We were broken up," he said hoarsely, looking like he'd aged ten years since the video started.

"Were you broken up? Or had she just said no to your latest marriage proposal and said she needed more time?" I drawled, cocking my head…not really interested at all in whatever his explanation was going to be.

I would rather die than touch another woman after meeting my future wife, so I couldn't relate.

And if she said no to my marriage proposal…I'd just have to be really persuasive in getting her to change her mind.

"Look. I was drunk. Blacked out. I got shitfaced after she said no. I thought we were done. I woke up in bed with…with Carlie and…" The words tumbled out in a jumble. I had to work to piece them together.

His whole body was shaking and big tears were streaming out of those eyes of his.

But the good news was he was now blinking a lot more.

So we'd fixed one problem.

"She targeted me. Waited until I didn't even know my fucking name. She'd been trying to flirt with me since I met

Maddie. I—I never, never would have done it. I've never done it any other time. I haven't even been tempted. It was a mistake! The only reason that happened was because I was blacked out!"

A sob wracked through his body and I nodded, hopefully looking sympathetic.

"Well, that sounds all well and good. I mean, honestly, I myself got drunk and made some questionable decisions the other night, so I get it…I really do," I told him, lying through my teeth—though the questionable decision thing was not a lie, my dick situation was not fun right now. I was quite positive though that even if my brain wasn't coherent, *Hercules* understood it was an only Olivia's pussy kind of guy now. "But…the reality is that you didn't tell Maddie about the fact that her best friend was trying to get your dick, did you? Andddd you definitely didn't tell her *after* her best friend *got* your dick."

He stared at me as if I was destroying his entire world. Honestly, props to Lincoln for getting ahold of the footage. I had no idea *where* he'd gotten it, but I figured don't ask, don't tell was the best course of action in this situation.

"You can't show her that video. It will ruin us. She will never, ever forgive me. I—I love her. I love her so much that I don't think I can survive without her."

I pretended to be thinking about it as I replayed the video *again*…just to drive home the situation he was in.

He flinched and jumped from the couch, grabbing his hair like he was trying to pull it out.

"Well, I think we both know what you can do to make sure that she doesn't see this video," I told him.

His eyes widened. "You want to be one of my groomsmen…"

I sighed again. "I mean, yes, but the important part is that I'm paired up with Olivia. That *is* the whole point of it."

"You have no idea what that girl's been through," he whispered, obviously torn about betraying his cousin to save his own skin. It was something I certainly wouldn't forget about Harley Jacobs.

"It's kind of an awkward situation, right? Because Carlie is her maid of honor. I mean, it's really a *problematic* thing."

"You're a fucking piece of shit," he hissed, but he didn't lunge at me. He collapsed back into the cushions, looking like I'd just told him he had five weeks to live. "How did you even get a hold of that?" he asked, sounding completely defeated.

I waved his question away. "Not important," I answered as I stood up. "Alright, let me just put my number in your phone. You can text me all the info. I'll pay for my tux since it's such late notice, of course." He didn't even glance up as I grabbed his phone from the couch. He just continued to stare desolately at the floor. I typed in my number and tossed him the phone.

"Is there anything I can give you to convince you to delete that," he whispered as he finally glanced up at me pleadingly, his entire body shaking.

"Just don't fuck this up and there won't be any issues," I said sweetly as I strode toward the door. "What time's the first event?" I called over my shoulder.

When there was only silence, I stopped and turned around, my lip curling as I gave him my scariest glare. "If you do anything to fuck this up for me...if you even think about mentioning it to another person...or trying to block me from the wedding...I'll send this video to every news outlet in the country. Have I made myself clear?" My voice came out cold and a little scary, and man—I wish Linc could have seen me now.

"There won't be any issues," Harley murmured, his entire body slumped over like he was in physical pain.

"Great!" I said brightly. "And again, *huge* congrats on the wedding. It's going to be the best weekend ever."

I strolled out of the house, making it down the sidewalk and back into the truck right as Maddie got home.

Perfect timing.

Ari was grinning at me through the windows as I went around the truck to hop in.

"I'm like a proud papa, Linc. Look at our boy, just out in the world, blackmailing people like a psychopath," he gushed as soon as I'd gotten in.

I blinked. "Lincoln's still on the phone?"

"I've hung up five times," Lincoln growled through the speaker. "But he keeps on texting me 9-1-1, and I keep thinking you've been arrested or something."

Awww. I was a little emotional. I think Lincoln Daniels likes me.

"Don't get any ideas, Disney. Golden Boy is still *my* best friend."

I smirked. "I would never...but I think I'm your best friend too."

Ari scoffed like such an idea was preposterous. "Possibly, Disney. Possibly," he finally said, and I did an internal fist pump.

"So will you be attending a certain wedding in two weeks?" Lincoln asked. "We need details here."

"I *will* be attending the wedding. As a motherfucking groomsman, baby. With my girl. Fuck yeah."

Ari made a loud whooping sound that reverberated through the cab of the truck.

"Linc, I'm just asking...do you have some kind of secret room out there filled with things to blackmail people with?" I asked.

There was a long silence.

"Is he still there?" I asked Ari, who was nodding his head to whatever Justin Bieber song he'd just put on.

"Hmm? Oh...yep, he hung up. Those kinds of questions are *privileged*, Walk. You can't just ask them."

I cast him a perplexed look, but he wasn't paying any attention, he had a video up of Blake playing with their dog, Waldo, and he was watching it avidly.

I would examine why I no longer thought that was weird behavior at another time.

But not right now.

I had a wedding weekend to plan.

CHAPTER 11

OLIVIA

Stepping onto the private plane felt like freedom.

And freedom…felt fucking great.

Even the bodyguard sitting nearby couldn't ruin my mood. Despite the fact that his main job was to make sure I wasn't doing anything Jolette and Marco wouldn't want, rather than to keep me safe.

He was at least the silent type.

Settling into a leather chair, I pulled out my headphones and settled in for the ride, watching the L.A. skyline disappear from view.

I wished that I could say goodbye to it…permanently.

I'd once thought L.A. was the most magical city on earth. I'd thought it was the key to making Jolette's dreams for me come true.

I hadn't realized that it would become my prison.

Not even its sunshine and palm trees could outweigh that.

It would be good to get away. I had gotten used to living in a cage, and that was not good.

Not good at all.

Since I was having a moment…I let my thoughts drift to… that night.

I'd gotten off more times than I'd like to admit to those

memories. And with Mr. Hulk Wannabe watching my every move, now wasn't the time to get turned on.

But the way Walker had looked at me.

"Would you like some coffee, ma'am?" a voice asked.

I startled in my seat and turned towards the flight attendant who was standing in the aisle with a tray. The smell of coffee washed over me.

"You wouldn't happen to have a shit load of creamer and vanilla syrup...would you?" I asked hopefully.

She winced and sneaked a side eye at Mr. Sir Hulk A Lot who was pretending not to listen to us. "It's not on the approved list for the flight, ma'am," she murmured, not looking me in the eye.

"That's fine," I said in a fake, weirdly high voice. For a minute I'd gotten carried away...thinking this weekend was something it wasn't. Being reminded of Jolette's approved list of foods when I was on official "Olivia Darling" business was just what I needed to make sure I didn't forget myself.

"Sorry," she whispered as she set down the mug full of tar black coffee on the table in front of me.

I didn't touch it.

A few minutes later she came back with a covered tray. "Your egg white omelet and salad, ma'am," she murmured, casting a furtive glance at my keeper once again.

"Thanks," I muttered, as she slid another cup of coffee next to the tray even though I still had a full mug in front of me.

"I—" I began, before noticing that the new cup was a creamy tan color, signifying it was loaded with all my favorite things.

I glanced up at her and she winked at me as she casually walked back up the aisle with the other coffee cup.

A tear slid down my cheek.

I let myself feel it for a moment, that small glimmer of kindness. Let it soak into my sorrow filled veins, gold tinged, with the capacity to bleat out some of my pain.

And then I wiped it away.

Picking up the mug, there was a small smile on my lips for at least another hour.

Maybe this weekend could be what I dreamed after all.

————

The humid heat of Dallas was a balm on my skin, washing over me like a warm blanket as I stepped down the stairs and walked towards the waiting car. Stepping onto the tarmac felt surreal.

Dramatic.

But a true statement.

Mr. Bodyguard followed me into the car, getting into the front seat with the driver while I slid into the back.

"Yes. We're in the car. Security is in place at the hotel," he said into his phone, and I could hear the soft murmurings of Jolette on the other end. Even the whisper of her voice was like a bucket of nails being thrown on my good mood.

I pulled up the itinerary, glancing through it. There was an engagement party tonight, followed by the bachelor/bachelorette parties. Tomorrow was a spa day for the girls, a small shower for Maddie, and then the rehearsal dinner. Sunday was the big day.

I wasn't going to know anyone this weekend but Maddie and Harley, and I wasn't expecting to see them very much under the circumstances. Hopefully there would be at least a few people to hang out with. I'd never had much luck with that—meeting new people who were actually interested in *me* and not the Olivia Darling part.

Harley had told me that cameras and phones were banned for the event, but someone always managed to sneak one in. So I couldn't ever *really* relax.

Hopefully the person I would be paired with for things wasn't a complete tool. Maddie had seemed so smug on the phone this week when she'd mentioned it, but she'd refused to tell me who it was. It's not like I would know them. I hadn't ever met any of Harley's teammates on any of his teams, college or NHL.

Driving down the Dallas streets was a rip to the heart—an excruciating trip through the past. It was amazing all the memories you could create in a small amount of time. The way they could burn inside you with an ever present ache that never quite healed…even after years.

We turned down a street and my gaze widened as I saw a bar where I'd done one of my first performances. Obviously it had been way against the rules for a kid to be in a bar, but somehow Jolette had gotten me in for open mic night.

I had felt like I was flying that night…

I'd clutched my guitar with trembling hands, ready to pee my pants as I stepped onto that dimly lit stage—I'd been so fucking nervous. But then…the soft, warm glow of the stage lights had brushed against my skin, and it was easier all of a sudden…like I was in my own little world.

The hushed chatter of the audience had gradually faded as I strummed my guitar, and then, as I started to sing, everything else had melted away. It was just me and the music, and the words and melodies I'd created that were a piece of me, pouring out like I was gifting the people watching a part of my soul.

I could still remember their applause. It was different than it had been at the end, when I was supposedly at the top of my game. And people loved the idea of me more than anything that was coming out of my mouth.

I didn't know why…but it had meant more to me, the applause that tiny crowd had given an unknown stranger.

It had felt more real.

Maybe I'd been wearing rose colored glasses back then. Or maybe it was just that my world was now gray-tinged, everything sullied by the last few years. The neon sign hanging above the entrance seemed to flicker with a tired looking glow now. The wooden facade of the outside looked weathered and worn…like it had been forgotten like the dreams of countless aspiring musicians who had crossed its threshold, hoping to make it big. I wondered how many of those people had succeeded, or if they, too, now felt like they'd left behind echoes of their songs and broken dreams in that bar.

I tried to push the dread away, but something about seeing that bar stayed with me for the rest of the drive. And by the time we arrived at the Rosewood Mansion, I was *not* in the headspace I would have liked for my weekend away.

We passed the entrance since I needed to go in the back if I was going to keep any anonymity this weekend. The hotel stood tall and elegant, exuding an air of timeless luxury with its ivy-covered walls, and the row of towering oak trees, their branches swaying gently in the breeze. The wrought-iron gates opened to reveal a cobblestone courtyard and the soft glow of lantern-style lights.

"Good job, Maddie," I whispered, since everything looked like a dream. I could already tell the wedding was going to be perfection.

Someone had checked me in, per Jolette's protocol, so I walked into my hotel suite, glancing around at the softly elegant furnishings as the door closed behind me and I was finally out from under the eye of Jolette's guard dog.

A big grin creeped on my face.

Because weirdly…this place already felt much more like home than my L.A. penthouse ever did.

I threw myself onto the bed, squeezing the pillows around my head. And I screamed into the fabric, muffling the sound of my complete and utter relief.

———

Hopefully this was alright for an engagement party. Maddie had said it was a dress to impress kind of event—whatever the hell that really meant.

But standing in front of the mirror, staring at myself in my black cocktail dress...I felt a little naked.

It covered way more than my old concert outfits ever did. But without my ball cap and sunglasses...or a wig...it felt like I was a poor, distressed mallard, about to fly out in the middle of hunting season.

Just breathe, Olivia, I murmured to myself, wondering how I'd gotten to the point of my life where it felt more natural to talk to myself...than it did to talk to other people.

My phone buzzed.

Behave.

That was the word Jolette chose to send.

Sir Hulksalot was going to be following me all night, so I wasn't sure how it would be possible for me to do anything other than *behave.*

The word still scalded my insides.

My hands were trembling and I fisted them, hating how I was desperate for one of my pills. I'd let myself go comatose basically for two days after Marco, and then I'd flushed the rest of them down the toilet.

I was certainly regretting that decision right now.

Taking a deep breath, I stepped outside, where unfortunately my guard was waiting for me.

"What's your name?" I asked, sick of making up names for him in my head—even though he was such a caricature it was far easier to do than it should have been.

"Toby," he finally said, after a long exaggerated pause, like he wasn't sure if he should text Jolette for permission first.

I didn't tell him it was nice to officially meet him. Because that would have been a lie.

Toby led me to the gardens through the back way, a route that avoided the main arteries of the hotel. We stepped outside and I smiled, because the set up was fucking gorgeous.

A large white tent stood in an open area, its billowing fabric shimmering in the soft glow of the setting sun. The tent was adorned with delicate drapes and floral garlands, and twinkling lights hung from the ceiling, casting a warm and inviting radiance upon the guests already teeming inside of it. The tables were meticulously arranged on one end, covered with crisp white linens and adorned with centerpieces of fresh flowers in shades of soft pink and ivory. At the other end of the tent, a small stage had been set up for live music. A talented band played soft, melodic tunes that filled the air. The sound of laughter and conversation floated on the breeze.

It was very fairytale-esque.

If those were to actually exist.

I turned to stare at Toby, suddenly desperate to have a night of normalcy. Although he was probably going to tell Jolette that I was doing this, and it was going to bite me in the ass.

It was still worth a try.

"Look, as you can see I'm not in any danger out here, at this private party…if I give you a thousand dollars…and promise not to say anything, can you just wait for me upstairs?" I would have offered him more money, but that was my limit right now, what Jolette and Marco deigned to give me from my own fucking money.

He scoffed, like I'd insulted him with my offer.

"I'll give you my rolex. It's a collector's edition, owned by Darius Jane herself," I spit out, feeling sick as I did so. Darius Jane was my musical idol. She'd died tragically in her prime from an overdose. I'd thought her life mirrored mine, and it had been one of my first purchases once I'd started making real money.

"You are fucking crazy," Toby said, as he extended his hand out for the watch.

Asshole.

"You have to stay away all weekend," I pressed insistently, "and report to them that everything's fine."

"You've got it," he said greedily, eyeing the watch.

I handed it to him and he all but ran away, probably thinking I'd come to my senses and ask for it back.

Maybe I was losing my mind.

"Liv!" Maddie whisper-yelled from nearby, and I turned, watching as her gaze darted around dramatically, like she was trying to keep me a secret even though her voice was definitely too loud for that. She threw her arms around me and gave me one of her trademark squeals.

"I'm so fucking glad you're here!" she purred. Maddie glanced over her shoulder. "Harley, get your delectable butt over here. She's here!" She motioned frantically at Harley who was talking to a group of very well-built men that I would take bets were from his team.

The asses on hockey players could not be beat.

I watched, a little confused when Harley froze at Maddie's comment, and then seemed to take his time walking over to us.

"Hi cuz," he grinned…but the way he said it…seemed a little frostier than usual. I attributed it to nerves as he slung an arm around me and gave me a squeeze. But Maddie was studying him too, looking as confused about the general vibe he was throwing off as I was.

"Everything okay, baby?" she asked, watching as Harley's gaze danced around the garden like he was looking for someone.

"Oh yeah. Is it hot out here though? There's fans going, but I swear it's fucking hot. Or is it just me?"

"Babe," Maddie said in an unimpressed voice. "*What* is going on?"

He pulled her into his arms and pressed a hard kiss on her lips. "Absolutely nothing," he murmured as he pulled away from a now dazed looking Maddie who had been completely distracted from Harley's suspicious behavior. "But I think we should go check on the fan situation—for the guests."

Evidently that was the magic word because Maddie's eyes widened and she started to look around anxiously. "Where is the wedding planner? We can get her on the cooling situation—oh!

There she is!" She began to pull Harley towards a harried looking woman surveying the party with a clipboard.

"Glad you're here, Liv," Harley murmured, but he sounded more...sad about it than anything.

I watched in confusion as they walked away, wondering why it felt like I'd made a huge sacrifice...given up my last remaining bit of power to Jolette and Marco...for nothing.

———

So far the party was a bust. Granted, it had been ten minutes. But I didn't think anyone was a fan of sipping champagne in a corner by themselves while everyone else had a good time.

"You look like you need company," a deep voice said from behind me.

I turned around to see a mildly attractive guy standing there. A lot of girls would probably think he was actually *incredibly* attractive with all that shaggy dark hair of his.

But I was feeling a little broken since sleeping with Walker. Like I'd touched the sun, and everyone else was just...nothing?

That was a depressing thought.

"Hi," I said, forcing a brightness to my voice, honed from years of having to be fake in public. What I really wanted to say was, "Is that really your pickup line?"

But I probably shouldn't be rude to the one person who was talking to me at the party.

"Has anyone ever told you that you look like that singer, the one that was in the news a few years back for going batshit crazy."

I blinked, a little bit of me wanting to die at the reminder that most of the world did think I'd gone "batshit crazy" so to speak.

"You know, it's a funny thing...I get that all the freaking time. But I honestly don't see the resemblance. At all," I responded politely, trying not to give myself away even if my head was full of snark.

"I mean, that's what I thought," he chuckled, like he'd told a particularly funny joke. "I'm Ryan, Ryan Taylors," he added, extending his hand...but instead of holding it out for me to shake...he put it on my waist.

I raised an eyebrow and drained the rest of my champagne.

"Ryan Taylors...from the Seattle Strikers?" he pressed, like I should have had Seattle's roster memorized.

I stared at him blankly, pretending I hadn't watched Seattle play L.A. a few months before.

He coughed and swept his hair out of his face as he tried to recover from the fact I hadn't thrown myself at him the second he said who he was.

"Want another drink? I think the idea is that we get trashed and make lots of bad decisions tonight," he told me with what I'm sure was his attempt at being charming.

"Here's your drink, baby," a voice murmured as a strong arm wrapped around my waist and pulled me from Ryan's grasp.

I froze, wondering if I'd fallen and hit my head.

Because I knew that voice.

It was ingrained in my memory like the etching of constellations in the velvet canvas of a starlit night.

And the body I'd just been pulled against, the one who was sparking up my insides like fireworks on a July night?

Walker Davis was here.

CHAPTER 12
WALKER

I'd been watching her since the moment she'd arrived, prowling around the edges of the party, feeding my addiction as I stared at her perfection.

No one seemed to have realized who was in their midst yet. Understandable, since you didn't exactly expect music royalty to show up to an engagement party. People should have known she was something special though. Regular people didn't glow like that, didn't light up the air around them like a rare and radiant comet, streaking through the night sky.

She'd shed her disguises for the night. I'd gotten used to seeing her in L.A. always wearing a hat and sunglasses...sometimes even that blonde wig. So seeing her like this...it was mind-blowing.

Her black dress hugged her curves just right, leaving enough to the imagination that she was making every male in her vicinity fucking crazy wondering what she had hiding under that dress.

Her dark auburn hair cascaded down her back in perfect waves, catching the light in a way that made it seem almost otherworldly. Her golden eyes flickered like distant stars beneath the strands of lights.

And I wanted those eyes staring at me. I wanted to fist that long hair in my hand, pull it back as I fucked her from behind.

Shit, I was getting hard.

Fuck, that hurt. I was definitely still not healed.

I sent a text to both Lincoln and Ari.

> Me: My dick hates you both.

Ari's response was of course...immediate.

> Ari: What a rude thing to say, Disney...

> King Linc: You're not going to be saying that for long after Oliviaaaaa sees it.

> Me: You're taunting me.

> Ari: You can thank us later...what was that your brother calls you...Walkie-poo?

And with that the convo was over.

I was debating the smooth way that I was going to "run" into her randomly, shocked to see her there of course.

But then Ryan fucking Taylors moved in, and well...that was not happening.

I grabbed a glass of champagne off a tray and moved in, swooping to wrap my arm around her in a clear "she's mine" kind of way.

"Here's your drink, baby," I said, trying not to *die* at the fact that I was *finally* touching her again.

She had stiffened against me, and I could feel her flipping the fuck out.

I mean, I got it. She'd never expected to see me again.

That fact burned my insides though.

I'd spent the last month learning everything I could about her, immersing myself in all things Olivia. From her music, to every interview she'd ever done—recorded and written...I'd also watched *every* performance I could find.

I knew that didn't mean that I knew her, knew her...but it meant that she'd been on my mind almost every second of every day.

I'm sure that hadn't been the case for her.

I guess I just needed to be more memorable, up my game so to speak.

The new additions to my dick were probably going to help with that.

Didn't think she could forget about me once she saw *those*.

"Davis, you two know each other?" Taylors said, a tic in his cheek as he stared daggers at me.

"You could definitely say that," I answered with a grin, brushing a kiss across her forehead that had her tensing even more. "She's my *date*."

Taylors cocked his head. "Did I hear right that you're one of Harley's groomsmen? I didn't know you two were friends."

Olivia glanced up at me, her eyes wide and questioning. I winked at her, a little dazed as a beautiful blush spread across her cheeks.

"Yeah, we go way back," I drawled, when I managed to drag my eyes away from her long enough to answer.

He lifted an eyebrow at that, but didn't try to fight me on it. "Well, uh, it was nice meeting you—" Taylors paused as he stared at Olivia, and I realized she hadn't given him her name.

"Violet," she said quickly, with a cute little wave, giving him what was obviously her stage smile. It was impossible not to smirk at the fake name...and the fact he'd only gotten her *fake* smile.

I'd seen her real smile as I fucked in and out of her body.

I could tell the difference.

Taylors nodded and left, finally getting the hint he wasn't welcome.

I mean, I doubted I was welcome either, but the difference between Taylors and me was that I wasn't a quitter.

"Fancy seeing you here," I said, turning my attention back to her and feasting on the sight of her beautiful face. Up close, the golden hue of her eyes intensified, like the flickering flames of a mesmerizing fire, and I didn't think I could look away.

"What are you doing here?" she murmured, fidgeting and glancing around…almost like she was embarrassed to be seen with me.

That was not happening.

I grabbed her arm and she squeaked as I abruptly pulled her towards the hotel, not caring about the inquiring stares as we passed by.

I made it into the entryway and down a corridor that said "bathrooms", and then I couldn't hold back anymore.

Before she could say anything, I pushed her against the wall, making sure my hand was behind her head to cushion the impact. Her chest was heaving, the tops of her breasts a delectable tease that had me wanting to tear at her dress so I could see them, suck those fucking perfect nipples in my mouth —to stop myself from doing anything *too* crazy, I smashed my lips against hers. It didn't take any coaxing to get her to open up and let me in, and I moaned as I got a taste of her, my tongue fucking in and out in the way that my dick was desperate to do with her pussy.

I felt drugged by her kiss, by the soft sighs emanating from her, from the way her hands pulled at the front of my dress shirt like she'd been just as desperate for this as I had been.

She ran her hands over my neck and shoulders and I shivered, wondering how I had lived without this for so many months.

My hand slid under her dress, bunching it up so that I could run my fingers over the seam of her soaking wet panties.

Fuuccck. She was perfect, so wet she'd be soaking my balls if I was inside of her.

I slid my fingers under her underwear and then plunged them inside, her breath leaving her in a gasp as I caught her moan in my mouth.

"This fucking wet, perfect pussy," I said between more of her addicting kisses. "You're dripping for me, angel. Fucking dripppping."

I rubbed that spot inside of her that had driven her crazy that night, massaging her clit with my thumb until she was shaking against me. Her pussy clenched down on my fingers as she came, and she bit down on my lower lip to muffle her cries.

I was bleeding when I pulled away, my fingers still sliding in and out of her, and her eyes widened, her hand coming to her mouth in shock. "I'm—I'm so sorry," she murmured.

"I'm not," I growled, kissing her again and sucking on her tongue so she could taste my blood. I mean, I wasn't a fucking vampire, but there was something about having a part of me inside her.

My fingers, my dick, my cum, my blood...my baby.

I was desperate for it all.

I hadn't been lying to Ari and Linc. I was gonna be a daddy. If our one night hadn't done the trick, I was gonna fill Olivia with my cum until her belly rounded with our child.

"We shouldn't be doing this," she gasped, as she writhed against my hand, another orgasm building.

"I can't think of a single reason why not, Olivia," I told her, watching in awe as she came...immediately. Like me using her real name was a magic password to her pussy.

A magic password pussy. Sounded about right.

Reluctantly, I withdrew my fingers, wanting to replace them with my dick, but having enough brain function to realize that probably wasn't a good idea.

"You know my name," she whispered, her face paling as she stared up at me.

I kept eye contact with her as I rubbed her cum on her bottom lip and then chased the taste of it with another kiss.

Delicious.

But fuck...my dick hurt.

"I know your name *now*...had to figure it out when you snuck out...and I love it," I finally murmured, watching as her golden gaze flashed with emotion. "Much better than Violet. Although I'm fine with you giving that one to all the fuck boys trying to get in your pants..."

"And you're not a fuckboy?" she asked dryly.

"Mmmh. I'm not a fuckboy at all. Unless we're role playing in bed and then I can totally be a fuck boy for you. Your wish is my command, baby."

She stared at me for a second before a nervous giggle popped out of her mouth.

She was so fucking cute.

"That's okay..." she finally said. "I don't think 'fuck boy' is what I'm going for in bed...or should I say 'puck boy.'" Olivia giggled again.

I snorted, falling even more. My girl was kind of corny.

And I loved it.

She pushed gently against my chest then, and I didn't love that.

"We really can't do this though. You know my name, so you probably know my life is...complicated. I'm just here for Harley and Maddie and...then I'll go home," she said the last part quickly, like she couldn't bear to keep the words inside of her. Olivia took a deep, sniffling breath. "But trust me...I'm doing you a favor. You don't want any of *this*," she said, gesturing to herself as tears filled her eyes.

"We'll talk about that little statement later," I said, the sounds of people talking and laughing as they came in from outside *assaulting* my eardrums—because honestly, how dare they disrupt this moment. There was wooing taking place, damnit.

I leaned down and pressed my forehead against hers, just wanting to touch her. How did you explain to someone that didn't know you, that you breathed for them? That the blood in your veins surged with every beat of *their* heart, and that their presence was the very essence of your existence.

Especially when you were still trying to figure out the why of it all yourself?

Not a problem for tonight.

Tonight was going to be about reminding her what my body could do for her. Then I'd start working on her heart.

"I have a lot of opinions on that particular subject, but for now I'll just say...I'm not worried about any of that. I—I think you're perfect," I stuttered out, completely losing the cool and collected I was going for.

She flushed, staring up at me like I was some kind of alien from a far off planet.

Olivia opened her mouth like she was going to argue with my assessment of her, and then snapped It close, letting out a garbled sounding "okay" instead.

I kissed the tip of her nose and pulled away...reluctantly might I add, before grabbing her hand and leading her out to the throng of people coming in from outside, assumedly heading to get ready for the bachelor/bachelorette parties.

Many of them were already staggering and swerving around, so tonight was guaranteed to be a shit show.

Harley and Maddie were by the door chatting with an older, gray-haired couple, the smiles on their faces radiating joy. Harley caught sight of me though, and his expression turned cold. He glared at me, obviously still pissed about the little blackmail incident.

He was coming off a little strong honestly...what was a little blackmail in the name of true love?

I smiled at him, going for friendly and disarming since I was going to marry his cousin...but evidently that didn't work... judging by the way his face contorted, a hint of fear sliding across his features before he quickly averted his gaze. He tucked his fiancée into his body, like that would protect her from the information I had in my possession.

"So, a groomsman, huh? That means I guess we'll be seeing each other all weekend," Olivia said, dragging my attention away from Harley as we followed the crowd towards the elevators. I noticed that she stayed a few steps behind everyone, deliberately dragging her feet so she wasn't with the group. When we got to the elevators, she motioned for everyone to go ahead, keeping her head down.

"I have to say, the blonde may have been good for a disguise, but I'm obsessed with this color," I told her, reaching out and smoothing her hair across my fingers as I admired the dark, rich strands.

"I feel like you're just saying that," she muttered as the elevator dinged and opened in front of us. We stepped inside and I quickly pressed the close button so no one could join us.

And then I crowded Olivia against the mirrored wall.

"Why would I just say that?"

She rolled her eyes, not trying to push me away at all.

That was a good sign.

"Bleach blonde, big boobs, silent...that's what they all want, Olivia," she snarked, obviously quoting some asshole from the past.

I growled and her gaze snapped to mine. "I'm staring at what I want," I told her solemnly, wanting her to get how serious I was. More serious than I'd been about anything in my life before, even hockey.

And I'd been fucking serious about that.

I leaned forward, making sure my lips brushed against her ear as I spoke. "I want that hair all over me as you suck my dick. I want that hair falling in my face as you ride me. I want to fist that hair as I fuck you for hours from behind." I moved one hand between us, plucking at her very erect nipple through the thin lining of her dress and bra. "And I fucking loooove these gorgeous tits. I've never seen a better pair."

The doors opened then and I pulled away, acting nonchalant as a couple joined us, ignoring the knowing smiles on their faces and the way Olivia bolted out of the elevator like her ass was on fire.

"See you later, sweetheart," I called as the doors began to close to take me to my floor. She didn't say anything back.

I whistled as the elevator continued up, congratulating myself for a very successful reunion.

As Ari was always saying...it was important to celebrate your accomplishments.

While I waited for the elevator to get to my floor, I checked my text messages, grinning when I saw what I'd been sent.

> Cole: How's Operation Act Crazy and Get a Popstar.

> Me: Is that what we're calling it?

> Parker: I voted for "How to Be a Psychopath: a novel by Walker Davis" but Cole shot me down.

> Me: I'm not a psychopath.

> Parker: Said like a true psychopath.

> Me: I just know what I want. To me, that says "winner."

> Cole: Just don't tell us if you lock her in a basement or something. I want to have plausible deniability.

> Me: I'm not going to lock her in a basement.

> Parker: Why can I imagine you pausing before you typed that.

> Me: This is real time...you would have seen if I'd paused.

> Cole: That's true.

Parker: But seriously, she's walking around right, she's not…tied up anywhere?

Cole: You seemed to have given this a lot of thought, little brother. Have anything you would like to share with the class?

Weirdly…Parker took a long time to respond to that one. Long enough that I'd walked all the way down the hallway, and into my room before my phone buzzed.

Parker: No. I'm the sane brother, remember?

Cole: I'm side-eyeing you, Parker.

Me: Big time.

Parker: I'm not the one that has a famous singer tied up in my basement!

Me: This hotel doesn't even have a basement!

Cole: Said like a person who's looked for one.

I threw my phone on the bed, exasperated.

But amused.

At least a few people thought that my sudden, life altering obsession was funny.

I changed out of my suit, dreading the next part of the night. The bachelor and bachelorette parties were being held in side by side rooms at a bar, but being forced to play nice with Seattle players while Olivia was in the next room over was not my favorite thing. Somehow I was going to have to figure out how to get her out and back to my room before the end of the night, but I figured I would come up with something along the way.

CHAPTER 13
WALKER

The guys going to the bachelor party were all bussed over to the bar—unfortunately without the ladies even though we were going to the same fucking place. The bar was alright, with the usual dimly lit interior, vintage décor, and the faint scent of spilled beer mingling with the aroma of fried food. But having Olivia separated from me by a wall made the place feel like actual hell.

I'd had enough of being separated from her.

I was ready to move on to where we spent every waking— and sleeping—second together forever and ever.

Walker, you sound like a psycho.

"Hey Davis, want to play pool?" one of Seattle's defenders, Mike O'Connell, called to me when we'd gotten inside.

"Let's do it," I responded, grabbing a beer off a waiter's tray as he passed by. I was going to need it. I generally got along with most of the players in the League, but there had always been something about Seattle.

Both Seattle and Soto were great about getting under my skin.

I could play nice for a night though.

If it all led me to the girl.

An hour passed, and the clinking of balls and raucous laughter filled the air as we settled into the party.

"Not surprised you're bad at this, Taylors, considering all the shots you fucked up that game," I told him with a smirk when he missed an easy shot.

He growled at me as the rest of the guys playing laughed, but someone threw another shot into his hands, and he shrugged and tossed it back without a retort.

We continued to line up shots and shit talk before the conversation inevitably turned to the bachelorette party happening in the room next door—the *only* topic I was actually interested in at the moment.

"I can't believe the girls are getting a stripper," one of the guys whined, shaking his head incredulously. "And our boy Harley has decided it's a bros only party tonight."

I stood up straighter, my gaze darting to the wall like it was going to open up and reveal the debauchery happening next door.

I didn't like the idea of a stripper around Olivia. Not at all.

She'd be the obvious one to get the attention, even with the bride to be in the room. The guy would take one look at how hot she was and start bumping and grinding...or whatever it was that they did.

Laughter erupted around the table about something else, but I could only pretend to laugh along with everyone.

I had a *no other dicks* policy when it came to Olivia's golden pussy. And I might go crazy tonight if a stripper's dick came around. I bet her cum was still smeared on her lips. They'd lean in close, and smell her perfection.

Or what if they fucking tried to kiss her? And they could taste her?

"Excuse me, boys," I murmured, trying to sound cool instead of like I was freaking the fuck out. I kept my walk even as I strode out to the hallway...immediately greeted by the sight of two oiled down guys lugging an old-fashioned boombox. One was dressed as a cowboy, the other as a police officer, looking a bit snug in his uniform.

Not fucking happening.

"Oh fuck, no one told you," I exclaimed, acting chagrined. "The groom canceled your gig—he got cold feet about another guy's balls all over his bride-to-be." I shook my head. "We called your company…"

The cowboy and the cop sighed. "Fucking hell. That's twice in the past week," the cop grumbled, setting the boombox on the ground.

I eyed it, where had they even gotten something like that? It was basically a collector's edition at this point.

"Yeah, I feel awful about you guys coming out here. Let me pay your fee. There was probably some late cancellation bullshit anyway. How much do I owe you?"

The guys glanced at each other, still looking unsure about the late cancellation. I made a big show of getting money out of my wallet and handing it to them. "How about this, here's $300 for each of you, because I'm assuming you would have gotten tips tonight." I pressed a wad of bills into their hands.

Both of their eyes lit up and they took the money without question, so evidently I'd overpaid. I wasn't exactly up on what male strippers were making nowadays.

I eyed the cowboy hat, wishing I had my own. My new Dallas Knights ball cap was going to have to do though, there was no way I was going to ask that guy for his hat. I could only imagine where it had been.

This might have been the most ridiculous thing I'd ever done in my life. Thank fuck the guys were not here, because I would never live it down.

Although knowing how possessive Lincoln was over Monroe, he probably would have just burned down the bar so that the bachelorette party had never happened in the first place.

Food for thought if I was ever in this situation again.

Not that Olivia would be having a bachelorette party where I wasn't there.

Taking a deep breath, I turned on some random song from a "stripper playlist" I'd found on Spotify—that was literally what it was called. And then I sauntered into the room, ignoring all of the girls but Olivia, who was whispering with Maddie at one of the tables, a tray of shot glasses in front of them. I grinned as I stared at her, because how could you not in the face of all that perfection.

She'd changed into some kind of black halter top and tight jeans get-up and it was doing something to me...and my balls.

"I heard you all are causing trouble, and someone called for backup," I announced, my voice laced with playful authority.

The room erupted into cheers and catcalls, no one seeming to recognize that I was actually a guest at this wedding. I'd been very incognito at the engagement party though, basically lurking in the shadows like a creeper while I waited to make a move on my girl—so that was understandable. I locked eyes with Olivia now, her cheeks flushed with surprise, confusion...and wariness as she stared at me.

"Let's get this party going, y'all," I yelled, turning my hat backwards, a move that for some reason made all the girls go crazy. Women were weird.

I turned on "Don't Blame Me"...which was not on the "stripper playlist," but was definitely fitting for my current life situation, and I began to move my hips.

What I'd forgotten with this master plan of mine...was that I was actually an awful dancer.

So this was going to be fun.

Tay-Tay, please don't fail me now.

———

Olivia

It felt like I had stepped into an alternate universe—one I

didn't want to leave. As "Don't Blame Me" blared from Walker's phone, he did some weird shaking move that reminded me of jello bouncing in a bowl.

A giggle slipped out of my mouth because he was *terrible*, and he grinned at me, like he'd been waiting for that.

And then things fucking changed.

His movements suddenly became hypnotic, each sway of his hips and twist of his body sending a surge of heat coursing straight to my core. I couldn't tear my eyes away from him. The smirk on his lips was driving me crazy—he knew he was the hottest thing on this fucking planet.

Even that was hot.

I was jealous for a second-wondering how he'd gotten so good at this kind of thing. I didn't know him very well obviously, but it seemed doubtful that he moonlighted as a stripper after hockey practice.

A part of me wanted to tear out everyone's eyes because they were getting to see something I wanted just for me.

I hadn't had much of that before.

But I was finding that out of everything I'd wanted in my life, that I never could keep...Walker Davis was moving his way to the top of that list.

He wasn't playing the crowd, flirting it up with all the women to get some cheers...instead, his gaze was locked onto mine...the entire time.

"Holy fuck," Maddie whispered from nearby.

But I couldn't tear my gaze away from him to look at her.

"Cover your eyes," I muttered instead.

And her answering snort shook the table. "Not for a million dollars, ma'am."

Rude.

Jolts of electricity—and lust—were shooting through me. It kind of felt like we actually *were* alone, like he was dancing just for me, his eyes smoldering with desire as he moved closer.

It kind of felt like I could *come* just from watching him long enough.

Another pang of jealousy sparked in my chest. Like my body had already decided he belonged to me, and no one else should have the privilege of seeing him like that.

"I think I need a volunteer for this next one," he announced, that slight southern drawl of his making me weak in the knees.

Me and everyone else.

I stared, wide-eyed as he stripped off his shirt in that universal hot guy move that I swore guys must go to school for —because the move was perfection.

Walker's shirt peeled away from his frame, revealing the taut contours of his chest and the defined lines of his abs.

My mouth dropped and I was suddenly...hungry. I'd dragged my tongue across those abs. I'd sunk my fingers into that skin. I'd bit down on that chest as he'd made me come.

Every flex of his muscles rippled with raw power as he moved. His abs were like a roadmap to my happy place, leading down to the part of him that was probably my favorite...

The bar could have burned down around me at that moment and I wouldn't have even cared.

Ignoring the other women screaming like we were at a boy band concert, he ambled straight towards me, his features cocky and delicious.

I was frozen in place as he stopped right in front of my chair, unable to even move. I was pretty sure this portion of the performance was supposed to involve the bride to be, but his hand wrapped around mine as he leaned over me.

"Come here, angel face. Let's have some fun."

I followed him up to the stage at the far side of the room like he held my life in his hands, like I would have followed him anywhere, to whatever end.

After getting me up on the stage, he grabbed a chair and set it beside me.

"Go ahead and sit down," he purred as I continued to gape up at him like a frog caught in the glare of headlights.

Having his attention like this, like I was the only person that existed for him…it was a heady…powerful feeling. I was used to having attention, but not like this, not the kind of attention where I was really seen, beyond the "Olivia Darling" veneer.

It was a dangerous thing, this feeling….

A girl could get addicted to it.

And that was the last thing that I needed.

Walker fiddled with his phone and then a second later "Candy Shop" was playing.

I grinned because I used to love this song. I had a feeling that it was going to make a comeback for me after this little moment.

Walker gave me a sexy wink, like he could read my freaking mind.

He began to dance around me, trailing his hands across my skin, his gaze seeming to explore every curve of my body. I melted in my seat, forgetting for a second we were in a crowded room, that there was anyone around but us.

His body moved in sync with the sultry melody. With each flick of his wrist and twist of his hips, I got caught further under his spell—

Wow…and there was his dick in my face…even with his jeans that monster was loud and proud.

I wanted to lick it.

He grabbed me and spun around, sitting down so I was straddling him on the chair. His cock was pressed against the seam of my pants and it was all I could do to hold in my groan as he thrust against me.

A hand went to my hair and he massaged my head for a second before he suddenly dipped me down, bumping and grinding his dick against my core.

Holy mother of all fucks.

He popped me up like I weighed nothing before swinging me back into my seat and falling to the ground in front of me as he pushed my legs apart, mimicking eating me out before he stood, grabbed me, and hoisted me into his arms.

I wrapped my legs around his waist, gasping as he thrust against me as the last notes of the song faded away.

There was a long beat of silence as we stared at each other.

"Wow," I whispered, and his answering grin threatened to light up my life.

And then the whole room was screaming and dollar bills were literally falling all around us.

I now understood better the phrase "make it rain."

"Want to get out of here?" he grumbled, his hips still making small movements against my core.

I glanced over at Maddie questioningly, who was standing on top of her chair, jumping up and down like she'd been possessed. "Go, go, go! Take that man to *Pound Town!*" she yelled, and I couldn't help but grin.

"Please," I finally gasped at Walker, feeling like I was burning from the inside out and the only cure was his dick.

Walker kept me in his arms as we walked toward the hallway, stopping at the threshold and turning back to the crowd of rowdy women. He flipped his ball cap back around and tipped it, a sexy smirk still on his lips. "Ladies," he called. "Another round on me."

Their answering screams and catcalls almost cost me my hearing.

As soon as we'd gotten out of the room, his lips crashed against my mouth, one hand tangling in my hair as his other arm kept me wrapped around his waist.

"Fuck," he groaned, his tongue fucking into my mouth desperately. "If I don't get inside of you, I think I might die."

I giggled against his lips, but he didn't laugh back. And I wasn't so sure that had been a joke.

He started to walk us down the hall towards the exit and I buried my face in his neck, trying to get a hold of myself. Why did he have to smell so fucking good?

"Olivia?" Harley's voice called to us. I lifted my face and glanced at my cousin over Walker's shoulder. Walker didn't stop walking even though there was no way he hadn't heard him. "Where are you going?"

"Back to the hotel," I told Harley, grinning and thinking he would be happy for me.

Harley didn't look happy at all though. His brows were furrowed and there was a scowl on his face. "You should stay for the party, Davis," Harley...snarled. What in the world?

"See you tomorrow, buddy," Walker responded in a friendly, easy voice, finally stopping and turning around to face him. "But don't worry! I'm keeping that video safe. I know how special it is."

"What video?" I asked, unable to stop myself from snuggling further into his chest.

I didn't even recognize myself right now. I'd had a few shots but I couldn't blame how I was behaving on alcohol.

"Oh, just a fun video Harley boy's thinking about showing at the wedding," Walker murmured, brushing a kiss against my forehead. He raised one hand in farewell, still somehow keeping me perfectly in place.

I soaked up the affection desperately, waving at Harley as well as Walker started back down the hallway. Hmm, he looked a little green around the edges. Maybe he'd already drank too much. "Get some water!" I shouted, but he was already walking away.

Walker chose that moment to lick along my pulse...and I forgot all about Harley.

Once we got out into the humid, night air though, I found my head. "Set me down," I murmured anxiously. His hands gripped my hips for a second, like he couldn't bear to let me go...and then he slid me down his body until I was standing on my own.

"How are we getting back to the hotel?" I asked, well aware that I sounded snippy all of a sudden.

But this was all I needed, for someone to see us and snap a picture.

He murmured something about an Uber, but I was still freaking out.

Holy fuck. And I'd just let him dance on me in what was probably a room full of social media savvy women. There were at least thirty women in there. Once they realized who I really was...

Well, you can't change anything now, I thought to myself...

But also...did I want to? Walker was holding my hand, pulling up the Uber app on his phone.

He was the kind of guy I would have fantasized about once upon a time. Who I would have thought didn't actually exist.

I *had* been fantasizing about him since the moment I'd met him.

The night that we'd met, I'd told him I'd wanted one night.

Would it be so bad to have one perfect weekend now? To give myself a few more memories to keep me warm at night before I went back to my miserable life?

Walker might be worth some pictures, or a gossip article....for one weekend.

That decision made, my shoulders relaxed and I was able to accept his arms when he pulled me against his chest as we waited for the car.

"Good girl," he murmured, as his embrace made me feel safe for the first time in a long time.

I ignored the way the butterflies soared in my stomach at his words.

Because I knew from experience that those butterflies...they always died.

CHAPTER 14
OLIVIA

The car ride had been quiet, but the underlying tension was thick enough to cut. I gripped the leather seat, trying to keep myself from doing something crazy like jumping him.

Sex in the backseat of an Uber was probably a step too far.

Walker's fists were clenched in his lap, like he too was having to do everything he could to stay away from me.

I liked that. Desperation like this shouldn't be experienced alone.

If I was going to ache for him, he'd better ache for me.

Once to the hotel, we both walked quickly to the elevator, me with my head down of course. I was learning though, that there was something about hiding in plain sight. It seemed that when I popped up in a place that no one would expect me to be, it was like I was wearing a disguise.

I could only hope that it kept up.

The elevator doors opened and we got inside, and Walker immediately plastered himself against the wall across from me. I raised an eyebrow as we began to ascend.

"It's everything I can do to keep myself away from you right now, angel. If you don't want to be fucked against the wall, than I fucking need to keep myself over here."

I bit my lip and he groaned, staring up at the ceiling like he was praying for deliverance.

The elevator dinged.

"Fucking finally," he growled, and I squeaked as he scooped me up and threw me over his shoulder as he practically sprinted down the hallway.

It took him three tries to get his key to work on the door and then...we were inside.

Walker set me down softly, and I tore at his shirt, ready to get that thing off and touch all that delicious skin.

But he grabbed my hands and stilled them. I glanced up, puzzled.

"Tell me you've been thinking about me. Tell me you've been obsessing about every touch, every kiss, every sigh...every fucking second of that night," he begged as he held my wrists tightly against his chest.

I yanked my gaze away from his. It was too much.

"Look at me," he growled, grabbing my chin so I was forced to. "Look. At. Me."

"The same rules apply," I whispered. "It's just this weekend. That's all I—that's all I can give you."

He shook his head but didn't say anything right away, a tic in his cheek and fire in his gaze as he stared down at me.

"I'm going to make you burn for me."

The words floated around us, and a part of me was worried...because I of all people knew that words had power, and what he'd just said...well, those words terrified me.

Because what if they came true?

Walker growled as he pulled my head back and bit down on that spot between my neck and my shoulder that he seemed to be obsessed with. His blue gaze glimmered with satisfaction as he released me and saw the mark he'd left.

"I want to mark you all over. Every inch of you. So there's no doubt in anyone's mind that you're mine," he said in a rough voice. "I've been *aching* for you."

I got on my tippy toes and tried to kiss him but he turned his head away. The move made me irrationally hurt.

"Tell me something real about you. If you're not going to give me anything else. Give me something real," he finally said, his forehead resting against me as he rubbed his nose against mine.

A second later he *finally* gave me the kiss I'd been craving.

The kiss burned my insides and it felt prophetic...like his earlier words were already coming true.

"Tell me," he whispered again after we'd come up for air.

"I'm not crazy," I blurted out, wanting to *die* that *that* was what my brain had decided to think of.

He snorted, "I already know that. Tell me something else." One of his hands slid up my front until it was loosely holding my throat. "Tell me something no one else knows."

I tried to move my head again, because when he stared at me like that, I was sure he was seeing too much. I couldn't have him running for the hills when the weekend had just begun.

But of course...he didn't let me go.

"I just want to get laid, okay. We don't need to do this." The words sounded hollow and wrong coming out of my throat, but I couldn't let him continue to make this something it wasn't.

Something it couldn't be.

He smiled at me like I'd said something adorable. "You will get laid, but you're going to give me everything I want while we're doing it. You're going to be cuddled and wooed, my lady. But these are my terms. Any time you want my dick...you have to give me something real."

"You're blackmailing me with your dick?" I scoffed.

He grinned unrepentantly, pressing the said dick into my stomach.

"Fine, but only because it's a really, really good dick."

Walker scoffed, his smile widening.

"I hate performing for large crowds. I don't feel like a real person when I'm up there. It feels like I'm a puppet or a machine, doing tricks to entertain. I had to numb myself before every single show, just so I could get through it."

He frowned. "I never would have guessed that. You're amazing up there."

"You've been to one of my shows?"

He blushed. "I might have watched all of the performances that I could find online, just so I could feed my addiction."

Now I was the one blushing, a warmth spreading across my chest. "It's not real though, that's the real thing I'm giving you. Nothing about 'Olivia Darling' is real."

"Is that why you stopped performing? Because you hate it so much?"

I closed my eyes, pain lancing my insides. Taking a deep breath, I opened my eyes...and my mouth...because what was one more truth tonight?

"I gave up performing because it was the only thing *they* wanted from me that they couldn't *force* me to do. Evidently, even in a place where they can strip you of your rights, your money, and everything else...they can't *force* you to sing in front of thousands of people. It's a funny thing actually." But obviously there was no humor in my voice.

He opened his mouth and I pulled my wrist from his grasp and placed a finger on his lips.

"You wanted my truth. Now give me your dick."

Walker frowned especially hard at that comment, but I was feeling particularly vulnerable at the moment and I was ready to not talk anymore...

"You want my dick, Olivia?" he drawled.

I stared up at him, a shiver running down my spine, my core absolutely throbbing.

"You want my big dick to fuck that perfect fucking pussy, angel? Want me to stretch your cunt, make you feel me for days?"

An involuntary moan slipped from my lips and he chuckled darkly.

"Turn around," he ordered, and just like last time, his take charge attitude was like catnip for my pussy.

I wanted to feel, not to think.

He unbuttoned my pants and his hand slid into them. He palmed my slit, a finger sliding lightly through my folds.

"This is what you need?" he growled.

I whimpered and his thick finger plunged into me.

"You're fucking drenched," he announced, deep male satisfaction in his voice. His other hand yanked at the strings of my corset top, his breath sounding a bit uneven as he revealed my chest. After my breasts were bare, he gave himself a minute to palm my breast before he shook his head and pulled his finger out of my core.

"Turn around."

I turned obediently until my cheek was pressed against the cool wall. Walker pulled my pants down, and then he snapped my lace thong once before massaging one of my ass cheeks.

"Ouch," I gasped as his teeth sank into my skin.

"Fucking perfect."

Walker tore my thong off and jerked my pants again. "Step," he commanded, and I obediently lifted my foot so he could get my leather pants down all the way. "Spread your legs and bend over."

"So eloquent," I teased, pretending that my voice wasn't all breathy and embarrassing sounding.

He ignored me, and I glanced back, only to see him dropping to his knees behind me. Before I could say anything, his mouth descended on my sex. He sucked and licked, separating my folds with his tongue as he pushed two fingers into me.

Walker pressed his face into my cunt, his mouth and tongue licking me *everywhere*.

"Oh," I cried out as his tongue slid along my slit and then circled my asshole. I straightened at the foreign sensation and he spanked me in response.

"Don't fucking move," he said roughly, his stubble scratching along my skin as he continued to devour me. I bent back over and arched my back, my hips writhing against his face, trying to get more friction. Walker thrust another finger inside me and I sobbed as I came, my cum dripping down my legs as his tongue slid to my clit. My knees weakened, tremors wracking through my body as he growled into my core, continuing to use his fingers and mouth to fuck me into another rolling orgasm. It was somehow even more intense and a tear slid down my cheek as my pussy clenched around his fingers.

I was gasping for breath as his fingers slipped out of me and then a second later, the thick length of his cock was pushing inside. I sobbed as something hard grazed over that spot inside of me. He felt different than he had before...he seemed almost bigger...and I hadn't thought that was possible. His hand wrapped around my throat and he pulled me until my back was pressed against his front.

"This pretty pussy's all mine, isn't it baby?" he said as he thrust up into me. His free hand grabbed one of mine, bringing it to my core as he used my own fingers to play with my clit. "That's it, sweetheart. That's my good girl."

I gushed around his cock again and he groaned, like that was the hottest thing he'd ever experienced.

"Someone likes being a good girl," he murmured as his hand tightened briefly around my throat, his thumb brushing against my pulse.

"Just yours," I whispered, the words slipping out only because I was drunk with pleasure.

Or at least that's what I would argue if he ever brought it up.

I could admit to *myself* at least that I did like being Walker's "good girl", even if I hated being a "good girl" for everyone else.

"Yes," he moaned. "Just mine."

"Keep touching yourself," Walker growled as he moved his hand from my pussy to my breasts, kneading and massaging and pulling at my nipples while he fucked me.

I was a writhing, desperate mess. Desperate for more, desperate to come, desperate for...him.

"My sweet girl. You're so perfect. Fuck...I—"

I didn't have time to think about what he'd been about to say as he grabbed my chin and angled it up so he could devour my lips as he continued to push in and out.

A wet sound filled the room as I soaked his thighs with my cum.

Walker's arm clamped around my waist so that I couldn't move, all I could do was feel. Feel so full I could scream, cry, die, if he ever dared to leave me.

I shattered, the edges of my vision darkening as my cries lit up the room, Walker's hips still pumping in and out of me at a brutal pace.

He was owning every inch of me, using me for his own pleasure even as he gave it back to me ten fold.

We fell forward onto the bed, somehow staying connected as he leaned over my body, completely covering me as he fucked me onto his cock.

His rhythm faltered and he shuddered as his dick pulsed inside me. Liquid heat flooded my insides, spilling out and dripping down my legs.

I collapsed on the bed and he followed, carefully rolling us so that he was behind me, his dick still inside my pussy, slowly moving in and out as if he couldn't bear to stop.

His lips trailed down my neck as his fingers played in our combined mess.

When he finally pulled out, he continued to play with our cum, pushing it back inside me like he didn't want me to lose any of it.

My eyes flew open when I realized we didn't use a condom.

Thank fuck for birth control.

Except...an image of him wrapped around me just like this, his hand cradling my stomach...it filled my thoughts, and I had to shake my head because that...that was so crazy.

He brushed another kiss against my neck and I relaxed against him in the afterglow, forgetting about anything except the ache between my legs, that deep satisfaction in my soul… and the fact that I'd never been more at peace in my whole fucking life than I was in that moment.

CHAPTER 15

OLIVIA

As I blinked awake, the soft morning light filtering through the crack in the curtains, a familiar sense of disorientation washed over me. It took a moment for my groggy mind to register where I was, and when it did, a thrill fluttered in my chest—a thrill and a terror.

I was in bed…with Walker…

Again.

Rolling onto my side, I found myself gazing at his still sleeping form, the gentle rise and fall of his chest a soothing rhythm in the quiet of the room. His features were softened in slumber, any lines of tension smoothed away in the vulnerability of sleep.

For a brief moment, I allowed myself to indulge in a daydream of what it would be like to wake up to this sight every day—to feel his warmth beside me, his steady breathing, his reassuring presence.

But of course it didn't take long for reality to crash over me like a wave, pulling me back from the edge of my fantasies.

I couldn't afford to let myself fall for him—not when the stakes were so high, not with what my life was like.

I rode the edge of complete destruction every single day.

Walker could break me, destroy all I'd done to survive like it was nothing but fragile glass.

Not wanting those kinds of thoughts to mess with my "perfect weekend", I moved to get out of the bed and use the bathroom. Some cold water on my face would do wonders.

As I went to slide out of the sheets though, something hard bit into my wrist.

Confused, I glanced down to see...a handcuff.

Walker had handcuffed me to him.

What the hell?

I glanced up at his face only to see a sleepy, roguish grin playing on his lips.

"I was making sure you couldn't sneak out on me again," he murmured, his voice low and husky with sleep as he pulled me towards him by my cuffed wrist so I tumbled onto his hard chest.

I stared at him in disbelief.

"I can't believe you handcuffed me!" I grumbled, not sounding as indignant as I would have liked. "And why the hell do you even have handcuffs with you?"

He winked at me and I tried not to let it affect me. Who would have thought that I'd like being handcuffed...because the guy was desperate to keep me.

"I don't know that there's much I wouldn't do to keep you," he murmured, his free hand softly stroking my cheek until I was leaning into him like a purring cat as we continued to stare at each other.

"It's just for the weekend," I reminded him, and he flinched as if I'd struck him before finally taking a deep breath.

"Whatever you say," he told me lightly, like there wasn't any part of him that believed me.

Unfortunately, I was beginning to not believe myself.

The fact that I had to pee hit me hard then, and I shook the handcuff so the rattle filled the air. "Are you going to let me out of this?"

He lifted an eyebrow. "Depends...are you going to run away the second I do?"

I huffed. But also...I had no plans to run this weekend.

I wanted to soak every second up.

Awe washed over me as I gazed at his gorgeous face. It was like he'd been made for me, perfectly designed to be my biggest weakness.

His features were chiseled and rugged, his jawline sharp and defined. His eyes were a piercing shade of blue, a depth and intensity to them that drew me in like a beacon in the darkness.

"I'm not going to run," I said softly, and his answering grin was heartbreaking...because I loved it so much. It was equal parts charming and mischievous, with just a hint of vulnerability lurking beneath the surface. Just enough to set me at ease that he wasn't as confident about all of this as he came across.

Maybe he was scared too.

"That's what I needed to hear," he murmured back, brushing a kiss against my lips that had my insides fluttering even though my body definitely needed a break.

That monster dick of his could also be called a pussy destroyer.

He grabbed a small key from the nightstand next to him and he unlocked the cuffs, pressing another soft kiss on my wrist where there was a light mark.

I hopped off the bed, trying not to be self conscious about the fact that I was still naked as I walked into the bathroom.

Glancing back, I saw that he was watching me, his head propped up in a tattooed hand.

As his gaze held mine, a silent promise of safety and security in his blue depths, I couldn't help but wonder if maybe—just maybe—taking a risk on him might be worth it in the end.

———

Walker

While Olivia went through her morning routine, I threw on a pair of briefs—not ready for her to discover the...surprise on my dick.

There was a reason I'd fucked Olivia from behind last night, and it didn't have anything to do with the fact that she had the most perfect ass I'd ever seen.

Although that was a bonus.

She might not have run after the handcuffs...but she was probably still at the stage where she'd run if she saw...I adjusted my cock, groaning because it was fucking sore.

I grabbed my phone off the nightstand to voice my complaints to the parties responsible.

> **Me:** My dick fucking hurts.

> **Ari:** That's what she said.

> **King Linc:**...

> **Ari:** What? Didn't like my "she said" joke?

> **Me:** It didn't make sense at all in that context.

> **Ari:** Fair. I"ll keep workshopping.

> **King Linc:** How about instead of "workshopping" you take a vow to never attempt a "she said" joke again.

> **Ari:** How dare you. I'm trying to master my craft and you're being a Negative Nancy. No one likes a Negative Nancy, Golden Boy. NO ONE!

> **Me:** Actually I 100% agree with Lincoln on this one.

> **Ari:** And that surprises no one.

> **Me:** Can we get back to my dick.

> **Me:** I mean not literally get back to my dick. But...

King Linc: I've told you this before, I don't want to know about your dick, Disney.

Ari: I'm sorry. I have to do it.

King Linc: Don't do it.

Me: Please don't do it.

Ari: That's what she said!

King Linc: ...

Olivia distracted me from the ridiculousness happening on my phone by stepping out of the bathroom, a robe wrapped around her fucking perfect body. "I need to get ready for the shower," she said, a blush on her cheeks, probably because of the way I was eye fucking her. "Can you do something about that?" she asked, gesturing wildly with her hands.

"What?" I asked, frowning as I glanced at my chest. I mean, yes, I had an erection, but that was to be expected if she was in the room.

"Put a shirt on. And then maybe eat a donut or something, so the rest of us mere mortals can feel better about ourselves," she griped, like she wasn't perfection incarnate herself.

I was totally going to tell Cole about that line though. *Eat your heart out, rockstar. Hockey players were the shit.*

It hit me then that I wasn't going to see her for another part of the day and I frowned, wishing she hadn't taken the handcuffs off and we were snapped together in bed right now.

I wanted a lifetime of that.

Maybe not the handcuff part, but the spending every second together part for sure.

"I'm going to go take a shower, I'm a mess," she explained as she gathered up her clothes.

"If you're referring to the state of your pussy, I think it's the best kind of mess," I told her, my dick getting harder just thinking about my cum being inside her. I wanted to keep that pussy full of me.

I reluctantly rolled out of bed so that I could walk her back to her room. I probably had some groomsman shit I was supposed to be at—not that Harley would want me there. But I had to keep appearances…or at least keep up the reminder that he needed to play a part too.

Last night's near bitch fit on his part was totally unacceptable.

"Oh, you don't need to come with me. I promise I'll see you later," she rushed out as she watched me pull on a pair of jeans.

"Yeah, that's not happening. I don't plan on letting you out of my sight unless I have to. You did tell me I could have *all* weekend. You're not trying to get out of that, are you, Jones?"

Olivia took a second to respond, her gaze was too caught up with the sight of me slipping on my shirt.

"Jones?"

She shook her head, like she was trying to shake herself from a trance. "I would never."

"Good," I called as I walked into the bathroom to throw some water on my face and maybe use some hair gel. "Because I would hate to have to use those handcuffs again."

She giggled like I'd said something funny.

I totally wasn't joking.

Once inside the bathroom, I stared at myself in the mirror as I washed my face and brushed my hair, thinking I looked…alive. Maybe for the first time.

I'd always been relatively laid back, sane.

It kind of felt now like that had been a mask I'd been wearing, and who I was with Olivia was who I was always meant to be.

A crazy thought for sure.

But if you weren't crazy in love…were you actually in love?

Food for thought for all the haters.

When I came back, she was sitting on the bed, her mouth

pinched and unhappy as she stared at her phone like it had personally wronged her.

"Everything all right, angel?" I asked, bending over to kiss her, because I couldn't help myself.

"Just the usual reminder," she murmured, pulling away from the kiss and staring out the window despondently. "That all this isn't real."

Olivia was silent the whole trip to her room and I could feel her withdrawing from me as we walked.

I wanted to tell her that it was real. It was the realest fucking thing I'd ever felt.

But I also needed to read the *room*—and Olivia's *room* was telling me that that kind of comment wasn't going to get me anywhere right now.

"I'll see you after the shower?" I told her, hoping the desperation wasn't seeping out of my pores as I stood there.

"Bye," she said simply, not answering my question as she slipped inside, and making me feel like a complete failure because I hadn't yet figured out how I was going to make her happy.

I stood at the door for a long moment, hoping she'd throw it open and pull me inside, just as desperate to be near me as I was to be near her.

It took me a couple of minutes to finally resign myself to the fact that wasn't going to happen.

I walked back to my room, checking my email to see where I was supposed to be today.

Pool Party: 2:00 pm.

Alright, I could wrap myself around the idea of a little sun.

My phone rang and I saw that it was Parker calling.

"What's up, little brother?" I asked.

"Mom's not eating again," he answered solemnly, and I cursed...because wasn't it always something?

"Did you call Dr. Calloway? Can he see her?"

"She's been seeing Dr. Calloway. She's just..." he sighed, and

I heard everything he wanted to say.

Like the fact that our mother was broken.

Irreparably it seemed—since our dad had been gone for ten years now, and she'd never recovered.

Sure, there had been some months where she seemed like she was...okay.

But that never lasted long.

"Do—" I swallowed because the last thing I wanted was to leave. "Do you need me to come home?"

Parker had taken a football scholarship at University of Tennessee instead of on the west coast, so he could stay close to Mom and help out if needed. He got the brunt of her...issues.

Cole and I hadn't handled it well...we'd just left.

"Aww, you must love me, if you're offering to leave your looooover to come help me," he teased, easing the tension that had built in my shoulders. If he could still joke around, things weren't dire yet.

Or at least that was what I was telling myself.

I'm not sure that Olivia was prepared for me to kidnap her and take her to Tennessee.

Baby steps and all of that.

"You get your girl...Disney. And try not to get arrested while you do it." he drawled. "I'll get Mom to eat...one way or another."

"I'm sorry," I finally said, because that's all I could say. My little brother was my hero on most days. Doing what Cole and I couldn't stand to do—watch our mother rot away.

"K, you're getting weepy on me. Cut it out," Parker said, and I chuckled...because it was true.

But as I hung up, all I could hope was that my mother could keep her shit together long enough for me to figure out my current situation. The last thing that Olivia needed in her life was a problem like my mother.

She had enough problems with her own.

Another thing on my list to solve.

CHAPTER 16
WALKER

O livia was acting like nothing had happened last night or this morning.

And it was driving me crazy. She'd tried to sit between two bridesmaids at dinner, instead of by me, not happy at all when I'd smiled at one of the girls and she'd given me her seat without a thought.

"You're running again," I murmured as she stared at her dinner plate as if it held the secrets to the universe.

"I just decided that I was an idiot," she responded, her voice blank. She fisted the skirt of her dress. "Every second I spend around you gets harder. I—I can't do hard…"

Fuck. She sounded like she was near tears and it was going to make me go insane.

It was also the closest she'd come to admitting that she was feeling something for me too.

"There's something we could do about that," I said carefully, and her gaze shot up at me, a dash of resentment there that I suddenly felt *very* wary about.

"Tell me, Walker. Is there something about me that screams idiot?"

I blinked at her, not understanding what she was talking about.

"Sorry, angel face, but I have no idea what you're hinting at right now."

She gestured to me like she had that morning, kind of crazy like.

"Look at you. You could have anything, have anyone. Why would you want me?" She was being quiet, but her gaze darted around us, suddenly remembering we were surrounded by people.

It hit me then, for the first time—because apparently I was an idiot.

She blamed herself for what had happened to her.

She thought something was wrong with *her*, that *she* was ruined because of those assholes.

We couldn't have that.

"I've got to go. I—I forgot something in my room," she stammered suddenly, standing up shakily and rushing out. I frowned after her, catching Harley's gaze and trying not to roll my eyes at the death glare he was sending my way.

Seriously, dude.

I counted to twenty, which honestly showed I had the patience of a fucking saint...and then I headed towards her room.

She must have been sprinting, because she was nowhere to be seen.

I tried to take my time getting up to her room, giving her a second to calm down...but it didn't seem to help.

I got to her door and knocked.

No answer.

"Olivia, it's me. Let me in," I growled.

Silence.

"Let. Me. In."

Still nothing.

I sighed patiently, because honestly...a little thing like a door wasn't going to keep me from her.

I'd swiped a card from a maid's cart yesterday...just in case my original plan didn't work. And it was certainly going to come in handy right now.

Her eyes were comically wide as I walked in. She was sitting on the edge of the bed, biting down on that damn bottom lip again.

"What? How!" she exclaimed, her mouth wide, like a beautiful little guppy fish.

"I want to be with you." I said roughly. "I want you to give me a fucking chance."

Olivia remained wide-eyed...and wide-mouthed.

I wanted to make a joke that I could put something in her mouth if she wanted and immediately cursed Ari Lancaster— because that was *his* influence.

I was a gentleman, damnit!

She finally scoffed at me like I'd said something crazy.

"Oh you mean besides the obvious that I don't have any control of my fucking life?"

"I can help you with that," I insisted.

———

Olivia

Hope was a dangerous thing. I'd said that before.

And there was nothing more hopeful feeling than the sight of Walker Davis as he stood in front of me right now. Telling me he wanted to be with me.

That he wanted...me.

Just thinking of the conservatorship left a bitterness on my tongue, but he was clearly not understanding the reality of my life. "Everything about my life is suffocating, my mother and my agent control every aspect of my existence. I have no freedom, no autonomy. I'm a puppet, trapped in an ivory tower unless I give them what they want."

When he didn't say anything...I continued on.

"And then there's the paparazzi," I continued, my voice trembling with pent-up frustration. "Two years ago they hounded me day and night, invaded every shred of privacy I had. They made up lies about me, and there was no one to stop them. I just had to put on a smile and pretend that it meant nothing to me when they called me a druggie, and a slut, and everything else." I glanced away because this was when he was going to leave.

"And some of those things they weren't wrong about," I whispered.

I snuck a look at Walker, noting the way his jaw was tightened with anger, the way his hands were clenching into fists at his sides.

"And if all of those weren't enough reasons why you should run from the *stranger* you've spent two nights with...you should think about yourself." The words caught in my throat. "You deserve someone who can give you everything, not just shattered pieces."

"Can I talk now?" he asked, his voice so gentle...and caring...that a piece of my armor chipped away. "I feel like I've been searching for something real, darlin', for a long fucking time. And I don't know how to explain it...but when I met you that night. I found my *real*."

My nose scrunched because I didn't understand...I didn't understand how things could be happening so quickly.

I'd always been told you shouldn't trust something that rises too fast.

And this thing between us...it was moving like lightning.

"How do you do that?" I whispered, staring up at him in wonder.

"What?" he asked, leaning over and kissing away the tear that had been falling down my cheek.

"How do you make me feel like nothing bad's ever happened to me...like I've never been broken before?"

He gazed at me, his expression unfathomable, a tic in his cheek like he was trying to hold himself in. "You make me feel like that too. Like now that I have you, all the sad things are gone. Like now that I've got you, all the bad things don't exist anymore."

He brushed a kiss against my lips.

"So what do you think, angel face? Are you going to give me a chance?" he sighed against my skin.

"Maybe," I answered. Because I think that was the only answer I *could* give.

"I can work with 'maybe'," he said with a triumphant grin, like he'd won.

As his lips covered mine and he pushed me back on the bed...it felt like maybe I'd won too.

———

Walker

If she was fucked up...then I was fucked up too. Because everything about her called to me.

I was still inside her—her pussy was still clenching my dick.

I was basically in heaven.

Olivia shifted, a strange look on her face.

"What's wrong?"

"I'm just realizing we didn't have *the talk*," she said...looking a little sick all of a sudden.

"The talk?"

"Like, um. If we're clean? I mean—we should have said something before we had unprotected sex multiple times...but... just give me the bad news."

"The bad news?" I knew I sounded stupid with every word out of my mouth, but I was really confused.

"Do you have...something?"

Ohhhh. I understood now. And I was kind of offended.

Especially because my dick was still inside her.

"Um, I don't have anything. We get checked constantly in physicals on the team...and I haven't been with anyone in months." Hercules flexed inside of her like it was trying to convince her too.

Her face filled with relief...and then confusion.

"Is there...a certain reason that you're asking that?" I asked.

I flipped her over so that I was on my back and she was straddling me. Fuck, she was sexy.

Focus, Walker. She thinks you have an STD. This is definitely not the time to think about her perfect tits.

"It's just...you...there's...there's something bumpy on your dick now." She held up her hands. "Don't get me wrong, they feel really, really good...but I don't think they were there the first time we...the first time we had sex."

Shit. She'd noticed.

I mean, on the plus side, she said they felt good. But I'd handcuffed her this morning, I'd just walked into her hotel room with a stolen room card...and now I was going to show her...my decorated dick.

Decorated for her.

I was either going to be cursing Lincoln Daniels and Ari Lancaster after this....or I was going to tell them I was madly in love with them.

It was definitely touch and go at the moment what it was going to be.

"I think this is proof that I'm very invested in us," I said cautiously as I lifted her off my dick, groaning a little as I did so, because I would live inside her if she'd let me.

"Why am I nervous all of a sudden?" she murmured.

I got up on my knees and presented her with...

"Are those...beads," she said slowly, staring at my dick with huge eyes.

"Not just beads," I said proudly, feeling a little more confident because she looked more awestruck than anything. "Look closer."

"Oh! They're the beads that are on friendship bracelets! I've never seen them like this, but I—" It hit her then…what the letters on the beads spelled out.

You see, in my blacked out state, Lincoln and Ari thought it would be *hilarious* for me to get Olivia's name…pierced rather than tattooed on my dick. I literally had beads spelling out her name, speared down the base of my dick.

"That's my name," she said with a gulp. "You have my name pierced through…your dick." She started to back away. "Please tell me this isn't where I end up as like a skin suit or something."

I snorted, my dick bobbing in front of me. "I don't know what a skin suit is, but it sounds like something I definitely wouldn't be interested in." I could tell she was trying to look away from my dick, but every time she tried, her gaze went right back to it immediately.

She was silent for another long minute, and I was beginning to plot Linc and Ari's deaths—well, maybe just Ari's. I wasn't sure I could actually follow through with ending Linc.

Suddenly, a small smile crept across her lips, and the next second a giggle slipped out. "Um, you really like me…don't you?" she finally said, before a few more *adorable* giggles filled the air.

I grinned, feeling a little light headed with relief because it's kind of a risky venture piercing your dick with someone's name when you've only had one night with them.

Of course, I also had been stalking her every day for months, but I definitely wasn't going to be gracing her with that little tidbit.

"I'm fucking crazy about you, angel face. Fucking crazy."

Her expression softened, and she finally was able to look away from Hercules and meet my gaze. And then she made my fucking day.

"Me too."

I wasn't sure how to describe the feeling I was experiencing at the moment.

Ecstatic?

Gleeful?

Melty inside?

Definitely that last one.

I pushed her onto her back and slid my fingers into her pussy, groaning because I couldn't wait to be inside her again. I spread her wetness across her lips, chasing the taste like it was my favorite drug.

I was about to slide inside her, when I realized I should probably double check something. I paused at her entrance. "You said that...the beads felt good, right?"

I really didn't want to have them torn out, but I would do it for her if she wanted me to.

Please don't want me to.

She bit down on her lip in that way that made me crazy and gazed up at me. "I fucking love them."

I slammed into her and made a mental note to never tell Ari and Linc that they'd been right.

I didn't want to encourage any more dick accessories when I was under the influence.

But also...I loved those guys.

Circle of Trust all the fucking way.

CHAPTER 17

OLIVIA

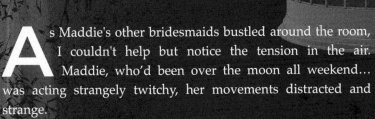

A s Maddie's other bridesmaids bustled around the room, I couldn't help but notice the tension in the air. Maddie, who'd been over the moon all weekend... was acting strangely twitchy, her movements distracted and strange.

"Are you okay?" I whispered, and she nodded, biting down on her lip in a very worried looking way. Her leg was tapping a million miles an hour underneath her gorgeous dress, and I gently touched her knee, trying to calm her down.

"Can you come into the bathroom with me?" Maddie suddenly asked, her voice suspiciously loud as she grabbed my hand and started dragging me to the door.

As soon as we got inside, she locked the door behind her, her gaze darting around the room like someone was hiding inside here with us.

"What's going on?" I asked, concern lacing my voice as I studied her pale face.

Maddie took a deep breath, her hands shaking as she met my gaze. "I took a pregnancy test this morning," she confessed, her voice barely above a whisper. "And...it was positive."

My heart skipped a beat at her words, I was completely shocked.

I also was...jealous.

That was a weird thing to think.

I realized she was waiting for me to say something. "You're going to be a mom," I whispered, my eyes getting all watery with the weird emotions I was feeling. I was so happy for her. Harley and her were going to be the best parents.

But I was also feeling a little sad for me.

No matter how much Walker thought this was going to work, there was no way I was going to be having a family while I was under the conservatorship.

I reached out to her, wrapping her in a comforting embrace. "And I'm going to be a freaking aunt," I squealed. "A cousin aunt," I amended, as I thought about the family semantics.

She laughed, but it sounded hollow.

"Are you okay? How does Harley feel about it?"

Maddie let out a shaky laugh, the sound tinged with uncertainty. "I'm not sure," she admitted, her eyes clouded with worry. "When I told him, he got really pale and quiet. I can't tell if he's happy or not."

I hugged her tighter. "I'm sure he's thrilled. Harley wants everything with you. He was probably so excited, he was trying not to pass out."

"Oh, I think he was definitely about to pass out," she snorted. "He was literally shaking...and then I left the room."

"You left the room?"

"I was scared," she whispered. "I didn't know what he was going to say. I kept him waiting for so long. I gave him so much crap when he just wanted to marry me. I'm afraid that this is going to be too much."

Just as she said that, there was a knock on the door.

"Yes?" Maddie called, her voice a little high-pitched.

"It's me," a voice called.

I cringed, because unfortunately the voice belonged to Carlie, her maid of honor. I'd never liked the girl. There was something about her that rubbed me the wrong way, something fake and insincere that made my skin crawl.

"Come in," Maddie said, straightening up and wiping at her eyes.

Carlie breezed into the room with a saccharine smile plastered on her pretty face, her gaze flickering over us with a hint of curiosity. "Hey, girls," she chirped, her voice too bright to be genuine. "How's everything going?"

Maddie forced a smile, her eyes still red from crying. "We're fine, Carlie," she replied, her tone surprisingly clipped. "Just catching up before the wedding."

Carlie didn't seem to notice the tension in the air, her gaze lingering on Maddie for a moment. "You're not second guessing anything…are you?"

For some reason, she didn't sound too upset about the idea of that.

I bit back a sarcastic retort, forcing myself to let Maddie handle it since I barely knew Carlie.

"No, of course not! Just having an emotional moment with my soon to be cousin," Maddie said in a bright voice that almost sounded real.

Carlie nodded, her expression almost…disappointed. "Good. That's good," she murmured slowly.

"I'll see you out there, okay?" Maddie said, nicely telling her to get lost.

Thankfully Carlie got the message. "See you soon," she responded as she walked out the door and I closed it behind her.

"Why didn't you tell her?" I asked. "I thought you guys were best friends."

Maddie's fake smile had dropped and she sighed. "I guess at one point we were, but over the years it's felt more like she was a thousand pound leech, hanging onto me for dear life so she can hang around NHL hotties. It just seemed like what I was supposed to do, having her be my maid of honor…since she's my oldest friend."

Before I could dwell on that information further, there was another knock at the door.

"I guess it's time to get out there and start hoping Harley shows up to the ceremony," she tried to joke as the knock sounded on the door again.

"Maddie, let me in, sweetheart," Harley said, and Maddie's eyes widened comically as she stared at me.

"What do I do?" she mouthed frantically.

"I'm going to let him in," I whispered, because I knew my cousin…he was so in love with Maddie. There was no doubt in my mind, they were going to be alright. If they weren't, I would officially be convinced that true love did not exist.

Harley stepped through the open door, his eyes filled with so much love and adoration as he stared at Maddie, I immediately began to tear up.

"Hey, baby," he murmured, his voice soft with emotion. "You ran away before I could say anything."

A hiccuped sob fell from Maddie's mouth, and I knew I should leave and let them have this moment alone, but I was frozen in place.

"I just wanted to tell you," he began, his voice trembling with emotion as he stared at her as if his life depended on it. "That I've never been happier in my entire life than when you told me you were having my baby. All these years, all I've ever wanted was…you. And now, with this baby on the way, it feels like all my dreams are finally coming true."

Maddie seemed unable to form words at the moment, just staring at him as if she'd never been more shocked.

I couldn't believe she'd thought he would reject her.

Her tears fell like raindrops, and he took a step towards her, his own tears streaming down his cheeks. "Can—can I hold you?" he asked.

She nodded as she started crying harder.

I felt a lump form in my throat as I stood there, watching as he hurried over and wrapped her in his arms.

This was what love looked like—a bond so deep and profound that you couldn't imagine your life without that person, that you didn't know where their happiness began and yours ended.

I watched them embrace, their tears mingling with their laughter and joy...and that longing twinged inside me once again.

Seeing them made me want to jump headfirst into something with Walker. Rip out my soul and give it to him, just for a chance at a love like that.

I left the room, closing the door behind me, a sense of peace floating over me for the first time this weekend that maybe... what I was dreaming of wasn't completely out of the realm of possibilities.

Maybe happily ever afters could exist after all.

———

Marco had officially announced the concert was happening tomorrow. He'd texted me as soon as the news went out.

I was standing at the reception when the whispers began— evidently, it was going viral online already. And evidently, guests weren't abiding by the no phones rule.

Shocking.

That had been Marco and Jolette's plan, to create a commotion, so I hoped they were happy.

Or at least as happy as miserable people like them could ever be.

Marco had figured it would be a bigger deal if it was announced last minute, that it would make people terrified they would be missing out if they didn't drop everything to go to a "once in a lifetime" concert. "Olivia Darling", practically back from the dead.

It was amazing how fast being back in the headlines could make people connect the dots. Literally no one had recognized me all weekend. And now, as I was dancing with Walker, it felt like everyone was staring, like everyone was talking about me.

That familiar itch under my skin began. The one that made me want to claw at my flesh until it was unrecognizable...

Someone's phone flashed nearby and I shrank against Walker's chest, like somehow he could protect me from what was about to happen.

"News spreads fast," Walker murmured, slipping his phone out of his tux and staring at it. I'd told him about the concert yesterday so the news wasn't a surprise.

"Don't google my name," I begged under my breath. "You won't like what you see."

He huffed as if I was being ridiculous. "I've had Google alerts on you from the second I discovered who you were. There's nothing about you I don't want to know, that would change my mind."

Now I was the one laughing. But the sound of my voice was harsh and sarcastic. "We'll see about that."

He squeezed me tighter against him, like his embrace could prove me wrong.

I closed my eyes, forcing myself to pretend that they weren't all staring at me. It had been a beautiful ceremony. Maddie and Harley had cried the entire time. And Walker, looking like a dream in his tux, had stared at me throughout it, like he was making the same vows that they'd made to each other.

Or at least that's what a deranged part of me was imagining. The one that was more and more desperate to keep him with every passing hour.

I'd stay like this for a little longer, stay in his bubble and pretend like tomorrow's concert wasn't going to change everything.

"You're not doubting me, right?" he said suddenly, anxiety sharp in his voice.

"I don't know what I'm feeling at the moment," I told him,

keeping my face nestled in his chest. "Or at least I don't know what I'm feeling besides dread."

"I was hoping that my little reveal last night would make you feel better today."

I snorted, as his "little reveal" pressed into my stomach. Walker's dick was a sight to behold on a regular day. But seeing my name beaded down the underside of his length…well, I still wasn't sure about that.

I'd never heard of something like that before. I especially didn't know what to think about the fact that he'd done that after only one night with me.

I wasn't *that* impressive in bed.

The psycho part of me did feel much better about the reveal though. The part of me that was desperate for someone to love me…to want me—that part of me loved the fact that he'd done something so permanent, so outlandish to himself.

The psycho part of me needed obsession. And your name on someone's dick had to be the definition of that.

"I'm still analyzing how I feel about your…friendship beads," I finally teased, and he wrapped me tighter, like he was afraid I would run away.

"Can I cut in?" a deep voice said from behind me.

"No," Walker responded succinctly, keeping me plastered against him.

I glanced back to see it was that guy that had tried to talk to me at the engagement party—the one on Harley's team. What was his name again?

"Come on, man. Give the rest of us a shot with her. Olivia Darling's never been a one man kind of girl anyway."

I froze at that, irrational hurt and embarrassment flooding my chest. Here we go again. I guess two years wasn't enough to make people forget all the rumors about me.

It took me a second to realize the way Walker had stiffened as well.

"What the fuck did you just say?" he hissed, his voice dark and...a little terrifying.

I hadn't heard that tone from him before.

Walker pulled me to his side, still keeping me tucked under one arm.

The guy took a step back, clearly intimidated by the sudden shift in Walker's demeanor, but he mustered a nervous laugh. "Davis, I was just joking around," he stammered, his bravado faltering under Walker's intense gaze.

Walker's eyes flashed with barely-contained rage, his fists clenched at his sides. "Oh, you think that's a fucking joke?" he growled, his voice rising to a guttural snarl. "You think you can say that, and I'll let you get away with it?"

Walker closed the distance between them, dragging me with him even as he towered over the guy. "Let me make one thing clear," he murmured, his voice low and dangerous. "Olivia is mine. If you ever even think about disrespecting something that's 'mine' again...I'll fucking end you."

The guy's eyes widened in fear, his bravado crumbling under the weight of Walker's aggression. He stumbled over his words, trying to backpedal, but Walker wasn't having it.

"I think it's time for you to leave the party," he suggested in a voice that I was going to label as his "serial killer" voice from now on—because it was that terrifying. "It's going to be a lot of fun next time I see you on the ice."

The guy turned and fled the room, like Walker had pulled out a literal knife and waved it at him.

Walker stared after him for a second, like he was waiting for him to reappear.

He finally turned to me, his eyes softening immediately. "Are you okay?" he asked, his voice rough with concern.

"Yeah," I whispered in a shaky, awe-filled voice. "Thank you. You didn't need to do that."

He shook his head at me. "I'll prove it to you eventually," he said quietly in response.

"Prove what?"

"That you have a safe place now, Olivia. That *I am* that safe place."

He pulled me back into his arms without waiting for a response, and his heartbeat felt like a ticking clock, counting down the moments when the real world returned...and I would see if that was true.

CHAPTER 18
OLIVIA

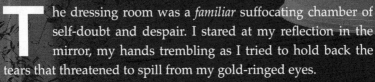

The dressing room was a *familiar* suffocating chamber of self-doubt and despair. I stared at my reflection in the mirror, my hands trembling as I tried to hold back the tears that threatened to spill from my gold-ringed eyes.

Why had I agreed to this?

Walker's face immediately came to mind.

Not that I'd known he would be a part of this weekend.

The room felt too small, like the walls were closing in around me. My mind raced, and it hit me, that craving.

One pill and I'd be able to go out there and not feel anything.

One pill and I could pretend in front of all those faces that there wasn't anything wrong with me.

That I was having the time of my life.

One pill.

I squeezed my eyes closed and counted to ten. And then I counted again. Over and over again until it felt like the desperation had diminished.

At least a little bit.

At least enough to say no.

Fuck, I was glad Walker wasn't in here to see me like this.

The door opened and I didn't have to look to see who it was.

It's not like anyone else but she and Marco would just barge into the room.

The smugness was emanating off of her like toxic fumes.

Jolette.

Her presence alone was enough to make my blood run cold. She wore that cruel smile that always made my skin crawl, her voice dripping with sarcasm as she spoke. "Do try and not embarrass yourself out there," she purred, her words laced with venom. "Who knows, you do well enough, and maybe the public will forgive you for being such a pathetic excuse of a human."

I didn't respond.

The words carved at my insides, like they always did, but I wasn't going to show her that. She had always been the vampire, sucking out every ounce of love I'd ever had for creating and singing until I was left hollow and broken. I didn't know if there would ever be a time when she couldn't hurt me, when the little girl inside me—the one that still held out hope she was worthy of love from someone—didn't want that someone to be my mother.

But maybe I was feeling a little bit stronger after a weekend in Walker's arms, where he'd memorized every dip and curve of my body like it was his sole mission in life. Because for once, I was able to keep my face perfectly blank.

After an awkward minute, where she just stood there, waiting for me to fall apart...she finally made a hmmph kind of sound and walked out without another word.

As soon as the door slammed behind her, I released a breath, leaning over the vanity in front of me, trying not to be sick. I felt dizzy, overwhelmed by the memories and the emotions that only she had the power to summon with just a few words.

Shaking my head, I finally straightened up and reapplied some red lipstick, slapping it on like it was war paint and had the ability to transform me into someone else.

As I stared into the mirror, I *forced* myself to become Olivia Darling.

However much I hated her.

———

Stepping out onto the stage, I felt like an imposter in my own skin. The lights were too bright and the crowd too loud, their energy draining, like a succubus taking my life force. This was the kind of crowd that I'd told Walker I hated. The kind where they took from me without giving anything back.

The band that accompanied me was a far cry from the familiar faces I used to perform with. My old crew had moved on obviously. I couldn't exactly ask them to wait for me after I'd said I'd never perform again as long as I was under the conservatorship.

The fact that I'd said that made me feel like a liar as I pasted on a smile for the screaming fans.

Taking a deep breath, I tried to find my voice and my composure.

"Hi y'all. How's everyone doing? My name's Olivia. And I'm going to sing some songs for you tonight," I said into the mic.

It was a phrase I'd said countless times before, but it had never felt so wrong.

Even with the monitors in my ears, I could barely hear the first chords of the music filling the air—the crowd was screaming so freaking loud. I almost missed my cue as I had to force myself to sing. The lyrics felt foreign on my tongue, and I stumbled through them, the weight of my past destroying the fact that these lyrics had been dragged from my bitterest depths.

That these words were me.

I wanted to look for Walker in the crowd. I wanted to see what he thought of this version of the girl he said he was falling for. If he understood the pain that bled from my lyrics like a blade tearing through my skin.

But the stage lights were blinding, the deafening roar of the crowd ringing in my ears as I sang. And I didn't have it in me to do anything but sing.

Survive.

Each song feeling like a weight around my neck, dragging me down into a sea of discontent.

Things only improved when I strummed the first chords of my acoustic set, a sense of calm washing over me, the familiar strings of my guitar soothing my frayed nerves without the clang of the other instruments barging in on my peace.

I closed my eyes, letting the music wash over me like a gentle wave, the soft strains of my guitar filling the air with a bitter-sweet melody. And as I opened my mouth to sing, the words spilled out like a long-forgotten prayer, each note tinged with longing and regret.

"In the stillness of the night, I search for you in dreams,
But you're just out of reach, like a whispered memory,
I wonder if you feel it too, this ache that won't subside,
Or if I'm just a fool, lost in the high tide."

My voice wavered slightly as I glanced out and somehow caught Walker's gaze in the crowd, a few rows back, his eyes burning with an intensity that left me breathless.

I stumbled over a word as we stared at each other, my heart pounding in my chest as I began to sing the song…to him.

"And though the distance may divide us,
And time may steal our days,
I'll keep holding onto hope,
In this tangled maze."

The words flowed effortlessly from my lips as I sang of love and longing, of heartache and redemption. It was easier to sing when I pretended like it was just us, and I was sharing a piece of my heart with him.

The only piece I had to give.

The final chords rang out, and the crowd erupted into applause, their cheers bringing me back to reality and the fact that I was playing to a sold out crowd…and not just Walker.

But that moment was enough to keep me going.

A few songs later and I was *done,* the final notes of my last song fading away and the applause filling the air. I offered a shaky smile and a quick wave to the crowd before darting off the stage. The adrenaline that had fueled me through the performance began to ebb away, replaced by a gnawing sense of unease that clawed at my insides.

With each step, the panic rose within me like a tidal wave threatening to engulf me. My heart pounded in my chest, my breath coming in short, shallow gasps as I fought to hold myself together long enough to make it to my dressing room.

The corridors of the backstage area blurred around me as I stumbled forward, my vision swimming with a dizzying haze. I could feel the walls closing in on me, suffocating me with their oppressive weight.

I burst into my dressing room and slammed the door behind me...just in time for my panic attack to hit me with full force. My knees buckled beneath me, and I sank to the ground in a trembling heap, the world spinning wildly around me.

I clutched at my chest, my fingers digging into the fabric of my dress as I struggled to draw in a lungful of air. But no matter how hard I tried, I couldn't regain control.

I squeezed my eyes shut, willing the panic to subside, but it only seemed to grow stronger with each passing second. Tears pricked at the corners of my eyes, hot and bitter against my skin.

And then...he was there...

Walker.

His strong arms wrapped around me, holding me close, and immediately a sense of peace thrummed in my heart. His chest rose and fell with the steady rhythm of his breathing, and I found solace in the warmth of his embrace.

And suddenly, everything didn't seem so bad anymore. Like somehow he was my own personal...good thing.

I turned in his embrace and buried my face in his chest as the tears streamed down my cheeks. I couldn't even find it in myself to be embarrassed at how I was acting.

"Shh," he whispered softly, his palm cradling my head, his voice a soothing balm to my shattered nerves. "It's okay, Liv. You're okay."

I clung to him tighter, my body trembling against him. "I'm sorry. I'm not sure what's wrong with me," I choked out, refusing to let go of him.

"It's the adrenaline, you're not used to it. And on that scale. Fuck, angel. That was incredible. Insane. But incredible. I've never seen a crowd like that."

I was still shaking, but at least my heart didn't feel like it was going to beat out of my chest anymore. Instead...something else was taking over.

Something that felt a lot like...lust.

Before I could think too hard, I lifted my head and pressed my lips against his. He didn't respond for a second and a throb of panic lanced through me.

"I'm sorry," I choked out, moving my head away. I'm sure he was experiencing the worst kind of whiplash from me right now.

"I don't want to take advantage of you—" he started and I shook my head, reaching between us to rub against his already hard dick.

"I need you," I told him, totally aware of how desperate I sounded.

"Fuck. I'm going to hell," he growled, but his lips crashed against mine as he lifted me, forcing me to wrap my legs around him.

Walker's fingers pushed under my dress, sliding up my leg and along the edges of the shorts I was wearing to make sure no one in the crowd saw something under my dress that they shouldn't.

He cursed as he briefly set me down, ripping off my shorts and my underwear before he lifted me again, walking towards the wall and pressing me up against it as his fingers glided over my sensitive flesh.

I moaned, my head rocking back into the wall as he rubbed my clit slowly.

"More," I begged, and he laughed wickedly, like he was enjoying seeing me like this.

Desperate for him in a way I hadn't been for anything else in my life.

"You're so fucking wet, angel. You're desperate for my big, fat cock..aren't you, baby?"

I whimpered in response, crying out loudly as his fingers speared into me.

"That's it, baby. Give me one just like this, and then I'll give you what you want. I'll fill you up, let that sweet pussy choke my fucking dick."

"Yes," I breathed, riding his fingers as he pressed me into the wall, holding me in place like I weighed nothing.

He lowered me to the ground as he tugged down my dress enough to free a nipple, his perfect fingers still thrusting in and out of me. I sobbed as he took my peak in his hot, wet mouth, suckling it with the perfect amount of pressure.

It was only seconds before I was coming, panting and shaking against him.

"Fuck yes," he hissed, his blue eyes watching me. The dressing room was dimly lit, nothing on but a small lamp in the corner. A lock of his hair had fallen into his face, and I'd never seen anything more beautiful.

More beautiful, or more dangerous looking.

He pulled his fingers out of me and licked them, moaning as he took in my taste.

I wasn't sure why that was so hot to me. Maybe it was because he was taking part of me inside that perfect body. I liked knowing that my essence was inside of him now.

Hopefully forever.

He unbuttoned his jeans, his gaze feverish and wild looking

as he pulled out his cock, the mushroom head red and angry looking, milky cum already seeping out of it.

I dropped to my knees in front of him, finding myself *starving* all of a sudden. I waited for the panic to creep in, the sense of dirtiness and despair that I'd always gotten when Marco had made me do this.

But there was nothing as I knelt in front of Walker. Only pure, aching, desperate lust to make this beautiful man cum.

"Fuck, what are you doing?" he gasped, his hand gripping his cock and slowly sliding up and down while he stared at me.

"What does it look like?" I murmured, my tongue darting out and licking at the head, moaning as I took in his musky taste.

"Please," he begged, his voice thick with arousal, and my pussy gushed at the thought of having this gorgeous alpha male desperate for me.

My tongue lapped at his slit, enjoying the sounds he was making as I finally pulled the head into my mouth.

My lips sucked him deeper, my tongue caressing his length as I tried to get as much of him in my mouth as possible.

The feel of the beads on the underside were a little weird, but they somehow made the whole thing even hotter.

"Yes, suck it. Please don't stop." I sucked harder, craving more of that ache in his voice.

I tried to work more of him past my gag reflex...but I wasn't exactly sure how to do that. He was so fucking big.

I pulled at his length, finding a rhythm that had him gasping as I pushed to open my throat more.

"Enough," he growled a moment later, yanking me off his dick and into his arms, his cock thrusting into me a second later.

My head fell back as he stretched me open, the ridged underside of his cock hitting all the sweet spots as he slid into my core.

"Fuck yes," he murmured, grabbing my bare ass as he slammed in and out of me at a punishing pace like he was trying to batter into the entrance of my womb. I was delirious with pleasure, tears gathering in my eyes because it felt so fucking good.

"Walker," I cried out.

"I know, baby. I know," he answered in a strained voice as his thrusts grew faster.

He captured my lips in a fierce kiss, his tongue thrusting against mine, aggressive, deep licks that I felt all the way to my cunt.

It felt too good. I couldn't take it. I thrashed against him, trying to keep in my cries as he fucked me hard and fast.

My pussy throbbed around him and I chanted his name against his lips as I violently came.

He ripped his lips away from me, licking down my throat until he was marking me with his teeth in his favorite place in the crook of my neck. I whimpered as he licked away the pain of his bite.

One of his hands moved to my stomach and he applied pressure right above my pubic bone, immediately igniting another round of pleasure. Walker pressed his forehead against mine, staring deep into my eyes as he fucked in and out of me, still pressing on that perfect spot.

"What is that?" I gasped as I spun closer to another orgasm.

"Relax, angel. Give me one more," he coaxed, and the sweetness in his tone was my undoing. My body jerked and shook as I came, the pleasure so intense I couldn't breathe.

"Fuuuuck," he growled as I milked his length, his hot cum exploding inside of me in bursts until it was once again dripping down my thighs.

My head fell back and I was a mindless, weak mess, completely held up by his strong arms.

"You're so perfect," he whispered as he slid in and out of me slowly until I was whimpering from the sensation. A second later he pulled out and his fingers were replacing his dick, pushing his cum back into me.

"Why do you do that?" I murmured, still not opening my eyes as I let him hold me up. "You know I'm on birth control."

"Wishful thinking, I guess," he drawled.

And my eyes did fly open at that.

Before I could question him about what he'd meant by that... there was the sound of voices from nearby.

"Fuck," Walker murmured, pulling his fingers out and setting me down carefully before adjusting my dress so my breasts were once again covered. He tucked his dick back into his pants and stepped away as a knock sounded on the door.

I breathed a sigh of relief because that knock was a good thing. That meant that Jolette had gone to celebrate the money she'd made tonight and I was dealing with one of her underlings instead.

"Yes," I called out, proud that my voice didn't sound like I'd just been fucked against a wall.

The door opened an inch and Becky, one of Jolette's assistants, peeked her head in. "Your car is waiting outside to take you to the hotel." Her eyes widened when she caught sight of Walker, her gaze darting back and forth between us as she connected the dots about what had obviously just happened in here.

"Thank you," I said, still feeling oddly calm even knowing Becky was definitely going to tell Jolette about this.

It was like Walker had fucked all the panic out of me.

I could get used to that. It was much more effective than the drugs had ever been because it didn't have the nasty aftermath and self loathing attached to it.

At least not yet.

The door closed behind her and a second later Walker's arms were wrapped around me. "Ready to go back to the hotel?" he asked, and I nodded, savoring the feel of his warmth.

Walker tangled his hand in mine as we walked out of the dressing room. I still couldn't get over how good I felt. I never felt like this after a performance. It was as if the dread I'd felt throughout it, had never actually happened.

We walked down the tunnel that led to the exit door.

"What are you hungry for?" Walker asked as the door to the outside swung open and—

Flashes.

What seemed like a million of them. Coming from all directions.

I came to a complete stop, not able to see where I was going because of all the cameras blinding me.

"Olivia, over here!"

"Is that Walker Davis?"

"Give us a smile, Olivia!"

"Are you high, Olivia?"

"Did you have a panic attack?"

"Hey, Walker, how do you feel about dating someone with so much baggage?"

"Olivia, smile!"

I hadn't expected this.

Not at all. I'd gotten comfortable—forgotten what it was like to be stalked, and hounded by the leeches of the entertainment world.

I put up a hand to try and block out the flashing lights.

A familiar feeling of helplessness fell over me as my heart started to race.

Everything was chaos.

"Don't let go," Walker yelled to me, reminding me that for the first time...I wasn't alone.

He wrapped his arm around me, holding me close as he walked us through the sea of photographers towards the waiting SUV.

I squeezed onto his arm, holding it like it was a lifeline.

"Olivia, are you pregnant?" one of them called and I stumbled, caught off guard by the question.

"Keep going, sweetheart," Walker urged as the photographers rushed toward us, their cameras clicking and flashing with an almost deafening intensity.

Walker continued to position his body as a shield between me and the advancing horde.

"Back the fuck off," he snarled as they continued to yell out questions.

Finally, we reached the car. Walker threw open the door and practically threw me inside as he slid in behind me. It was quieter inside, but the cameras continued to flash through the windows, capturing our every move, our every expression.

A cameraman battered on the window as the driver cursed and pulled away, trying to avoid running them over and causing another news story.

I sank back into my seat, my hands trembling in my lap as the adrenaline slowly began to ebb away, leaving behind a hollow sense of disbelief. That had been a...nightmare.

Except...

I stared down where my fingers were still intertwined with Walker's, his presence beside me a comfort I'd never had before.

"Fuck, sweetheart. That was intense," he muttered, and a giggle slipped from my lips. Because I wasn't sure that "intense" was the right word for what had just happened.

Bedlam perhaps?

"Welcome to my world," I told him, searching his face for a sign that he was about to run away screaming.

Instead, he brushed a kiss against my lips and then our connected hands.

"Happy to be here," he told me.

And the funny thing was...I thought he was telling the truth.

CHAPTER 19
WALKER

"**M**y bro, the up and coming Hollywood *starlet*," Cole drawled as I picked up the phone. I was walking down the sidewalk towards the restaurant where my PI had told me Jolette and Marco were currently dining.

A man on a mission so to speak.

"Starlet?" I muttered, pulling my phone away from my ear to see where the hell I was going.

"Didn't know you had such a pretty face for the camera, Walkie Poo."

"I'm literally on TV every time I play," I reminded him, trying to relax my shoulders and walk through all the reasons I couldn't just shoot both of them when I got to the restaurant.

Prison time.

Lack of conjugal visits with Olivia.

That last one being the important one.

"You have that ugly mask hiding your face though. No one knew the legend that was hiding underneath. You're like the girl in the movies where the guy takes her glasses off and suddenly she's the hottest girl in school."

"Why exactly do you keep comparing me to girls?" I complained, glancing down at my GPS again.

"What can I say, I've got women on the brain."

"Is that different than usual?" I asked, going ahead and putting him on speakerphone because now I needed to check the camera feed I'd had installed in Olivia's apartment. I'd submitted a complaint about a gas leak for her floor and then had my guy show up pretending to be the contractor hired to check it out. When he'd "inspected" Olivia's apartment, he'd installed the little cameras that Lincoln and Ari had told me about.

I didn't know what it said that my two best friends also had cameras in their places so they could see their girls whenever they weren't there...but I figured it was a circle of trust thing. Like the dick decorations.

A circle of trust thing that we would never tell another living soul.

She was sitting on her couch, playing with her guitar, and I traced the screen like a fucking lunatic, wishing I was there listening to her right now.

Baby steps though. This "meeting" was necessary for Olivia and I to move to the next level.

Sacrifices must be made.

"I'm on a pussy break," Cole announced, reminding me he was still on the phone. "Walker?" he pressed when I didn't respond for a second.

"Sorry, I just about dropped dead with shock. I needed a second to process what you just said."

He huffed like he was mortally offended.

"I accidentally bedded a stage five clinger last night, Walk. She tried to rip a hole in the condom...while it was on my dick... so I could get her pregnant. She pulled up wedding dresses on her phone while I was still inside her." He sounded completely terrified just telling me about it.

It did sound...kind of terrifying. If the girl wasn't Olivia. I'd gladly look at dresses with her while she was on my dick. I'd gladly do anything she wanted in that position.

"Sounds like you weren't doing a very good job if she was

bored enough to start surfing the web, Cole. Maybe that legendary Davis stamina skipped you."

"Har, Har. That was not the case," he snapped. "It's because I was so good that she was doing that. She was trying to trap me!"

"Keep telling yourself that, brother," I teased. "She wasn't properly dickmatized is the only thing I'm hearing right now."

"I hate you," he muttered as I finally got to the restaurant.

"Love you too, Coco Bean," I told him, smiling as he snorted at my use of his childhood nickname. "I gotta go though."

"Fiiine," he complained, "go get your picture taken again. Try the left side this time though, because the right side was a little lacking." I was chuckling as we said our goodbyes and hung up.

The smile on my face faded right off when I remembered what I was about to do.

It hadn't been my favorite thing to tip off the photographers about where Olivia was going to be coming out, but I needed to be seen with her...and I needed it to be everywhere.

It had worked out exactly as I wanted it to. The gossip headlines had been full of us.

"Has Love Tamed Music's Wild Child?"

"Rebel with a new cause?: Olivia Darling and NHL's Prince Charming Dating?"

"Prince Charming and the Frog Princess?"

The headlines infuriated me, but they served my purpose. Me dating Olivia was good for her reputation.

And I knew of two people who were desperate for that.

Even though they had been the ones to ruin and trash Olivia's reputation in the first place.

Fuckwads.

I put on my *Lincoln Daniels* face as I walked into the restaurant. The one that said I was the king of badassery, a prince among men. And all these fuckers were just lucky to breathe the same air as me.

Wasn't sure I quite had it down, but I'd been practicing in the mirror and I believed it was an achievable goal.

And as we all knew...achievable goals were important.

I didn't need to ask the hostess where they were sitting. As usual for two people who craved the spotlight but didn't have an ounce of talent between them, they were seated at the most visible table at the restaurant.

Not my favorite thing since I did need this part of the plan to be incognito, but at least this place wasn't a paparazzi hotspot. And everyone around didn't seem to give a damn who was sitting around them, they were just here for the food.

I only got a little satisfaction from their shocked expressions as I slid into the empty chair at their table.

Jolette gaped at me for a second before remembering she was a frigid ice bitch and was supposed to play it cool. Marco recovered quicker, probably seeing dollar signs since I knew from doing research on him he'd recently picked up some gullible athletes to add to his clientele.

He was probably frothing at the mouth having me here.

I took a second to examine them.

I couldn't see any of Jolette in Olivia, but maybe the bitch had gotten so much plastic surgery you couldn't tell what she really looked like anymore. Her ice blonde hair was perfectly coiffed, her skin stretched tight over her bones, giving her the appearance of a porcelain doll with a cruel smile. Her eyes, cold and calculating, swept over me, and I held in my shiver because she honestly looked like she wanted to eat me alive.

"What can we do for you, Walker Davis?" she purred, and the sound of her voice was like a knife in the ear.

My dick was shrinking listening to her. I would have to measure it when I got home because I might have just lost two inches just being in her presence.

Olivia would be furious. I was pretty sure I was making her addicted to my dick.

Jolette cleared her throat and I put my bad bitch mask back

THE PUCKING WRONG DATE **223**

on, deciding that thinking about fucking her daughter was probably not a good idea at the moment.

Disinterested. That's what I needed to go for.

"Quite the contract you recently signed," Marco simpered, and I mean simpered. He resembled a scavenger, ready to pounce on any opportunity. He stunk of desperation, practically reeked of it as a matter of fact.

"I have a little proposition for you," I said, settling into my seat and grabbing a breadstick.

Their gazes were locked on me, waiting for me to continue. Marco leaned forward, eager to hear what I had to say, while Jolette remained composed, her cold blue eyes studying me intently.

"I'm sure you've seen the recent headlines. They've been quite good for your daughter." I threw down my phone, scrolling through the articles that I'm sure they'd already been through at least twice this morning.

I could feel their energy shift, both of them frothing at the mouth as they began to realize where I was going with this.

"I'm offering that I date Olivia. I need the publicity for my new gig with Dallas, and she needs the reputation boost." I flashed them what I hoped was a brilliant looking smile, the words I'd just said feeling like ash on my fucking tongue. "And we all know that dating someone like me would be good for her."

"I'm sorry," Jolette giggled, and it was too high pitched, like she'd practiced how to sound like a demented clown child for hours before this moment. "I'm struggling to understand what Olivia can offer you. Besides her most likely diseased *cunt*."

I blinked slowly, because...I knew she was an evil bitch, but I had *not* expected those words to come out of her mouth. I clenched my fists under the table, struggling to keep a calm facade and not knock her out.

As a rule, I was against hitting women, but this "cunt" in front of me wasn't a woman.

She was a monstrous bitch.

"Now Jolette, try and keep calm. I know it's difficult with everything she's put us through," cooed Marco, smoothing his slicked back hair like he thought he was some kind of Bond villain.

I pasted on a smile, this time not channeling Lincoln because I didn't want Jolette to start humping my leg...something she felt dangerously close to doing.

"Easy. I need a little something to set me apart in Dallas. The team's full of All Stars. It's easy to fade into the background with people like Lincoln Daniels and Ari Lancaster in the building."

"Don't forget about Camden James. That was quite the offseason for Dallas," added Marco.

I nodded because Camden was a baller.

I shrugged though, like all of it meant nothing. "What better way to do that than to date Olivia and be the man responsible for bringing her back in the limelight?"

Jolette's gross flirty smile remained in place, but I could see the gears turning in her mind. Marco, on the other hand, looked positively ecstatic at the idea, as if he could already see the dollar signs in his future.

This whole conversation made me feel the worst kind of dirty, and I was hoping it could hurry up so I could get as far away from these people as possible.

I was going to destroy these two fools. Make them wish they'd never been born.

"Do you understand, Mr. Davis...that we *own* Olivia?" Jolette finally asked slowly as she stared me down, holding a finger up when Marco tried to interject something.

I swallowed down my rage...and kept my face blank. "Why do you think I'm here?" I said lightly.

She tipped her head at me, obviously liking that answer.

"It *will* mean she has to move to Dallas. I can't have a relationship with someone in L.A. during the season. That's not going to do anything for me."

I'd brought up the idea of moving and Olivia had refused to even talk about it, thinking it was impossible.

Hopefully she'd be pleased with this little change.

Jolette's nails tapped on the table.

"That's fine," agreed Marco, sounding like he was getting bored with the conversation as he picked up his phone and fired off a text. "Her Dallas gig went perfectly. I'll plan a few more of those and that, combined with new headlines with you, and we'll be golden."

Jolette nodded, her piercing gaze still trying to dig a hole into my forehead.

I stood up to leave and Jolette held up one taloned red fingernail. "Why were you with my daughter the other night, Mr. Davis?"

I plastered on another smile.

"Getting a meeting with you," I winked, pretending her answering blush and cackle didn't make me want to be sick.

I walked out of the restaurant, their numbers in my phone, feeling like I needed to take a scalding hot shower to wash off the nastiness of what I'd just done.

As I was learning though...sometimes when you found the *right* girl...to get her...you had to do all the *wrong* things.

———

"Would you move to Dallas if they agreed?" I asked later as she was laying in my arms on her couch while we watched a movie.

She froze, and then finally laughed, the sound fake and wrong in my ears. "It's a little early to talk about something like that," she finally said.

I frowned, wondering how much I should push this issue. She *was* about to move to Dallas. It would be nice if she was happy about it.

"What's early? I'm in. You're in. We're good to go," I pressed.

She glanced up at me with wary eyes. "Why are you pushing this? What's the rush?"

"I have to leave soon for Dallas. I'd like for you to come with me," I answered quietly.

She sighed, and I hated the sound of it. "I'm sorry. I can't—I can't rush this thing between us. I have too much to lose."

I understood what she was saying. But it didn't mean that I had to accept it.

"Olivia—"

"Don't," she sprung out of my arms and turned to face me, the soft flicker of the television playing across her beautiful features. "You don't understand. I'm a *mess*. Every day I'm just holding it together. You've seen me at my best, believe it or not, and what's happened between us? A couple of panic attacks... lots of crying. That's just the beginning."

I opened my mouth to tell her I didn't care about that, that I was there for her no matter what.

But she shook her head ferociously.

"I had to distract myself for hours today because I wanted those pills. The same pills that I took every day for *years*. The same ones that made me an idiot, and let them take everything from me little by little because I was so high." Olivia shook her head and my chest *ached* seeing how much she hated herself. She stood up. "I can't jump headfirst into something with you, Walker. Even if you seem like 'Prince Charming'. Even if you seem like the best fucking thing that's ever happened to me. Moving to Dallas is definitely jumping in headfirst," she ended quietly.

"Come here," I growled, watching her lower lip tremble.

"Why?" she whispered.

"Come *here*," I pressed again, and this time she practically threw herself into my arms, burying her face in my neck, her whole body shaking.

Oh sweetheart, I'm going to take care of everything, I vowed silently.

No matter what it took.

———

Olivia

"I'd like to think there is a place for us, all the people that walk around perpetually empty, with something missing inside of them. Somewhere where we can belong, and exist without this...pain," I murmured against his skin as he held me through yet another one of my meltdowns.

He gently lifted me off his chest, his stare burning into my tear stained gaze. "There is a place," he told me fiercely, making me want to die with the devotion in his eyes. "I was put on this earth to be *that* place. To be those missing pieces."

I just continued to look at him. I wanted to believe him. But every person I'd ever met had only made those missing pieces bigger.

I'd *like* to think that place actually exists.

But I don't tell him that I don't.

"I want to be wrapped in your skin...in your bones. I want every piece of you, all over me. There isn't anything about you that I don't want. That I don't covet," he whispered. "There's nothing you could show me that's going to make me change my mind."

"Change your mind?"

"That you're mine. Your body belongs to me. Your heart belongs to me. Your soul. Is. Mine."

He kissed me like he owned me.

And as I settled back into his chest...I was a little afraid that he did.

CHAPTER 20

OLIVIA

"**W**e're moving you to Dallas," Jolette said, a minute in to her unexpected visit.

Walker had held me all night after my emotional collapse before leaving to go work out this morning.

But I was feeling very…exposed at the moment. Like all of my work keeping my emotions under wraps the last two years had been destroyed.

"What?" I almost slapped myself because there was no way I'd heard her right.

"Marco and I have decided L.A. isn't the place for you. You've been floundering here. One weekend in Dallas and you transformed. Look at the blush in your cheeks." She gestured to me as if I was able to see myself. "It's clear this is the right move."

I opened my mouth to say…to say what?

It felt like kismet almost. Like the universe had taken the wish I was fighting against, and wouldn't admit I wanted…and was somehow giving it to me.

"Why Dallas?" I murmured.

"Doesn't your cousin have a house there? Isn't that why they held the wedding there? And besides, it's where you grew up. Besides L.A., it's the closest thing to home you've ever known."

I frowned, because she'd never cared about that before. A sly smile crept up on her lips.

"And isn't that where that boy you're seeing will be living?"

My heartbeat spiked. It was the first time she'd mentioned Walker to me since the weekend in Dallas. I'd been waiting for it every day. And here it was.

"That is where he's living. But I—I just met him," I told her.

She was telling me what I wanted to hear—or at least what I thought I wanted to hear...but she was *almost* being nice.

I didn't have a single memory of Jolette being nice to me. Not even when I'd sang that first day and caught Marco's eye. What the hell was going on?

"Well, regardless. Let's think of Dallas as a fresh start. If you can turn it around there, who knows...maybe the conservatorship won't be necessary anymore."

I was dreaming. That had to be what was happening.

"I'm sorry—I still don't understand. You've barely let me leave in two years. And now...now you're just letting me go?" I whispered, very suspicious. Last time I'd thought she was being *reasonable*, I'd ended up drugged with my entire life taken away.

What was the catch?

She sighed, and sat down on the couch, looking dare I say...tired?

"Nothing has gone to plan these past few years. And... you've won. You've quit life. You haven't cared about anything...I'm just...done fighting with you," Jolette said stiffly, her face blank as she stared at me.

It was happening. Hope was creeping into my chest, set to destroy me once again.

But fuck. I wanted it. I'd refused to admit it to Walker last night, but I did want it. The thought of actually escaping the suffocating grip of L.A...I hadn't even let myself dream it.

"Do I have a choice?" I finally said, when other words failed me, even though I regretted them as soon as they came out of my mouth.

"Do you want a choice?"

She got up from the couch, letting that question stew in the air, and for the first time since this whole hell had started...I wasn't sure.

Jolette left without another word, leaving me to stress over what had happened.

It only took a little bit for a small smile to finally tug at the corners of my lips.

I picked up the phone and called Walker.

"Hi, angel," he said, his sexy voice hitting me all the way to my core.

"You still want me to move to Dallas?" I asked hesitantly, nervous excitement building inside me.

"Are you serious?" he growled. "Because this isn't a funny joke, baby."

"I'm serious. I'm moving to Dallas."

"I'll make sure you don't regret it," he swore.

"This is me diving in headfirst," I whispered, and I could hear his answering sigh of relief like it was a physical caress.

"I'm diving right in there with you."

Walker

I watched Olivia sleep, marveling at her perfection, counting the freckles on her olive skin, tracing her lips with my gaze....falling more and more into obsession.

She looked so peaceful right now, all the sadness and anxiety bled out of her.

But that peace would disappear when she woke up. I knew that for a fact.

There was a storm inside of her, and although she may have sounded excited about moving today, I knew that her mood could change with the wind.

I'd held her last night, saw the misery in her eyes, the hesitation...the lack of belief in me...in us.

I'd said this before, but it was more true than ever. She was a flight risk, always on the edge of running away.

It hadn't been a long time, the rational part of my brain was well aware of that...but there was a part of me that wasn't sure she'd ever be able to trust.

Sometimes broken things stayed broken no matter what you did.

My mom was proof of that.

I wasn't prone to panic, but there was nothing that got me closer to the edge than imagining her leaving me.

As I lay there beside her, my resolve settled in my chest.

It wasn't enough for her to move.

It wasn't even enough for her to move in with *me*.

It wouldn't even be enough for me to get her to marry me.

I needed to tie her to me forever...and there was only one real way to do that.

I slipped out of bed, careful not to wake her up. Making my way to the bathroom, my steps were silent against the cool tile floor. The small package of birth control pills sat on the counter —she kept it out so she never forgot to take it.

I stared at the packet for a long moment, knowing this was way different than poking a few holes in a condom.

I reached for the pills with a steady hand though, carefully replacing the contents with sugar pills I'd gotten online, the act feeling completely exhilarating. I needed to research how long it took for birth control to wear off.

Looks like there was going to be a new "Daddy" in the Circle of Trust.

And it was *not* Lincoln Daniels.

I made sure to put the packet back exactly where she'd had it, a sense of satisfaction washing over me. Satisfaction and peace.

A snort slipped out of me and I wondered if I'd actually gone mad.

Because I was totally pulling the goalie so to speak.

Look at me go.

I returned to the bed, a big crazy grin on my face as I slipped beneath the covers and nuzzled into her warm, perfect body for a second before I propped myself up on my arm, and continued to watch her sleep.

The night stretched on, and as I lay there beside her, I let the madness settle in, becoming who I was.

This girl was mine.

CHAPTER 21
WALKER

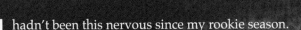

I hadn't been this nervous since my rookie season.

That was a fact.

The Dallas Knights logo loomed large before me on the wall, somehow looking way more intimidating than a Cobra.

Despite the fact that I was nervous as fuck, there was a sense of rightness in the air.

This was where I belonged.

"As I live and breathe," Ari announced in an exaggerated southern accent the second I'd stepped into the locker room. "Is that Walker Davis?"

"I literally just saw you yesterday for tacos," I said with a raised eyebrow.

Ari's gaze flicked from me to Lincoln, who was getting dressed.

"Don't do it," Lincoln muttered, already shaking his head.

"Seriously don't," I pleaded as I set my stuff down in front of a locker with a shiny new nameplate above it.

"That's what she said," Ari burst out, while everyone in the locker room groaned.

Lincoln snapped him with his towel. "It's your first fucking day of practice."

Ari crossed his arms and leaned against the wall behind him.

"I like to think of last season as an extended vacation," he drawled. "It's like I never left."

I began to get dressed, still nervous, my gaze darting around the locker room to all the faces. Most of them were familiar from playing against each other in the league, but I didn't know everyone. Plus, despite the fact that you would have thought I would be desensitized about playing on the same team with Lincoln, I was very much freaking the fuck out.

"I'm in the building," a voice announced, and I glanced over with one eyebrow raised to see one of the new rookies, Logan York, strutting his way into the locker room.

"Lord, spare me," a voice said from next to me, and I glanced over to see Camden James, also a new addition to the team, settling onto the bench next to me.

"You mean you didn't think you were God's gift to hockey when you first started, James?" Lincoln said sarcastically, shooting Logan an annoyed look that the guy must not have noticed...because I would have been shitting myself if he'd stared at me like that.

"He probably doesn't remember that far back. You've been in the League for what, a million years?" Logan said, coming to sit on the other side of Camden.

Camden scoffed and rolled his eyes so far back in his head, I was a little amazed.

Logan lifted off his shirt to change, revealing the fact that every inch of exposed skin seemed to be covered in ink, the intricate designs weaving their way across his arms and creeping up his neck. And he had...I blinked, my eyes catching on the fact that he had piercings in both nipples.

"Is there anywhere you don't have ink?" Ari asked, the question we probably all had on our minds.

Logan winked, a smirk creeping on his lips. And then his gaze shot to Lincoln. "I'm saving my dick."

Ari and I cracked up, but Lincoln looked decidedly less amused.

"I don't get it," Camden whispered to me, staring at Ari as he cackled.

"Oh...you haven't heard, Hero? Lincoln Daniels here has his girl's name tattooed on his dick," Logan drawled.

Lincoln huffed, a small smile on his lips that looked a little psycho, like he was already imagining Logan's punishment.

"Real men have dick tattoos, York. You'd do well to remember that," drawled Camden, of course getting *all* of our attention.

"Well, well, well...this is going to be an interesting year," Ari snorted, his gaze bouncing all over the room. "They'll probably want us to make some kind of calendar or something. A '12 Months of Decorated Dicks' kind of motif."

I shifted in my seat grumpily, thinking about the fact that Olivia had thought I had a fucking STD thanks to *my* "decorated dick." A tattoo would have been much better.

I glanced up and Ari was smirking at me. "You're like a true 'Swiftie' with yours, Disney," he whispered, and Lincoln snorted, shaking his head again, because sometimes...that's all you could do with Ari Lancaster.

"Is your nickname, 'Hero', or is Logan trying to be funny?" Lincoln asked as he began to put on his skates.

Logan grinned, answering before Camden could. "Oh it's 'Hero' alright. He once jumped off the ice in the middle of a game because he'd passed a fan who was choking. Gave her CPR and everything." He cocked his head mischievously. "She was really hot, so maybe it wasn't entirely selfless though, was it, James?"

Camden's cheeks were red.

"Oh my gosh. You totally fucked her after that," snorted Ari, staring at Camden with a little awe.

Camden stood up from the bench. "She *was* really hot and wanted to show her appreciation. Who was I to say no?" He turned to Logan who was grinning from ear to ear. "But also, how do you even know about that?"

"I was at that game sitting in the stands, old man. Saw the whole thing."

There was a moment of silence and then everyone in the locker room burst into hysterics.

"Yeah, yeah, laugh at the old guy," growled Camden, flipping us all off.

"Stop fucking around and get on the ice," one of the coaches growled from the doorway, and I snapped to attention, freaking out a little because I wanted to make a good first impression.

"Relax, Walker," murmured Lincoln, clapping a hand on my shoulder as we walked down the tunnel that led out onto the ice. I nodded, not sure why I felt fucking sick all of a sudden.

"How's 'Operation Become a Disney Dad'?" Ari whisper-yelled as we got onto the ice, causing me to trip and almost bite it.

"Thank you for that," I hissed as I skated to where the coaches and players were gathering at center ice.

"Well?" Lincoln asked, a smirk on his face.

"It's in operation," I said vaguely.

"Wait! You're actually doing it?" Ari's face was complete shock.

I stared at him, bemused. "Of course."

Lincoln clapped me on the back with a confusing chuckle, but evidently I'd pushed Ari over the edge.

"I thought you were kidding. I thought it was a joke," he said, skating next to me.

I raised an eyebrow. "Ahh. You must have been distracted by the queso that night. Or the tequila shots. Or somehow convincing me to get a fucking dick piercing—Yep, it was probably that."

Ari's gaze darted between Lincoln and I. "Golden Boy, you are a bad, bad influence. I blame you for warping poor Disney's mind."

"Who's warping Disney's mind?" asked Camden as he skated up behind us.

"One second, Hero. This is a meeting between the 'Circle of Trust.' Inner circle members only," Ari said belligerently, holding up a hand.

Camden cocked his head. "What the hell is the 'Circle of Trust'?"

Before Ari could answer, Coach Porter cleared his throat, and I ignored Ari's mutterings, my ginormous contract feeling like a million pound weight on my head.

"Alright, Knights, listen up," he began, his voice echoing across the rink. "Today marks the beginning of a new journey—a new journey filled with a lot of new faces. There's going to be growing pains, challenges, triumphs, and everything else in between. But make no mistake, gentlemen, we...are here to win."

"Fuck yeah we are!" yelled Logan, and Coach smirked.

"You've put in the work. You're the best of the best or you wouldn't be a Dallas Knight." His gaze hovered on me for a second like he could see my current headspace. "Now it's time to show the world what we're made of." He held up a finger. "Success is not given, it's earned. It's earned through hard work, dedication, and unwavering commitment to the game. So let's show those motherfuckers this season what Dallas Knights are made of!"

Lincoln immediately started up a Knights! chant, and we huddled together before breaking to begin practice.

As practice started, I settled into my position between the pipes, the weight of my goalie pads providing a sense of comfort and familiarity. The sound of pucks clacking against the boards and the rhythmic thud of skates on ice surrounded me, grounding me in the moment.

This wasn't so different. I could do this shit.

As the forwards and defensemen began their drills, I focused on warming up, stretching my muscles, and loosening up my joints. The first few shots that came my way were routine, easily deflected with a quick flick of my glove or a swift kick of my leg pads.

"Atta boy, Walker," Lincoln said as he skated behind the net.

I really needed to examine this praise-kink thing. Olivia giving me a few "atta boys" might be the death of me judging by my reaction anytime Lincoln Daniels said...well, anything.

Practice progressed, and I got my ass kicked in a rapid-fire shooting drill that consisted of half the team sending a barrage of shots at me from all directions.

I'd just begun to find my rhythm when Coach decided on a series of breakaway drills that required me to face off against the forwards one on one.

I braced myself as Lincoln charged towards me, the puck dancing on the blade of his stick as he closed the distance between us. His movements were fluid and calculated, each stride carrying him closer to the net with purpose and precision.

As he reached the hash marks, he unleashed a lightning-quick deke, shifting the puck from side to side in an attempt to throw me off balance. Instinctively, I tracked his movements, my eyes locked on the puck as I anticipated his next move.

He burst forward, attempting to slide the puck between my legs and into the net. I dropped into a split, my pads closing off the five-hole just in time to deny his shot.

The puck ricocheted off my pads with a satisfying thud, sending it flying harmlessly into the corner of the rink.

"Fuck," Lincoln muttered, tipping his head at me.

"Walker 'Disney' Davis you are a mother fucking wall," yelled Ari as he skated by.

I grinned.

"Why does he look so happy about blocking Lincoln's shot? He's stopped like five of mine," Logan complained.

"Have you met Disney? He'd eat Golden Boy's lunch leftovers if he'd let him," announced Ari.

"You sound jealous, Lancaster," Logan drawled, ducking at the puck Ari shot at him.

The whistle blew and we skated to the bench for a break. I

glanced at the clock. It had been two hours. I wondered what Olivia was doing.

I watched as Lincoln slipped his phone out from under a towel and Monroe popped up on the screen.

'What?" he asked without looking at me. "You think I'm going to go hours without checking up on her? That's a rookie mistake, Walk. A rookie...mistake."

Note to self, hide my phone next practice so I could stalk Olivia during breaks. Wouldn't want to be a rookie.

"Oh, shoot, let me help you with that," said Camden from nearby. I glanced over to see him awkwardly trying to pick up towels that a female employee had dropped. Ari snorted as Camden almost fell over as he grabbed one.

"I'm getting it now," he mused. "I'm definitely seeing the 'Hero' nickname."

"Right?" Logan said, crossing his arms and cocking his head as he stared at the girl giving moon eyes to Camden for his help. "It's very, very effective with the ladies, though. The amount of ass that guy gets is legendary."

Camden waved at the girl, looking nothing but polite, and then turned and hopped back onto the ice.

"Note to self, Camden James is not allowed near my lady," Ari said breezily, playing with a puck as we started back with practice.

I made a mental note as well. You know...just in case.

———

I was dead tired, but eager to get back to Olivia. She'd been staying at my house while she worked to find a place. Usually Jolette would have arranged all her housing accommodations, but since the whole goal was for her to be around me as much as possible—that hadn't happened. Olivia had no idea about that, of course, and since I was paying her realtor to *not* find a place for her to move into, I had myself the loveliest, most perfect roommate of all time at the moment.

Lincoln had parked near me in one of his sports cars, and he was silent as he walked, texting someone—i.e. Monroe—as we walked.

"See ya," I told him as I unlocked my truck.

"Hey, I just wanted to say something," Lincoln said, before I could climb in the cab.

He sounded like he had his "Captain Linc" voice on, and I was immediately nervous.

"What's up?"

"I don't know everything that's happened with Olivia, but what I do know is that most likely she's going to find out someday all about it."

Well, fuck. Hadn't expected this conversation today.

I eyed him warily.

"Just be prepared," he said. "She'll want to run...and I'd suggest not letting her."

With those wise...and foreboding words...he walked to his car and got in.

I had fucking goosebumps.

I was deep in thought the entire drive home, going well over the speed limit because his words had made me fucking anxious.

What if she wasn't there when I got back?

What if one day she left, and I never found her again?

As I pulled into the driveway and threw the truck into park, I'd all but convinced myself I was going to walk in and she wasn't going to be there.

All my worries disappeared when I walked into the house.

And there she was.

Olivia was sitting in one of my t-shirts on the couch, strumming on her guitar. The way her eyes lit up when she saw me...if I hadn't been in love already, I would have been now.

"Honey, I'm hoooome," I called to her dramatically as I set

my bag on the floor, trying to cover up the fact that I'd been freaking out for the past twenty minutes.

Her answering laugh settled something inside me.

"How was practice?" she asked as I stood there hesitantly.

Finally, I decided, "fuck it", and embraced my desperation by walking over to the couch and lifting her up, settling her on my lap so I could wrap myself around her.

I took a second to breathe her in, until my heart stopped pounding and I'd convinced myself she was really here.

She was quiet, probably sensing my mood even though I was trying my best to hide it.

"How was practice?' she asked softly, as the mood in the room drifted into some sort of dreamy subspace.

"The team's fucking incredible. I can just feel it, ya know... this year is going to be special." She laid her head back on my shoulder and softly stroked my arm.

"Stanley Cup all the way."

"Shhh. You can't say that. It's bad luck!" I said, putting a hand over her mouth. She bit down on my hand and I growled, hardening underneath her.

I was learning all sorts of things about my sexual preferences lately. Biting included.

"Have you been working on a new song?" I asked and she nodded, shyly almost, like she didn't know what I'd think about that.

"Am I allowed to hear it?" I murmured.

She paused for a moment. "Of course."

I picked her up and cradled her in my arms, her guitar still in her hands.

"What are you doing?" she said with a laugh.

"I have an idea. I think you should sing while we're in bed."

"In bed, huh?"

"Yep, in bed. While I'm inside of you. This might be the best idea I've ever had."

She snorted.

"Well, what do you think?" I asked, kicking the door of the bedroom open since I didn't want to let her go.

"It's definitely worth experimenting with," she said seriously.

"I like that attitude, Jones," I murmured, gently laying her on the bed. She stared up at me, her features softened in the fading light. Every time I saw her she took my breath away.

Sometimes I wondered if she'd stepped out of a dream, a dark dream, where all of the things I wanted most in life had been captured inside one person—a person I had to sell my fucking soul to get. With her hair splayed out around her like a halo, and her delicate features illuminated by the softening light, she really looked like an angel.

Every curve of her face, every line and contour, was perfect, a testament to the sheer artistry of her existence. I traced the curve of her face with my fingertips, marveling at everything about her —the way her lashes brushed against her cheeks, the way her lips arched into a smile. She surpassed anything I had ever known. Sometimes it felt like I'd been granted a glimpse of paradise—a paradise that was destined to lead me to hell as I chased after it.

"I'm obsessed with you," I murmured, and she smiled, because she thought I was joking.

Leaning down, I brushed my lips down her neck, the answering sigh making my cock even harder.

I stood up.

"Now get undressed."

———

Olivia

Looking at him up close like this…it was almost overwhelming. It should be outlawed for a man to be so pretty. I wanted to lick him all over…and I'd finally decided…that wasn't weird.

Considering I spent today alone, it was one of the best days that I had experienced in a long time. Being in a place where Jolette and Marco weren't allowed to barge in. Feeling safe. Having Walker's things around me…It was a level of comfort I hadn't had maybe…ever.

Seeing all the pictures online of myself around town with Walker hadn't even bothered me. I had even saved some of them because I loved how we looked like we belonged together in them.

That had certainly never happened before. The headlines had even been, dare I say…nice.

For the first time in a long time, I'd picked up a guitar…and the words had just come.

I hadn't even realized how much time had passed until Walker was unlocking the door and he'd walked in.

"What are you thinking about right now, angel?" he murmured, his hand stroking down my skin.

"That I feel happy," I whispered, biting down on my lip because the words felt strange to say.

His answering grin was blinding.

"That's my only goal, nowadays, so I'm glad that I'm inching closer."

I pulled on his shoulders so he was leaning over me, pressing a soft kiss against his lips. I'd never imagined I could feel comfortable with someone like this. So quickly.

I was already hating the thought of moving out when I found my own place.

"Tell me something no one else knows about you, and then I'm going to fuck you while you sing to me," he said in that same soft, romantic tone he'd been using since he got home.

My mouth dropped open, and he had the audacity to wink at me, like he hadn't just *ruined* my panties.

"You first," I ordered.

Walker straddled me and pulled on the t-shirt, yanking it off. "One of these days I'm going to fuck you in my t-shirt…and then in my jersey…but that's going to have to wait for another day. I've got a specific fantasy of you playing the guitar naked, and that's what I'm hoping you'll give me today."

I could feel my skin heating up as he removed the jean shorts I'd been wearing as well.

A second later, the panties and bra somehow seemed to magically disappear, and I was lying naked underneath him. Luckily for me, he'd undressed as well this time.

"There," he said, with an air of satisfaction. "Now everything's perfect."

I rolled my eyes but made no move to cover myself. I liked him looking at me as if he'd die if he looked away.

I got hungry looks from people all the time, but it was for 'Olivia Darling'. Walker had seen all the broken parts of 'Olivia Jones' and he was still looking at me like the sun rose and set because I existed.

He made me feel different. Like the world didn't have to be gray anymore. Like it was possible for me to live in a world where colors existed.

I wondered what it would be like if I got to keep him—at the same time hating that he'd made me think of things like that.

"Let's see. What's a new thing for you to know about me?" he mused, dragging me out of my darkening thoughts like he always did.

"You mean what's something no one knows about you," I corrected him, and he kissed me, like my sassy mouth turned him on.

That or he was trying to shut me up.

Regardless, I was a big fan of his methods.

"Ready for this one, because there's a 'before' and there's an 'after' you find this out. And there's no going back," he told me, his tone very serious.

"Alright, give it to me, Davis."

"Last names, I like your style."

"I'm learning from the best," I said with a wink, as his gaze dipped from my face to my boobs for a second.

I'd kind of forgotten I was naked for a minute.

"Here it is. I'm scared of…pineapples."

I stared at him for a second. "Sorry…what did you just say?"

"Well, only when they're on my pizza but…"

I poked him in the stomach and huffed. "I thought we were being serious. I'm literally laying here, butt naked, desperate for you to fuck me."

"I'm well aware. But please feel free to say "fuck me" again. Because that was fucking hot."

"Tell me something real," I insisted softly as his fingertips dragged along my sides.

He was quiet for a moment, seemingly lost in thought—that or he was staring at my breasts, I couldn't really tell.

"My dad died ten years ago. He woke up one day, kissed my mother, got out of bed…and then just died. And my mom…she might as well have died too. She's basically a zombie. A sweet, sad zombie. Every day."

I stared at him in shock. And then…in shame. How had I not known that? He seemed to know everything about me…and this was kind of a big thing.

"I'm so sorry," I whispered.

He shook his head. "I mean, it's a terrible story. And it fucking sucks for my mom. But I—I get it now."

"You get it now?" I said, confused.

"Losing you, I couldn't come back from that. So I get it. How she feels."

I stared at him, words completely failing me, as they seemed to do quite often since I'd met him. A tear slid down my face and he watched it, fascinated for a second before he did that thing…

And licked it off.

"Tell me your something real now," he said, looking nonplussed as he lifted his tongue from my face.

"Why do you do that?" I asked, wrinkling my nose.

"What?"

"Lick my tears," I said, a weird giggle coming out of my mouth.

"I think that should be obvious, sweetheart."

"Nope, not obvious." His dick was pushing into my stomach, precum leaking out onto my skin.

He leaned over me again so that his lips were brushing against my ear. "Because I want all of you. I covet you. I want your tears, your cum, your words, your breath. I want everything."

My entire body reacted violently to his words, and my core fluttered. I was pretty sure I could have an orgasm just from the sound of his voice...especially when he was saying crazy things like that.

"I want to hear your song now, and I want to fuck you," he murmured.

And how could I argue with that?

In one smooth move, he rolled us over so that I was now lying on top of him. I grabbed his dick, my hand barely fitting around it as I eased my hand up and down his long, perfect length. I could see my name beaded down his dick from this angle.

And like usual, the evidence of his crazy made me so fucking hot.

He squeezed and played with my nipples as I played with his dick, his half lidded gaze watching my hands move.

A hand moved to my clit and he lazily caressed it, his fingers grazing over the sensitive bud and driving me crazy. I squeezed his dick harder as my insides lightly spasmed, watching as beads of precum slid down the head of his dick.

So. Fucking. Hot.

"Ride me, sweetheart. Squeeze my dick with that perfect cunt, and ride me."

I slid his tip along my wet slit, moaning at the sensation. He was watching me avidly, that awestruck look in his gaze again.

"Stop teasing me, sweetheart," he groaned as his hands slid along my skin.

I lifted up and slowly lowered myself onto his dick, inch by inch, groaning as he stretched me far beyond what was comfortable.

My head fell back, my breath coming out in gasps as his balls fit against the curve of my ass.

"Wow," I muttered, and he laughed, the vibration of his body too much for my current position.

"You're so tight. How are you so tight every fucking time?" he growled. "Fuck."

I rocked up, a squelching sound filling the air because of how completely *soaked* I was. And then I slammed down, the head of his dick hitting so freaking deep. My hands dug into his chest and I leaned forward, trying to ride him harder. My clit rubbed against the base of his dick as he massaged my breasts.

My core clenched and he growled.

"Fuck. Look at you. Riding my cock like a fucking queen. You're soaking my dick. You were made for me." He pumped up into me, perfectly in sync with the roll of my hips.

"Yes, yes, yes," I chanted, my orgasm approaching. His abs were clenching underneath my fingertips and I whimpered as his hips thrust into me. "Almost," I cried as he did some kind of hot guy sit up move and sucked on my nipple, biting down softly and pushing me into an orgasm.

My core squeezed around his length as pleasure surged down my spine. I fell forward and he continued to fuck into me.

"I love you," he murmured, and my eyes flew open.

What had he just said?

His cum filled me in hot bursts as he came. It spilled out, wetting my thighs and the base of his cock.

I was still staring at him, and he cocked his head, reaching up and smoothing my hair out of my face as his thrusts slowed.

"Still want me to play?" I whispered, and he nodded, a tiny

smirk on his lips, like he knew I was freaking out about what he'd just said and trying to distract us both from the fact of it.

"Please," he said, his dick twitching inside me.

I carefully grabbed my guitar that was somehow still intact on the bed beside us, more liquid seeping out as I moved.

He groaned a little and began to stroke the outside of my thighs, his aquamarine stare burning as he watched me. He was hardening inside me again, but I ignored it...for now. I loved being connected to him like this, filled up completely. I closed my eyes and strummed the familiar strings, and then I started singing the song that I'd written just for him—the first time I'd ever written a love song that was actually about a real someone...

In shadows deep, I wandered lost,
No shelter found, nor bridge to cross.
Then you appeared, a guiding light,
Leading me from the darkest night.

I swayed as I sang, realizing at some point that I was actually making love to him as I moved.

I couldn't call it anything else.

How could you call it "fucking" when you were baring your soul while you were doing it?

My eyes opened and I saw there was a light sheen of sweat across his forehead. His eyes were bright, his pupils blown out... almost like he was high...which maybe he was. Maybe he was high on us...high on me.

I felt the same way.

This...this was better than what any pill had ever given me.

You're my safe place, my shelter in the storm,
With you by my side, I feel reborn.
In your arms, I find my solace and my grace,
With you, I've found my hope, my love, my safe place.

I sang and my pussy clenched around him, and I felt like he'd become a part of me. Like we were two halves of one soul, somehow separated, and now we'd found our way back to each other. I stared down at him in wonder, another tear sliding down my cheek as our bodies moved together. This is what music was meant to be. This is what they meant when they said mind, body, and soul.

I felt him everywhere.

In your arms, all fears cease,

With you, my love, I find my peace.

The last notes of the song reverberated around the room and he gently pulled the guitar away from me, tossing it on the other side of the bed as he rolled us over and began fucking me in earnest.

"I love you. I love you. I love you," he chanted, his soulful gaze locked on mine.

He owned me.

He owned my body.

He owned my heart.

He owned *everything*.

I started to cum, shockwaves of pleasure everywhere, like I'd touched a livewire that energized me rather than burned.

His thrusts picked up, like if he fucked me hard enough, he'd be imprinted inside me forever.

I wasn't opposed to that idea.

"Say it," he begged, cradling my face as he kissed me desperately. "Say it," he whispered.

"I love you," slipped out of my mouth, and something happened that I never would have predicted.

I didn't regret it.

That fact was my something 'real.'

My feet dropped onto the asphalt and I glanced at the crowd of teeming people as I walked to the other side to help Olivia out of the truck. I couldn't wipe the grin off my face at seeing the horde of people trying to get in.

My big brother had hit the big time.

My lady had said "I love you."

Finally.

And my best friends were hanging out at the concert with us today.

The only thing that would be better is if Olivia had a positive pregnancy test.

This morning's test had been a *negative*...while also being one of the weirder experiences of my life.

I was in multiple pregnancy Facebook groups under an alias so I could research all this pregnancy stuff. I couldn't remember any information about ovulation cycles being taught in school— or maybe I'd blanked it out because it had been ingrained in me since almost the first time I'd picked up a stick...don't get a girl pregnant.

That was probably more likely than a hole in my education.

Regardless...I was having to play catch-up. Read weird

science articles that talked about eggs releasing, and fallopian tubes, and twenty-eight day cycles.

It was a lot.

I loved how helpful all the moms were. They were just willing to give out all this free information to whoever asked.

I didn't know how women kept track of it all. I was marking dates on my phone calendar and watching her body carefully for any signs...swollen boobs, wild emotions, dry vs. wet pussy... timing of her period. I had code words in my phone for when I thought she was supposed to ovulate...and when you could start testing with early detection pregnancy tests.

And *that* had been this morning...

"Olivia!" I burst into the bathroom, right as she'd finished peeing. She stared at me in shock. "Hurry, you have to see this... this news story!"

I was making this up as I went...but I had to get access to that toilet. As inappropriate and ridiculous as it was.

But if I was willing to poke holes in a condom to use on a girl I'd just met...this seemed like the obvious next step if I was being honest.

"Walker, I thought we talked about boundaries in the bath-room," she giggled as she pulled up her pants.

I lunged forward and tugged on her...before she had a chance to flush and realized there was a baggie spread out in the bowl.

I'd read that you couldn't test diluted pee in water accurately, so a baggie to catch her pee was all I'd come up with.

And yes, I realized how fucking weird this was.

It would have been weirder though if I'd figured out a way to catch it fresh out of her...

Lord help me.

"Go on...I'm right behind you," I urged.

"I'm just going to wash my hands first," she said, turning on the water. I gave her like two seconds before I hurried her out the door and I stabbed the pregnancy test in the baggie, setting the timer on the phone.

"I don't see anything?" her voice called.

"Keep watching!" I yelled, hoping I didn't sound as crazy as I felt.

Had that been seven seconds yet? Some of the chat groups recommended longer than that.

"Walker?"

"Coming!"

I pulled the pregnancy test out and stabbed on the lid before stuffing it under my sink to check in three to five minutes.

Scrambling to dump the baggie, I flushed the toilet and then washed my hands before heading down the hallway to the living room where Olivia was standing in front of the TV.

"There was a news story about the resurgence of killer bees, and an injury report on the Dallas Cowboys…thrilling entertainment no doubt…but why exactly did you want me to see it?"

"Hmm, they said they were about to give updates on the team. I thought you'd be interested," I lied through my teeth. Although, really, it wasn't out of the realm of possibility. We were about to have our first game.

She frowned. "Oh, I should keep watching. Maybe it's still coming," she said, because she was such a fucking supportive sweetheart. I wrapped an arm around her waist and pulled her back against me.

"Nah, I must have heard wrong. Don't worry about it, angel face."

She melted into my arms as I kissed her. "Go get ready," I said, slapping her on her perfect ass.

"I think I'm going to heat up those breakfast burritos that Mrs. Bentley gave you. I'm obsessed. Do you want one?"

Cravings were a sign of pregnancy, right?

Although anyone would crave Mrs. Bentley's burritos. They were the best thing in the world.

Well, second best thing. Obviously Olivia's pussy took the top spot.

"Yes, please," I purred, giving her another kiss before I slipped away to the bathroom to check the test.

Closing the door behind me, I stalked to the cabinet and pulled out the stick.

One blue line. One blue line…what did that mean again?

I pulled out the instructions and frowned.

Negative.

Well…I had no problem with continuing to try. It happened to be my favorite thing to do actually.

Olivia Jones *was* going to have my baby.

———

My brother had made it. He was living his dream.

That's all I could think as we pulled into the AT&T parking lot and I saw the mass of people all here to see him…and the Sounds of Us of course.

But I was pretending all these people were just here to see my brother.

Adrenaline beat beneath my skin, the same jittery feeling I got before a big game. I'd seen him start in bars, summer festivals, and now he was here…

Fuck yes.

The air around us buzzed with anticipation as I helped Olivia out of the truck, my dick stirring with how hot she looked…even with the oversized glasses and hat she was using to try and stay incognito. She was wearing a tight leather miniskirt that showed off her mile long legs, and a crop top that literally had me drooling.

I wasn't sure that the hat and sunglasses were going to do the job when you couldn't help but stare at her because she was so fucking hot.

I adjusted my dick with my free hand and she had the nerve

to smirk at my pain. She *had* stared at me for an extra long time when I'd come out with a backwards ball cap earlier though, and I'd probably given her a similar smirk. So I guess we were even.

We headed towards the VIP entrance where I could see Lincoln, Monroe, Ari, Blake...and Camden all gathered. 'Hero' was starting to grow on me...as long as he kept arms length from Olivia, of course.

"Are you okay?" I asked, checking in with her. She hated crowds, and I'd offered to miss the concert and stay home, but she'd wanted us to be there for Cole. She seemed to like the idea of supporting my family members. Probably because she'd never had anything like that. Parker and Cole had started on insisting she was on our FaceTime calls because the bastards liked to talk to her more than they liked to talk to me.

But it also made me really, really happy. As hard as it was for me to share, Olivia needed more people in her life who saw her magic.

"I'm good," she promised, laying her head on my arm as we walked.

Fuck...I was the luckiest.

As soon as I had that thought, my phone buzzed and I pulled it out, frowning and deleting the text right away. It was from Jolette—the cunt. She was "congratulating" me for the recent pictures that had been posted of Olivia skating with me on center ice at the Dallas Knight's family night.

My PI had been busy collecting everything I could on the two of them, like the doctors they'd paid off to write reports about Olivia's condition. Jeff thought he was close to finding proof of some big skeletons of Marco's as well.

I just hoped he could hurry the fuck up.

Olivia squeezed my hand, seeming nervous all of a sudden as we got to the group.

They all loved her already. Hence why we were now getting Tupperware containers filled with Mrs. Bentley's burritos. Olivia still got nervous every time we hung out though, her brain programmed to believe she couldn't have real friends.

"Olivia," Ari crowed, striding forward with his arms outstretched. It took me a second to realize what he was doing, and I immediately pulled Olivia behind my body.

"What are you doing?" I asked, horrified. Wasn't it a rule in the Circle of Trust, "Do Not Touch The Girl?"

Ari snorted, his arms still outstretched. "What's going on, Walker? I'm just trying to hug one of my new best friends."

"Lancaster, I'd rather you not die and make me be out on the ice for every second of the first game," Camden tossed out, watching the interaction like it was funny.

This was not funny.

Lincoln was also grinning though. "My, how the turntables have turned," he drawled.

Ari got sidetracked with that comment. "Turntables have turned? That was what you came up with?"

"It's in 'The Office', it's hilarious."

Ari stared at Lincoln, disgusted. "Zero points for originality, Golden Boy. Go back to the drawing board."

Blake giggled and Ari grinned as he turned his full attention to his wife. Sometimes I was pretty sure he acted so ridiculous just to make sure she was paying attention to him.

A real "Circle of Trust" move if I'd ever heard of one.

"You look so pretty," Monroe murmured to Olivia, coming over to give her a hug, side eyeing me the whole time like I was going to stab her with a fork or something.

I allowed the comment because Olivia loved Blake and Monroe..but I was still twitchy. Judging by the way Lincoln scooped Monroe back into his arms the second she'd released Olivia...he was twitchy too.

"Can we go now that all of you have successfully proven you're all psychos?" Camden casually asked.

"Listen, *Hero*, just you wait...one day you'll wake up and you'll be crazy. Just. Like. Us," commented Ari, slinging his arm around Blake and heading towards where an employee was manning the VIP entrance.

Olivia snorted at Camden's look of alarm.

We flashed our badges to gain access, and I grinned again the second we were through—there were so many fucking people here. I didn't know how Cole didn't shit his pants.

Inside the stadium the corridors were alive with the hustle and bustle of crew members preparing for the night's event. The sound of footsteps echoed off the walls, mingling with the distant hum of conversation and the faint strains of music drifting from the first opening act.

We reached the backstage area, and I snorted when I saw Cole surrounded by women. One was draped across his lap, feeding him...were those Cheetos?

I was definitely telling Parker about this.

"Walkie-poo!" Cole called when he saw me, holding up his arms before he unceremoniously dumped the girl in his lap onto the couch and stood up.

He was dressed to impress today, a cowboy hat, leather vest and tight jeans. Oh, and a feather. He had his usual enormous feather in his hat.

Might I add that my brother was not a country singer...so he kept the world guessing with his...unusual fashion choices.

"I feel like the nickname of 'Disney' shouldn't offend you so much, *Walkie-Poo*," Lincoln commented.

I didn't bother flipping him off.

Because it was true.

Cole walked right past me and then...he was scooping up Olivia. "How's my favorite girl?" he practically cooed.

"Okay, okay. Set her down," I growled.

And maybe Cole was actually Ari's long lost brother and not my own...because he fucking winked.

"Wow, Walker, I've never noticed that vein in your forehead before," Camden commented.

The rest of them chuckled and I sighed, still trying to tug Olivia from my playboy brother's clutches.

Cole finally set her down, pulling me in for a hug. Our family had always been affectionate with each other. My dad had set the tone for that. Sometimes hugging my brothers felt like I was hugging him.

"I'm glad you're here," he murmured, and another surge of pride welled up inside me.

"I'm so fucking proud of you," I replied, clapping him on the back.

Both of our eyes were suspiciously shiny when we parted, but because these guys were the best, no one commented.

"Oh. My. Gosh," squealed Monroe a second later. We all stared at her and watched as she transformed into a fan girl. "Oh my gosh, oh my gosh, oh my gosh," she whispered, her hands coming up to cover her mouth as she did this weird little jig thing.

"Monroe?" Lincoln asked, only for Blake to start doing the same thing!

It was like watching a contagious disease spread across our women.

Except instead of a disease, they were one of the world's biggest music groups.

The Sounds of Us.

I glanced down at Olivia, and at least *she* seemed relatively calm. Which was good because having Lincoln, Ari, and me going psycho right now was probably not ideal for my brother's show.

Lincoln snapped his finger a few times near Monroe's face. "Hey, remember me, your gorgeous hockey player husband who has your name tattooed on my—"

"I can't believe I'm in the same room with them," Monroe whispered as she stared at Jesse Carroway, Tanner Crosby, and Jensen Reid as they walked into the room. The girls that had just been all over my brother literally screamed. One of them burst into tears and started babbling.

"Alright, we're leaving," Lincoln growled, scooping Monroe up into his arms and taking a step backwards like he really was going to leave.

"Lincoln 'mother-fucking' Daniels, you put me down right now," Monroe said in the most fierce voice I'd ever heard her use.

Lincoln scoffed, but he stopped walking. Instead, he covered her eyes with his hand so she couldn't see the band anymore.

Olivia started laughing into the side of my shirt, her whole body shaking as she watched Blake and Monroe freak out about the band, and Lincoln and Ari freak out about their reactions to other men.

"Oh hey, that looks heavy. Need some help?" I heard Camden say as a pretty brunette walked in with a large roller bag. He'd no sooner taken a step towards her when Jensen Reid popped out of nowhere, an arm going around the woman's waist as he grabbed the suitcase from her.

"You were supposed to wait for me to help you," Jensen purred into her ear. All of a sudden, Jesse came over and pressed a kiss into her neck.

"That's Ariana Kent...she's with the band. The *whole* band," Olivia whispered to me, and I shook my head. I mean, good for them...but the idea of sharing Olivia made me feel bloodthirsty.

I would die before I ever let another man have her.

"Hey guys. You've met my brother, Walker. But that's his girl, Olivia, and these are his friends," Cole said, gesturing to the rest of the group.

"That's Lincoln Daniels," I said helpfully, pointing to the golden god.

Ari rolled his eyes. "Disney, you little simp."

"Can I have your autograph," Monroe all of a sudden squealed, her face resembling a lovely beet.

Jesse gave her wide grin that had Blake and Monroe looking

like they were going to pass out. "Yeah, of course. What do you want me to sign?"

"Your shirt," it sounded like Monroe whispered, before she shook her head. "Uh, I mean—a shirt. I'll go get a shirt, and you can sign it!"

Lincoln whispered something into her ear then and she somehow got even redder.

"Holy shit. You're—you're Olivia Darling," Tanner suddenly whisper-yelled.

"I just introduced her," Cole said with a laugh. "Also, why isn't anyone reacting like this to me? I feel left out."

"You didn't say "Olivia *Darling*!" Tanner said, his voice kind of high and squeaky. His girlfriend, Ariana, started giggling as she watched one of her boyfriends completely fall apart over my girlfriend.

I'm sure they were all very devoted to each other...but I still wrapped an arm around Olivia's waist and pulled her into my body...you know, just in case.

"Hi," Olivia said shyly, pushing a strand of hair behind her ear as she removed her sunglasses.

"How are you guys?"

"How are we?" Jesse scoffed. "How the fuck are you?"

There was a small beat of silence. "It's complicated," she finally said awkwardly.

"Here, can you sign my guitar?" Jensen asked, presenting it to Olivia eagerly, completely starstruck.

"Yeah, of course," she murmured, her voice sounding almost...touched.

She signed her name with a flourish and I decided right then and there to have her signature tattooed on me.

I couldn't believe I hadn't thought of it yet.

I was even obsessed with her handwriting.

A harried looking employee dressed in a black polo ran over. "Mr. Davis, you're up," he said to Cole.

Cole did a weird little spin move that for some reason had his female admirers swooning. I just thought he looked like an idiot. "I'll see you guys in a bit," he said with a head nod before stalking off towards the stage.

Jesse, Jensen, and Tanner needed to do some more prep before their set so we parted ways as the rest of us walked to watch Cole.

"I'm really hungry," I muttered as we looked out at the frenzied crowd waiting for my brother to come on. "Are you hungry?" I asked Ari.

"I'm a little too *traumatized* to have a hotdog, Walker," he griped.

"What's wrong with you?"

"He's jealous his wife has the hots for a world famous rock band," Camden offered, snacking on a tub of popcorn he'd literally pulled from thin air.

I frowned because I wanted some of that.

Ari scoffed, but he didn't deny it as he wrapped himself around Blake like a fucking boa constrictor. Probably to make sure a hot rockstar didn't abscond with her while his back was turned.

"I watched a clip of you performing here," I told Olivia, who'd gone silent as she stared out at the crowd, deep in thought.

She grinned, as usual looking bemused that I was such a fucking fan-boy.

"I always thought of it as my home-town crowd, ya know? So it always felt a little special," she murmured.

The crowd suddenly went wild as a guitar melody began and I glanced at the stage. A second later, my brother walked out from the side entrance across from us.

Cole's voice soared through the stadium, rich and powerful, filling the air with its soulful resonance. His voice had always captivated me, just like it did for everyone else.

It wasn't just Cole's vocals that had the crowd in a frenzy—it was his stage presence, his charisma, his undeniable star quality.

He moved across the stage with effortless grace, his dance moves fluid and confident, commanding the attention of everyone in the audience.

It gave me chills to watch him. We'd dreamed of these things as kids, me playing pro sports...him singing for crowds. Everything seems possible when you're young, but it was still crazy to see us now.

The crowd roared with applause as Cole launched into the chorus of one of his hit songs, his voice ringing out clear and strong. I nodded along to the rhythm—it was one of my favorites. I especially loved it when Olivia rubbed her ass on my dick to it.

As the final notes of the song faded away and the crowd erupted into applause, I beamed at Cole. For a second, we locked eyes, a silent acknowledgment of the fact that we'd fucking made it.

The moment passed and he started the next song, and I once again pretended I wasn't emotional.

———

Olivia

Cole had been amazing, but somehow the crowd had taken it up a notch as The Sounds of Us took the stage. I stood on the sidelines with the rest of the group, Walker's arms around me as I watched Jesse, Tanner, and Jensen command the attention of tens of thousands of adoring fans.

"Walker, I owe you my first born child," Monroe said as she watched the band perform with huge eyes, her hands over her heart as she mouthed the words to every song.

"That's not happening," Lincoln snarled as he pressed a kiss against the side of her head.

I snorted and Walker's arms tightened around me.

The song ended, and Jesse, the lead singer for the band, stepped close to the mic.

"You guys are never going to believe who came to watch us fucking play tonight," he announced, his voice carrying over the roar of the crowd. I stared out into the rows of fans like I could find the star he was talking about.

"Should we get her to come out here?" Jesse asked, grinning as the mass of people continued to scream. He glanced over to where I was standing and gave me a smirk.

"Olivia, why don't you join us?" he called out to me as my heart started beating in my ears and adrenaline began to pulse.

Walker froze as Jesse waved me forward like he'd been possessed.

"You don't have to go out there," Walker said fiercely, looking like he was ready to jump Jesse Carroway if I didn't want to do this.

I pressed a kiss to his lips and took a deep breath before pasting on my stage smile and walking out.

The cheers of what felt like all eighty thousand people swept over me with an overwhelming force, like a powerful surge of energy as I met Jesse at the microphone. Another polo wearing employee ran out and handed me a guitar.

"Hello!" I called out, pretending I wasn't terrified at the moment to have thousands of pairs of eyes staring back at me. "I'm Olivia. It's so great to be here tonight."

As I spoke, I couldn't help but steal a glance at Walker, who was watching me with a mixture of pride and concern. I offered him a reassuring smile before turning back to the crowd, my fingers trembling as I strummed a random chord.

"Imagine our surprise when the queen herself showed up tonight. Lucky us, right?" Jesse crowed as everyone continued to scream. I waved at the fans again, my smile turning...genuine as I listened to their adoration.

"Let's see if you guys know this one," I said in the mic as I strummed the first notes of one of my biggest songs. Their screams about knocked me over.

"I think they do," Tanner said with a laugh.

"Sing along then, Dallas!" I yelled. "This one's for Walker."

I winked at him and I swear he swooned.

Lost in the world, caught in the fray,

Searching for something to light my way.

But in the chaos, I found my truth,

I'm only free when I'm with you.

Usually with this big of a crowd, I wouldn't be able to lose myself. I'd be stressed and anxious, especially without any pills.

But something seemed to have changed since I'd met Walker. The songs that I used to sing about—the ones that came from me imagining my dream man, or my dream life...they weren't dreams anymore.

The lyrics poured out of me effortlessly, each word imbued with emotion as I poured my heart and soul into the song, the Sounds of Us following along smoothly like they'd been secretly practicing just in case I ever showed up to one of their shows.

The final notes faded away, and the stadium erupted into cheers and screams, the sound echoing all around me and filling me with a sense of...elation. I basked in the glow of the moment, my heart soaring as I drank in the adulation of the crowd.

Waving one last time, I gave Jesse a hug and walked offstage.

Walker scooped me into his arms the second I got within reach. "You are fucking incredible," he told me, kissing me until I wanted to climb him like a tree.

"Way to go, *sis*," Cole said, giving me a wink at my shocked expression. I side-eyed Walker to see what he thought of that, but he looked freaking ecstatic.

Blake and Monroe rushed me at once, but evidently Ari and Lincoln were a little touchy about their fan girl moment because they were only allowed to hug me for a second before they were pulled back to them.

Camden reached out an arm like he was going to hug me, but Walker pulled me back. "Disney, what's up?" Camden smirked.

"You need to stay far away from Olivia's ovaries," he

responded matter of factly, making me blush and everyone else cackle like hyenas.

"I'll put that in the 'circle of trust' rulebook I'm compiling," Camden responded. "Stay away from Olivia's ovaries."

Ari scoffed. "You are not in the 'circle of trust.'"

"I will be," Camden said with a grin.

We watched The Sounds of Us continue to rock the stage, and the hope that I'd been trying my best to keep away…

It fucking grew.

———

"Olivia!"

"Olivia! Over here!"

"Is that Blake Lancaster?"

"Holy shit," Ari commented as he put a hand in front of Blake's eyes to block the lights.

We'd just stepped out of the stadium and there were flashing cameras and reporters *everywhere*.

Walker immediately went into protector mode, his body trying to block the reporters. I glanced around though, feeling oddly numb to the onslaught.

"Olivia, can you tell us about your performance tonight?"

"Walker, how does it feel to be dating a superstar?"

The questions were almost nice, and for once, I found myself smiling…or at least not grimacing. Maybe it was the adrenaline from performing on stage, or perhaps it was Walker, but whatever the reason, I felt strangely…at ease.

Walker hustled us to the truck, everyone splitting up to escape the cameras. He climbed into the cab and was quieter than usual, his brow furrowed with concern as he navigated the truck through the horde.

"I'm okay," I promised, reaching out to him and squeezing his hand reassuringly. "They were way nicer than usual."

He nodded, but his expression remained guarded, and he still didn't say anything.

"Are you okay?" I pressed quietly, starting to feel nervous—worst case scenarios blooming in my brain...like what if everything became too much for him...

"I'm fine, angel face. I just hate those guys, and I hate that they stalk you." There was a pause and then he laughed, almost to himself as we finally got out of the parking lot. "I'm the only one who's allowed to stalk you."

I laughed too, and he finally seemed to relax.

"I really mean it. You're amazing. Incredible. The most talented person I've ever met," he said softly, his hand grabbing mine.

I blushed and laid my head back in the seat.

"I love you," he said tentatively, like he thought the other night was a fluke and I was going to reject him.

"I love you," I immediately answered back, the smile he gave me better than anything I'd ever seen.

CHAPTER 23
WALKER

Game day, baby.

My first game with the Dallas Knights.

And I was a fucking nervous wreck.

I sat in the locker room doing my visualizations.

I was a wall. A fucking wall.

"You look a little green, Disney," Camden said, plopping down on the bench as he pulled on his skates.

"I feel a little green," I grumbled. I glanced over at him and he looked fresh as a daisy. "I hate you."

"I would say I was offended, but I would be more offended if you puked on me right now," he said, scooching away from me.

"Walker's fine. He just needs a little dance party," Ari said, shaking his hips in my face. I batted him away and he jumped back right before I got him in the balls.

"Dance party?" Logan said, popping from behind a wall like a damn groundhog. He did a little shimmy like the words "dance party" got him going.

"We're not doing a dance party," I told Ari, and he chuckled like I'd said something funny.

Ari did a spin move. "Golden Boy, tell them all what a fantastic dancer I am."

Lincoln was pulling on his jersey. "We're not dancing. I—am not dancing."

"No one likes a pooper, Linc," Ari commented.

Lincoln raised an eyebrow.

"Sorry, scratch that. No one likes a *party* pooper. Knew I'd forgotten something there."

Logan went over to the speaker system, and a second later, "Sexy Back" was blaring from the speakers. He immediately began doing some kind of hip move that I had no doubt Justin Timberlake would approve of.

"Fucking rookies," Lincoln growled, going over to the system and pressing buttons.

"Hey!" Logan retorted.

"When you grow hair on your chin, you can pick a song, Rookie," Camden drawled.

Logan scoffed. "Ugh, I can't even comment on your hair, because you still have a head of luscious locks."

Camden flipped his hair out of his face dramatically before frowning. "I'm not a fucking dinosaur, York!"

Logan raised an eyebrow condescendingly.

Camden flipped him off and the whole locker room erupted into laughter.

A second later, a club beat of "Love Story" filled the room.

"That's what I'm talking about," Ari crowed as he snapped his fingers and slid from side to side.

"Okay, I can get behind this," Logan said as he resumed his smooth moves.

"We don't really care, rookie," Ari drawled.

The whole team was trying to show off, and I had a little foot tap going, some of my nerves drifting away.

After an entire season with Ari and Tay-Tay, this felt normal. That was kind of weird in and of itself.

Twenty-three grown ass men having a dance party to get themselves hyped.

"Come on, Disney. This is your jam," Ari said, shaking his ass at me.

I glanced over at Lincoln who was leaning against the wall, a small, cool smirk on his lips as he watched everyone make an idiot of themselves.

"Ooooh, Golden Boy. I think you're going to have to dance to make Walker feel better," Ari commented, shimmying up to Lincoln.

Lincoln looked at him in disgust...and then finally sighed.

My jaw dropped when Lincoln unleashed a flurry of smooth, slick moves that left us all gaping in awe. He spun and twirled and I was mesmerized.

"Ugh, you disgust me," Ari called out. "Now, Disney's going to simp even harder."

I was up now, because if Lincoln 'Fucking' Daniels was going to dance like an angel...I was going to dance too.

Camden whooped as I pulled out my electric slide and the moneymaker—the running man.

Coach Porter walked in and stared at us all, aghast. "Get your fucking heads in the game and get out to warm-ups," he growled, shaking his head as he stormed towards the tunnel.

"You alright, Davis?" Lincoln asked, slapping me on the back. I nodded, feeling muchhh calmer after that nonsense. "That's my goalie."

I was fucking beaming as we made it out on the ice.

———

The game was about to start and I looked over to where Olivia was sitting with Blake and Monroe. She wasn't wearing any disguises this time around, and best of all...she was wearing *my* jersey.

I immediately started thinking about *after* the game...when I was for sure going to fuck her in nothing but that jersey.

Don't get hard now, Disney.

Fucking hell...I'd just referred to myself as *Disney*.

I blew her a kiss and she blushed, and unlike the last time she'd been sitting at one of my games...she didn't flip me off.

What a difference a few months could make.

The puck dropped and we were off.

Midway through the first period, Denver executed a perfectly timed cross-ice pass, setting up a one-timer from the faceoff circle. As the puck came in, I kicked out my left leg in a sweeping motion, deflecting it away from *my* net.

Ari slapped my head as he passed by. "Yes!" he yelled with a fist pump.

I grinned and glanced over to Olivia...just to make sure she was paying attention. She was on her feet screaming and clapping, perfect in every way.

What the hell...I glared at a guy near Olivia that was definitely staring at her ass. But of course, he didn't notice he'd gotten my attention...my helmet made death glares a bit difficult.

The crowd roared with excitement as the puck flew back and forth across the ice. As Denver moved in again, Camden slammed one of the forwards into the glass, sending him sprawling to the ice afterwards.

"That's a fucking cheap shot, asshole," Clayton hissed as he scrambled to his feet. Camden's grin was all teeth. "How's it feel to be a fucking prick?"

"Let's see...what am I feeling? It's not bittersweet. Hmm. Oh, got it. It's sweet. *That's* what I'm feeling," said Camden.

I snorted and he gave me a wink before skating away.

"He is kind of dreamy, Disney," Ari commented as he came up from behind me. "I'm going to tell Blake she'd better gird her loins."

"What does that even mean?" I mused. "I hear it all the time. I think I fucking use it. But I have no idea what it means."

"Hey, Golden Boy, what does 'gird your loins' mean," he called out to Lincoln who was skating by to line up for a face off.

"It means get in your fucking spot, Lancaster," he scowled, coming to a stop by the ref.

"Touchy, touchy. We'll have to table that discussion. Just keep being a wall, Disney!" Ari yelled as he raced forward.

I checked on Olivia again, stiffening when I saw that the same guy was leaning in so close to her that she was having to lean into Blake to have some space.

"Walker!" Ari growled, and I glanced up to see a Denver forward skipping past Fredericks and bearing down on me, the puck hurtling towards the net. I lunged towards the puck, managing to snag it just inches before it could cross the goal line.

Holy fuck, that had been close.

The clock was ticking down the final seconds of the period. Ari sprinted down the ice with the puck on his stick. With a flick of his wrist, he sent the puck sailing across the ice toward Lincoln, who streaked forward, receiving the pass before sending it hurtling towards the goal.

The entire arena seemed to be holding its collective breath as the puck soared through the air. A second later, the goal light lit up as the puck collided with the back of the net right as the buzzer sounded, signaling the end of the period.

The crowd roared its approval. Lincoln raised his arms in triumph, a cocky grin spreading across his face before he skated over to Monroe, made a heart sign, and then pointed right at her just like he'd done since they'd started dating.

Only then was he swarmed by our teammates.

"Disney, stop simping after Golden Boy, and compliment me on my assist," Ari snapped as we headed towards the bench.

"Should I give you an ass slap, Lancaster. Or what are you looking for?" I huffed as I glanced over to Olivia's seat, happy that the guy was nowhere to be found.

"I love you," I mouthed at her, and her smile about did me in.

"Oh shoot, let me help you with that," Camden suddenly called out, picking up a foam finger that a little girl had dropped over the glass into the tunnel.

Logan rolled his eyes dramatically and pretended that he was throwing up.

"What?" Camden asked, when he noticed we were all waiting for him to move down the tunnel.

"Keep moving, Hero, I gotta piss," Logan snarked.

"Just helping out the fans," Camden said defensively.

"Sure, had nothing to do with the hot as fuck mom she had with her."

Camden winked and Logan shook his head…all the way into the locker room for the break.

———

"Oh shit, does your coach know you're out here," Logan said in a shocked voice to the Denver guy he was facing off with.

I scoffed and he winked at me.

Cheeky little rookie.

We were halfway through the second period, still up by only one. But so far I hadn't allowed a goal.

Logan won and took the goal down the ice, so I took a second to check on Olivia.

Seriously, what the fuck.

The guy was back. He was *again* sitting way too close. She was doing her best to pay attention to the game, but the fucker wouldn't stop talking to her.

Crap, the puck was back on our side.

Denver took it behind the net, and I hugged the left pole, tracking the back and forth as our guys tried to get the puck back. A split second later the puck was on the edge of the crease, Denver trying to push it towards my backhand side. I quickly shifted my weight to cover the angle, snapping my glove down to grab the puck.

The crowd cheered, but my focus was back on Olivia, watching as the guy reached over and touched her fucking arm.

The ref blew the whistle, but instead of giving the puck back,

I dropped it to the ice and then smashed it towards the glass with a forceful smack of my stick.

The guy jumped as the puck cracked against the barrier in front of him, his eyes wide in shock. Someone next to him said something and his gaze shot to mine. I ripped my helmet off and gave him my best death glare, making a cutting motion across my throat as I mouthed the words: "She's mine."

The guy's expression faltered, a mixture of fear and uncertainty flickering across his face. A second later he scrambled out of his seat and ran up the stairs, glancing back every couple of steps like he was afraid I was coming after him.

Pussy.

Olivia's mouth was open, a cute little shocked expression on her face, and I winked at her before pulling my helmet back on to get back to the game.

My teammates were watching me, stunned.

All except Lincoln and Ari...who were...slow clapping for me?

"That's how it's done, Disney. True 'Circle of Trust' behavior right there. I mean, you might get suspended for threatening to end someone in a nationally syndicated program...but that is how it's fucking DONE," Ari whooped as he skated by.

The refs must have been too stunned to know what to do since I'm pretty sure nothing like that had happened in the history of the league...so play resumed.

The guy never came back and I was able to keep my head in the game, secure in knowing Olivia was safe from douchebags... for at least the rest of this game.

Which we won.

CHAPTER 24

OLIVIA

Security led us down to the tunnel to wait for the players to come out.

"I love hockey," Monroe said dreamily as she stared at a poster of Lincoln on the wall. Monroe and Lincoln were intense together and it made me wonder what Walker and I looked like to other people. I kind of hoped we looked similar, like we were in our own little world.

"Game day sex is the best day sex," Blake murmured, and there was a slight pause before Monroe and I started giggling.

"What? You know it's true. All that adrenaline. It's the *best*." She eyed me speculatively. "I bet it's the same after a show, isn't it?"

I blushed, thinking of that show in Dallas where I'd practically attacked Walker afterwards like a nut case.

"Yep, look at that blush. She's thinking of hot sex right now," joked Monroe.

"And after that game...where he went all caveman on you..." Blake made a kissing sound. "It's going to be hot."

Walker came out right then and made a beeline towards me, sweeping me up into his arms and burying his face in my neck like we'd been separated for days instead of a few hours.

Blake raised her eyebrows up and down. "Bow chicka wow wow," she purred, Ari obviously having rubbed off on her.

"You were amazing!" I whispered as he continued to hold me.

"Let's get out of here?" he said, his voice gruff, and I nodded.

He set me down and grabbed my hand, leading me down the tunnel towards the player's exit. "See you guys later," I called behind me because Walker hadn't even said hi.

"Have fun!" Monroe called, and I snorted, thinking it was amazing that I'd never had any girl friends…and now I had two that seemed pretty great.

Walker was silent as we drove out of the parking lot.

"So, how was it playing in your first game for Dallas? I thought you would be more excited."

He grabbed my hand and placed it on his hard cock. "I am excited, Olivia. It's just all I can do not to fuck you in this truck right now. So I'm going to stay quiet until we get home…alright?"

I inhaled and nodded, my skin flushing at the growly tone he had going.

We didn't speak and he didn't touch me the entire ride home.

Walker unlocked the door and stepped inside the dark hallway, and I followed him.

"Get on your knees," he suddenly said, in a silky voice.

"What?"

"Get on your fucking knees, angel."

"Okay," I whispered as I sank down to the floor.

"Good girl," he said, running a hand down my cheek. "You're going to open that perfect mouth and suck my dick until my cum is dripping down your face…and after you've taken the edge off…I'm going to fuck you. In my jersey. First in your pussy, and then in that perfect ass."

I stared up at him, shock and arousal slipping through my bloodstream. My panties were drenched.

I wanted that.

I wanted *all* of that.

Now.

"Open up," he growled as he pulled his dick out of his Knights sweatpants. "Wider."

He made a pleased sound of approval when I obeyed.

I'd worn my hair up in a high pony for the game and Walker wrapped the ponytail around his hand, pulling my head back more.

"Fuck you're hot," he hummed.

He rubbed the tip of his cock along my bottom lip, spreading pre-cum across it before he slid his cock into my mouth.

His sweet musky smell had my pussy gushing, and I swallowed down the cum that was leaking steadily from his dick.

"Good girl, sweetheart. Suck my cock."

I moaned around his length and tried to open my throat more. I wanted to please him. The beads of his piercing slid along my tongue and I pressed on them, making him moan and surge further into my mouth until I was gagging around his cock.

"All of it," he ordered as he thrust in deeper, hitting the back of my throat.

Walker caressed my jaw for a second, his other hand still holding my ponytail taut.

"Relax your throat, angel," he rasped, the head of his dick somehow pushing deeper.

I was pretty sure that *this* was the textbook definition of "deep throating" if there was one.

And I thought I was doing it pretty well.

Walker pulled out slowly and eased back in, his gaze glued to my mouth as I sucked on him eagerly.

My hands pushed up under his shirt, desperate to touch his warm skin, wanting every piece of him I could get.

"That's it, baby. Suck my cock. You're gonna swallow every last drop, aren't you, Olivia?" he growled, his hand tightening in my hair. His thrusts became rougher and harder, and without warning, his cock was pulsing, and warm cum shot into my mouth, thick bursts that I couldn't swallow fast enough. It spilled from my lips down my chin as he continued to fuck into my mouth for a few more thrusts before finally pulling out.

He gathered up the cum that had dripped down my chin and pushed it back into my mouth. "I want you to have it all." There was cum on my neck too, and he smoothed it under the collar of my jersey, caressing my breasts as he covered my chest.

His dick bobbed in front of me and my mouth watered.

He was still hard.

"I told you I just needed to take the edge off. Seeing another man touch you, angel. It makes me *feral*. I'm going to be spending the rest of the night fucking your every hole, until you're so full of my cum that you can't get rid of it. You're going to be my good girl tonight, aren't you baby?" he teased, playing with my breast through my jersey.

I nodded, absolutely desperate to be his good girl tonight. Once again, I wondered why it felt so good to submit to him, to do exactly what he wanted...when I hated it in every other part of my life.

"Take off everything but my jersey," he murmured, releasing my hair and taking a step away, his blue eyes glimmering in the dark hallway.

I stood up and slipped off my leggings and panties, before reaching under the jersey and taking off my bra. Who knew the trick that every girl seemed to learn at some time or another would be so useful?

Walker palmed his cock, fisting it from root to tip while he stared at me.

"That's going to be your last name soon, so I suggest you get used to wearing it, angel. Get used to having it on when I fuck that perfect pussy."

A bead of arousal slid down my thigh as we stared at each other and he smirked, like he knew.

Walker stalked towards me, and for some reason I stepped back, matching every step he took until we'd made it out of the hallway and into the living room.

"Don't take another step, sweetheart," he rasped. "I want you to crawl the rest of the way to the couch, slip that jersey over that perfect ass so I can watch your pussy as you move."

Holy fuck. My man had a dirty mouth...and I fucking loved it.

I found myself sinking to my knees for the second time tonight. I bent over and pulled up the jersey so my ass cheeks were bare, and then I slowly crawled my way to the couch, his gaze burning into my skin.

"I could cum just staring at you, baby. I'm not sure you're even real. I worry sometimes that I'll wake up and you'll be just a figment of my darkest dreams." His voice sounded pained.

I slid onto the couch, making sure the jersey stayed up as I spread my legs so he could see how wet I was for him.

Walker leaned against the wall across from me, stroking his dick slowly as if he was in a trance.

"Play with yourself," he said hoarsely, and his eyes tracked my fingers as I slid them through my folds.

"How does that feel?"

"So good," I whispered, moaning as I slid a finger into my cunt for a second before using it to spread wetness around my clit.

His hand was moving faster along his shaft, a sight that was turning me on even more.

"Taste yourself. Suck all that sweetness off," he growled.

I obeyed, sliding my fingers in my mouth, licking off my taste like it was candy.

He lunged off the wall and stalked towards me. "Pull the jersey up. I want to see those perfect tits."

Once again, I did as he asked, shaking as he dropped to his

knees in front of me, his lips closing over one of my nipples and sucking hard as he pushed two fingers into my core. He squeezed my other breast as his teeth lightly bit down on my sensitive tip. I moaned as he forced a third finger in before he pulled them all out and trailed them down to my other hole, spreading my wet desire all around it.

His mouth moved to my other breast and he licked and sucked as he began to push two fingers into my ass. I gasped as he stretched and wet my hole, shaking from the sensations.

"Fuck, I love your tits," he said as he went back and forth between my breasts, licking and sucking and driving me crazy.

A hungry noise rattled through him as he continued to stretch my ass. An orgasm hit me, unexpected and hard, and I cried out as my cum dripped down my pussy, further wetting my hole. Walker withdrew his fingers and I whined at the emptiness.

"I'm going to take such good care of you," he murmured as he leaned over me.

My hips arched towards him and I gasped as his dick brushed against my asshole. "Just relax, baby," he whispered as he massaged my clit. The head of his cock felt huge as he pressed against my opening, pushing into me inch by inch until he was halfway inside.

"Fuck," I gasped, the words barely coming out because it felt like I was too full to breathe.

"You're doing so good," he praised, and I preened under his compliment, like it was my life goal for him to love taking my ass.

I cried out as he pushed in further and further, until somehow he'd worked himself all the way in, his balls seated against me.

Tears were sliding down my cheeks and he kissed each one, murmuring praises that barely filtered into my consciousness since all my focus was on the huge pole currently in my ass.

I'd thought I'd felt owned before...but this was on another

level. The beads of his piercing felt like they were brushing up against my nerves and I'd never felt pleasure like this. It was so much.

"Tell me you're mine," he growled.

"Yes," I whispered.

"I want it louder. I want the whole fucking world to know it. I want you to tell me you're never going to leave me."

"I'm not going to leave you. I'm yours," I sobbed, more tears falling down my face because it felt like I was being transformed at that moment, remade into something I wasn't going to recognize.

He pulled out and slammed back into me, one hand playing with my clit while the other one massaged my breasts.

"You take it up the ass so fucking good, sweetheart," he purred. I couldn't say anything back though, I was too lost to the sensations.

"Going to fill up that cunt next, drown you in my cum."

I was half aware that what he was saying was a little scary... but the rest of me was unopposed to what he was proposing.

High on lust, I wanted him to own every part of me.

My hips moved against his, chasing the high that only he could give me. I could feel it building, almost there, and then it hit, euphoria pulsed up my spine as he rammed into me...his seed coating my insides. It was the last thing I felt as the edges of my vision darkened and I slipped into unconsciousness.

Fucked to death indeed.

CHAPTER 25
WALKER

Ari: Helloooo Daddy.

Me: It sounds creepy when you say it like that.

King Linc: He didn't say it. He texted it.

Me: Same difference when it comes to Lancaster.

Ari: Would you prefer 'Daddy Disney'? Daddy… actually that's as far as I got.

Me: I'll find out today.

Ari: Oooh. I'll totally act surprised when Olivia tells Blake.

Me: She won't exactly know today…

King Linc: She won't exactly know? How the fuck are you going to find out without her knowing?

Me:…

Ari:…

King Linc:...

King Linc: Good boy.

"What is that smell?" Olivia groaned as she walked into the kitchen.

"Eggs?" I asked, confused as I turned towards her with the skillet of breakfast I was about to spoon onto our plates.

"I think I'm going to be sick," she said, her face pale as she scrambled from the room.

I froze for a second before a big grin lit up my face.

And then I hustled into the bathroom to hold my girl's hair.

An hour later, I had the news I wanted.

Two pink lines on a stick.

Pregnant.

Best fucking day of my life.

———

I watched Olivia rummage through the kitchen cabinets, wearing nothing but one of my tees that completely drowned her. The collar had slid off one of her shoulders and my dick twitched as my gaze traced her smooth skin. I couldn't help but grin at the sight.

She was looking for the coffee, a morning ritual she cherished almost as much as I cherished her. Unfortunately for her little ritual, I had disposed of every last coffee bean in the house.

I'd read that caffeine was a no go during pregnancy, so I'd rid the kitchen of all of her coffee and Diet Coke. I would also be giving up coffee during her pregnancy...just in case somehow the caffeine could be transferred in my cum.

I was not taking any risks.

"Hey, babe, did you finish off the coffee yesterday?" she asked with a frown, pushing some hair out of her face. Her brow furrowed in confusion as she turned to face me, her hand still hovering over the empty coffee canister.

That she had just filled for the third time in a week.

I leaned against the counter with practiced nonchalance. "No, I thought we had a bunch left."

Her frown deepened. "So did I. Didn't we just get some yesterday?"

I shrugged. "I'll grab some after practice."

"Let's go to Starbucks," she said, sounding a little panicked. "I need my fix."

Olivia's caffeine addiction was going to be a problem.

"How about I make you a smoothie instead?" I asked. "Oh, and Mrs. Bentley's burritos. She sent some to practice with Lincoln."

"We should try and steal her away from Lincoln," she murmured, temporarily distracted from her quest for caffeine with the mention of Lincoln's housekeeper's burritos.

When I was silent, she turned and glanced at me. "Disney, you simp," she said in what I assumed was her best attempt at Ari's voice, "You're quivering in your shorts just thinking about taking anything away from Lincoln."

It was true. I would never ever try to steal Mrs. Bentley. Even for the love of my life. I grinned unrepentantly and she laughed.

I started pulling out ingredients for smoothies. I had become an expert over the last week at pregnancy smoothies, blending together fruits, veggies, and a healthy dose of prenatal vitamins. Olivia had no idea that her morning pick-me-up was now laced with all sorts of ingredients meant to nourish a growing baby.

I was desperate for her to realize she was pregnant, but so far she hadn't seemed suspicious at all about the nausea, increased breast size, and missed periods. I'd specifically searched pregnancy topics on her phone so now all her ads were baby related.

Still nothing.

Apparently getting pregnant was so far out of the realm of possibility for her that she was missing even the most obvious signs.

She went to get some water out of the tap and I hurried to "accidentally" knock her glass over so it all spilled out.

"Oh babe, use the filtered water in the fridge, sink water sucks," I told her, grabbing the glass and filling it for her. I'd paid to have a super fancy filter put in the fridge that got rid of everything bad because I'd read that tap water had a bunch of toxins in it.

Who knew?

According to my five baby books, apparently everything was bad for you while you were pregnant. Which made my job really hard at the moment keeping *everything* away from her.

I finished making the smoothie and handed it to her, feeling even more crazy as I stared at her perfection. I wished I knew how she would react to the news. Having a baby with her was the best thing I could ever imagine...but I wasn't sure she would feel the same way. I could have pointed out her missed period, but I was trying to enjoy this little calm before the storm...just in case she freaked out.

At least she'd never know exactly *how* she came to be pregnant. That would be far harder news to deliver.

I laughed at that little thought and Olivia raised an inquiring eyebrow. She didn't ask me what I was thinking about though, since I tended to do that a lot—laugh at random things in my head.

"Drink your smoothie," I ordered, and she wrinkled her nose.

"What all do you put in these? They taste a little different than usual," she commented as she took a long draw from her straw.

"Just some vitamins," I answered innocently, obviously leaving out the fact that she was gulping down the most expensive prenatal supplements that money could buy.

Nothing was too good for my two babies.

I was pretty sure that the role of the smoothie-making, coffee-banning, overprotective partner was my life calling.

Hopefully she was cool with that.

———

Later that day, as we headed out for a walk in the park after my practice, I made sure to keep a close eye on her. I insisted on carrying the heavy bag with our picnic essentials, brushing off her protests.

"You're glowing today, baby," I murmured, watching her with adoration as she told me about a song she'd been writing that afternoon.

Her cheeks flushed pink, and my mouth watered. My sex drive had been even more insane knowing she was pregnant, like I had some kind of pregnancy kink.

Another thing for me to examine later.

We settled down on a patch of grass, and I pulled out the blanket and spread it out, making sure Olivia was comfortable before joining her. My gaze kept dipping to her flat stomach, wishing the bump was already there.

A large and in charge sign that she was mine.

I opened the basket and freaked out when I saw that she'd packed sandwiches for the picnic. Our cook, Marsha, had gone grocery shopping this week before the positive test and our fridge had been full of contraband items before I went through it.

How the fuck had I missed the deli lunchmeat?

"This looks good," I said, leaning over the basket so that my body was blocking what I was doing, and grabbing the sandwiches so I could slip them behind me. "Let's see what we got. Fruit salad, chips, pasta salad, and holy fuck....are these Marsha's german chocolate brownies?"

"Yeah, she made a batch for us this afternoon. But aren't there sandwiches in there?" she asked, trying to look into the basket.

"What's that kid doing?" I muttered, throwing the sandwiches as far as I could behind me when she turned her attention over to where I'd been staring.

"Which one?" she asked, confused because there were tons of kids at the park right then.

"He was eating some grass. Really weird," I answered, shrugging my shoulders when she looked back over to me. "Now what were you saying before that?"

"What? Oh, um. Sandwiches. There were supposed to be sandwiches in the basket."

I made a big show of moving items and looking around. "I'm not seeing sandwiches, but the rest of it looks amazing."

"Crap. I'm sorry," she muttered, her nose wrinkling when I opened up the pasta salad.

"What's wrong?"

"I don't know. Maybe don't eat that. Something smells off about it."

"Oh," I answered, immediately closing the lid while mourning the chance to eat pasta salad. It was my favorite.

"Apparently I didn't do a very good job with this picnic," she huffed as I pulled out what was left.

"Looks perfect to me," I told her as I stared at her hungrily.

She swooned like I'd said something particularly romantic before she grabbed a chip and took a bite.

It was nice to be out here like this with her. I'd stopped leaking where we were going to the paps last week when Jeff had finally come up with more evidence against Marco and Jolette and I could stop with my ruse.

I'd been ignoring texts from them all week, all of them complaining about the lack of recent stories.

The stupid fools had no idea what was coming.

It was nice to have a break from the cameras, although I had liked the pics. I had a folder on my computer with all of them.

A few more weeks and I'd have everything in place so that we could have a lifetime of days like this.

After we'd eaten what was left in the basket—excluding the pasta salad of course, she laid in my arms.

And I pretended it was completely normal for me to cradle her stomach the entire time.

CHAPTER 26

OLIVIA

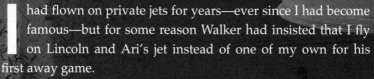

I had flown on private jets for years—ever since I had become famous—but for some reason Walker had insisted that I fly on Lincoln and Ari's jet instead of one of my own for his first away game.

Lincoln and Monroe's private car had picked Blake and me up and we'd driven to the private airstrip to get on the plane.

And that's when things got weird.

It was a gorgeous plane, top of the line and fitting with the fact that Lincoln had more money than God, but he had a very strange flight crew.

Everyone was female.

And not just female…they were…elderly.

Commercial airlines had rules of retirement of sixty five for pilots. I wasn't sure that this crew was under seventy. Perhaps that was why there was a third pilot…maybe for emergencies if one of them bit the dust while in the air.

The flight attendants, Mabel and Edna, were wearing cat sweaters, and they greeted me with warm cookies as soon as I stepped onto the plane.

We settled into our seats and Blake and Monroe were being really quiet.

I glanced at both of them and they had suspiciously blank faces.

I pulled out my phone.

> Me: I'm surrounded by grandmas...and I'm really confused.

> Walker: Grandmas?

> Me: The flight crew, the pilots...does Lincoln rent this from a retirement home or what is going on...

> Walker: Aren't they great? Did they give you cookies yet? Can you grab a couple for me?

> Me: Why isn't this weird to you? I've never seen this before!

> Walker: Just bring me some cookies, angel face. I fucking love you.

"You're asking Walker about 'Grandma Airways,' aren't you?" Monroe asked innocently.

"Grandma Airways?"

Blake extended her arms at the plane. "Lincoln and Ari's answer to making sure that no male or age appropriate female can get near us."

Monroe smirked. "Jokes on Lincoln, I would marry Edna or Mabel in a heartbeat just for their cookies."

A strange, shocked laugh burst from my mouth...right as Edna and Mabel came down the aisle rolling a cart that had a full tea service on it as well as a tray of chocolate chip cookies.

"Here dearie, these just came out of the warmer, take as many as you like." She picked up the tray with a weathered hand and offered it to me.

I'm sure I looked a bit crazy, my gaze going from the cookies to their cat sweaters...to Blake and Monroe who were watching me with huge smiles on their faces. I just wasn't sure if this was a joke or not.

"Thank you," I finally said as I slowly brought the cookie to my mouth and took a hesitant bite...My taste buds immediately exploded because oh my holy cookie.

"I"m in love," I exclaimed, my eyes widening in disbelief. "This is incredible!" I shoved another bite into my mouth—I couldn't help it. I was already wondering how many was too many for me to eat before I'd even finished one.

Blake and Monroe exchanged knowing glances, their lips twitching with suppressed amusement.

"Told you," Monroe smirked. "Mabel's cookies are legendary." She took a cookie for herself. "I would rather have access to these than man candy any day."

"Same," Blake said with a full mouth, some cookie crumbs sticking to her pink lipstick. "I dream about these babies."

"Okay, so let me get this straight...Lincoln and Ari bought this plane...and then hired a"—I glanced at Mabel and Edna who were pouring us all tea—"*mature* flight crew, all so that other guys wouldn't talk to you?"

Blake nodded. "Well, technically Lincoln started it all."

"He was spending so much money buying out every seat in first class that eventually he decided I should fly private. And only a 'mature' crew would do." Monroe giggled like what she'd just said hadn't been crazy.

Blake snorted at the expression on my face as she pulled her gorgeous blonde hair into a clip. "You do remember your goalie boyfriend, stopping play and smacking a puck into the glass...all because a guy dared to talk to you...right?"

"Our guys are kind of...a lot," I finally said in a bemused tone.

"'A lot' is one way to describe them," agreed Monroe, stuffing another cookie into her mouth.

I picked up the phone to text Walker.

> Me: Sorry, there aren't going to be any cookies left.

Walker immediately responded.

> Walker: That's okay, I know of one thing that tastes better, and I intend to eat it soon.

My pussy. He was definitely talking about my pussy.

I sat back in my seat, trying not to blush as Mabel and Edna handed us tea and we stuffed ourselves on cookies.

As I happily munched on my food and sipped my tea, there was one thing I knew for certain..."Grandma Airlines" was the best.

———

The plane touched down in St. Louis, and we were met with a waiting car ready to whisk us away to the arena. The three of us chatted excitedly as we drove, Blake and Monroe telling me ridiculous stories of things that Ari and Lincoln had done to win their hearts.

I still couldn't believe what Lincoln did to get Monroe to go on a date with him. I was understanding Walker's adoration a little bit more now. That man was a king.

While we drove I put on my Knights cap and sunglasses, although at this point I wasn't sure how effective a disguise was. The photographers had been relentless up until a week ago, and I didn't know if there was anyone that followed pop culture gossip that didn't know Walker and I were together.

Arriving at the arena, we made our way through the throngs of people to our front-row seats, eager to cheer on our guys. We made our way down the aisle, and I couldn't help but notice the two imposing females already occupying the seats on either side of ours. Dressed in all black and exuding an aura of strength, they looked like they could bench press a small car without breaking a sweat.

Monroe exchanged a puzzled glance with Blake and me, because the women could have passed for twins. They seemed like they should've been seated together. Neither of them seemed to notice us staring at them though.

Before I could think about that little mystery, Walker skated up to us and took off one of his gloves, pressing his hand against the glass. I shyly pressed my hand in the same spot. "I love you," he said, and I flushed even more as I stared at his gorgeous face.

"Love you too!" I called through the barrier. He winked at me and skated back to the net.

Lincoln passed by next and made a heart sign at Monroe, his gaze drifting to the imposing women seated on either side with a small grin on his face.

And Ari…Ari did not skate by. Instead, he sent an employee over to us with a sign that said "I'm obsessed with Mrs. Lancaster."

Blake blushed and hid her face for a second before shaking her head in amusement at Ari who was grinning at her.

"They're kind of crazy," I mused, staring at the three hotties as they finished warmups.

Monroe glanced at me like I was the crazy one. "I don't think there's any 'kind of' about it," she said. "Luckily, I love crazy."

I thought about that for a second before acknowledging to myself…I kind of loved crazy too.

The game began, and I kind of felt like I was flanked by human fortresses on either side. I glanced at them from time to time, before realizing something strange.

They weren't watching the game.

Instead, they were watching the crowd, their eyes scanning everyone with a careful intensity.

Odd.

Walker seemed much happier about my seat mate this time.

He still looked at me constantly in between plays, but he seemed much more at ease than he had at the last game.

Halfway through the game, Blake burst into a fit of laughter. "I can't believe it," she exclaimed between giggles. "Walker totally hired these women as bodyguards!"

I glanced between the two women...feeling a little dumb. They definitely fit the bill of bodyguards. The all black look they were rocking, the capability to bench four thousand men with one hand, the fact that they weren't watching the game...the signs were definitely all there.

I started giggling too. "How do you know it was my man?"

"Because Ari keeps poking Walker and grinning every time he passes by and looks over here. He totally thinks it's a 'circle of trust' move," said Blake.

I side-eyed the woman next to me, but she kept her gaze averted, clearly not wanting to talk. There was a tiny smirk on her lips, though, that told me she was listening to every word we said.

Walker had totally hired these women.

After the game, we met the guys outside the locker room to say goodbye before we flew back on "Grandma Airlines" and they flew back on the team plane.

Ari came out first and made a beeline for Blake, scooping her into his arms and kissing her with an exaggerated smacking sound before he turned his attention to Monroe and me.

Ari was exceptionally good looking, so was Lincoln. Maybe it was a requirement for the "circle of trust" that Walker was so obsessed with getting into...they all had to be hot.

If so, Walker definitely had that going for him.

"Don't even think about it," said Monroe, a grin slipping onto her lips even though she was trying to be stern.

"Please," he whined. "Just for a second."

Monroe sighed. "Fine, but one of these days, he's going to go crazy." She was silent for a minute, seemingly deep in thought.

"Actually, I don't think he could get crazier than he already is. You're probably safe."

Before I could ask what was going on, Ari let go of Blake and slung his arms around Monroe and I's shoulders. "Hello besties," he purred, right as Lincoln and Walker came out of the locker room.

Lincoln literally growled. But before he could say anything, Walker had yanked me out of Ari's grasp, and moved me against the wall, shielding me with his body before he smashed his lips against my mouth.

"Mine," he murmured silkily, biting down on his favorite part of my neck.

"You're acting like a caveman," I whispered. "Or like a vampire, I'm not sure which one at the moment."

"I'm acting like a man who literally has found the most perfect angel face sweetheart in the whole world, and I'm not about to let anyone take it."

I wrinkled my nose at how over the top he was being, but I was definitely swooning.

"Spoiler alert. I don't think that Ari is taking anyone. Blake and Monroe told me some of the things those two did to get them…" I huffed and lowered my voice. "I mean, they're *obsessed*…"

Walker got a funny look on his face as he stared at me and studied my face.

"You're totally right. *They* are crazy," he finally said, giving me one more kiss as the guys walked us down the tunnel to where the car was waiting to take us back to the airport.

———

We were fifteen minutes away from touching down in Dallas when Monroe came out of the back bedroom, her beautiful face scrunched up in pain. "Ugh. My period started. I'm bleeding everywhere."

"Oh shoot, do you need a tampon?" I asked, already reaching for my purse...only to realize...when was the last time I'd had a period?

I pulled out my phone, searching for when I'd made a note because I'd always kept track of my cycle religiously.

Panic. That's what I was feeling as I realized that I hadn't been keeping track for months...basically since Harley and Maddie's wedding.

What the fuck.

Ok, think...I'd had my period...when was it?

Two months ago?

Fuck. Fuck. Fuck.

I'd been taking my birth control perfectly. I know I hadn't fucked that up. But Walker probably had some kind of freaking super sperm. And he pushed it back inside me every single fucking time we had sex. Which was constantly.

There was a ringing sound in my ears. Monroe said something and I remembered I was supposed to be grabbing a tampon.

A useless tampon.

I handed it to her with a weak smile.

"Liv, are you alright?" Monroe asked sweetly, her gaze concerned.

"Fine," I said in a voice that sounded strangely high pitched. "Just fine."

Monroe looked like she wanted to say something else, but she must have decided otherwise because she went back into the bathroom with the tampon.

Blake and Monroe gave me surreptitious glances for the rest of the flight, and the drive to my house.

I did my best to keep my face blank, and I stayed quiet, inwardly freaking out.

When we got to the house, I moved to open the door and Blake softly touched my shoulder. "Did we do something?" she asked worriedly. "Because I'm sorry if we did."

I tried to give her a smile, because these two women were the nicest girls I'd ever met. "I promise it's not you. I just—I just realized something and I need to work through it for a little bit. You guys are the best, I promise you."

She grinned at me, relieved, and I waved goodbye to both of them as I trudged to the door.

I couldn't be pregnant…right?

And why didn't that seem like the worst thing in the world?

CHAPTER 27

OLIVIA

I sat at the kitchen table, staring at the burrito in front of me. Walker had just left for weights, and I was still trying to convince myself that I was indeed *not* pregnant.

If I could eat Mrs. Bentley's burrito, I wasn't pregnant.

Or at least I was trying to convince myself of that.

The problem was, I couldn't even pick the damn thing up. My stomach was churning at the smell, and wave after wave of nausea was hitting me.

And when I really thought about it...I'd been having weird food aversions for a while.

Like the eggs the other morning.

Denial, your name is Olivia.

Setting down my fork, I pushed my plate away and took a deep breath, willing the queasiness to pass. But it only intensified, twisting and turning in the pit of my stomach until I couldn't ignore it.

I threw back my chair and hurried towards the bathroom, barely making it in time.

I doubled over the toilet, my body convulsing as I retched violently. Tears stung my eyes as I clung to the porcelain bowl, the bitter taste of bile lingering on my tongue.

As I sat there, trying to catch my breath, I was still trying to figure out any other reason for my sickness…and my sensitive breasts…and the headaches I'd been getting.

It was just a stomach bug, I tried to reason. Or maybe all those cookies I ate yesterday.

And the eggs the other day had been bad. I was sure of it.

But as I stumbled back into the kitchen, my hand pressed against my queasy stomach, I finally let myself admit the truth.

I needed a pregnancy test.

With trembling hands, I fumbled for my phone, searching frantically for the nearest pharmacy. I needed answers, and I needed them now.

The drive to the pharmacy felt like an eternity. I only remembered it was a bad idea for me to make unplanned public appearances when I'd pulled into the parking lot of the CVS.

But it was too late to go back now. I wasn't leaving without that test.

I got out of the car, keeping my head down as I made my way into the store, my heart pounding in my chest.

I glanced around the store, ducking behind a nail polish display when I heard a teenage girl's voice—they'd been particularly *excitable* since the news had come out I was dating Walker. Once her voice had faded away, I made a beeline for the family planning aisle, my hands shaking as I reached for a box of pregnancy tests.

Thank fuck for self checkout stands.

I quickly paid for the tests, my mind racing with a thousand different thoughts and fears.

I'd almost made it to the automatic doors when my luck ran out.

"Holy crap. Is that Olivia Darling?" someone commented from nearby.

Leave it to me to get recognized at a CVS when I'd escaped notice in a ton of more public places.

"Is it really?" another voice asked, and I scurried out the doors before they got the nerve to try and talk to me.

Back at home, I locked myself in the bathroom, trying to keep myself semi-together as I tore open the box and unwrapped one of the tests. Taking a deep breath, I followed the instructions carefully before I set the stick on the counter and I waited.

Turns out three to seven minutes can actually feel like an hour.

The timer on my phone went off and I stared at the stick for a second longer, knowing that I could never go past this moment. The *before* of knowing. I was just going to live in the *before* for a second longer.

Finally, I picked up the stick.

Two pink lines. Two freaking pink lines.

The proof stared back at me from the small plastic window. My heart skipped a beat as tears welled up in my eyes, a mixture of joy and fear singing through my veins.

I was pregnant.

I collapsed onto the bathroom floor. My mind was complete chaos, a thousand worst case scenarios hitting me hard—the fact that I didn't even have control over my body under the conservatorship top of mind.

What was I going to do? I should have been smarter than this. What was Walker going to think? He'd joked about getting me pregnant before, but that's all it had been...a joke, right? I reached for self-loathing, something that had always come so easily to me...but it didn't come.

Because amidst the fear...a word was burrowing its way into my psyche.

Mommy.

I was going to be a mommy.

I'd always wanted to be one. I'd never admitted that exact thing before now, but when I'd been traveling from city to city, alone in hotel rooms or on a bus, I'd dreamed about what it would be like to have a real family, of what I would be like as a mom—how I would be the opposite of Jolette and be the best mom I could be.

A weird thing for a teenager to think for sure—but loneliness made you think about things like what it would be like to have someone that loved you. And really loved *you*, not just the idea of you.

There was that thing again, the one thing I hadn't dared to have all these years. The one thing that kept popping up ever since Walker and I had locked eyes at that first game.

Hope.

CHAPTER 28

OLIVIA

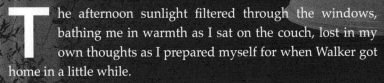

The afternoon sunlight filtered through the windows, bathing me in warmth as I sat on the couch, lost in my own thoughts as I prepared myself for when Walker got home in a little while.

And I told him he was going to be a daddy.

A sharp knock on the door startled me back to reality. Frowning, I rose from the couch and made my way to the door, thinking it was probably a package.

I glanced through the glass, seeing the outline of a woman. Freezing, I slowly peered through the peephole, panicking when I saw who it was.

Jolette.

"I can see you there. Open up the damn door, for fuck's sake," she snapped and I cringed, any gumption I carried with me rapidly shrinking at the idea of her presence.

I could do this though. I hadn't seen her for months. It had given me time to build up a little armor. Right? This was probably just a check-in, a little reminder of who owned me.

I opened the door, resigning myself to misery for however long she decided to stay. Jolette stood on the doorstep, her coiffed hair and designer attire perfect as usual.

My stomach clenched as we took each other in.

"Jolette," I greeted her tersely, my voice carefully blank of any emotion. "You should have called.."

Jolette's lips curved into a sly smile, her gaze sweeping over me with a hint of disgust. "Just thought I'd drop by for a little in-person chat," she replied, pushing her way in. "Although I see I should have brought your dietician with me. You're getting fat."

Fuck you is what I wanted to say...but I kept quiet, knowing from experience that any pushback only made things worse.

And what if I made her mad and she decided to try and force me to leave?

I couldn't leave Walker.

I wouldn't.

Jolette sauntered in like she owned the place, her heels clicking against the hardwood floor as she took everything in.

I hated her here. I hated it even more than I'd hated it in L.A. This was my safe place. My sanctuary. Where Walker made love to me. She wasn't supposed to be here. She would ruin it.

"So, what's this all about?" I asked, still trying to keep my tone neutral.

She turned to face me, her expression unreadable as she fixed me with a piercing gaze. "I was thinking we should start talking about a tour," she began, her voice measured and controlled. "Between your little romance with Walker, and your perfor-mance at the Sounds of Us concert, our phones have been ringing off the hook. It's the perfect time to resurrect your career."

Panic spilled into my chest and I stared at the floor, not wanting her to see what I was thinking. As much as I'd enjoyed singing lately, as much fun as I'd had at the concert...there was no way I was ready to go back out on the road.

Especially considering...I was going to be a mom.

It took me a second to realize that Jolette had gone extremely quiet. Usually she'd already be screaming at me for not immedi-ately agreeing with her. I glanced over to see what she was doing and...

She was staring at the table, where I'd laid the small plastic stick in preparation for Walker coming home. Recognition was dawning in her eyes, along with horror...and disgust.

Stupid. Stupid. Why hadn't I hid it?

"What's this?" she demanded, her voice rising in pitch as she reached for the pregnancy test.

I felt my cheeks flush with embarrassment as I struggled to come up with a response. "It's...it's nothing," I stammered, my voice barely above a whisper.

I reached for the test but before I could get to it, she snatched it up, holding it aloft like a damning piece of evidence.

"You're pregnant," she hissed, her eyes ablaze with fury. "How could you let this happen? How could you be so careless?"

I bristled at her accusatory tone, my own defensiveness rising to meet hers. "It's none of your business," I shot back, my voice trembling with indignation.

"We're leaving. Right now," she growled.

"What?"

"We'll make an appointment with the doctor. No one will know." She reached for my arm like she was prepared to drag me out.

I backed out of reach.

"You think I've worked this hard to let you ruin everything! To let you have a baby? No!" she growled. "You're getting rid of that thing...even if I have to stick a hanger in you and do it myself!"

"What? No!" My voice trembled as fear leached in. Staring at her, it wasn't hard to believe she would do it. Knock me out and drag the baby out of me if it was the last thing she did. Her eyes were crazed, her cheeks red and pinched. I covered my stomach protectively and backed away.

"You need to leave. I'm going to call the police!" I told her, backing towards the kitchen, where I'd left my phone on the bar.

Her laughter sliced through the air like shards of glass, each cruel note piercing my ears and settling like a weight in the pit of my stomach. "Like anyone will believe anything you have to say," she hissed, taking a step toward me.

―――

Walker

"Liv?" I called out the second I opened the garage door and stepped inside the house, eager to see Olivia after a fucking *grueling* practice session.

I frowned as I walked down the hallway, hearing the murmur of voices. I'd checked the camera thirty minutes ago and no one had been here. No one was supposed to be here.

Turning the corner, I froze when I saw Jolette standing in the middle of the living room—Olivia a few feet away, cradling her stomach as she stared wide-eyed at her bitch of a mother.

It didn't take a rocket scientist to realize I'd just stepped into a very tense conversation.

"What's going on here?" I demanded, as I crossed the room to stand in front of Olivia, not wanting Jolette to even be able to look at her.

Jolette's eyes narrowed, her face curling up in disgust, her tone laced with venom as she addressed me. "You know exactly what's going on. How dare you, you fucking piece of shit."

"Language," I commented, still trying to figure out what was going on. My gaze dropped to her hand where she was clenching something…was that…?

I glanced behind me at Olivia who stared back at me with a wide-eyed pleading expression.

Guess the cat was out of the bag. She knew we were having a baby.

"This was not part of—"

"How are those frozen accounts doing, Jolette?" I interjected before she could let *another* cat out of the bag—one I was not interested in my pregnant soulmate learning about.

I watched with satisfaction as her face paled in response.

"They only left one open...right?"

Jolette's face aged ten years in a matter of seconds, and she sputtered in disbelief. "How did you—"

"How did I?" I repeated mockingly. "The details aren't really that important. Only that the judge is going to find all sorts of proof of fraud and misuse of those accounts. And...since you decided to piss me off...I think I'll just go ahead and make sure that last account is closed too." I pulled out my phone and sent off a text for Jeff to send more evidence to the lawyer I'd hired for Olivia. Based on how good the guy was, I would have Marco and Jolette completely cut off from Olivia's money before the day was gone.

Jolette was scrambling to the door. "I'm leaving," she said hoarsely. "There's no reason to do something stupid."

"Maybe you should have thought about that today before *you* did something stupid," I called after her with a smug smile.

She threw open the door and lurched through it.

"Oh, and Jolette," I called after her, making sure my voice carried to her. "That's only the beginning. There's plenty more fun where that came from."

She threw me a look of complete terror before she literally scrambled down the road, one of her ridiculous heels breaking as she went. I watched her crash to the ground with a grin. Hopefully a car would hit her.

I closed the door and turned towards my girl.

Because we had something to celebrate.

CHAPTER 29

OLIVIA

I watched Jolette flee the house like Walker was chasing after her with a butcher knife. It was one of the most satisfying things I'd ever seen. Only possibly trumped by the knife being actually included in the scene.

But I couldn't feel completely relieved.

It was out there now, the news about the baby.

And I had no idea how he was going to react.

He shut the door and paused for a second before he spun slowly towards me, his blue gaze hard to read. His hair was sexily tousled from practice and his shirt was tight enough that I could easily take in the fact that his body was perfect.

Perfect and mine.

At least before this news.

"You're going to have my baby." His words hung in the air, and I wasn't sure if he'd asked a question or just said it, but I nodded my head anyway.

I held up trembling hands, my heart racing. "I know it's soon, and I know we didn't plan this…but..." My voice trailed off, choked with emotion, and I struggled to find the right words to express the depth of my feelings since I'd see those two pink lines. "I already love it," I finally whispered. "I understand if you need time—"

In one swift motion, Walker scooped me up into his arms, spinning me around with a whoop of excitement that filled the room.

"You're having my fucking baby!" His words rang out, a declaration of love and happiness that washed over me like champagne bubbles, giddiness drowning out the doubts and fears that had plagued me moments before.

A laugh spilled out of me, tears of relief streaking down my cheeks.

I took a mental picture of his face. The pure elation written across his features. Elation that he'd created something with me.

Me. Olivia Jones. The girl who ruined everything she touched.

Walker set me back down, his arms still wrapped tightly around me.

"I love you. I love you. I love you," he murmured, each word punctuated with a kiss to the tip of my nose.

I'm sure the grin on my face was ridiculous, but I couldn't help it. I'd thought that I was happy before with him...but this... this was on a whole other level.

"Our little Shmoopy," he sighed, stroking a hand over my flat stomach.

For what seemed like my entire life, I'd been worried about my weight, monitoring everything that went into my mouth so I looked perfect up there on the stage. It was kind of crazy to think I couldn't wait to have a bump.

Wait a minute.

"Did you just call the baby a 'shmoopy'?" I asked, aghast.

"We can workshop it. But it just came to me. Or should we call it 'lover bean' or 'googly bear'? Either of those would be good," he commented innocently.

He was handling this so well. Why wasn't he freaking out more?

"Why aren't you acting...surprised?" I asked, my voice tinged with curiosity and a hint of disbelief, as I searched his face.

Walker's grin widened, his eyes twinkling mischievously as he pulled me even closer, his warmth seeping into my skin. "I knew already," he confessed, his voice low and intimate as he pressed a soft kiss on my lips. "You were nauseous, throwing up, your boobs grew at least one size bigger, and you cried at a McDonald's commercial." He chuckled softly, pressing a tender kiss to my forehead. "It was pretty obvious."

I blushed, feeling like an idiot. Because in retrospect, those had been very obvious signs that I must have been trying really hard to miss.

"I just wanted you to figure it out yourself so you didn't freak out," he said smoothly.

"You're handling this so much better than I thought you would," I murmured, tears clouding my vision. *Again.*

"There's nothing to handle. I've been thinking about you having my baby since the first night I met you. I was giving my penis daily pep talks that my sperm could find a way."

"That's a really weird thing to say," I muttered, strangely giddy about everything he'd said.

"It's called manifestation, angel face. And I...happen to be a master at it."

I didn't have anything to say to that. I totally agreed. He was a master...at many things.

"You know what I think we should do?" he said as he picked me up and began walking towards our bedroom.

"What?" I asked the question, even though I was already starting to feel him up.

"We should celebrate," he said.

And once again...I totally agreed.

———

"Don't make me beg," I gasped as he ran his huge cock along my slit.

He'd been torturing my pussy for what felt like hours with

his tongue and there was a light sheen of my essence all over his gorgeous face as he stared down at me.

"It's your fault you taste so fucking good, angel. It's your fault you're so wet." He pushed the tip of his thick head inside me before he withdrew it, and it felt a little bit like he was trying to torture me. "It's your fault you're so tight." Again, he pushed just the tip inside, and I whimpered because I wanted him so much.

"Please," I begged.

"You want my big dick, sweetheart? You want me to slide inside this tight, perfect cunt, show you just how happy I am you're having my baby?"

Yes, I wanted that.

It took me a second to realize that I'd said that out loud and I was currently whimpering the word "please".

He pushed into me, and I felt every bump and ridge of his piercing as he moved all the way inside.

My hands dug into his skin, my body already drenched in pleasure from the three orgasms he'd given me.

I arched my back as he pulled out and then slammed back in, his body wrapped completely around me.

No matter what happened, I would own a piece of this man.

He'd put a baby in me, and for the rest of my life we'd be connected.

No matter what.

The thought was dizzying.

Magnificent.

All I could ever want.

His blue eyes were lust drenched as he slid his gigantic shaft in and out of me, feeling like, somehow, he was driving deeper every time.

"I love your body. I can't wait to fuck you when you start showing. I'm going to cum all over you," he commented as my pussy clamped around him at the thought.

"I want you to say it," he commanded, his hands gripping my ass, a finger sliding around the rim of my asshole. I whimpered against his lips as he fucked in and out of me hard and deep, thrusting relentlessly until I was close to the edge.

"I want you to say you can't wait to have my baby. That you'll let me fill you up like this again and again...breed you so you can never leave me."

I came. Hard. Pure bliss exploding through my body as he slid his tongue in my mouth, capturing my cries as my muscles fluttered around his dick.

"You feel so good, angel," he whispered. "And now you're mine. Forever." Walker pushed my legs wider, one hand on my thigh while his other hand lightly wrapped around my neck. Leaning over, he licked along my aching breasts, his mouth finally suckling on my nipple.

"I'm going to feed from these fucking perfect tits. I want everything from you," he growled.

His cock stretched me, rubbing against every sensitive place in my core as he continued to drive in and out.

"Say it," he ordered.

"I'm yours," I gasped as another orgasm crested inside of me.

"Say you'll let me fill this perfect body with my cum every single fucking day."

"Yes," I cried out. "Whatever you want."

"Fuck, you are so sweet. I can't believe you're having my baby," he gasped as I fell over the edge again, this time the orgasm somehow even more intense.

Walker stared into my eyes, and it felt like a piece of my soul reached out and wrapped around him at that moment. It felt like I couldn't survive without him. He'd become as necessary to my existence as breathing, as a beating heart. I took everything from him that I could, my body squeezing and pulling on his dick, desperate to keep it, his cum...*him* inside me.

"Fuck, fuck, fuck. I love you," he gasped as his hips stuttered against me and his cum filled me in warm bursts.

He moaned against my lips, and it was the most erotic thing

I'd ever heard, the sound enough to keep every woman's spank bank alive and well if they ever were lucky enough to hear it.

Which they weren't.

His hips moved in and out of me in a few more lazy, languid slides, and then he rolled us carefully over so that I was laying on top of him. His cum spilled out of me, most likely making a huge mess.

But I didn't care.

I just wanted to stay like this, with him...Forever.

"I'm yours," I murmured and he growled in pleasure. "And you're mine," I continued.

"All of me. Forever," he said, and then he put his hands over my stomach.

"And this baby is *ours*."

If a person could have died from happiness, it would've happened to me then.

But it was a good thing that it didn't, because for the first time...I wanted to *live*.

CHAPTER 30
WALKER

"Well, helloooo there, B.D.," Ari drawled as I strolled into the locker room.

Camden racked his weights and stared at him, clearly ready for whatever 'tomfoolery' Ari had planned—tomfoolery had been the "word of the day" in my dictionary app...who knew I'd have a chance to use it so soon. Olivia would be impressed.

"Alright, I'll bite. What does B.D. mean?" I asked, starting some stretches.

"Besides the obvious?" Ari said, gesturing to the front of his shorts.

Lincoln groaned as he pushed his barbell up. "Can we please not talk about your dick this morning—especially not when you got stuck. Again. You have to do something about that." He racked his weights, glaring at Ari who was supposed to be spotting him.

Ari rolled his eyes. "Focus. That's not important right now."

Camden looked intrigued. "Where exactly did you get stuck?"

"That's private information, Hero," Ari said haughtily.

Logan started cackling like a hyena as he started a set of jump squats. "That piercing of yours totally got stuck, didn't it?"

Ari flushed. "I said to focus. I brainstormed for hours for this."

"Please tell me your dick did not get stuck in..." Camden pressed.

"Big Daddy! Disney's new nickname is Big Daddy!" Ari spit out frantically, glaring at Lincoln who was smirking unrepentantly.

Logan stared at him, appalled. "It took you hours to come up with the name 'Big Daddy'? Also, why wouldn't it be 'Big Disney'? And why are we giving Disney new nicknames anyway? He already has one!"

"I prefer 'Walker Texas Ranger'," I told everyone seriously, but the conversation was clearly off the rails because no one was paying attention to me.

"Logan apparently wants a nickname," Camden commented as he did a bicep curl.

"He already has a nickname, it's 'Rookie,'" Lincoln drawled.

Logan grimaced. "That can't be my nickname...it would be good for one season. And I'm going to be around for longer than that."

"Why did we move on from Disney's new nickname so fast? That took a lot of time and energy!" Ari said, sounding appalled.

"Why did we move on from whatever your dick was stuck in so fast?" asked Camden calmly.

"Thanks, Golden Boy. 'Why don't you just feed me to the lions? Step on my head when I'm drowning,'" Ari snarked at Lincoln who had resumed lifting. "I hope that barbell falls on your head."

"*Wedding Crashers*. That's where that's from," Logan huffed as he did another squat jump. "Maybe be original, Lancaster."

Ari grinned, looking a bit evil. "Maybe score a goal, York."

We all laughed as Logan told us to fuck off with both hands.

"Why are we calling Walker "Big Daddy?" Camden asked, cocking his head.

"Sorry, Camden, you've moved past your 'Big Daddy' time

of life, and moved right into "Big Grandpappy," Logan said seriously.

Camden sighed and did that crazy eye roll of his again. "I'm literally 31, asshole. I definitely can still be a 'Big Daddy'!"

"If I don't see all of you asswipes dripping sweat in the next minute, you're doing *bag skates* on the ice until you fucking pass out," the strength and conditioning coach, Coach Wheeler, barked as he entered the weight room from his office. "What is this...fucking gossip hour?!"

Ari winked at me and mouthed "B.D." as he started lifting, and I snorted.

I would stick with *Disney*, thank you very much.

Although Ari had one thing right...I was going to be a "Daddy."

————

I bustled around the kitchen, blending fruits and vegetables into her smoothie. I'd been doing research about the best ones to use, and this one was a pregnancy "hydration" blend. I also had some Mozart playing because I'd read that babies could hear music in the womb and supposedly, classical music helped with the development of their brains.

I was pretty sure that T-Swift would do the same thing, but regardless...I was going to kill this whole daddy thing.

With a flourish, I poured the smoothie into a tall glass and carried it over to the bar area where she was seated, watching me work with a bemused expression on her face.

"Voilà, here you go, princess," I quipped, my tone light and teasing.

She stiffened as soon as the words came out of my mouth, the color draining from her cheeks as she stared at the smoothie like it was poison or something.

"Olivia?" I murmured. "Sweetheart, are you okay?"

A knot formed in the pit of my stomach as I watched her completely shut down.

What had I missed?

"Don't call me that ever again," she finally whispered, getting up from her chair and walking away without another word.

Of course, I followed her all the way into the bedroom because this wasn't something I could just let go.

She sat on the bed and stared out the window into the backyard.

"Olivia?"

"You said that there was nothing I could say that would change your mind about me," she said softly, her shoulders hunched over and defeat all over her.

"And I mean that," I swore fiercely. "There's nothing that would ever cause me to not want you...to not need you. Nothing."

There was another beat of silence.

"How about the fact that I allowed my manager to beat and sexually assault me for years. And when he finally raped me, I didn't tell a soul."

Her words hung in the air, suffocating and clawing at the oxygen in the room until it felt like there wasn't anything left.

More silence descended upon us, broken only by the out of control pounding of my heart.

This. This was what rage felt like. This was what real hate felt like, the kind that could consume your whole life until there wasn't anything else left.

Without a word, I staggered out of the bedroom and into the bathroom, where I doubled over the sink, retching violently as the bile rose in my throat.

Each heave was accompanied by a surge of raw, primal, terrifying anger.

I was going to kill him. I was going to cut off his dick and shove it down his throat.

And then I was going to kill him.

I straightened up, staring at the crazy eyed man in the mirror that I barely recognized.

With a roar, I lashed out, my fist connecting with my reflection. Pain exploded through my hand, blood spattering out onto the glass as it broke.

I welcomed the pain, relished it actually.

Even though nothing could take away what I was feeling knowing what had happened to her.

I leaned over the sink, forcing down the vomit that was threatening again. Finally, I realized what a dumb ass I was, and that I'd practically run into the bathroom right after she'd admitted something like that to me.

Fuck.

I dashed out to the bedroom, relief flooding me when I saw she was still there.

Walking around the bed to go to her, I felt like I might die when I saw the silent tears dripping down her gorgeous face. Tears blurred my own vision as I slumped to the floor in front of her, my chest heaving with the effort of trying to contain the emotions raging inside me.

"Angel..." My voice was hoarse, choked with tears and unspoken anguish. "I swear to you, I'm going to make him pay for what he's done. I'll tear him apart piece by piece until there's nothing left but dust and ashes."

She stared at me, her gaze...confused. "What?"

"I've been working on a plan to destroy them both. I will get them, I promise."

Olivia sighed. "Don't make promises you can't keep," she said in a dead voice that made me flinch.

I stood up, cautious in my movements in case this conversation had brought up triggers from the past. When she didn't flinch or move away, I stepped closer to her.

"It's a promise I'm going to keep," I growled, my hand closing gently around her chin so she couldn't turn away.

The blankness in her gaze broke, and her gorgeous gold eyes filled with even more tears. "How can you touch me, knowing what—what he did?" A harsh sob ripped out of her.

"What?" I asked, in total disbelief. "How would anything that fuckwad did change how I feel about you?"

"Because you can fully see now how—how weak I am! I let them dictate every inch of my career. I let them get me hooked on painkillers. I let him abuse me. I let him rape me. I let them take over my fucking life." She sobbed again, her eyes squeezing shut. "I let them ruin me." Those last words came out in a whisper.

Another tear slid down my cheek as I stared at my beautiful, broken love.

She didn't get it at all.

"You were a child. You didn't *let them* do anything," I growled. "These assholes were supposed to protect you. Take care of you! Nurture you! And instead, they took advantage. They took and they took and they took some more. You are not responsible."

She just looked at me, clearly not agreeing with me. But that was understandable. Years of blaming yourself didn't disappear overnight.

My hands softly trailed down her face, wiping up the tear tracks staining her perfect cheeks. I didn't know if she was crying because of *them*, or if she was crying for herself. But I hoped it was the latter.

They didn't deserve her tears.

And I was going to make sure they wouldn't get anything else from her ever again.

"I don't have anything to give you that you don't give me more of," she whispered. "I'm weak, and maybe...I'll always be weak."

Another sob slipped her lips.

"Our baby deserves better," she finally whispered.

A growl ripped from my lips but she didn't jump or act

scared, she just stared at me, silently begging me to prove her wrong.

"There's no one better," I told her fiercely, every cell in my body focused on getting her to believe me.

"Only a person without a mother could understand how much a child needs one. Only a person who's been broken can fully understand how to make someone whole. Only a person who has been without love can understand why it's so necessary. Only a person who's had to fight for their life could understand how precious it is. Our baby is going to have the most perfect mother in the world because you know all of those things, and you're going to give our baby everything you didn't have."

"How can you be so sure?" she murmured, a glimmer of what looked an awful lot like hope starting to shine from her golden gaze.

"Because I happen to be an expert on all things relating to my stunning, perfect angel face. So I know it for a fact."

"Is that so?" she huffed.

I brushed a kiss against her lips. "Yes. So don't question me. I know *everything*."

A small smile appeared on her lips, and I swore, I'd never seen anything more gorgeous in my entire life...than the sight of Olivia Jones stepping out of the darkness that had followed her for years...and coming out into the light.

Cole: So…Olivia being kept in an ivory tower yet?

Me: What?

Cole: I just assumed that your beastliness will have gotten even worse now that she's pregnant.

Parker: How can it get worse? He was already insane.

Me: No, I haven't locked her in an ivory tower…

Me: I don't think high altitudes are good for pregnancy anyway.

Cole: I don't like that you seem to have already looked that up.

Parker: It's the hotel basement moment all over again.

Me: Pot meet kettle. I'm still convinced you're having your own basement moment, Parkie, and there's some poor girl locked in your dorm room as we text.

Parker:...

Cole: Why do you keep doing that? Just say no.

Parker:...

Me:...

Cole: My brothers are both psychopaths.

———

The thing about evil people…is that they always messed up eventually. At one point or another, they lost the ability to think rationally. They start to think that they're untouchable, that they can get away with anything…

And luckily for me…Jolette and Marco had reached that point years ago.

It's just that there hadn't been anyone in Olivia's corner that had been looking for the evidence of it.

But now she had me.

And I guess Jeff.

Which was still a really weird name for a P.I.

I would someday have to tell him that.

After he finished his job for me, of course.

Freezing the accounts had been easy actually. Jeff had gotten a look at the books, so to speak, and there was basically nothing being spent that had anything to do with Olivia. Jolette spent all her money on botox and massages and lavish vacations that Olivia obviously wasn't a part of. And while California law allowed that to a certain extent, the sheer amount of money she was spending pushed her way over the edge.

There was also her gambling addiction that was fair game. She'd been jetting off to Vegas almost every weekend since the conservatorship began, and her debt was astounding.

Jolette was truly an awful gambler.

She was paying it off in small amounts to try and keep it under the radar...but the hotel casino accounts did no such thing. It was an astonishingly easy thing to get the full balance sheet of her debts to multiple casinos in front of the judge. And of course include proof that the bank account and credit cards being used in the casinos were all tied to Olivia's accounts.

Marco was an even bigger idiot, and I was a little surprised that he was still alive...or that his dick hadn't fallen off yet. Between the drug addiction and the hookers, he couldn't have been doing very well. The fact that he was making Venmo payments to high end escorts with the money from the fund was like shooting fish in a barrel...

And when we found out that many of those girls were underage....

It just made it that much easier to submit the evidence and have a judge do an emergency order for everything to be frozen.

"You're paying me triple for this," Jeff growled through the phone. "My eyes are never going to recover from what this sick bastard does on a nightly basis. Watching hookers snort blow out of his ass crack is not my idea of a good time, Davis."

I grimaced at the mental picture and replaced it with Olivia's face.

Instantly better.

"Aww, come on, Jeffrey, you're doing it for the greater good," I cajoled.

"For the millionth time, it's Jeff," he snapped. "And if you think that watching him get fucked by a big purple dildo was 'for the greater good'..." He stuttered a little. "Well, you're wrong."

That was fair.

"So Sharbrooks and Wrench have all the files for the hearing?"

He sighed impatiently. "How many times you going to ask me that?" he asked.

"As many times as I want since you're charging me triple."

"Alright then," he said. "Fair point…yes, they have all the files. You should have updates in your email…"

I was already reading through them, satisfaction hitting me right in the gut.

I loved when a good plan came together.

"Alright, keep me updated," I said needlessly, since I would most likely text him ten more times tonight to make sure everything was going smoothly.

He grumbled something and I hung up, taking a deep breath before I stepped into the locker room.

"Everything good?" asked Lincoln as I walked in, still making me fucking *shake* like a giddy schoolboy because he was watching out for me.

"The lawyers have all the stuff. They said this was enough to get another emergency hearing to examine the conservatorship," I explained, worrying for a second that I was missing something.

"What about the…mental illness claims," Ari said quietly, uncharacteristically serious in the moment, which only made me love the guy more.

"That doctor evidently lost his license a year ago…for falsifying documents. He's already admitted it on other cases, so the lawyers will be dragging him into this one, and somehow they'll get him to talk. Hopefully," I added with a frown, hating that every part of my plan depended on other people.

It felt a little bit like having really bad teammates and trying to win.

"We're here for you, buddy," Ari said, lightly clapping my back before he walked over to grab his stick for practice.

Lincoln stared at me for a second. "And she's happy…about the pregnancy?" he murmured, so softly there was no way that any one could hear him.

"Fucking ecstatic," I told him with a grin, my mood brightening just thinking of the ever present smile Olivia wore lately… when she wasn't throwing up, of course.

"And she still doesn't know?" he pressed, and I smiled at the reminder of another good plan that had also come together.

"Nope. And that's one secret I'll carry to the grave," I told him.

"Good boy," he said with a blinding smile that had me feeling a bit woozy for a moment.

That praise kink may have become a praise addiction...

Something to think about later.

Lincoln fucking winked at me as if he knew how glorious he was, and Ari came back up to me shaking his head. "Fucking simp," Ari muttered with a smirk.

And for the first time, I didn't deny it.

How could I?

———

Olivia

I wanted ice cream.

Actually, it wasn't a want. It was a need. And if I didn't get some soon...well, I wasn't sure what was going to happen. It seemed dramatic to say that I might die without it.

But that was kind of how I was feeling at the moment.

Walker had promised me tubs of it the second he was home. But I didn't have that kind of patience.

I needed it now.

Long shadows stretched across the garage as I walked out of the house and pressed the garage door opener.

Let's see...did I want mint chocolate chip or moose tracks?

Or did I want both?

"I'll definitely get both," I muttered to myself, slipping into the driver's seat. The familiar scent of leather and gasoline enveloped me as I turned the key, a sense of freedom accompanying the revving engine. After years of never driving myself, I still got a thrill every time I did it now.

I reached for my seatbelt and my door was suddenly yanked open.

"What?!" I froze, fear clogging my throat.

"Hello, *princess*," Marco grinned.

"What are you doing here?" I demanded, my voice betraying my rising anxiety. "I heard you were having some...legal problems."

He chuckled darkly, ignoring my comment.

Marco looked nothing like the smooth and polished man I was used to. He was disheveled, his usually immaculate hair in disarray and dark circles etched beneath his eyes. There was a wildness to his gaze...a desperation. His clothes were rumpled and unkempt, and the scent of stale alcohol and cigarette smoke clung to him like a second skin.

"I just wanted to catch up, Olivia," he replied.

My gaze darted around, looking for some kind of escape route as my hand drifted towards my Apple watch. If I could just get to the SOS.

Right before I could get to my watch, he grabbed my wrist and yanked me out of the car.

"Your little boyfriend thinks he's so smart," Marco said mockingly as he pulled me against him. "Tell me, princess. Does he know that I've had this cunt?" His hand darted between my legs, pushing against me as I began to struggle. "Does he know that I know what you sound like when you cum?" He pressed harder against my core, and I sobbed as I continued to thrash, rejecting everything he was saying.

I hated the reminder of how many times my body had betrayed me.

"He thinks that he's got me all pinned down. That a little thing like an 'investigation' is going to do anything to me." He laughed, no semblance of sanity in his voice. "I'm Marco fucking Davine. I'm untouchable."

I was suddenly yanked away, falling against the car as Walker threw himself at Marco with a roar, slamming his head against the garage wall with a loud thump.

"I'm going to fucking kill you," Walker breathed, smashing his fist against Marco's face.

Blood sprayed through the air as the crunch of Marco's nose shattering filled the garage.

Marco feebly tried to hit Walker, but Walker laughed, as if he'd been tickled rather than punched.

"Did you touch her here?" he asked, slamming his fist against Marco's lips so blood dribbled down his chin.

"How about here?" he continued, pointing at Marco's ribs. He struck at Marco's side until at least some of his ribs snapped.

Marco was moaning and tried to push him away, but Walker punched him in the gut and he fell back against the wall.

"Angel, did he touch you here?" he asked me, pointing to Marco's forehead. I nodded, and Walker punched him so hard in the eye, the ridge of his eye popped open, showing all the way to the bone.

Marco's howls filled the garage, and Walker laughed again.

I made no move to interfere, or tell him to stop. This felt like cosmic justice, like Superman had come to life and was saving me for hopefully the last time.

"And I *know* you touched her here, you fuckwad," Walker seethed, right before he kneed Marco in the dick. Marco screamed and a giggle slipped from my lips.

Marco fell to the ground, writhing in agony on the concrete floor as blood poured from his face. I stared at him, memorizing the moment and every cry he made.

Just like I'd bet he'd done whenever he'd touched me.

Walker calmly walked over to the toolkit that was on a shelf in front of my car, and he grabbed a hammer.

"What are you going to do with that?" I asked, wide-eyed, finally realizing that Walker really couldn't kill him—as much as I wanted him to.

"Making sure he pays for what he did to you for the rest of his life," he told me, pressing a fierce kiss against my lips before he slammed his knee into Marco's gut, holding him flat while he lifted the hammer in the air...

And smashed it against Marco's dick.

Thwack, Thwack, Thwack. He hammered away until blood had soaked the front of his pants. And still he continued.

"Holy fuck, Disney. His dick is gone," I heard Ari's voice comment, right before he grabbed Walker around the waist and pulled him off of Marco's limp form.

I wasn't sure at what point he'd passed out.

Walker kept struggling, his breath coming out in heaving gasps as he tried to lunge back to Marco.

"Walker, it's done. You got him," Lincoln said, a grin on his lips as he stared down at Marco's destroyed body.

"I'm good," Walker huffed.

"You sure?" Ari asked, still holding him around the chest. "Because one more crack with that hammer, and I'm pretty sure he's dead. And you're too pretty for prison. They would like you too much." Walker scoffed and Ari slowly let him go, watching him closely like he expected Walker to lunge back at him at any second.

It was me that did the lunging though. I fell to the ground besides Marco and started slamming my fists anywhere I could reach, tears suddenly streaming down my face.

"I hate you! I hate you! I hope you die, you worthless cunt!" I screamed, my body racking with sobs.

A strong pair of arms wrapped around me and I turned and threw myself into Walker's chest, hysterically crying as I gripped at his shirt.

"Shhh. It's okay, angel. It's done. You did so good. You're safe. He's done," Walker murmured, over and over again until my sobs finally quieted.

Police sirens sounded in the distance.

"Fuck! Walker, tear Olivia's shirt," Lincoln ordered, wrapping the bottom of his shirt around the hammer and carefully moving it into Marco's hand, closing Marco's fingers around it.

"What's going on?" Walker asked, confused.

"Just do it!" Lincoln snapped. "The police are about to be here. There's a little legal term called 'reasonable force' and I'm pretty sure we've flown way past that here. Like Ari said... you're too pretty for prison."

I swear I felt Walker preen at the compliment, and I locked eyes with Ari for a second. He shook his head and mouthed, "fucking simp."

It *almost* made me smile.

"Sorry, sweetheart," Walker muttered as he took my shirt and ripped it down the front.

"Mess with her hair," Lincoln continued. "Make it look like he got farther than he did. Tear her shorts too. They need to see that more...force was necessary."

"Fuck, Golden Boy. You're a fucking genius," Ari commented as Walker messed with my hair before ripping my shorts open and the top of my underwear. "Put a lot of thought into these sorts of things?"

Lincoln scoffed. "Olivia, sweetheart. Keep crying, okay? Don't let those tears dry up."

I nodded, thinking that request was at least easy.

The sirens got louder, and a minute later two squad cars were pulling up to the front of the house, officers leaping out and rushing towards the garage.

"We got him!" Lincoln said. "He's over here!' I stared at Lincoln in shock because of the change in his voice. He was perfectly executing the part of someone who was scared and a victim.

"Shit," one of the officers said, grimacing when he saw Marco. His hand went to the front of his dick, like he was trying to protect his balls from the same fate.

I held in my grin like a champ.

"What happened here?" another officer asked, frowning as he stared at the four of us. "Hey, wait a second, are you guys

Knights players?" His voice got excited. "Holy shit. You're Lincoln Daniels!"

Lincoln's smile was polite but he was still holding back his usual alpha energy.

The officer's gaze fell to me, no recognition in his eyes—just how I liked it. "Ma'am, are you alright? Do you need an ambulance?"

For some reason, that question led to another round of hysterics as it hit me what really could have happened if Walker had been just a few minutes later. My hand went to my stomach, cradling it instinctively as Walker pulled me back into his arms.

"I came home from practice and he was trying..." Walker's voice choked up for a second. "He was trying to rape her."

The officer's gaze dipped to my torn shirt and pants before flicking respectfully away. Walker pushed his hair out of his face, a faint grimace on his lips. "I might have gotten a little carried away," he growled, staring down at Marco. "But my fiancee's pregnant. I—might have lost my head."

"We don't tolerate rapists here in the state of Texas," one of the officers said, prodding Marco's body with his foot in disgust.

"Is that what happened?" the first officer said, rubbing his pot belly as he scrutinized Lincoln, Ari, and Walker. He didn't seem as convinced as the others. "What happened to the man's —" he gulped, "the man's groin area?" He gestured to the blood soaked mess Walker had made of Marco's dick.

"I grabbed the hammer to defend myself and I hit him there," I said through another sob. "I just wanted him to stop. He'd just taken the hammer from me when Walker came home." I wiped at my eyes, feeling shaky as my adrenaline began to crash.

The officer stared us down for a few seconds longer as the other officers lifted Marco's upper half off the floor and cuffed his arms behind his back.

Somehow, Marco began to come to, his eyes slowly blinking until he finally opened them all the way. Walker slipped me behind his back even though there was no way that Marco was in any condition to come at me.

His eyes were hazy and confused as he glanced around, taking a second before he seemed to remember where he was. His gaze met mine as I peeked out behind Walker's body. "Why —" he spit, an inhuman cry coming out of him as he laid there, seemingly unable to move at all. "Don't you..ask him about…the deal." His garbled words cut off as he passed out once again.

What had he said? A deal? I shook my head, confused.

The officers stared at Marco in disgust as an ambulance barreled down the street, its sirens going off. "Get him out of here, boys. Try not to let him die on the way to the hospital," the first officer said. He turned his attention to me, his gaze gentling. "Ma'am, do you need medical treatment? Did he–"

I shook my head, the effort making my head pound. "No," I whispered. "He was stopped in time."

The officer breathed out a relieved sounding sigh and nodded. "We're going to need to take your statement then, if that's alright," he said.

"Later. *After* she's checked out at the hospital," Walker growled.

The officer startled, staring at Walker's face…a faint flicker of fear in his eyes.

"Later," he agreed. Walker and the others gave him their contact information and finally…what seemed like forever later…he left.

"Thank you," I murmured to Lincoln and Ari, taking a step towards the house.

"Not so fast, sweetheart. We're going to get you checked out at the hospital," Walker said anxiously, scooping me up into his arms before I could take another step.

"I'm fine. I just need a nap," I insisted, my words sounding weird in my ears.

He paid me no attention as he carried me to the passenger side of my car and set me down on the seat.

"Let us know how she is," called Ari as Walker hopped into the driver's seat and threw the car in reverse.

Walker waved at them as we drove away.

I was shaking in my seat, a full on crash happening. "You're okay, sweetheart," he murmured soothingly, flipping on the heater and rubbing his hand over my leg as he drove.

I was faintly aware of him continuing to speak to me, but the words sounded like he was muttering them underwater.

And eventually...I couldn't hear them at all.

CHAPTER 32

WALKER

I paced back and forth in the hospital room, my heart threatening to beat out of my chest. The doctors had assured me that Olivia was going to be fine…that the baby was going to be fine too…but the sight of her…laying there.

I wanted nothing to do with this world without her in it.

I'd come full circle evidently. Because I understood now how much my mother had felt all these years. Without the other half of your soul…what were you?

Nothing.

The answer was nothing.

A faint moan was like music to my ears, and I rushed to Olivia's side as she *finally* stirred awake. Relief flooding me as I saw her beautiful eyes flutter open.

I gently laid my head on her chest, listening to the steady rhythm of her heartbeat.

"Please don't ever leave me," I murmured into her skin, an ache in my voice that I couldn't hide.

"I'm okay," she said in a groggy voice as she touched my hair, softly stroking it. I closed my eyes, trying to reassure myself…she was okay. She was here.

I'd never allow her to go somewhere I couldn't follow.

Never.

The door opened and a doctor popped her head in. "Oh good, you're awake," she said warmly, stepping inside. The woman had a kind smile with silver streaked hair that was pulled back into a neat bun, and I didn't immediately want to throw her out for getting near Olivia.

So I guess that was a good sign.

"My name is Dr. Rochelle. How are you feeling?" she asked as I held a cup of water up to Olivia's lips for her to sip.

'Tired," Olivia answered before she glanced at me. "How long was I out?"

"Two hours," I responded shakily, not wanting to think about that fact, or else I might go crazy.

Or at least crazier than I already was.

"Well, your vitals look great. I'm not worried at all," the doctor reassured. "Would you like to see your baby before we get you out of here?" Her eyes twinkled with excitement.

I blinked, my mind trying to wrap around what she'd just asked.

"Yes!" Olivia said, anticipation threaded through her voice as she shifted in the bed.

"I'll help you!" I insisted quickly, jumping up to pick her up.

"I'm fine," she murmured. "I'm just tired, remember?"

I forced myself to sit back down even though all I really wanted to do was grab her and pull her into my lap.

Calm down, Walker. The doctor is looking at you like she's concerned.

"So, Olivia," Dr. Rachelle started, her tone gentle yet probing, "How long has it been since your last period?"

Olivia bit her lip, a furrow forming between her brows as she thought back. "I think at least two months...maybe more," she finally replied, her voice slightly strained. "It's been a busy fall. I guess I got distracted."

Olivia was right. She'd missed two periods. I would know... I'd been tracking her cycle religiously for months. If she wasn't pregnant, her period would have been about to start.

The doctor nodded sympathetically, jotting down notes on her clipboard. "Understandable," she murmured, clearing her throat. "Your records say Olivia Jones...but you're Olivia Darling, aren't you?" Olivia stiffened before finally nodding. "Yes, that's my stage name," she finally answered.

The doctor nodded again, looking kind of like one of those bobble head dolls since she'd been doing it so much. "And were you using any form of birth control during this time?"

Olivia frowned. "Yes, and I took it religiously...but I guess it didn't work."

"Strong swimmers," I joked, but neither Olivia nor the doctor laughed.

Tough crowd.

"Well, birth control methods aren't always 100% effective, but it's still unusual. Can you tell me which one you were using, so we try another one next time?"

"They are still in my purse actually. Did you bring it in by chance?" Olivia asked, turning towards me. "I had put it in the car before...everything."

I froze, pure panic hitting me with a jolt. Her pills were in her purse.

The doctor was going to take one look and *know*.

I slowly reached for her bag, feeling like there was a ticking time bomb attached to every move I made. "Here you go, baby," I said lightly, proud of myself for keeping my voice so controlled.

She rummaged through it, eventually finding the little birth control packet.

My hand slipped into my pocket. I'd started doing a slightly weird thing when I'd begun working towards her pregnancy... I'd taken to carrying...handcuffs.

Although there were only three people in the world who knew what I'd done, Lincoln had drilled into my head that you never knew when things could fall apart.

For example...this was not a situation I'd ever envisioned—our baby doctor about to blow my whole scheme.

I was fully prepared if it came down to it, to handcuff Olivia to me...until eventually she just gave up and decided to love me despite what I'd done.

Not an ideal situation, but beggars couldn't be choosers. There was no scenario where she and that baby weren't mine.

I rubbed the metal of the cuffs, my nerves practically vibrating with tension as the doctor took the packet from Olivia. "This is usually a very dependable brand," she murmured. Popping one of the pills out of the package, she examined it closely. "Hmmm. These are all placebo pills," she remarked, her surprise evident in her voice.

The place I'd bought them from was very good. Everything was sealed, in the same packaging as the regular pills. So there would be no evidence it had been tampered with.

They just happened to be the sugar pills you were supposed to take the last seven days of the month.

Blank. I was a blank slate, I told myself.

"What?" Olivia whispered. She turned to me, her gaze wide. "Can you believe this?!"

A bead of sweat rolled down my back.

Fuck. Fuck. Fuck.

I opened my mouth, and then closed it, swallowing the bitter taste flooding my taste buds as I feigned surprise. "I can't believe it!"

There, that sounded shocked...right?

I watched Olivia's body language closely, trying to read into what she was thinking.

The doctor leaned in close, like she was telling her a secret, and I wondered for a second if I was going to have to knock her out and then kidnap Olivia.

What was a traumatic brain injury in the name of true love?

"Mistakes happen," Dr Rochelle said in a low tone, "but between you and me, you probably have a *very* good chance at winning in a lawsuit against whatever pharmacy filled this. I've never seen anything like it."

Olivia nodded, staying quiet.

What the fuck was she thinking? Should I just get the cuffs out now?

She glanced at me again...and then winced. "I swear I had no idea. I've never paid attention to what my birth control pills have looked like before. I'm an idiot."

I immediately relaxed, loosening my grip on the cuffs as I used my other hand to softly stroke her cheek.

"It was meant to be. All that manifesting worked like a charm," I said with a wink.

Her grin was blinding and perfect and...she didn't suspect a thing.

"I don't think we need to sue the pharmacy though, Doc. I'm not sure they award damages for being *blissfully happy* about something," I drawled.

The doctor's cheeks blushed and Olivia rolled her eyes at me because evidently...Dr. Rochelle had a little crush.

Which was honestly great because that meant she didn't suspect a thing either.

I finally let go of the cuffs in my pocket, feeling like I might have aged ten years in the process.

The doctor finally turned her attention to the ultrasound machine, and my heart started racing again. This was it—the moment I'd been waiting for, the chance to catch a glimpse of our baby for the first time.

She applied the gel to Olivia's stomach and began to move the wand. I held my breath, anticipation humming through my insides.

And then, there it was—the unmistakable sound of a heartbeat, strong and steady, filling the room with its rhythmic cadence.

Olivia's eyes widened in wonder, her hand flying to her

mouth as tears welled up in her eyes. "Oh my God," she whispered, her voice choked with emotion. "That's our baby."

"It looks like you're around thirteen weeks along," Dr. Rochelle said as she moved the wand across Olivia's skin.

I squeezed her hand, my own eyes shimmering with tears as I gazed at the monitor, drinking in the sight of our tiny miracle.

It was the second time I'd been reborn in my life.

The first being when I saw Olivia, of course.

The emotions I was feeling were complicated, life-changing. I loved this baby. I loved it so much.

"Our little Shmoopy," I sighed happily.

Olivia groaned. "*It's* not a little shmoopy!" she said indignantly.

"It's not an "it" at all," the doctor said with a smile. "You're having a girl."

Word to the wise…passing out onto a hard, tile floor when you're 6'4 and you weigh 220 pounds…it hurts like fuck when you wake up.

CHAPTER 33
WALKER

 Ari: I'm going to start calling you Thor with the way you worked that hammer.

King Linc: That was a ridiculous attempt at humor, Lancaster. Even for you.

Ari: I'm not even joking. I'm a little nauseous… and turned on…every time I think about it. I mean, you literally smashed his dick.

Me: That's what she said.

King Linc:...

Ari: Perfectly executed, Disney.

Me: Why are you being so nice?

King Linc: That should be obvious…

Me:?

King Linc: He's scared of what you can do with your hammer.

Ari: I have to do it.

King Linc:…

King Linc: Fine.

Ari: That's what she said.

Me: Anyways, you can't call me Thor.

Ari: Why not?

Me: Because Hercules and Thor don't mix. They aren't the right mythology or whatever.

King Linc: Hercules?

Ari: His dick, Golden Boy. It's his name for his dick.

King Linc: Why do all of these conversations end up with discussions about dicks?

Ari:...

Me:...

King Linc: Sigh.

———

O*livia*

"I'm ready to make my ruling."

The judge's words seemed to echo around the L.A. courtroom where my attorneys had spent the last hour presenting all the evidence Walker's P.I. had collected over the last few months.

It helped that Marco had admitted in prison to drugging me that first night—-that he and Jolette had orchestrated it *all.* Evidently the loss of his dick and his freedom had fully convinced him that it wasn't worth attempting to lie anymore.

He'd already lost everything.

Jolette was sitting in the courtroom, her attorney mostly silent thus far except for an attempt at arguing that Marco had been the mastermind behind everything that had occurred—and Jolette just a victim.

That argument hadn't gone well with the Court.

She sat slouched in her seat, a pitiful sight devoid of all her usual pretentious glamor. Her once impeccably styled blonde hair had grown out since that day she'd come to the house, revealing gray roots—a sight I'd never seen on her before. Without the façade of designer labels and ostentatious accessories, she appeared utterly diminished, a hollow shell of a human being unworthy of any sympathy. Like her mask had finally been removed.

"What has happened to Ms. Jones is a miscarriage of justice," the judge began, her expression stern as she surveyed the room, her keen eyes seeming to miss nothing as they darted over the spectators filling the rows behind me. She frowned for a second, like she didn't like so many people in her courtroom. "It is a sad and unfortunate truth that the conservatorship process is not perfect. That sometimes it can be wielded like a weapon, instead of as the healing stopgap it was originally intended to be."

Dressed in a black robe that billowed around her like a cloak of authority, she finally turned her attention to me.

"I know there is nothing that I can say today that will remedy the past and the harm that's befallen you…that will bring back the years that you've lost. But I hope that it will at least allow for you to flourish in the present. The Court's order is that from this day forward, the conservatorship is ended, all rights are returned to Ms. Jones; legal, financial, and otherwise. I also order that Jolette Jones and Marco Davine will pay restitution for the appalling misuse of Ms. Jones's funds. In all my time as a judge in L.A. County, I have never seen such an abuse of a conservatorship. Although I predict that they will spend the majority—if not all—of their lives in prison for the fraud and abuse and other crimes they have committed, any money they do earn will go to reimburse Ms. Jones, and any assets they currently possess will be liquidated to assist with that reimbursement."

The judge's words echoed in my ears, and a rush of emotions swept through me like a sudden downpour, drenching my senses and leaving me reeling in its wake.

Relief, disbelief, and a profound sense of *freedom* swelled in my soul, mingling with the pounding of my heart and the tight knot of anxiety that had been lodged in my chest for so long it was all I could remember.

I glanced at Walker in disbelief, wondering if I was dreaming. If I would blink and I'd wake up in bed, alone and miserable in that L.A. apartment.

It felt like I'd been in chains all these years, and the weight of them had suddenly fallen away. It was a heady sensation, exhilarating and terrifying all at once, like stepping off a precipice into the unknown depths below.

Tears pricked at the corners of my eyes as I stared around the courtroom, taking in the faces of fans that had shown up to show support once news had begun to leak out about what Marco and Jolette had done to me. I could have used their support years ago, but I guess it was a nice enough gesture now.

The judge banged her gavel, adjourning the hearing, and I stood up, unsure for a second what to do with myself. My gaze fell on Jolette and I walked towards her, unable to stop, Walker trailing behind me with his comforting presence.

"My client does *not* wish to speak to you," her lawyer mumbled, sounding embarrassed as he spoke the words.

It must suck to represent a piece of trash, one that I was sure wouldn't be able to pay him. His fee was certainly not coming out of my bank accounts.

"That's fine. I just have one thing to say to *her* though," I said sarcastically, staring at my mother as she tried to avoid my gaze. "This will be the last time I think about you," I told her. "But unfortunately for you...I'm quite positive that you will think about me for the *rest* of your life." Jolette flinched at that statement...because she knew it was true. She may not have spent much time thinking about me all these years, but that was definitely going to change.

She was about to have a lot of time on her hands.

I turned to leave, satisfied with that ending.

"He came to us," she called after me. "Your *precious* boyfriend came to us and offered to date you in exchange for publicity. How about you *think* about that."

I scoffed at the ridiculousness of what she'd said, and I didn't bother turning around to look at her. Walker had gone still at her comment though, his fingers pressing into my lower back as he led us out of the courtroom.

There was no way she'd been telling the truth…right?

The sidewalk outside the courthouse was insane, teeming with a frenetic energy, cameras flashing everywhere, like strobe lights in a darkened club. My lawyer's voice cut through the chaos. "I'll handle the statement," he said, his tone brimming with confidence. "You need to get out of here."

"Thank you," I told him, and he smiled and nodded for a second before he turned towards the crowd.

"Car's over there, angel," Walker murmured as he huddled close behind me, his arm outstretched in front of my chest to prevent anyone from getting too close.

I kept my gaze down, trying to avoid the eyes of the reporters who'd taken such joy in my downfall all these years.

We made it to the other side of the sidewalk where the driver already had the door open of the SUV we were taking to the airport—I was ready to get out of this hellish town as soon as possible.

I was about to slide onto the leather seats when a ripple of applause suddenly echoed through the crowd, like the first drops of rain after a long drought.

I froze, one foot in the car, my heart hammering in my chest as I glanced around in disbelief.

The crowd of paparazzi were clapping and cheering for me.

These were the same people who had once reveled in my

downfall, the same faces that had gleefully spread the lies and rumors Jolette and Marco had used to tarnish my name.

And yet, here they were, applauding me, offering their support in a way I had never imagined possible.

I flipped them off and got in the SUV.

Because *fuck them* for deciding to be decent *now*.

The engine roared to life, the steady hum of the vehicle a soothing backdrop to the emotions raging in my chest.

At least we were on the way to the airport. I'd always been able to think more clearly outside of L.A.

"Do you want to talk about what she said?" Walker finally asked.

"No. Not right now," I murmured, my gaze drifting to the driver who was pretending not to listen. I'd had enough of strangers knowing everything about my business for today.

For my life…

"We *are* going to talk about it," he insisted. "When we get home."

I finally turned to look at him, taking in his gorgeous, concerned face. Home. Was it still my home?

There couldn't be a world where he'd betrayed me. That couldn't be the plot twist of my story.

"Was she telling the truth?" The words slipped past my lips before I could stop them, my voice barely above a whisper but ringing loud in the confined space of the car.

Walker's eyes flickered with a myriad of emotions, his features contorting with conflict as he struggled to find the right words. "It's complicated," he finally said, his voice strained as he met my gaze. "But no…"

Complicated. The word echoed in my mind like a discordant melody, leaving me reeling. Anger, hurt, betrayal—all vied for dominance as I searched his face for answers.

But his expression remained inscrutable, a mask of conflicting emotions.

The rest of the car ride to the airport was eerily silent, the tension between us tangible and suffocating.

As we boarded Lincoln and Ari's private plane, aka "Grandma Airways", Mabel and Edna greeted us with non-alcoholic sparkling cider and cookies.

"Congratulations!" they cried, their cheerful demeanor and cat sweaters at odds with the knot of dread that had settled in the pit of my stomach. I forced a polite smile and accepted a glass of the drink, but the bubbly liquid tasted wrong on my tongue.

We settled into our seats and the plane took off. I had thought every mile away from L.A. would be healing.

But so far the journey hadn't been what I'd thought.

Walker tried to talk to me, his voice gentle as he reached out to touch my arm, but I pulled away, the ache in my chest too raw to bear. "Not now," I whispered, my voice barely audible above the hum of the plane's engines. "I can't...not yet."

His brow furrowed with concern, but he nodded, his expression reflecting the turmoil that mirrored my own. We retreated to our seats, the silence between us heavy with unspoken words and unanswered questions.

I buried myself in my thoughts, and the hours stretched on, each minute somehow feeling like an eternity.

How was he going to explain this?

CHAPTER 34
WALKER

"You need to eat," I coaxed her as we walked into the door of the house. She hadn't eaten anything this morning before the hearing because she'd been too nervous. And on the plane, I hadn't even been able to get her to eat Mabel's cookies.

She and the baby needed nutrition, damnit.

"I can make you a smoothie…"

"I'm not hungry," she muttered, heading towards the bedroom.

I followed after her…of course. Where she went I was always going to go.

Olivia walked into the closet and stopped in front of her side, staring at her clothes.

"What are you doing?" I asked. "Can we talk now?"

"I think we should take a minute. Maybe I should get my own place for a little bit," she said in a dead voice. "I'll probably need a new realtor since the one I've been using clearly sucks." She glared at me. "Or was that part of your plan too?"

Fair point about the realtor…but what had she just said? There was a buzzing in my ears and I was thinking I'd finally lost my mind because there was no way she was saying she needed some space. The farthest space she could have was the other side of the bed. "Space" was not happening.

"There's no plan," I said patiently. "If you would just listen to me. There's a very reasonable explanation for what she said."

Her golden eyes had lost their shine, and her expression was...defeated.

She pulled one of her favorite shirts off a hanger and I shook my head.

There was a lot that Olivia could want to leave me over...the foremost being *our daughter* in her stomach right now...but my deal with Jolette and Marco to smooth the way for our relationship was not one of them.

Sighing, I shook my head as I pulled the handcuffs out of my pocket.

I reached over and fastened them around her delicate wrist, the metallic click echoing loudly in the room.

Olivia glanced down at her arm, staring at the cuffs for a second before she gaped at me in disbelief.

"What the hell are you doing?" she demanded.

I stared back unflinchingly, my jaw clenched tight as I secured the other side of the cuffs to my wrist. "Making sure you don't try to run from me before we talk about what that bitch said," I replied, my voice low and intense.

She huffed. "Seriously, Walker, undo these *right* now." She didn't seem scared or alarmed yet...that was good. This was a perfect practice run for if she ever figured out the birth control... and everything else I'd done.

"We need to talk," I insisted, my voice tinged with urgency.

"You unhook me right now or...or..." her voice faded away as she failed to come up with something she would do to me.

My girl loved me too much to be mean.

I went to touch her cheek and she jerked away, a cute little growl coming from her lips.

"I met with them after Harley's wedding," I began. "You seemed to think that there wasn't any reasoning with them, and that we were dead in the water." I shrugged. "So I reasoned with them."

Her lip trembled. "And what did *reasoning* with them look like?"

I gently pulled on her arm, taking her into the bedroom so she could sit on the bed. I needed to check her ankles for swelling too, see if I needed to massage them or anything. I'd read that airline travel and pregnancy sometimes weren't fun.

"Sit down," I told her, and she huffed and tried to cross her arms in front of her...before remembering her left arm was still attached to mine.

When I continued to stare at her demandingly, she flopped down on the bed, trying her best to make her irritation known.

"I told them that I was starting a new team, and dating you was the perfect opportunity to get some publicity. They thought that you dating me was good for your reputation, so it was an easy sell."

She nodded, tears gathering in her eyes.

"Sweetheart," I said, appalled at the sight of her crying. "Obviously that wasn't true! It was all to make sure they wouldn't get in the way of us being together. It's not like I could have just *reasoned* with them."

She nodded again. And I was beginning to hate that move.

"So the move to Dallas...that was you?" she asked quietly.

Shit. This web was going to untangle really quickly.

"Yes," I said hesitantly.

"And the paparazzi magically knowing where we were most times we went out...you again?"

"I had to hold up at least part of my bargain," I responded.

"And I assume the goal was to improve my reputation enough for me to perform to sold out crowds again?"

"I would assume that was their goal...yes."

She stared down at the handcuff again and rattled it. "You know this is crazy, right..." she muttered, her voice barely a whisper.

"Some would call it that, yes," I responded, trying to hold in my grin...because it seemed like she was softening.

"Why didn't you tell me?" she whispered after another long pause. "When you knew all they'd done to control and manipulate my life...why didn't you tell me?"

"Because of the situation we're in right this very second," I responded fiercely.

"What?" she asked, confused.

"Angel face, you're questioning me after *months* of us being together. After everything I did to get you free of the conservatorship. After I made Marco's dick a pancake. After you got pregnant with my baby... Telling you the truth after we'd spent *one* weekend together was not going to go well."

She bit down on her lip sheepishly...a small smile appearing. "That's—that's probably a good point."

I grinned triumphantly. This was going swimmingly.

"It's safe to say I may have issues with trust," she admitted, and when I tried to reach out to touch her cheek again, she didn't move away.

"That is safe to say," I snorted. "But for completely valid reasons," I hurriedly added, not wanting her to feel bad about that.

There *were* lots of things about me she shouldn't trust at all... being with her for the wrong reasons though...that wasn't one of them.

"I'm sorry you have to put up with me," she said softly. "I know it's a lot."

I stared at her in shock.

"Sorry?" I echoed, my voice filled with incredulity. "Olivia, I'm the one that's *sorry*. Because clearly I've been doing a shitty job of showing just how much I love you. You're not a burden, you're my *everything*. Everything," I repeated fiercely. "I breathe for you. I covet you. I spend every second of every day thinking about you. A burden?" I scoffed. "The way I love you goes beyond any love story you've ever heard. There isn't anything I wouldn't do to keep you. I burn for you, in the way that only someone can when you're holding a piece of their soul."

She was staring at me like she was entranced, and I leaned in slowly and brushed a kiss against her lips.

Olivia's answering sigh was one of relief. Like she hadn't been able to handle the last couple of hours either. Hope was gleaming in her eyes, pushing out the fear she sometimes had that she wasn't worthy of love.

"A little handcuffing is the least of what I'd do to keep you," I told her, my forehead meeting hers as I breathed her in.

"Sometimes it sounds a little...crazy when you say things like that," she murmured.

I laughed because...if she only knew.

"Good thing you love crazy."

She nodded. "For some reason, I do."

"If you can believe anything I say, believe this, angel. I will never let you go."

"Can you take this off now?" she asked finally, rattling the handcuff, because she still thought they were some kind of a joke. That's okay, it was better if she thought that way.

"Not quite," I murmured, unhooking the cuff from around my wrist and snapping it on her free one.

A blush appeared on her cheeks and her gaze grew heavy-lidded. Evidently my girl actually liked cuffs...

That would be a fun thing to experiment with.

I laid her down on the bed, feeling a bit deranged as I stared at her. She was still wearing the prim and proper little skirt that she'd put on for the hearing—the one that reminded me of an Audrey Hepburn movie. And, I was just glad that I was the only man who was going to know that underneath that suit was a body built for pure sin.

I gripped my gigantic hard on, which was pressing against the zipper of my suit slacks, thinking that I might die if I didn't get inside her soon.

"Put your hands above your head," I growled as I pushed her

skirt up, not having the patience to bother with trying to take it off, and then I ripped her thong away, my dick gushing pre-cum all over my briefs as I stared at her perfect pussy, her lips already glistening with her arousal.

"Please fuck me," she murmured, her eyes gleaming because she knew what it did to me when she talked like that.

"I don't know, angel face. I'm not sure you're ready for me. Should I check if you're wet enough for my big cock?" I purred as I slid a hand up her thigh, lightly stroking her skin until I was inches away from her cunt.

"Please," she whispered, still holding her hands above her head, like the good girl she was.

I slid my fingers through her dripping folds, moaning at how she was already gushing for me.

Before I fucked her, I needed a taste.

I dove between her legs, unable to take it slow as I forced her legs wider, pushing her knees so that she was completely open for me. The sight of her like this...skirt bunched up around her waist, hands over her head...her bare fucking cunt.

This was my heaven.

I licked up her slit, gathering every drop of essence I could.

"Fuck," I moaned. "Sweetest thing I've ever tasted."

She squirmed and I grinned before I swirled my tongue over her clit, licking and sucking on it until she was fucking her hips against my face.

Just how I liked it.

But I could think of another position that would be fun.

I sat up and she whimpered at the loss of my mouth.

"Turn over, baby," I murmured, helping her onto her knees so her perfect ass was on display. I pushed up her blouse so that more of her back was bare to me. "Keep your hands above your head."

She obeyed and I stroked my hand down her skin, imagining for a second what it would be like to fuck her like this with her belly huge beneath her.

Fucking perfection.

I licked her from clit to asshole, rimming the pucker of her hole, my fingers dipping into her folds as I spread her moisture around so that I could work her clit and her ass at the same time.

She writhed against my face and my fingers, and my cock felt like it might die if it didn't get inside her soon.

Just a little more....

She came, gushing all over my face, and I lapped up everything desperately, not wanting to waste a drop.

"Yes, fuck," I groaned as I gave her one more lick before I finally unbuttoned my slacks and pulled out my throbbing cock.

It was still a little strange to fist it and feel the beads of her name pierced through my shaft...but she seemed to like how it felt...so I guess it was okay.

Fucking Ari.

"I'm going to fuck this perfect cunt. And then I'm going to fuck this perfect ass so every part of you knows who you belong to..sound good, baby?" I growled as I pushed my dick through her slick folds, wetting it so I could get inside her tight pussy.

No matter how many times I fucked her...it was a tight fit.

I almost blacked out when I slid all the way to the hilt... because the way she took me. This is how I wanted to die, choked by her pussy.

I gripped her hips and started to fuck in and out of her, adjusting my speed and rhythm based on the noises she was making. I knew when I hit the right spot..because just like always...she started to beg.

"That's it, sweetheart. You feel so good."

I kneaded and massaged her ass, knowing I was going to have to pull out soon and fuck her there before I came.

"Yes, yes. Walker. Fuuuck," she moaned, her pussy clamping down on me as she orgasmed...hard.

I gritted my teeth, trying to hold in my own release as I pulled out, my fingers dipping inside her cunt so I could spread it around her ass and make what was coming feel good.

That was going to have to do.

My dick was already soaked from her pussy, but it was still an effort to push inside her ass, that tight ring of muscle gripping my dick so tight I thought I might pass out.

"Walker," she screamed as I thrusted all the way in, caressing her clit so I could push hard and deep.

"Milk my cock, angel. Choke it with your tight hole," I growled as she came again, her perfect whimpers and cries lighting up the room.

This time, I couldn't hold off. Bursts of pleasure licked up my spine as I pulled out and sprayed ropes of milky white cum all over her smooth skin. I stared at it dazed as I came down slowly from my high, reaching out and spreading it all over her ass cheeks so that she was covered with me.

She collapsed to the bed and I followed her, my hand moving to cradle her stomach as I licked a line up her shoulder and into her neck.

"I love you," I murmured, satisfaction thrumming through me because I didn't think it was possible for me to be happier than this.

"I love you," she whispered as she faded into sleep.

———

Olivia may have been able to go to sleep after our lovemaking, but I'd stayed awake, not able to tear my eyes away from her.

I reached for the small velvet box tucked away in my bedside table. Carefully, almost reverently, I slid the engagement ring onto her finger. I'd had it since right after her cousin's wedding. But it had taken until now to feel like she was ready.

I watched as she slept, the soft rise and fall of her chest, the way her lips twitched in a small smile as she dreamed. I counted the freckles on her cheeks for the thousandth time…waiting.

And then, slowly, she began to stir, blinking her eyes sleepily as she stared up at the ceiling. She rubbed at her face, and a second later she was gaping at the ring, her mouth open in complete shock.

Finally, her gaze turned to meet mine, tears already pooling in her golden eyes.

"You want me to marry you?" she whispered, her voice thick with emotion.

I couldn't help but smile at her, my heart soaring at the sight of her tear-streaked face. "Actually, I'm telling you that you are. I'll give you lots of choices in life," I replied, my voice barely above a whisper, "but not this one."

Her grin was radiant as she reached out to caress my face, her touch sending sparks straight to my dick—as usual. "Good thing I was going to say yes anyway," she teased…as usual thinking I was joking.

"Mine," I murmured, leaning in to brush my lips against hers. Olivia's tears mingled with our kiss, the taste of saltwater becoming my new favorite flavor.

"Mine," she replied back, her hand slipping to my already excited cock.

And then, as usual, our hands met on her belly. "*Ours*," I mouthed against her lips, before we didn't talk for a very, very long time.

CHAPTER 35
WALKER

Ari: It's time to resurrect my taco truck idea.

King Linc: What taco truck idea?

Ari: How could you forget about my best idea?

Me: A taco truck was your best idea?

CAMDEN "HERO' JAMES ADDED TO THE CHAT.

Camden: Where am I?

Ari: Welcome to the circle of trust. Actually, you're not in the circle yet. Your sole purpose is to tell these two how awesome my taco truck idea is.

Camden: I'm kind of offended.

Me: Welcome to the club. It's not "the circle", but getting dick punched by Ari is a club.

King Linc: I literally thought we discussed this. No dick talk today!

Ari: Ooh, he's using his growly voice again, Disney. I bet you're turned on.

Me: Fuck you.

Ari:...that's...

King Linc: Okay, your taco truck is a good idea. But please, for fuck's sake, don't say it, Lancaster.

Camden: I would just like to say that I haven't officially endorsed the idea of a taco truck. I'd like entry into the circle of trust before I make that kind of commitment.

King Linc: Bribing your way into the circle...I like it.

Ari: Although blackmailing is best practice in this group.

Camden:...

King Linc:...

Ari:...

Me: Welcome to the club.

Ari: But again...not the circle.

Camden: I'll get there.

O*livia*

The NHL All-Star Weekend was in full swing, and I was cheering from the stands as Walker took to the ice for the goalie skills competition.

Ari and Lincoln were standing on the side of the rink, waiting for their respective competitions to start. Ari reached over and grabbed something from the other side of the boards, pulling out a large sign that he hoisted above his head.

"Daddy Disney is a 10."

Blake erupted in giggles next to me, and I saw Walker shake his head before he turned his attention to the competition.

With each event, from the rapid-fire shots to the precision saves, Walker was a badass between the pipes, leaving everyone in the crowd in awe.

He was also turning me on. Pregnancy had made me a horny mess, and watching him block shot after shot like the number one goalie he was had me feeling particularly *thirsty*.

Lincoln lined up for his shot, he was last since he was the number one scorer in the league right now. There was a mischievous grin on his lips, and Monroe literally swooned next to me.

I snorted at her and she stuck out her tongue. "What can I say? My guy's hot."

It was a true statement, but not even Lincoln Daniels could live up to Walker Davis in my book.

My husband.

The thought still made me giddy.

Lincoln skated towards Walker with the confidence of someone who knew he was the best. He closed in on Walker, his stick poised and ready to strike. With a swift motion, he maneuvered the puck with finesse, aiming for the top corner of the net. I held my breath as the puck soared towards the goal, a blur of motion against the ice. In a split second, Walker dove to make the save, his body stretching to its limits as he deflected the puck away with his blocker.

The crowd erupted into cheers as Walker made the save, their applause echoing through the arena.

Walker did a little bow to Lincoln and Ari reached over the boards and grabbed another sign, this one saying.

"Disney, you're still a simp."

I giggled as I watched Walker skate off the ice, the clear winner of the competition.

My belly fluttered, and I softly rubbed the spot where our daughter was kicking the ever loving crap out of me. She did that, a lot.

And it happened to be Walker's and my favorite thing to feel it.

"Well, if it isn't my favorite sister-in-law," Cole drawled. I glanced up and saw him coming down the aisle towards us. He was performing for All Star Weekend, and I knew Walker was pumped to have most of his favorite people around for three days.

Right before he could get to me, Elaine leapt up from her seat. Walker still had two female bodyguards on me for every game—and every other time he wasn't with me, which wasn't often.

I thought they had a pretty easy gig since Walker's favorite thing in life was being close to me.

"Hey," Cole said indignantly when Elaine wouldn't let him pass.

"Sorry sir, you're not on the approved list," she said, crossing her arms in front of her, a sight that would be intimidating to anyone since her biceps were the size of small busses.

"Who's on the approved list?" Blake whispered, her gaze tracking Ari as he skated around.

"I don't actually think anyone's on the list except for Walker," I mused, my gaze also on the ice as Walker skated towards us.

Blake snorted, not surprised at all since Ari was just as bad.

"Walkie-poo, tell this fine lady that I'm allowed to talk to your wife. She's already pregnant. There's not much I can do."

Walker rolled his eyes at his brother. "Sorry, the last time you hugged my wife, it lasted five seconds. That should last you for the next five years."

Cole gaped at him, before turning his attention to me. "I swear our Mama didn't raise him like this."

I grinned. "I happen to like him exactly as he is."

Walker blew me a kiss and I reached out and pretended to catch it.

Cole made a gagging noise like he was about to throw up. "You guys are so sweet it makes me sick."

Walker smiled unrepentantly and skated away. "Keep everyone away from my wife, Elaine," he reminded her, and I swear her muscles hulked out even more as she stood there.

Thinking about Walker and Cole's mom made my grin slip a little. She'd been officially placed in a nursing care facility a month ago, having completely given up on life. Walker had taken me to Tennessee to meet her, and she had been a sweet, if incredibly sad woman.

Walker had made peace with the fact that she probably wouldn't get better. He'd told me that meeting me made him understand her better now.

I still held out hope for some kind of miracle for her.

I happened to be a big believer in those things nowadays.

The baby kicked again and I shifted in my seat, trying to get into a more comfortable position. Maddie leaned over from the other side of Blake, her own belly almost bursting. She was due in a month.

"Maddie Jr. giving you trouble?" she teased. Despite the fact that Maddie and Harley had a house in Dallas, we rarely saw them, so I was overjoyed she was with us this weekend since Harley had been named an All Star this year as well.

She seemed blissfully happy, and she and Harley still called me often, but Harley always had some kind of excuse for why we couldn't actually get together in person. Maddie couldn't explain Harley's attitude, but we were working on him.

"That joke's going to be funny until I accidentally say it in the hospital because you've said it so often," I said snarkily, and she grinned.

"That's obviously my plan," she responded with a wink.

Sometimes I still couldn't believe that this was my life. That so much sweetness could come after so much pain.

That I sang all the time now.

Of course I didn't plan on touring or performing tons of shows again, but my fans didn't seem to care. The album I'd just released—all love songs for Walker, might I add—had gone triple platinum.

I had nightmares sometimes, where I'd dream that nothing over the past year had happened, and I was still in that L.A. apartment...all alone.

Walker was always there though, waking me up and reminding me that I'd never be alone again, because he owned me body and soul.

If this was a dream, it was one that I never wanted to wake up from.

I would have gone through a million years of misery as long as I ended up with him.

I thought about fate alot, about how the tides could turn and change...about how one moment, one decision...could change your whole life...

Like what happened when I had the *pucking wrong date*...and I ended up with a happily ever after.

EPILOGUE

WALKER

Ari: Avengers assemble!

Lincoln: What?

Ari: Oh sorry, that's what this meeting kind of felt like.

Me: I just want to make sure everyone knows their role.

Camden: I think the question is, do you know your role...because I'm not going anywhere near your wife's cervix.

Ari: I have a horrified look on my face right now.

King Linc: Me too.

Me: Stay away from my wife's cervix, Camden.

Ari: You've been docked ten points for that comment. *-10 pts*

Camden: Wait, what's the point system for?

Me: Can we focus?

King Linc: Good fucking hell. I will handle this. Okay, Olivia's water breaks while you're at practice, Disney, and you get the call. What do you do?

Ari: Monroe is driving her to the hospital in this scenario by the way.

King Linc: Wait, why is Monroe at Walker's house?

Ari: Well, in this scenario, it's more of Olivia's house because Walker's not there, right? So you can probably hold off on the jealous caveman routine.

Camden: Can I remind everyone that this is a fake scenario we're discussing.

Me: Thank you, Hero.

Ari: But eventually it will be real, so we better have Blake drive Olivia. I can sacrifice for the greater good for my bestie.

Me: Aww, you called me your bestie.

Ari: I was talking about Olivia of course, Disney. It's like you don't even know me.

Me:...

"What are you guys talking about?" Olivia asked absentmindedly as she stared at the contents of the fridge, her nose wrinkled as she found its contents lacking. "I think you've snorted five times in the last minute."

"Planning for the baby, of course," I said, setting the phone down and walking up to her so I could hold her belly for a second. I couldn't get enough. "How are you feeling, angel face? Want me to take you to get something?"

She pouted and I kissed her, because how could I resist? I

grabbed her hand, tangling my fingers with hers, the feel of her wedding ring soothing something inside me. The ring was soothing in two ways actually. It represented that she was mine, obviously, but it also had a tracker so I knew where she was at all times...just in case the cameras throughout the house and in the cars, and the 24/7 female bodyguards I had on duty somehow lost her.

"I'm hungry, but I'm full. I'm tired, but I can't sleep. I'm a little ridiculous at this point," she said with a sigh, leaning her forehead against my chest.

Something wet suddenly splashed my foot.

I glanced at the floor, wondering what it was, when Olivia's grip tightened on my hand.

"Walker," she murmured in a slightly dazed...but excited voice.

"Yeah baby?" I asked, seeing a small puddle on the floor.

"It's probably time to go to the hospital."

I glanced at her face in shock. "What! Why? What's wrong?"

A gorgeous grin spread across her lips. "My water just broke."

———

As Olivia's contractions intensified, each wave of pain seemed to grip her entire body, contorting her face into a mask of agony. Her nails dug into my hand, her knuckles turning white from the strain as she fought to endure the relentless onslaught of pain.

I stood by her side, helpless and filled with a sense of urgency, my heart pounding in my chest with each labored breath she took. Beads of sweat formed on her brow, her breaths coming in ragged gasps as she pushed with all her might, her body trembling with the effort.

"Keep going, angel," I urged, my voice laced with desperation as I reached out to grasp her hand tightly. "You're doing great. Just a little bit more."

Olivia's cries filled the room, mingling with the beeping of the monitors and the hushed whispers of the medical staff. Her body arched with each contraction, her muscles straining as she fought to bring our daughter into the world.

I fucking hated this. I was rethinking my whole *breed Olivia kink*, because seeing her like this was one of the most fucking terrible things I'd ever seen.

And then, a cry pierced the air, sharp and piercing...and *everything*.

"Olivia and Walker, you have a daughter," Dr. Rochelle cooed, a huge smile on her face as she cradled our beautiful, *tiny* daughter in her arms.

I sobbed. Big tears streamed down my face because the two most beautiful things that had ever been created were in this room with me right then.

Olivia collapsed back onto the bed, her chest heaving with exhaustion as she gazed down at our daughter with her own tear-filled eyes, her face awash with a mixture of exhaustion and overwhelming love. She reached out a trembling hand, her fingers brushing against our daughter's cheek.

"Look at what you gave me," I whispered, smoothing her sweat soaked forehead as the doctor laid our daughter against Olivia's chest. "Look at our perfect little..."

"Isabella," she finished, saying our daughter's name for the very first time.

"Isabella," I repeated, murmuring the name in awe, my heart feeling like it might burst out of my chest as my arms wrapped around the new addition to my perfect world.

SECOND EPILOGUE

WALKER

> Camden: I'm here with the chicken tenders Olivia wanted.

> Me: You really are a hero, Hero. I'll be out in a second.

I got out of my seat and stretched, a smile automatically hitting my lips as I stared at Olivia and our baby girl sleeping in the hospital bed in front of me.

Olivia's eyes flew open like she'd felt me watching her.

"Hi," she murmured tiredly, a rockstar if there ever was one. Seeing her be a mom…well, let's say I was rethinking the ban on more children I'd instigated while I watched her during labor.

"Camden's here with the chicken tenders you wanted. I'm going to go out and grab it."

"Cain's chicken tenders?" she whispered excitedly, her eyes lighting up like I'd just promised her diamonds.

"Yes, Cain's chicken tenders," I told her, hoping Camden had listened to that part of my directive.

Twenty points off his circle of trust application if he didn't.

I brushed a kiss against Olivia's forehead, taking one more second to take them in as she started to softly sing to Isabella.

It was all I could do to force myself to leave the room.

Hopefully with the cameras I had in all corners of the room... and Elaine's presence by the door...I could make it down to the lobby and keep at least some of my sanity.

I'd given up on keeping it *all*.

Olivia + Isabella meant I was basically a psychopath 24/7.

Camden was sitting in a chair in the corner, staring at something on his phone when I got to the lobby. I was a little surprised that the guy wasn't at the front desk, flirting with reception, or helping organize medical supplies—with him it could usually go either way.

"Please tell me that's Cain's chicken you have in that bag," I drawled, staring at the cooler bag on the seat next to him.

"Wouldn't dream of messing up Olivia's order," he grinned, unzipping it and showing off a tray of chicken tenders, fries, and Cain's sauce.

"Ten points to Camden," I said dramatically, and he huffed.

"At this point, it feels like the three of you are actually secret Harry Potter nerds and this is your way of role playing it undercover."

"What are you talking about?" I asked, lifting an eyebrow.

"You know—" he said, gesturing around wildly with his hands like I was supposed to understand that. "Like how they say "Ten points to Gryffindor...It's like that."

"I have no idea what you're talking about, Camden. But I'll be sure to tell the boys how much of a big nerd you are."

He scoffed and scowled at me, checking his phone again for the fifth time in the conversation. His scowl grew and he handed me the cooler bag. "I gotta run, but let me know if you need anything else. I can bring you guys whatever."

What a good dude.

"What do you have planned for the rest of the day?" I asked, as he began to briskly walk away...kind of like his ass was on fire.

"I've got the love of my life locked in my room at the

moment," he grinned, glancing back at me with a wink. "Can't leave her alone for long, she's kind of grumpy."

You know, I wasn't really sure if he was joking...

I watched in shock...and a little awe...as he strode through the hospital with a parting wave.

I immediately pulled out my phone to text Ari and Lincoln as I turned to get back to my girls.

> Me: How do we feel about kidnapping when it comes to entry into the Circle of Trust?

King Linc:?

> Me: ...

King Linc:...

Ari: The answer is obviously fuck yes.

> Me: Good. I guess Camden's in.

THE PUCKING WRONG DATE BONUS SCENE & NOVELLA

Want more Walker and Olivia? Come hang out in my Fated Realm for an exclusive BONUS scene! Get it HERE.

Want to read a novella about Lincoln, Ari, Walker, and the gang before Walker met Olivia...get A Pucking Wrong Christmas here.

Mabel's Chocolate Chip Pudding Cookies

SERVINGS: 15 COOKIES

INGREDIENTS

- 2 ¼ CUPS (281G) ALL PURPOSE FLOUR SPOONED AND LEVELED
- 1 TEASPOON BAKING SODA
- ½ TEASPOON SALT
- 1 CUP (2 STICKS; 227G) UNSALTED BUTTER, SOFTENED TO ROOM TEMP (VEGAN BUTTER WORKS TOO)
- ¾ CUP (150G) LIGHT BROWN SUGAR PACKED
- ¼ CUP (50G) GRANULATED SUGAR
- 1 (3.4-OUNCE) PACKAGE INSTANT VANILLA PUDDING MIX
- 2 LARGE EGGS ROOM TEMPERATURE
- 1 TEASPOON VANILLA EXTRACT
- 2 CUPS SEMI-SWEET CHOCOLATE CHIPS

INSTRUCTIONS

PREHEAT THE OVEN TO 350 DEGREES F. LINE A COOKIE SHEET WITH PARCHMENT PAPER AND SET ASIDE.

IN A MEDIUM BOWL, WHISK TOGETHER FLOUR, BAKING SODA AND SALT AND SET ASIDE.

IN A SEPARATE BOWL WITH A HAND MIXER, OR IN THE BOWL OF A STAND MIXER FITTED WITH THE PADDLE ATTACHMENT, CREAM THE BUTTER, BROWN SUGAR, AND WHITE SUGAR ON HIGH SPEED UNTIL LIGHT AND CREAMY, AT LEAST 3 MINUTES. DO NOT SKIP THIS STEP.

ADD THE DRY PUDDING MIX, VANILLA AND EGGS AND BEAT ON HIGH FOR 2-3 MINUTES, UNTIL LIGHT AND FLUFFY.

SLOWLY ADD HALF OF THE DRY INGREDIENTS TO THE WET INGREDIENTS AND TURN THE MIXER ON LOW SPEED TO START SO THE FLOUR DOESN'T GET EVERYWHERE. TURN THE MIXER UP TO HIGH SPEED AND MIX UNTIL COMBINED. ADD THE REST OF THE DRY INGREDIENTS AND REPEAT UNTIL DOUGH IS JUST COMBINED. STIR IN THE CHOCOLATE CHIPS WITH A RUBBER SPATULA UNTIL INCORPORATED.

USE A LARGE COOKIE SCOOP OR ¼ CUP MEASURING CUP TO DROP THE COOKIE DOUGH BALLS ONTO THE PREPARED BAKING SHEET. BAKE FOR 10-12 MINUTES, OR UNTIL SLIGHTLY GOLDEN AND JUST SET ON THE TOP. ALLOW TO COOL ON THE BAKING SHEET FOR TWO MINUTES THEN TRANSFER TO A BAKING RACK TO COOL COMPLETELY

THE PUCKING
WRONG MAN

Want to read Camden's standalone story? Preorder The Pucking Wrong Man here.

THE PUCKING
WRONG GUY

Want to read Ari's standalone story? Get The Wrong Pucking Guy here.

THE PUCKING WRONG NUMBER EXCERPT

C urious about Lincoln Daniels and his red flags...keep reading for his story in The Pucking Wrong Number...

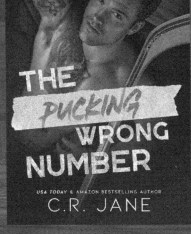

The Pucking Wrong Number by C. R. Jane

Copyright © 2023 by C. R. Jane

All rights reserved.

No portion of this book may be reproduced in any form or by any electronic or mechanical means, including information storage and retrieval systems, without written permission from the author, except for the use of brief quotations in a book review, and except as permitted by U.S. copyright law.

For permissions contact:

crjaneauthor@gmail.com

This book is a work of fiction. Names, characters, businesses, places, events, locales, and incidents are either the products of the author's imagination or used in a fictitious manner. Any resemblance to actual persons, living or dead, or actual events is purely coincidental.

Cover Design: Cassie Chapman/Opulent Designs

Photographer: Cadwallader Photography

Editing: Jasmine J.

PROLOGUE
MONROE

"Monroe. My pretty little girl," Mama slurs from the couch. She's staring up at the ceiling, and even though she's saying my name, I know she's not talking to me. Or at least the me that's standing right here, scrubbing at the vomit stain she left on the floor. She's talking to the me from the past, or wherever it is her brain takes her when she's high as a kite.

There's a knock on the door, and I glance at it fearfully, dread churning through my insides. Because I know who it is. One of her "customers" as Mama calls them.

The door opens without either of us saying anything. I'm not sure Mama even heard the knock. In steps a sweaty, pale-faced man that I've seen once or twice before. He has rosy cheeks and a belly that protrudes over his jeans. Like a perverse Santa Claus. Not that I believe in that guy anymore. He's certainly never come to our place on Christmas Eve.

The man's eyes gleam as he stares at me, but then Mama groans in a weird way, and his attention goes to her.

"Roxanne," he says in a sing-song voice as he makes his way over there.

I want to say something. Anything. Tell him that Mama's in no shape for company, but I know it's no use. Besides, Mama would be furious with me later on if she missed out on the money she needs to get her fix.

I leave the room and lock myself in the one bedroom we have in this place. Mama and I share the room, but more often than not, she can't make it any further than the couch.

The disgusting noises I've learned to hate start, so I turn on the radio, trying to drown them out. I fall into a fitful sleep, and my dreams are haunted by the image of a healthy mother that cares more about me than she does about escaping the life she created.

I wake with a start, panic blurring the edges of the room until I can convince my brain that everything's fine.

Except everything doesn't feel fine. It's so quiet. Way too quiet.

I creep towards the door, pressing my ear against it to see if I can hear anything.

But there's nothing.

I slowly open the door and peek out into the room. There's no sign of the man, or my mother. Thinking the coast is clear, I make my way out of my room, only to come to a screeching halt when I see my mother on the ground by the front door, a pile of green liquid by her face.

I sigh, thinking of the clean-up ahead. Again. I hate these men. Every time they come here, they take a piece of her, while leaving her with nothing. It's always like this after they're done with her.

When I walk over with a rag and bucket, I see Mama is shaking, tears streaming down her face. She's a scary gray color I don't think I've ever seen before.

"Mama," I whisper, reaching down to touch her face, only to flinch at how icy cold her skin is. Her eyes suddenly shoot open, causing me to jump. They're even more bloodshot than normal. Her bony hand claws at my shirt, and she frantically pulls me closer to her. Her lip is bruised and bloody. The bastard must've gotten rough.

"Don't let 'em taze your heart," she slurs, incomprehensibly.

"Mama?" I ask, worry thick in my voice.

"Don't...let a man...take your heart," she spits out. "Don't let him..." Her words fade away and her chest rises with one big inhale...before she goes perfectly still.

"Mama!" I whimper, shaking her over and over again.

But she never says another word. She's just gone, like a flame extinguished in a dark room.

And I'm all alone, with her last words forever ringing in my ears.

CHAPTER 1
MONROE

I sat on the edge of my bed, staring out the window into the dark, seemingly starless sky. Freedom was so close I could taste it.

18.

It felt like I'd been waiting my whole life for this moment. For this specific birthday. The thought of finally being able to leave this place, to start my life, on my own terms…it helped get me through each day.

I knew it would be difficult when I left. I only had my scrimpy savings from my after school job at the grocery store to start my life. But I'd do whatever it took to make something of myself.

Something more than the empty shell my mother had left me that day.

I'd been in the foster system since I was ten years old, the day after that fateful night where I'd lost her. Everyone wanted to adopt a baby, and a baby I had not been. I'd gone through what seemed like a hundred different homes at this point, but my current home was where I'd managed to stay the longest.

Unfortunately.

My foster parents, Mr. and Mrs. Detweiler, and their son

Ripley, seemed like nice people at first, but over time, things had changed. They were different now.

Mrs. Detweiler, Marie, had come to think of me as her live-in maid. I was all for helping out around the house, but when they got up as a collective group after every meal and left everything to me to clean up–as well as every other chore around the house–it was too much.

Someday, hopefully in the near future, I would never clean someone else's toilet again.

While I could deal with manual labor for another month, it was Mr. Detweiler, Todd, who had become a major problem. His actions had grown increasingly creepy, his longing stares and lingering glances making me sick. Everything he said to me had an underlying meaning…was an innuendo. He'd started talking about my birthday more, like he wanted to remind me of it for reasons far different than the promise of freedom it represented to me. I'm not sure it had even occurred to any of them yet that I was actually allowed to leave after that day. Both my birthday and high school graduation were the same week. Perfect timing. I just hoped he could control himself and keep his hands off me long enough to get to that point. Some people might not think a high school graduation was anything special, but to me, it represented *everything*.

Ripley was fine, I guess. He was more like a potato than a person, which was better than other things he could be. His eyes skipped over me when we were in the same room, like I didn't actually exist. And maybe I didn't exist to him. As long as his bed was made every day, and he had food on the table, and toilet paper stocked to wipe his ass, he could care less. He was much too involved in his video games to care about the world around him.

I glanced at the clock. It was 4:55pm, time to get dinner started before Mr. Detweiler got home from work. Sighing, I absentmindedly smoothed my faded quilt that Mrs. Detweiler had brought home from who knows where, and headed out to the hallway and down to the kitchen. The house was a three bedroom rambler in an okay part of town. It was nicer than other places I'd stayed, but I'd found that didn't matter all that much. The hearts beating inside the home held a much greater significance than how nice, or not nice, the house actually was.

I'm sure I could have been perfectly happy in the hovel I'd started life in with my mother...if only she'd been different.

I came to a screeching halt, and panic laced my insides, when I walked into the kitchen and saw Mr. Detweiler leaning against the laminate counter. How had I missed him coming into the house? I couldn't recall hearing the garage door opening.

He was nursing his favorite bottle of beer, which was actually the fanciest thing in the kitchen, costing far more than any of the other food they bought. Todd Detweiler was still dressed in the baggy suit he wore to the accounting office he worked at. He had a receding hairline that rivaled any I'd seen, so he brushed all the hair forward, carefully styling it to a point on his forehead right above his watery blue eyes.

He raised an eyebrow at the fact I was still frozen in place. But he usually didn't get home until 6:30, long enough for me to get dinner on the table and hide away until they were done.

"Well, hello there, Monroe," he drawled, my name sounding dirty coming from his lips.

I schooled my face and steeled my insides, taking methodical steps towards the fridge like his presence hadn't disarmed me.

"Hello," I answered pleasantly, hating the way I could feel his gaze stroking across my skin. Like I was an object to be coveted rather than a person.

I knew I was pretty. The spitting image of my mother when she was young. But just like with her, my looks had only been a curse, forever designed to attract assholes whose only goal was to use and abuse me.

I reached into the fridge to grab the bowl of chicken I'd put in there earlier to defrost...when suddenly he was behind me. Close enough that if I moved, he'd be pressed against me.

"Is there something you need?" I asked, trying to keep the edge of hysteria out of my voice. His hand settled on my hip and I squeezed my eyes shut, cursing the universe.

He leaned close, his breath a whisper against my skin. "You've been thinking about it, haven't you?" Todd's breath stunk of beer, a smell that would prevent me from ever trying it, no matter how expensive and nice it was supposed to be.

"I—I'm not sure what you're talking about, sir." I grabbed the chicken and tried to stand , hoping he would back away. But the only thing he did was straighten up, so our bodies were against each other. I tried to move away, but his hand squeezed against my hip. Hard.

"I need to get this chicken on the stove," I said pleasantly, like I wasn't dying inside at the feel of his touch.

"Such a tease," he murmured with a small chuckle. "I love how you like to play games. Just going to make it so much better when we stop." There was a bulge growing harder against my lower back, and I bit down on my lip hard enough that the salty tang of blood flooded my taste buds.

My hands were shaking, the water sloshing around in the bowl. An idiot could figure out what he was talking about.

"Have you noticed how much I love to collect things?" he asked randomly, finally releasing my hip and stepping back.

I moved quickly towards the sink, setting the bowl inside and going to grab the breadcrumbs I needed to coat the chicken breasts with for dinner.

"I have noticed that," I finally responded, after he'd taken a step towards me when I didn't answer fast enough.

How could anyone miss it? Todd collected...beer bottles. Both walls of the garage had various cans and bottles lined up neatly on shelves. There were so many of them that you could barely see the wall—not sure how social services never seemed concerned he might have a drinking problem with that amount of empties. But Todd was never worried about that. He added at least five to the wall every day.

"Virgins happen to be my favorite thing to collect."

I'd been holding a carton of eggs, and I dropped them, shocked that he'd outright said that, shells and yolk ricocheting everywhere.

Just then, Mrs. Detweiler ambled in, her gaze flicking between her husband and me suspiciously. "What's going on in here?" she asked, her eyes stopping on the ruined eggs all over the floor.

Marie had once been a pretty woman, but like her husband, her attempt to hold onto youth was a miserable failure. Right now, she was wearing a too tight flowered dress that resembled a couch from the eighties. It accented every roll, and there was a fine sheen of sweat across her heavily made up face, probably from the effort she'd had to make to get out of her armchair and storm in here. Her hair was a harsh, bottle-black color, and though she attempted to curl and keep it nice, it was thin and limp and I'm sure disappointing for her.

I usually didn't pay attention to looks; I knew better than most they could be deceiving, but Todd and Marie Detweiler's appearances were too in your face to ignore.

"Just an accident, honey," he drawled, walking towards her and pulling her into a soul sickening kiss that made me want to puke considering Marie most likely had no idea where else that mouth had been.

They walked out of the kitchen without a backward glance, leaving me a shaking, miserable mess as I cleaned up the eggs and tried to make dinner.

If that interaction hadn't sealed the deal that waiting for my birthday to leave wasn't an option...the next night would.

I was in bed, tossing and turning as I did every night. When your mind was as haunted as mine was, sleep was elusive, a fervent goal I would never successfully master. I'd never had a night where I could relax, where the memories of the past didn't creep in and plague my thoughts.

It was 3 am, and I was on the verge of giving up if I couldn't fall back asleep soon.

Light footsteps sounded down the hallway by my door. I frowned, as everyone had gone to bed long ago. I knew their habits like they were my own at this point.

Was someone in the house? Someone who didn't belong?

The footsteps stopped outside my door, and shivers crept up my spine.

"Hello?" I whisper squeaked, feeling like a fool for speaking at all when the doorknob tried to turn, getting caught on the lock I was lucky enough to have.

I felt like the would-be victim in a horror movie as I slid out of bed and yanked my lamp from the nightstand, prepared to use it as a weapon if need be.

The person outside fiddled with the lock and it clicked, signaling it had been disengaged.

There was a long pause as I stared breathlessly at the door, waiting for the inevitable.

The door creaked open and a hairy hand—that I recognized —appeared.

It was Mr. Detweiler's.

I didn't think, I just started screaming, knowing I had one chance to get him away from my room.

I needed to wake up his wife. With their bedroom right down the hall, I just needed to be loud enough.

Sure enough, a second after I started screaming, the door banged shut, and footsteps dashed away. A moment later, I heard the Detweilers' bedroom door fly open, and then a moment after that, my door cracked against the wall and Marie's harried form was there. Her chest was heaving, pushing against the two sizes too small negligee she was wearing–that made me want to burn my eyes–and her gaze was crazed as they dashed around the room, finally falling to me standing there in the middle of it, a lamp clutched to my chest.

A red mottled rash spread across her chest and up to her cheeks as anger flooded her features.

"What the fuck is wrong with you?"

"Someone was trying to get into my room. Someone unlocked the door."

I didn't say it was her husband, because that would give me even more problems.

A moment later, Todd was there, faking a yawn with a glass of water in his hand. "What's going on?" he asked casually. Our eyes locked, and in that moment, he knew I knew it was him. His features were taunting, daring me to say something, like his wife would ever believe anything that came out of my mouth when it came to him.

"The girl's saying someone was breaking into her room," Marie scoffed before pausing for a second and examining her husband. "Why were you up?"

The way her lips were pursed, the way her flush deepened—it told me a lot. Apparently, Marie wasn't so unaware of her husband's true nature after all.

Not that she would ever do anything about it.

"I was getting some water when I heard Monroe scream. But I didn't hear anyone else in the house." His gaze feigned concern. "Are you sure you didn't just have a nightmare?"

I stared at him for a long, tense moment before I took a breath. "Maybe that's all it was," I finally whispered, eliciting a loud huff from Marie.

"Get yourself under control, you brat. The rest of us need our sleep!" she snapped, whirling away and leaving, curses streaming from her mouth as she walked back to her room.

Todd lingered, a smug grin curling across his pathetic lips. "Sleep well, Monroe," he purred, a firm promise in his eyes that he would be back.

And that he would finish what he started.

I fell to my knees as soon as the door closed, sobs wracking through my body.

I'd never felt so alone.

He had ruined everything. A month away from a high school diploma, and he'd just torn it from my grasp.

If Todd got his hands on me, he would break me. And I wasn't talking about my body–I was talking about my soul.

The image of my mother's desolate, destroyed features flashed through my mind.

That couldn't be my story. It couldn't.

I had to leave. Tomorrow. I had no other option.

––––––

The Detweilers lived in a small town right outside Houston. I decided Dallas would be my destination, about four hours away. I'd never been there before, but the ticket price wasn't too bad, and it was big. Just what I needed to hopefully disappear. Surely the Detweilers wouldn't try and go that far, not with only a month left of state support on the line. I bet they wouldn't even tell anyone I was gone. They'd want that last check.

I didn't let myself think about what my virginity would be worth to Todd. Hopefully, "easy" was one of his requisites, and he would forget me as soon as I disappeared.

I went to school, my heart hurting the whole day. I'd never been one to make close friends—when you never knew when you'd be moving on, it was best not to make any close connections—but I found myself wishing I had longer with the acquaintances I did have. I walked the familiar hallways, wondering if it would have been hard to say goodbye at graduation, or if I was simply feeling the loss of my dream.

Mama had never graduated from high school. In her lucid moments, though, even when I was little, she would sometimes talk about her dreams for me. Dreams of walking across that stage.

I'd just have to walk across a college stage, I told myself firmly, promising myself I'd get a GED and make that possible.

After school, I went to the H.E.B. grocery store where I worked, putting even more hustle in than usual since I'd be a disappearing act after this shift. The timing worked out, because it was payday, and I was able to get one more check to take with me. Every penny would count.

After my shift, I bought a prepaid phone since I didn't want to take my Detweiler phone with me. Knowing them, they'd probably try and get the police to bring me back by saying I'd stolen their property. A part of me was a little afraid they could track me with it too. I knew I wasn't living in a spy thriller...but still, better to be safe than sorry.

Once I got home, I packed a small bag with some clothes, my new phone, and the cash I'd saved up. And then I sat on my bed, hands squeezing together with anxiety.

I didn't have a good plan. For as much as I'd been dreaming of getting away, my plans were more fluid than concrete. And all of them had depended on me having a high school diploma so I could get a better job, as well as not having to look over my shoulder every second for fear the Detweilers were after me. The state also had a support system for kids coming out of foster care, and I'd been hopeful I'd have that to lean on.

But I could do this.

I cleaned up after dinner. Marie had ordered pizza, so it didn't take as much effort as usual. And then I sat in the corner of the living room, biding my time until I could say goodnight. It was a tricky thing. I had to escape tonight–late enough that they'd gone to bed, but not so late that Todd decided to give me another late night visit.

My departure was the definition of anticlimactic. My mind had conjured this image of the Detweilers running after me as I escaped with my bag out the window, the sound of a siren haunting the air as I ducked in and out of the bushes, trying to avoid the police.

But what really happened was that I slipped out the window, and everyone stayed asleep. I walked for an hour until I got to the Greyhound station, and no one came after me. The exhausted-looking attendant didn't even blink when I bought a ticket to Dallas.

It was nice for something to go my way every once in a blue moon.

The bus ride took twice as long as a car would have. And although I tried to catch a few hours of rest, I kept worrying I'd somehow miss my stop, so I never could slip into a deep sleep. My mind also couldn't help but race with thoughts of what my future held. Would I be able to make it on my own?

Despite my worries, a sense of relief flickered in my chest as the distance between Todd and me grew with each mile that passed.

At least I could cross keeping my virginity safe off my list of to-do's.

When we finally arrived in Dallas, the morning sun was just peeking over the horizon. Even with the dilapidated buildings that surrounded the Greyhound station, I couldn't help but feel excitement. I was here. I'd made it. I may have never been to Dallas before, and I may not have known a single soul here, but I was determined to make a new life for myself.

This was my new beginning.

———

It took about twelve hours for the afterglow of my arrival to fade and for me to find myself on a park bench, debating whether I could actually fall asleep if I were to try. Or if it was even safe to attempt such a thing.

I'd gotten off the bus and was in the process of calling for a cab to take me to the teen shelter I'd found online. And then I'd been fucking pick pocketed while I looked the address up. They'd taken all the cash in my pocket that I'd pulled out for the cab, and swiped my phone right out of my hand.

You can bet I ran after them like a madwoman. But with a

backpack containing all my earthly possessions weighing me down, the group of boys easily outran me.

I hadn't dared to spend any of the rest of the cash I had left, except to get a bag of chips from a gas station that had seen better days.

I'd walked all over for the rest of the day, trying to find the shelter, scared to ask for directions in case anyone got suspicious and reported to the authorities that I looked like a runaway teen.

Obviously, I never found the place, because there I was, on the park bench. Cold, hungry, and pissed off.

And exhausted.

Apparently, when you hadn't slept for close to forty-eight hours, you could fall asleep anywhere, because eventually... that's exactly what I did.

———

I woke with a start, the feeling of someone watching me thick in my throat. Night had fallen, and a deep blue hue had settled over the park. The trees and bushes were indistinct shadows against the darkened sky. The street lamps had flickered to life, casting a warm glow on the path and the nearby benches. The light danced and swayed with the gentle breeze, casting long shadows on the ground. You could hear the rustling of leaves and the chirping of crickets.

I yelped when I saw a grizzled old man sitting next to me on the bench, a wildness in his gaze that matched the tattered clothing on his body. There was the scent of dirt and body odor wafting off him, and when he smiled at me, it was only with a few teeth.

"Oy. I've been a watchin'. Making sure you could sleep, my lady," he said in what was clearly an affected British accent.

I flinched at his words, even though they were perfectly friendly and kind, and scooted away from him.

"Oh, don't be afraid of Ole Bill. I'll watch out for ye."

I moved to jump off the bench and run away…but I also had a moment of hesitation. There was something so…wholesome about him. Once you got past his looks and his smell, obviously.

"This park's mine, but I can share. You go back to sleep, and I'll keep watch. Make sure the ruffians stay away," he continued. Even though I had yet to say anything to him.

I opened my mouth to reject his offer, but then he pulled a clean, brand new blanket with tags out of his grocery sack. When he offered it to me…instead of talking…I found myself crying.

I sobbed and sobbed while he watched me frantically, throwing the blanket at me like it had the power to quell hysterical women's tears. When I still didn't stop crying, overwhelmed by the events of the past few days…and his kindness, he finally started to sing what I think was the worst rendition of "Eleanor Rigby" that I'd ever heard. Actually, it was the worst rendition of *any* song I'd ever heard.

But it worked, and I stopped crying.

"There, there, little duck. Go to sleep. Ole Bill will watch out for ya," he said soothingly after he'd finished the song—the last few lyrics definitely made up.

I was a smarter girl than that, I really was. But I was so freaking tired. And everything inside of me really wanted to trust him. After all, he had called me "little duck." Serial killers didn't have cute pet names for their victims, right?

"Just a couple of minutes," I murmured, and he nodded, smiling softly again with his crooked grin that I was quite fond of at that moment.

I drifted off into a fitful sleep, shivering from stress and exhaustion, and dreaming of better days.

When I woke up, it was far later than ten minutes. It was the rest of the night, actually.

Bill was still there, watching over me, and whistling softly to himself, like he hadn't just stayed up all night. My backpack was still under my head, the cash still in it, and at least I didn't *feel* like anyone had touched me.

Fuck, I'd gotten desperate, hadn't I?

"Do you have a place to stay, lassie?" he asked softly. I shook my head, biting down on my lip as I thought about spending another night on this bench.

"Ole Bill will take you to a good place. It's not as nice as my castle, but it will do," he said, gesturing to the park proudly as if it was in fact an English castle complete with a moat, and he was its ruler.

Despite the fact that he'd at least proven trustworthy enough not to do anything to me after a few hours, it was still pure desperation that had me following him to what I was hoping wasn't a trafficking ring, or something else equally heinous.

I relaxed a little as he took me to a slightly better part of town than where I'd been walking the day before. He chattered my ear off, all in that fake British accent, regaling me with stories about places I was sure he'd never visited.

Before I knew it, we were standing in front of the entrance to what appeared to be a fairly new shelter. The sign read that it was a women's shelter, and the sight made me want to cry once again.

"When you get in there, tell 'em Ole Bill sent you...they'll give you the royal treatment," he chortled, and tears filled my eyes for what seemed like the hundredth time—causing him to take a step away–probably fearing I would burst into hysterics again.

I hesitated for another moment before I finally ascended the steps that led to the shelter doors. Stopping halfway, I glanced back at Bill, who gave me another charmingly snaggletoothed grin. "I see great things for you, little duck," he called after me when I continued to walk.

I knew I'd never forget him. He may have been homeless and slightly crazy, but he was also one of the kindest people I had ever met. He'd watched over me, a stranger, and helped me when I needed it the most.

As I walked inside, exhaustion still stretched across my

shoulders, I strangely felt at peace right then that everything was going to work out.

"Welcome to Haven," a kind woman murmured as I approached the front desk.

Haven indeed.

I could only hope.

Continue Monroe and Lincoln's store here.

THE SOUND OF US

Curious about the band Sounds of Us and how they got their girl? Get the complete series HERE.

COPYRIGHT

Remember Us This Way by C. R. Jane
Copyright © 2019 by C. R. Jane

REMEMBER US
THIS WAY

They are idols to millions worldwide. I hear their names whispered in the hallways and blasted through the radio. Their faces are never far from the television screen, tormenting me with images of what I gave up.

To everyone else, they're unattainable rockstars, the music gods who make up The Sound of Us. But to me? They'll always be the boys I lost.

I broke all our hearts when I refused to follow them to L.A., convinced I would only bring them down. Years later, after I've succumbed to a monster, and my life has become something out of a nightmare, they are back.

I'm no longer the girl they left behind. But what if I've become the woman they can't forget?

PROLOGUE
BEFORE

According to the Sounds of Us Wikipedia page, the band hit almost instant stardom as soon as they finished recording their first album. A small indie band that had gained only regional notoriety, Red Label had taken a huge risk by signing them. The good looks and the killer voices of the three band members combined with the chance at a larger platform ended up making Sounds of Us the Label's most successful band in history. They released their first album, Death by Heartbreak, in 2013, and the first single, Follow You Into the Dark, made it to the Billboard Top 100 immediately.

It was their second single that propelled Sounds of Us to legend status though. Cold Heart was number one on the charts almost the second it was released. That led to four other songs ending up in the top ten. Three of them reached number one, with a fourth hitting number two on the charts. That album was torture in its finest form for me. Partly because I had lost them, but also partly because every one of those songs was about me. And that was just the hits. There were a lot more references in the songs that never got released as singles. It was a sharp stab in the chest to hear songs blaring from radios – songs whose lyrics contained exact words each of them had said to me, and that I had said to them.

And while some of the songs were wistful and pained, others were angry. Pissed-off. Occasionally enraged. It was uncomfortable. Actually, it was excruciating. At least for the first couple of months. I stopped listening to music eventually, something that had meant the world to me my entire life. I just couldn't handle the reminder of them anymore. My heart couldn't take it.

But every so often, a car would go by with its window down, or I'd walk past a motel room playing the radio, and I'd hear one of their voices and it would be an unexpected jolt of pain all over again.

After the release of their album, the band embarked on a short European tour, then followed it up with a much larger American tour. They started selling out stadiums. They appeared on every late-night show there was. Everyone wanted a piece of them. They were like this generation's Beatles, probably even bigger. The next two albums certainly were bigger, although those were easier for me to listen to since the songs about me faded as time went on. They were the most celebrated band in the world and there was no sign of their success slowing down anytime soon. It was everything they had ever dreamed about and that I had dreamed about with them.

They lived up to the bad boy image their label wanted to sell. Rumors of drug use and rampant women kept the gossip sites busy. I tried to ignore the magazines in the store racks by the checkout stand, but some of the pictures of the guys stumbling out of clubs with five girls each were a little too damning to be completely unfounded. And of course, there were the rumors that Tanner had secretly been in and out of rehab for the last two years in between tours. Tanner had always struggled with addiction but had only dabbled in hard drugs when I knew him. It wasn't hard for me to picture him struggling with them now that he probably had easy access to whatever he wanted from people desperate to please them all.

I often wondered if any part of the boys I knew were still around after I let myself give into my own addiction of catching up on any Sounds of Us news I could find. And then I would hear about them buying a house for someone who had lost everything in a natural disaster or hear of them participating in a charity drive to keep a no-kill shelter up and running, and I would know that a part of them was still there.

I've never made peace with letting them go. I never will.

CHAPTER 1
NOW

I hear the song come on from the living room. I had forgotten I had read that they were performing for New Year's Eve tonight in New York City before they embarked on their North American tour for the rest of the year. I wanted to avoid the room the music was coming from, but not even my hate for its current occupant could keep my feet from wandering to where the song was playing.

As I took that first step into the living room, and I saw Tanner's face up close, my heart clenched. As usual, he was singing to the audience like he was making love to them. When the camera panned to the audience, girls were literally fainting in the first few rows if he so much as ran his eyes in their direction. He swept a lock of his black hair out of his face, and the girls screamed even louder. Tanner had always had the bad boy look down perfectly. Piercing silver eyes that demanded sex, and full pouty lips you couldn't help but fantasize over, he was every mother's worst nightmare and every girl's naughty dream. I devoured his image like I was a crack addict desperate for one more hit. Usually I avoided them like the plague, but junkies always gave in eventually. I was not the exception.

"See something you like?" comes a cold, amused voice that

never ceases to fill me with dread. I curse my weakness at allowing myself to even come in the room. I know better than this.

"Just coming to see if you need a refill of your beer," I tell him nonchalantly, praying that he'll believe me, but knowing he won't.

My husband is sitting in his favorite armchair. He's a good-looking man according to the world's standards. Even I have to admit that despite the fact that the ugliness that lies inside his heart has long prevented me from finding him appealing in any way. His blonde hair is parted to the side perfectly, not a hair out of place. Sometimes I get the urge to mess it up, just so there can be an outward expression of the chaos that hides beneath his skin.

After I let the guys go, there was nothing left for me in the world. Instead of rising above my circumstances and becoming someone they would have been proud of, I became nothing. Gentry made perfectly clear that anything I was now was because of him.

Echoes of my lost heart beat inside my mind as another song starts to play on the television. It's the song that I know they wrote for me. It's angry and filled with betrayal, the kind of pain you don't come back from. The kind of pain you don't forgive.

Too late I realize that Gentry just asked me something and that my silence will tell him that I'm not paying attention to him. The sharp strike of his palm against my face sends me flying to the ground. I press my hand to my cheek as if I can stop the pain that is coursing through me. I already know this one will bruise. I'll have to wear an extra layer of makeup to cover it up when Gentry forces me to meet him at the country club tomorrow. After all, we wouldn't want anyone at the club to know that our lives are anything less than perfect.

The song is still going and somehow the pain I hear in Tanner's voice hurts me more than the pain blossoming across

my cheek. Would it not hurt them as much if they knew everything I had told them to sever our connection permanently was a
lie? Would they even care at this point that I had done it to set
them free, to stop them from being dragged down into the hell I
never seemed to be able to escape from? At night, when I lay in
bed, listening to the sound of Gentry sleeping peacefully as if the
world was perfect and monsters didn't exist, I told myself that it
would matter.

"Get up," snaps Gentry, yanking me up from the floor. I'm
really off my game tonight by lingering. Nothing makes Gentry
madder than when I "wallow" as he calls it. As I stumble out of
the room, my head spinning a bit from the force of the hit, a sick
part of me thinks it was worth it, just so I could hear the end of
their song.

———

Later that night, long after I should have fallen asleep, my mind
plays back what little of the performance I saw earlier. I wonder
if Jensen still gets severe stage fright before he performs. I
wonder if Jesse still keeps his lucky guitar pick in his pocket
during performances. I wonder who Tanner gets his good luck
kiss from now.

It all hurts too much to contemplate for too long so I grab the
Ambien I keep on my bedside table for when I can't sleep, which
is often, and I drift off into a dreamland filled with a silver eyed
boy who speaks straight to my soul.

The next morning comes too early and I struggle to wake up
when Gentry's alarm goes off. Ambien always leaves me groggy
and I haven't decided what's better, being exhausted from not
sleeping, or taking half the day to wake up all the way.

Throwing a robe on, I blurrily walk to the kitchen to get
Gentry's protein shake ready for him to take with him to
the gym.

I'm standing in front of the blender when Gentry comes up behind me and puts his arms around me, as if the night before never happened. I'm very still, not wanting to make any sudden movement just in case he takes it the wrong way.

"Meet me at the club for lunch," he asks, running his nose up the side of my neck and eliciting shivers...the wrong kind of shivers. He's using his charming voice, the one that always gets everyone to do what he wants. It stopped working on me a long time ago.

"Of course," I tell him, turning in his arms and giving him a wide, fake smile. What else would my answer be when I know the consequences of going against Gentry's wishes?

"Good," he says with satisfaction, placing a quick, sharp kiss on my lips before stepping away.

I pour the blended protein shake into a cup and hand it to him. "11:45?" I ask. He nods and waves goodbye as he walks out of the house to head to the country club gym where he'll spend the next several hours working out with his friends, flirting with the girls that work out there, and overall acting like the overwhelming douche that he is.

I don't relax until the sound of the car fades into the distance. After eating a protein shake myself (Gentry doesn't approve of me eating carbs), I start my chores for the day before I have to get ready to meet him at the country club.

My hands are red and raw from washing the dishes twice. Everything was always twice. Twice bought me time and ensured there wouldn't be anything left behind. An errant fleck of food, a spot that hadn't been rinsed – these were things he'd notice.

Hours later, I've vacuumed, swept, done the laundry, and cleaned all the bathrooms. Gentry could easily afford a maid, but he likes me to "keep busy" as he puts it, so I do everything in this house of horrors. I repeat the same things every day even though the house is in perfect condition. I would clean every second if it meant that he was out of the house permanently though.

I straighten the pearls around my neck and think for the thousandth time that if I ever escape this hell hole, I'm going to burn every pearl I come across. I'm dressed in a fitted pastel pink dress that comes complete with a belt ordained with daisies. Five years ago, I wouldn't have been caught dead in such an outfit but far be it for me to wear jeans to a country club. I slip into a pair of matching pastel wedges and then run out to the car. I'm running late and I can only hope that he's distracted and doesn't realize the time.

As I drive, I can't help but daydream. Dream about what it would have been like if I had joined the guys in L.A. Bellmont is a sleepy town that's been the same for generations. I haven't been anywhere outside of the town since I got married except to Myrtle Beach for my honeymoon.

The town is steeped in history, a history that it's very proud of. The main street is still perfectly maintained from the early 1900s, and I've always loved the whitewashed look of the buildings and the wooden shingles on every roof. The town attracts a vast array of tourists who come here to be close to the beach. They can get a taste of the coastal southern flavor of places like Charleston and Charlotte, but they don't have to pay as high of a price tag.

It's a beautiful prison to me, and if I ever manage to escape from it, I never want to see it again.

I turn down a street and start down the long drive that leads to Bellmont's most exclusive country club. The entire length of the road is sheltered by large oak trees and it never ceases to make me feel like an extra in Gone With the Wind whenever I come here. The feeling is only reinforced when I pull up to the large, freshly painted white plantation house that's been converted into the club.

My blood pressure spikes as I near the valet stand. Just knowing that I'm about to see Gentry and all of his friends is enough to send my pulse racing. I smile nervously at the teenage boy who is manning the stand and hand him my keys. He gives me a big smile and a wink. It reminds me of something that Jesse used to do to older women to make them swoon, and my heart clenches. Is there ever going to be a day when something doesn't remind me of one of them?

I ignore the valet boy's smile and walk inside, heading to the bar where I can usually find Gentry around lunch time. I pause as I walk inside the lounge. Wendy Perkinson is leaning against Gentry, pressing her breasts against him, much too close for propriety's sake. I know I should probably care at least a little bit, but the idea of Gentry turning his attentions away from me and on to Wendy permanently is more than I can even wish for. I'm sure he's fucked her, the way she's practically salivating over him as he talks to his friend blares it loudly, but unfortunately that's all she will ever get from him. Gentry's obsession with me has thus far proved to be a lasting thing. But since I finally started refusing to sleep with him after the beatings became a regular thing, he goes elsewhere for his so-called needs when he doesn't feel like trying to force me. At least a few times a week I'm assaulted by the stench of another woman's perfume on my husband's clothes. It's become just another unspoken thing in my marriage.

Martin, Gentry's best friend, is the first to see me and his eyes widen when he does. He coughs nervously, the poor thing thinking I actually care about the situation I've walked into. Gentry looks at him and then looks at the entrance where he sees me standing there. His eyes don't widen in anything remotely resembling remorse or shame...we're too far past that at this point. He does extricate himself from Wendy's grip however to start walking towards me, his gaze devouring me as he does so. One thing I've never doubted in my relationship with Gentry is how beautiful he thinks I am.

"You're gorgeous," he tells me, kissing me on the cheek and putting a little too much pressure on my arm as he guides me to the bar. Wendy has moved farther down the bar, setting her sights on another married member of the club. It's funny to me that in high school I had wanted to stab her viciously when she set her sights on Jesse, but when she actually sleeps with my husband I could care less.

"My parents are waiting in the dining hall. You're ten minutes late," says Gentry, again squeezing my arm to empha- size his displeasure with me. I sigh, pasting the fake smile on my face that I know he expects. "There was traffic," I say simply, and I let him lead me to the dining hall where the second worst thing about Gentry is waiting for us.

Gentry's mother, Lucinda, considers herself southern royalty. Her parents owned the largest plantation in South Carolina and spoiled their only daughter with everything that her heart desired. This of course made her perhaps the most self-obsessed woman I had ever met, and that was putting it lightly. Gentry's father, Conrad, stands as we approach, dressed up in the suit and tie that he wears everywhere regardless of the occasion. Like his son, Gentry's father was a handsome man. Although his hair was slightly greying at the temples, his face remained impres- sively unlined, perhaps due to the same miracle worker that made his wife look forever thirty-five.

"Darling, you look wonderful as always," he tells me, brushing a kiss against my cheek and making we want to douse myself in boiling water. Conrad had no qualms about proposi- tioning his son's wife. I couldn't remember an interaction I'd had with him that hadn't ended with him asking me to sneak away to the nearest dark corner with him. I purposely choose to sit on the other side of Gentry, next to his mother, although that option isn't much better. She looks me over, pursing her lips when she gets to my hair. According to her, a proper southern lady keeps her hair pulled back. But I've never been a proper lady, and the guys always loved my hair. Keeping it down is my silent tribute to them and the person I used to be since everything else about me is almost unrecognizable.

Lucinda is a beautiful woman. She's always impeccably dressed, and her mahogany hair is always impeccably coiffed. She's also as shallow as a teacup. She begins to chatter, telling me all about the town gossip; who's sleeping with who, who just got fake boobs, whose husband just filed for bankruptcy. It all passes in one ear and out the other until I hear her say something that sounds unmistakably like "Sounds of Us."

I look up at her, catching her off guard with my sudden interest. "Sorry, could you repeat that?" I ask. Her eyes are gleaming with excitement as she clasps her hands delicately in front of herself. She waits to speak until the waiter has refilled her glass with water. She slowly takes a sip, drawing out the wait now that she actually has my attention.

"I was talking about the Sounds of Us concert next week. They are performing two shows. Everyone's going crazy over the fact that the boys will be coming home for the first time since they made it big. It's been what...four years?" she says.

"Five," I correct her automatically, before cursing myself when she smirks at me.

"So, you aren't immune to the boys' charms either..." she says with a grin.

"What was that, Mother?" asks Gentry, his interest of course rising at the mention of anything to do with me and other men.

"I was just telling Ariana about the concert coming to town," she says. I hold my breath waiting to hear if she will mention the name. Gentry's so clueless about anything that doesn't involve him that he probably hasn't heard yet that they're coming to town.

"Ariana doesn't like concerts," he says automatically. It's his go-to excuse for making sure I never attend any social functions that don't involve him. Ariana doesn't like sushi. Ariana doesn't like movies. The list of times he's said such a thing go on and on. I feel a slight pang in my chest. Ariana. Gentry and his family insist on calling me by my full name, and I miss the days where I had relationships that were free and easy enough to use my nick-name of Ari.

"Of course she doesn't, dear," says Lucinda, patting my hand. The state of my marriage provides much amusement to Lucinda and Conrad. Both approve of the Gentry's "heavy hand" towards me and although they haven't witnessed the abuse first hand, they're well aware of Gentry's penchant for using me as a punching bag. Gentry's parents are simply charming.

I pick at my salad and listen to Lucinda prattle on, my interest gone now that she's off the subject of the concert. Gentry and his dad are whispering back and forth, and I can feel Gentry shooting furtive glances at me. I know I should be concerned or at least interested about what their talking about, but my mind has taken off, thinking about the fact that in just a few days' time, the guys will be in the same vicinity as me for the first time in five years. If only....

"Ariana," says Gentry, pulling me from my day dream. I immediately pull on the smile I have programmed to flash whenever I'm in public with Gentry.

"Yes?"

"I think you've had enough to eat," he tells me as if he's talking about the weather and not the fact that he's just embar-rassed me in front of everyone at the table.

I shakily set my fork down, my cheeks flushing from his comment. I was eating a salad and I'm already slimmer than I should be. But Gentry loves to control everything about me, food being just one of many things. I see Lucinda patting her lips deli-cately as she finishes eating her salmon. My stomach growls at the fact that I've had just a few bites to eat. I have a few dollars stashed away in my car, I'll have to stop somewhere and grab something to eat on the way home. That is if Gentry doesn't leave at the same time as me and follow me.

When I've gotten my emotions under control, I finally lift my eyes and glance at my husband. He's back in deep conversation with Conrad, their voices still too soft for me to pick anything up. Looking at him, I can't help but get the urge to stab him with my silverware and then run screaming from the room. The bastard would probably find a way to haunt me from the grave even if he didn't survive. Still, I find my hand clenching involuntarily as if grasping for a phantom knife.

After that one terrible night when it became clear that I couldn't go to L.A. to meet up with the guys, I was lost. I got a job as a waitress and was living in one of those pay by week extended stay motels since there was no way I could stay in my trailer with *them* anymore. I met Gentry Mayfield while waitressing one night. He was handsome and charming, and persevered in asking me out even when I refused the first half a dozen times. My heart was broken, how could I even think of trying to give my broken self to someone else? I finally got tired of saying no and went on a date with him. He made me smile, something that I didn't think was possible, and every date after that seemed to be more perfect than I deserved. I didn't fall in love with Gentry, my heart belonged to three other men, but I did develop admiration and fondness for Gentry in a way that I hadn't thought possible. After pictures started to surface on the first page of the gossip sites of the guys with hordes of beautiful women, and the fact that my life seemed to be going nowhere, marrying Gentry seemed to be the second chance that I didn't deserve. Except the funny thing about how it all turned out is that my life with Gentry turned out worse than I probably deserved, even after everything that had happened.

Three months after we were married, I burnt dinner. Gentry had come home in a bad mood because of something that had happened at work. Apparently, me burning dinner was the last straw for him that day and he struck me across the face, sending me flying to the ground. Afterwards, he begged and pleaded with me for forgiveness, saying it would never happen again. But I wasn't stupid, I knew how this story played out. I stayed for a week so that I could get ahold of as much money as I could and then I drove off while he was at work. I was stopped at the state lines by a trooper who evidently was friends with Gentry's family. I was dragged kicking and screaming back home where Gentry was waiting, furious and ready to make me pay. Every semblance of the man that I had thought I was marrying was gone.

I had $5,000 to my name when I met him. I'd gotten it from selling the trailer that I inherited when my parents died in a car crash after one of their drunken nights out on the town. Gentry had convinced me that I should put it in our "joint account" right after we got married and stupidly, I had agreed to do it. I never got access to that account. Gentry stole my money, he stole my self-esteem. No, he didn't steal it, he chipped away at it and just when I thought I'd crumble, he kissed me and cried over me and told me he'd die without me.

I tried to get away several more times, by bus, on foot, I even went to the police to try and report him. But the Mayfield's had everyone in this state in their pocket, and nothing I said or did worked. I eventually stopped trying. It had taken me a year of not running away to get my car back and to be able to do things other than stay home, locked in our bedroom, while Gentry was at work.

Gentry stood up from the table, bringing me back to the present. A random song lyric floated through my mind about how the devil wears a pretty face, it certainly fit Gentry Mayfield.

"I'm heading to the office for the rest of the day. What are your plans?" he asks, as if I had a choice in what my plans were.

"Just finishing things around the house and going to the store to get a few ingredients for dinner," I tell him, waving a falsely cheerful goodbye to Gentry's parents as he walks me out of the dining area towards the valet stand. We stop by the exit and he pulls me towards him, stroking the side of my face that I've painted with makeup to hide the bruise he gave me the night before. My eyes flutter from the rush of pain but Gentry somehow mistakes it as the good kind of reaction to his touch. He leans in for a kiss.

"You're still the most beautiful woman I've ever seen," he tells me, sealing his lips over mine in a way that both cuts off my air supply and makes me want to wretch all at once. I hold still, knowing that it will enrage him that I don't do anything in response to his kiss, but not having it in me to fake more than I already have for the day. He pulls back and searches my eyes for something, I'm not sure what. He must not find it because his own eyes darken, and his grip on my arms suddenly tightens to a point that wouldn't look like anything to a club passerby, but that will inevitably leave bruises on my too pale skin.

He leans in and brushes his lips against my ear. "You're never going to get away from me, so when are you going to just give in?" he spits out harshly. I say nothing, just stare at him stonily. I can see the storm building in his eyes.

"Don't bother with dinner, I'll be home late," he says, striding away without a second glance, probably to go find Wendy and make plans to fuck her after he leaves the office, or maybe it will be at the office knowing him.

I wearily make my way through the doors to the valet stand and patiently wait for my keys. It's a different kid this time and I'm grateful he doesn't try to flirt with me.

On my way back from the country club I find myself taking the long way back to the house, the way that takes me by the trailer park where I grew up. I park by the office trailer and find myself walking to the field behind the rows of homes. Looking at the trash riddled ground, I gingerly walk through the mud, flecks of it hitting the formerly pristine white fabric of my shoes. I walk until I get to an abandoned fire pit that doesn't look like it's been used for quite a while. For probably five years to be exact.

I sit on a turned over trash barrel until the sun sits precariously low in the sky and I know that I'm playing with fire if I dare to stay any longer. I then get up and walk back to my car,

passing by the trailer I once lived in. It's funny that after everything that has happened, at the moment I would give anything
to be back in that trailer again.

Discover the rest of this **COMPLETED** series at books2read.
com/rememberusthisway

ACKNOWLEDGMENTS

A few thank you's…

When I started writing, I had no idea that this journey would bring me such beautiful friendships. This book came to be because of my friends. I've never been so stressed and overwhelmed and every day they put me on their shoulders and pushed me along.

To my beta readers, Crystal, Blair, and Ashton, You three are literal angels. Your messages kept me sane, your love of Walker kept me going, and I'm blessed to call you my dear friends. Thank you for being there for me so selflessly and wonderfully. ILY.

To Jasmine, my editor, thank you for always stepping up for me and getting the book done no matter what. I trust you with my book babies, and that says a lot.

To my PA and bff, Caitlin. You keep me sane. You keep me going. You make me feel loved and seen. ILY.

To Raven: Once again I couldn't have done this book without you. Thanks for putting up with my late night freakouts and being the friend that I need. You inspire me, you're always there for me. ILY.

To Mila: You've been my girl since almost the beginning. Thanks for your unwavering support and love. BFFs forever.

To Chels: Thanks for pretending it isn't weird when I ask you how long it takes for a goalie to get undressed. And for letting me have your wife as my bestie. And answering my 101 million hockey questions. You're a dime.

And to you, the readers who make all my dreams come true. It is a privilege to be able to write these words for you, and I will *never* take you for granted.

ABOUT C.R. JANE

A Texas girl living in Utah now, I'm a wife, mother, lawyer, and now author. My stories have been floating around in my head for years, and it has been a relief to finally get them down on paper. I'm a huge Dallas Cowboys fan and I primarily listen to Taylor Swift and hip hop…don't lie and say you don't too.

My love of reading started probably when I was three and it only made sense that I would start to create my own worlds since I was always getting lost in others'.

I like heroines who have to grow in order to become badasses, happy endings, and swoon-worthy, devoted, (and hot) male characters. If this sounds like you, I'm pretty sure we'll be friends.

I'm so glad to have you here…check out the links below for ways to hang out with me and more of my books you can read!

Visit my **Facebook** page to get updates.

Visit my Website.

Sign up for my newsletter to stay updated on new releases, find out random facts about me, and get access to different points of view from my characters.

BOOKS BY C.R. JANE

www.crjanebooks.com

The Pucking Wrong Series (Hockey Romance Standalones)

The Pucking Wrong Number

The Pucking Wrong Guy

A Pucking Wrong Christmas (a novella)

The Pucking Wrong Date

The Pucking Wrong Man

The Sounds of Us Contemporary Series (complete series)

Remember Us This Way

Remember You This Way

Remember Me This Way

Broken Hearts Academy Series: A Bully Romance (complete duet)

Heartbreak Prince

Heartbreak Lover

Ruining Dahlia (Contemporary Mafia Standalone)

Ruining Dahlia

The Fated Wings Series (Paranormal series)

First Impressions

Forgotten Specters

The Fallen One (a Fated Wings Novella)

Forbidden Queens

Frightful Beginnings (a Fated Wings Short Story)

Faded Realms

Faithless Dreams

Fabled Kingdoms

Forever Hearts

The Darkest Curse Series

Forget Me

Lost Passions

Hades Redemption Series

The Darkest Lover

The Darkest Kingdom

Monster & Me Duet Co-write with Mila Young

Monster's Temptation

Monster's Obsession

The Rich Demons of Hockey Duet Cowrite with May Dawson

No Pucking Way

Our Pucking Way

Academy of Souls Co-write with Mila Young (complete series)

School of Broken Souls

School of Broken Hearts

School of Broken Dreams

School of Broken Wings

Fallen World Series Co-write with Mila Young (complete series)

Bound

Broken

Betrayed

Belong

Thief of Hearts Co-write with Mila Young (complete series)

Darkest Destiny

Stolen Destiny

Broken Destiny

Sweet Destiny

Kingdom of Wolves Co-write with Mila Young

Wild Moon

Wild Heart

Wild Girl

Wild Love

Wild Soul

Wild Kiss

Stupid Boys Series Co-write with Rebecca Royce

Stupid Boys

Dumb Girl

Crazy Love

Breathe Me Duet Co-write with Ivy Fox (complete)

Breathe Me

Breathe You

Breathe Me Duet

Love & Hate Co-write with Ivy Fox (complete)

The Boy I Once Hated

The Girl I Once Loved

Rich Demons of Darkwood Series Co-write with May Dawson (complete series)

Make Me Lie

Make Me Beg

Make Me Wild

Make Me Burn

Make Me Queen